T0283069

EX LIBRIS

VINTAGE **CLASSICS**

WILD PLACES

KATHERINE MANSFIELD

Wild Places

Selected Stories

WITH A FOREWORD BY
Helen Simpson

WITH AN INTRODUCTION BY
Claire Harman

VINTAGE

1 3 5 7 9 10 8 6 4 2

Vintage Classics is part of the Penguin Random House group of companies
whose addresses can be found at global.penguinrandomhouse.com

This edition published in Vintage Classics in 2023

Foreword copyright © Helen Simpson 2023
Introduction and selection copyright © Claire Harman 2023

Katherine Mansfield has asserted their right to be identified as the author of this
Work in accordance with the Copyright, Designs and Patents Act 1988

penguin.co.uk/vintage-classics

Typeset in 10.5/12.5pt Bembo Book MT Pro by Jouve (UK), Milton Keynes.

Printed and bound in Great Britain by Clays Ltd, Elcograf S.p.A.

The authorised representative in the EEA is Penguin Random House Ireland,
Morrison Chambers, 32 Nassau Street, Dublin D02 YH68

A CIP catalogue record for this book is available from the British Library

ISBN 9781784878146

Penguin Random House is committed to a sustainable future
for our business, our readers and our planet. This book is made
from Forest Stewardship Council® certified paper.

No, no, the mind I love must still have wild places, a tangled orchard where dark damsons drop in the heavy grass, an overgrown little wood, the chance of a snake or two (real snakes), a pool that nobody's fathomed the depth of — and paths threaded with those little flowers planted by the wind.

Katherine Mansfield's *Journal*, 1920

Contents

Foreword

How and why did Katherine Mansfield provoke such violent extremes of admiration and hostility, both during her life and after it? Because clearly she did, and still does.

Fifty years on from her death, the BBC television series *A Picture of Katherine Mansfield* gave a fair example of her reputation in 1973. Tall, intense Vanessa Redgrave played Mansfield; short, baffled Annette Crosbie her devoted dogsbody-friend LM (Ida Baker); with Jeremy Brett as husband John Middleton Murry, taking off his glasses whenever he had to express emotional inadequacy – which was frequently. In an accompanying *Radio Times* interview, the 85-year-old LM, literal-minded to the end, said the series hadn't seemed realistic to her as Katherine had been shorter than her; *she* had been the tall one. (One of Mansfield's less-than-kind nicknames for LM had been 'The Mountain'.) The biopic broadly followed Murry's drive to establish his late wife as a sort of secular saint, and her final wish to make something visionary of her death, a line that enraged those who had known her and perplexed new readers who had found her work funny and beautiful before coming into contact with the myth.

A flock of biographies followed, the finest two presenting a startlingly different portrait of her. New Zealander Antony Alpers's epic 1980 life (a vastly fuller account than his 1953 study) was sympathetic to the point of avuncular. The reader cannot but flinch at his account of the passionate, gifted girl launching herself thousands of miles from home on a handful of Oscar Wilde's least helpful aphorisms – in an early notebook she had copied out 'Push everything as far as it can go' and 'The only way to get rid of temptation is to yield to it', and so on (with her own, too, written in imitation – 'Never relight a dead cigarette or an old passion').

After this, Claire Tomalin's *Katherine Mansfield: A Secret Life* (1987) was a shock. In her foreword she wrote, 'Hers was a painful life, and it has been a painful task to write about it,' and commended Mansfield's 'recklessness and scrupulousness', while in the biography itself she judged her to be, among other things, 'a liar all her life – there is no getting round this'. (For the naive young reader who had copied out lines from Mansfield's journal to pin above her desk, lines like, 'Honesty is the only thing one seems to prize beyond life, love, death, everything . . . At the end *truth* is the only thing *worth having*,' this was hard to learn; but then – grow up, girl! – life is complex, and so is art.) Earlier, Brigid Brophy had described Mansfield's 'cannibal imagination' as being governed by 'a furious impulse of aggression', even suggesting anger 'was probably one of the precipitators of her illness'. Reacting to similar judgments, Philip Larkin wrote, 'All this stuff about hate & rancour makes me wonder if they've got hold of the same book as I. Haven't they ever been cross? Haven't they ever let off steam?' and suggested any rage stemmed from having contracted tuberculosis and married a man who 'played up to all her all-for-love two-children-holding-hands line of talk but was quite content to live apart from her & indeed found actual cohabitation with her a bit of a strain'.

How to account for these violently clashing opinions?

One explanation might lie in Mansfield's keen sense of the absurd and the striking lack of anything deferential in her attitude – whether towards men or anyone powerful or rich or influential.

A 1917 journal entry describes how, preparing some sticks of rhubarb, she notices in its newspaper wrapping a line from Prime Minister Lloyd George's latest speech – 'that sentence wherein he tells us that we have grasped our niblick and struck out for the open course' – which prompts a page-long mock-heroic flight imagining how these words may in the fullness of time be inscribed on his tombstone beneath a pair of crossed niblicks. She ponders how they will strike the Allies, the crowds of patient Russians waiting in the snow to have the speech read aloud to them – 'what dreadful weapon will it present to their imagination?' – while as for France, 'Shall we read in the French papers next week of someone *qui manque de niblick*?' The 'ripple of laughter' (a favourite phrase of Mansfield's) at play throughout her writing could cause offence (particularly coming from a young, upstart, female New Zealander). A sense of humour for a woman is a double-edged sword. When one of her finest tragi-comic stories, 'The Daughters of the Late Colonel', was published, the reviewers found it 'cruel'; in a 1921 letter Mansfield commented, 'It's almost terrifying to be so misunderstood.'

Almost. Even her enemies commented on her courage.

Mansfield's relationship with the English literary world, and the Bloomsbury Group in particular, had been conflicted, to put it mildly. She was an outsider, treated as 'the little Colonial walking in the London garden patch – allowed to look, perhaps, but not to linger', as she wrote in her journal in 1919. Her accent was mocked by, among others, Rupert Brooke. Virginia Woolf infamously described her as smelling like a 'civet cat that had taken to street walking'; Dora Carrington judged her 'very much a female of the underworld, with the language of a fishwife in Wapping'; and Lytton Strachey as 'that foul-mouthed, virulent, brazen-faced broomstick of a creature'. At this distance the venom strikes one as verging on the insane, but after all she had been fearless in taking them on, mocking and witty and able to make rooms rock with laughter. 'I don't think anyone has ever made me laugh more than she did in those days,' wrote Leonard Woolf in his autobiography, 'with not the shadow of a gleam of a smile on her mask-like face, the extraordinary funniness of the story . . . increased by the flashes of astringent wit.'

Her story 'Bliss' is perhaps instructive here. It can be read relatively straight (poor, deluded Bertha with her cheating husband, but the pear tree is still beautiful); or as a sharply observed satirical portrait of the whole privileged crew, Bertha included, with their consciously bohemian sensibilities and their crassly entitled blindness to the inequalities of class. Mansfield is describing the London Metropolitan Elite of her time, Bertha's 'modern, thrilling friends, writers and painters and poets or people keen on social questions – just the friends they wanted'. Writer Eddie Warren arrives at the dinner party after 'a *dreadful* experience with a taxi-man; he was *most* sinister. I couldn't get him to *stop*. The *more* I knocked and called the *faster* he went. And *in* the moonlight this *bizarre* figure with the *flattened* head *crouching* over the *lit-le* wheel . . .' One does not need to have had personal acquaintanceship with the Blooms Berries (as Mansfield called them) to sense that some pretty sharp caricatures are being drawn. No wonder Virginia Woolf threw 'Bliss' to the floor on reading it. Mansfield was clearly a force to be reckoned with.

The two women maintained an uneasy friendship for the six years they knew each other. 'We have got the same job, Virginia,' Katherine wrote to the older woman, '& it is really very curious & thrilling that we should both, quite apart from each other be after so very nearly the same thing. We are you know; there's no denying it'; and in another letter, interestingly, that T. S. Eliot's poem 'Prufrock' is 'really a short story'. It is surely no coincidence that Woolf's story 'Kew Gardens' and most of her other experimental short pieces were written soon after they met in 1917, then petered out at about the time of Mansfield's death (at which point Woolf wrote, 'I was jealous of her writing – the only writing I have ever been jealous of.'). Mansfield died at the age of thirty-four; Woolf was forty at that point and had only just published *Jacob's Room*, the first of her novels to break free from tradition.

Across the Channel their consoeur Colette, Woolf's senior by nine years and Mansfield's by fifteen, was in her prolific prime. Mansfield had read her work early on while living in Paris and she shared Colette's respect for '*Ces plaisirs qu'on nomme, à la légère, physique*'; bored, fantasising schoolgirls Eve and Katie in 'Carnation' surely bear some relation to Colette's Claudine and Luce. Both writers show a hyper-responsiveness to beauty and write with vivid precision about the natural world, though Mansfield is less earthbound than Colette; skies shift, the light changes, clouds move in her stories; nothing stays the same and an awareness of mortality is ever present, if obliquely. On reading Colette's *L'Entrave* in 1914 Mansfield had commented, 'I don't care a fig for anyone I know except her,' and she would have been fascinated by Colette's stories of women struggling towards new inner and outward freedoms. Later, another Frenchwoman, Simone de Beauvoir, would quote Mansfield extensively in *The Second Sex* (1949), with long passages voicing unspeakable truths from 'Prelude' and 'At the Bay', including whole pages of wonderfully imagined ambivalence felt by a woman towards her husband and children.

Mansfield had admired Woolf's seriousness about writing but she had certainly not been in awe of her: she 'is not *of* her subject – she hovers over, dips, skims, makes exquisite flights – sees the lovely reflections in the water that a bird must see – but *not humanly*'. If anything, as a writer Mansfield had more in common with D. H. Lawrence – the recklessness, the multisensory immediacy, the reverence for what she called the 'warm sensational life'. Theirs was a stormy friendship; Mansfield was not in awe of him either. 'Whatever your disagreement is about he says it is because you have gone wrong in your sex and

belong to an obscene spirit,' she wrote, and when she and Murry
rented beside the Lawrences in Cornwall she suggested he call his cottage The Phallus. Frieda Lawrence remembered how 'sharp and quick
she pounced on anything funny that happened and gave you a swift
look, the rest of her face innocent', and later commented that Mansfield had 'the terrible gift of nearness, she can come so close'. Despite
Lawrence's intermittent unbearableness ('You revolt me stewing in
your consumption,' he wrote to her from Capri; ironic as it is now
thought probable that it was Lawrence himself who had given Mansfield tuberculosis), in the last year of her life Mansfield was to write to
S. S. Koteliansky (the close friend she had helped in translating Chekhov's letters) of Lawrence's latest novel, *Aaron's Rod*: 'I do not go all
the way with Lawrence. His ideas of sex mean nothing to me. But I
feel nearer L than anyone else.' And then again, 'It seems to me whatever he writes, no matter how much one may "disagree", is important.
And after all even what one objects to is a *sign of life* in him . . . It is a
living book; it is warm, it breathes.'

In the various lonely *chambres d'hôte* and *camere* in *pensione* where she
stayed in pursuit of a good lung climate during her last years, Mansfield would lie awake in the night and call on Chekhov, her fellow
tubercular and tutelary deity, not that long dead himself in 1904 at the
age of forty-three. She loved and revered his work, and is indeed cred-
ited with importing his so-called plotlessness to the short-story form
in English. In her journal in 1918 she wrote, 'Ach, Tchehov! [*sic*] why
are you dead? Why can't I talk to you, in a big darkish room, at late
evening – where the light is green from the waving trees outside. I'd
like to write a series of Heavens: that would be one.' She died on
9 January 1923 in the Russian George Gurdjieff's 'alternative' com-
mune in Fontainebleau.

As soon as she had breathed her last the reputation mill cranked into
action. 'This peculiar quality of her work I can only describe as [a]
kind of *purity*. It is as though the glass through which she looked upon
life were crystal-clear,' wrote John Middleton Murry in 1927, already
striking a quasi-religious note in his preface to the *Journal of Katherine
Mansfield* (which he published himself; her friend Koteliansky was to
regret the omission of Mansfield's jokes in Murry's edition of her *Letters* the following year). Also in 1927: she had 'the crystal clearness
which is needed if one is to write truthfully' wrote Virginia Woolf.

Then V. S. Pritchett in 1946 claimed, 'She made stories as clear as glass,' and praised her 'sparkling quality'. Ten years on, Elizabeth Bowen marvelled, 'The singular beauty of her language consists, partly, in its hardly seeming to *be* language at all, so glass-transparent is it to her meaning . . . Perception and language could not be kept too fresh, too alert, too fluid.' To this Cyril Connolly in 1965 added praise of her 'airy freshness . . . this is feminine writing at its best'.

Sparkling, fresh, crystal clear . . . Such comparisons make her stories sound as though they bubbled up artlessly from some mysterious female spring. This is not altogether the fault of the critics. There *is* an extraordinary directness, clarity and new-mintedness about them. It was deliberate: Mansfield's stated aim as a writer was to be 'warm, vivid, intimate – not "made up" – not self-conscious'. Her highest praise for a book would be that it was *alive*. Such apparent spontaneity, however, is deceptive. Katherine Mansfield was immensely dedicated and ruthlessly hard-working.

'You know how I *choose* my words; they can't be changed. And if you don't like it or think it is wrong *just as it is* I'd rather you didn't print it. I'll try and do another,' she wrote when sending 'The Young Girl' for publication. In another letter she described how she worked: 'I choose not only the length of every sentence, but even the sound of every sentence. I choose the rise and fall of every paragraph . . . I read it aloud – numbers of times – just as one would *play over* a musical composition – trying to get it nearer and nearer to the expression.' In her notebooks and journals she stored detailed observations: of back ache, 'So sudden, so painful. I must remember it when I write about an old man. The start to get up – the pause – the slow look of fury – and how, lying at night, one seems to get *locked*. To move is an agony; till finally one discovers a movement which is possible. But the helpless feeling about with the legs first!' Here too she would set down her thoughts about what she was aiming for: 'The truth is that one can get only *so much* into a story; there is always a sacrifice. One has to leave out what one knows and longs to use. Why? I haven't any idea, but there it is. It's always a kind of race to get in as much as one can before it *disappears*.'

Her writing possesses a steady, unshowy unexpectedness. Sentence by carefully calibrated sentence her stories proceed, wheeling through volatile shifts in mood, temperature and weather. She can segue between the past and the future in the blink of an eye; she presses into service dreamlike flashforwards (see the last half-page of 'The Wind Blows') as well as filmic flashbacks, all done in such a way the reader barely notices. This is very considered, condensed prose despite the initial impression it gives of ease, space, light. Even so, it is oddly difficult to quote any single particular sentence to useful effect, as they can't be pulled out like plums; they work together in a more gradual accumulation.

Plot was the story element that least interested her. Once, in a letter to Dorothy Brett, she made fun of a request from a man publishing an anthology of short stories: 'He is bringing out an anthology of short stories and he said the more "plotty" a story I could give him the better. What about that for a word! It made my hair stand up in prongs. A nice "plotty" story, please. People *are* funny.' Her stories could never be called plotty; but they are not mere episodes either. They are musically complete in themselves; they float like islands.

Actively opposed to what would now be called autofiction, Mansfield imagined her way into multiple lives. 'People today are simply cursed with what I call the *personal*,' she wrote. 'What is happening to ME. Look at ME. This is what has been done to ME. It's just as though you tried to run and all the while an enormous black serpent fastened on to you.' Yes, certainly Mansfield wrote in the close third person-person about teenage girls and young women (this is presumably what provoked early critics like H. E. Bates, who wrote, 'Her art is essentially feminine; she delights in making her characters show their thoughts by a kind of mental soliloquy, fluttering, gossipy, breathless with question and answer.'). She also wrote, however, in the voices of children and old men; retired office workers, charladies and ladies' maids; lone women on park benches; aged couples, married couples, honeymoon couples; nagging histrionic wives and stoical husbands; patient wives and callous, vain husbands; widows; widowers; selfish parents sitting on their grown children like dead weights ('The Daughters of the Late Colonel'); selfish children telling their parents to shut up and go to hell ('The Wind Blows' and 'The Young Girl'). The most striking element, perhaps, is that she will take as her subject a situation that one may reasonably assume to have been drawn from her own lived experience (an invalid wife and her husband abroad, as in 'The Man Without a Temperament' and 'The Escape'), and then she will tell it entirely from the viewpoint of the husband.

She 'became' other people, took other viewpoints; she really was interested in what it was like to inhabit existences other than her own. She wanted more life. It is a cruel fact that she was given so little of it herself, but in her short time she saw a great deal of the world (for a young woman then, anyway) – literally, as well as in other ways. She crossed the world twice in ocean liners between her native New Zealand and her new home, England. Her travels in search of health had her criss-crossing Germany, France and Italy (mostly in wartime too), and she has left luminous descriptions of places in her letters and notebooks as well as her stories. The movement and changing scenes of travel stirred her – the adventurousness of trains ('An Indiscreet Journey'); huge ships 'cutting sharp through the dark waves so that big white shavings curled to either side' ('The Stranger'); the rattle of carts and horses through open country ('The Escape'); the glamour of a fast car: 'We 'tore through the black-and-gold town like a pair of scissors tearing through brocade' ('The Young Girl').

She was brave and adventurous, a New Woman and a dedicated artist, and she paid dearly and from very early on with her health for the freedoms she had claimed. An outsider everywhere, she had the rare gift of nearness. The facts of her life were ultimately harsh, even tragic, but her talent was a comic talent and her prose is lit by its alertness to beauty and – most difficult of all to analyse – its unmistakable quality of delight in being alive and putting life on the page as near as she could get it. 'The amount of minute and delicate joy I get out of watching people and things . . . is simply enormous,' she wrote in her journal; 'the detail of life, the *life* of life.'

Helen Simpson, 2023

Introduction

When Katherine Mansfield died of tuberculosis in 1923, aged thirty-four, Virginia Woolf was one of the few people to appreciate how significant her work had been. Mansfield's was 'the only writing I have ever been jealous of,' Woolf wrote in her diary, 'probably we had something in common which I shall never find in anyone else'. But now Katherine was gone, leaving Woolf to ponder 'a rival the less?'

To other contemporaries, the brevity of Mansfield's career suggested she could be quickly forgotten. She had published a couple of books, but only of short stories, and quirky ones at that, with irregular forms and little or no plot. Raymond Mortimer thought her reputation could only decline from that point, and T. S. Eliot, who had been planning to critique Mansfield's work in his magazine *Criterion*, decided not to bother. Whatever interest the young New Zealander had aroused during her lifetime, her early death made everything about her seem brief and incomplete.

Things might have stayed that way if the instructions in Mansfield's will had been followed: to destroy her drafts and papers and 'leave no sign'. But her husband, John Middleton Murry, ignored her wishes in rather spectacular fashion, producing posthumous collections of stories both finished and fragmentary, a selection of journalism, two volumes of her letters and two editions of journals, showing a closely examined inner life. Critics accused him of both bad taste and a kind of idolatry, but the effect on readers was palpable. Mansfield emerged as a passionately committed and restlessly experimental writer, brilliant, funny and brave; someone who took her art with extreme seriousness and redefined what a short story could do. A hundred years later, Mansfield is widely acknowledged as one of the great innovators in twentieth-century fiction, on a par with her contemporaries Woolf, Lawrence and Joyce. Fellow writers in particular have held her in special esteem: Elizabeth Bowen, Willa Cather, Rebecca West, V. S. Pritchett, A. E. Coppard, Angela Carter, Alice

Munro. Bowen thought she possessed 'almost a touch of the miraculous', Cather an exceptional virtuosity and 'love for the medium she had chosen', while Pritchett felt Mansfield's work had marked 'a new point of departure' for a whole generation.

In this selection of stories from Mansfield's output of a hundred or so, I hope to show many examples of that virtuosity and dazzling range. It covers all Mansfield's mature writing years, from the age of twenty to the year before her death, and includes the most famous pieces – 'The Garden Party', 'Prelude', 'At the Bay', 'The Daughters of the Late Colonel', 'Bliss', 'The Voyage', 'The Fly' – and many other favourites such as 'The Doll's House', 'The Stranger', 'A Dill Pickle', 'Miss Brill'. It's hard to put one's finger on what might constitute a characteristic Mansfield story. Many readers will be familiar with the dreamlike impressionism of 'Prelude' and 'At the Bay', and the masterly black comedy of 'The Daughters of the Late Colonel', but what to make of an oeuvre that also includes 'Je ne parle pas français', a story so worldly that its original version (the one printed here) was censored for years; her brilliant alternative-reality account of the war in 'An Indiscreet Journey; dialogue stories like 'Late at Night' (written at a time when she was experimenting with play-writing); the unfinished, sinister 'A Married Man's Story; the small gem 'Carnation'? The constants in her style are spareness, lightness and the vivid evocations of light, colour, scent and texture that animate every page; she is a writer as sensual as Colette and as sure in her choice of detail as Chekhov. There is also a pleasing element of irregularity everywhere, from the types of people she writes about to the ways in which she weaves in and out of different points of view or enters the consciousness of infants, silent bystanders, animals. Mansfield professed herself uninterested in plot and avoided conventional 'closure', sometimes letting a story just drift away (as it does in 'Carnation') or stop, as when Raoul leaves the café at the end of 'Je ne parle pas français'. Has he been thinking aloud, talking to someone, writing the story we've just read? The man is so devious it is impossible to tell. Some stories have the quality of witty talk ('The Luft-Bad') while in others the narrative point of view is so opaque that you must constantly reposition yourself to keep up ('The Escape' is a fascinating example of this). And sometimes, just when you think a character or situation is pinned down, it develops and eludes you (as Ma Parker does, in the story about her). Each page brings a new kind of surprise, and though the stories in this collection appear in chronological order of composition, I would encourage readers to dip in and out at random without fear of missing some vital clue to her development. There were often long gaps between writing and publication and, besides, Mansfield never stopped learning, and never settled into just one mode.

What of her own story? Katherine Mansfield was born Kathleen Mansfield Beauchamp in Wellington, New Zealand, on 14 October 1888, the middle of a family of six, preceded by sisters Vera and Charlotte, and followed by Gwen (who died in infancy), Jeanne and Leslie, an adored son and brother. No one adored Kathleen, who was thought to be the least attractive and biddable of the Beauchamp girls, though her maternal grandmother, Grannie Dyer, provided a steady and reliable source of affection. The Beauchamps were on the rise: their father, Harold, had originally been a travelling salesman, but ended up as chairman of the Bank of New Zealand and was knighted in 1923. All through Kathleen's formative years, the family kept moving to bigger and better houses in and around Wellington with more garden, more things and more comforts. The world of 'The Garden Party' was exactly their world, of cheerful extravagance and display. When the eldest three sisters, Vera, Charlotte and Kathleen, went to boarding school in London (11,000 miles away) the whole family travelled with them in high style, taking over the entire passenger accommodation of the SS *Niwaru* for the six-week journey.

Kathleen's three years at Queen's College developed her taste not just for challenging art and literature, but for the excitements of cosmopolitan life; 'wizard London', as she called it. She was longing to be independent and creative – whether as a musician or writer she wasn't sure at this date – and when she went home to New Zealand in 1906, it was to prepare herself for the earliest possible escape. She had love affairs with both men and women, experimented with pseudonyms, personae and styles, wrote a lot of poetry and some innovative fiction in these years; Oscar Wilde and the decadent and symbolist writers of the fin de siècle were her models, but she was also forging her own style quite independently. 'The Tiredness of Rosabel', Mansfield's sly glimpse of a shop-girl's dreams, written in New Zealand in 1908, used flashbacks, 'moments of being' and stream of consciousness long before those things had been identified as quintessentially Modern.

When Kathleen returned to London as a music student in 1908, her life immediately became complicated and chaotic; she fell in love with a young friend from home, Garnet Trowell (having been formerly in love with his twin brother), but was denounced by his family when it became clear the young couple had slept together. In the spring of 1909, finding herself pregnant, she made a sudden marriage to an older man, a voice teacher called George Bowden (not the baby's father), and left him the same day. The rest of that year was spent abroad in and around the Bavarian spa of Bad Wörishofen, where the pregnancy and the love affair with Garnet both ended, and by the time Kathleen returned to London in 1910 she had reinvented herself as an independent woman writer, armed with a new seriousness and determination about her work – also a new name, 'Katherine Mansfield'. The stories she had been writing in Bavaria, characterised by a sharply satiric eye and female perspective, were published in quick succession and collected in her first book, *In a German Pension*.

She met the young writer and editor John Middleton Murry the following year, and they were to stay together – more or less – for the rest of her life. With Murry she edited and wrote for the avant-garde journal *Rhythm* (her New Zealand stories 'The Woman at the Store' and 'How Pearl Button was Kidnapped' belong to this period) and became well known in bohemian circles, close friends – for a while – with D. H. Lawrence and his wife Frieda, and later part of Lady Ottoline Morrell's Garsington set. Through Morrell, she became acquainted with Bertrand Russell (who found her 'full of alarming penetration') and 'the Woolves', Leonard and Virginia, but was often treated like a colonial interloper who needed to be kept at arm's length. Even the important connection she formed later with Virginia Woolf, in the year when they were near neighbours and both doing 'the same job', was too guarded ever to tip over into a real friendship.

The war brought enormous disruptions to Katherine's life, with displacement, impoverishment and bereavements. Murry was exempted from active service but worked in the War Office and many of their friends went to the Front and were killed. The death of Katherine's brother Leslie devastated her; it also provoked a radical change of purpose – trying to 'renew in writing . . . all the remembered places':

> I want for one moment to make our undiscovered country leap into the eyes of the old world. It must be mysterious, as though floating – it must take the breath . . . I shall tell everything, even of how the laundry basket squeaked as '75' – but all must be told with a sense of mystery, a radiance, an after glow . . .

She had already been experimenting along these lines, both with her emphasis on states of mind over plot, as in 'An Indiscreet Journey', and in a long story called 'The Aloe', written as a series of interconnecting scenes that follow the flow of ordinary life in one household, down to the tiniest details. 'I expect you'll think I'm dotty when you read it,' she warned Murry, 'It's queer stuff.' When she rewrote 'The Aloe' as 'Prelude', for the Woolfs to publish at their new Hogarth Press, it took them both by surprise with its loose structure, plotlessness and complex mixing of sensations, sounds and feelings (from which Virginia was to learn a great deal), but Mansfield was defiant about how the book might be received by the 'Intellectuals': 'They'll think it's a New Primer for Infant Readers. Let 'em.' Simultaneously but independent of her contemporaries Proust and Joyce, she had been finding her own way of 'making it New':

> one has these 'glimpses', before which all that one ever has written (what has one written?) – all (yes, all) that one has ever read, pales . . . The waves, as I drove home this afternoon, and the high foam, how it was suspended in the air before it fell . . . What is it that happens in that moment of suspension? It is timeless. In that moment (what *do* I mean?) the whole life of the soul is contained.

As for subject, she had all the riches of her imagination at her disposal: 'All my *feelings* are there and my *desires* and my ambitions,' she wrote in her diary; it was a sort of secret weapon, and also a kind of drug, dangerously alluring. 'One ought to merge into things,' she told Virginia Woolf, and tried to explain further what she meant in a letter to her friend Dorothy Brett: 'When I write about ducks I swear that I am a white duck with a round eye, floating in a pond,' a process 'so thrilling that I can hardly breathe'. You can see her using it all through her work, but perhaps nowhere so deftly as in 'Carnation', a deceptively simple and very short story evoking the drowsy atmosphere of a classroom on a hot summer's day. Amid the heat, the light (some of it given off by the schoolgirls' blouses, and the teacher whose white waistcoat 'gleamed like the belly of a shark') and the sense in which everyone, including the teacher, has put aside their usual behaviour, the central character, Katie, is half-attending to some sounds outside. Her mind's eye supplies the probable scene below the window:

> Now she could hear a man clatter over the cobbles and the jing-jang of the pails he carried. And now *Hoo-hor-her! Hoo-hor-her!* as he worked the pump and a great gush of water followed. Now he was flinging the water over something, over the wheels of a carriage perhaps. And she saw the wheel, propped up, clear of the ground, spinning round, flashing scarlet and black, with great drops glancing off it.

We see it, too; the horse in the yard and the water flying off the wheel, just as the girl in the story does. Mansfield somehow manages to make this trick feel utterly real, something bordering on a collaborative vision. 'I have tried to make it as familiar to "you" as it is to me,' she told Brett when she was composing 'At the Bay'. 'You know the marigolds? You know those pools in the rocks, you know the mousetrap on the wash house window sill?' Art isn't just a preservative of one person's creative idea; it can and should be a form of gift.

The deterioration of Mansfield's health, which had begun with the effects of undetected gonorrhoea as early as 1910, became critical after 1917, when she discovered she had tuberculosis. 'Oh, yes, of course I am frightened,' she wrote in her diary; 'perhaps it's going to gallop – who knows – and I shan't have my work written. *That's what matters*. How unbearable it would be to die, leave "scraps", "bits", nothing real finished'. Mansfield was advised to avoid cold climates and spent the last five years of her life wintering in a series of rented villas in Italy, France and Switzerland, often accompanied by Ida Baker, the doggedly devoted old school friend whom Mansfield both loved and loathed. Her three most productive writing years, which followed her diagnosis, were also years of invalidism and pain which she met with bravery, mordant humour, curiosity, art. 'I have consumption,' she wrote in 1920; 'There is still a great deal of moisture (& pain) in my BAD lung. But I do not care – I do not want anything I could not have. Peace, solitude, time to write my books, beautiful external life to watch & ponder – no more.' Not much more was granted: in 1922, she opted (desperately) for a course of the new 'Rayons-X' treatment in Paris, and when that failed turned to the more holistic approach of the controversial theosophist guru George Gurdjieff, at whose Institute for the Harmonious Development of Man at Le Prieuré, Avon, Fontainebleau, she died in January 1923.

The sense of time running out in those last years is evident in the urgency of her desire to work, and the physical speed at which she executed much of it, hurtling along towards the end of 'The Daughters of the Late Colonel' in a barely legible hand, 'for fear of dying before the story was sent'. The late journals are full of harsh self-analysis, but also a kind of relief at needing to face various truths head-on: 'My spirit is nearly dead . . . Can I walk? Only creep. Can I do anything with my hands or my body? Nothing at all. I am an absolutely hopeless invalid.' She was equally stark about her relations with Murry, from whom she felt increasingly detached: 'He dreams of a life with you *some day* when the miracle has happened. You are important to him as a dream.' But just writing this down made her feel 'a little calmer'; 'Thank God for writing.'

Thank God, indeed. One could argue that Mansfield's essential loneliness of mind was one of her greatest assets as a writer, however painful to her personally. It animates her diaries and flashes out in the stories in some of the most memorable moments: Beryl before the mirror in 'Prelude', for instance, contemplating her 'false self', Linda thinking about her marital relations in 'At the Bay' (a passage which fascinated Simone de Beauvoir, who singled it out for notice in *The Second Sex*), Connie at the end of 'The Daughters of the Late Colonel' wondering, 'What did it all lead to? Now? Now?' In company, Katherine Mansfield often seemed to be a poseur, a fabricator, a wearer of masks, but perhaps her most urgent and sincere opinions, her most profoundly truthful and unsentimental revelations, were reserved for her writing and addressed to a future reader, to us. A hundred years may have passed since her death, but she is a writer you can discover at any time or age because her presence is so vital, her eye so clear, and she is always hoping to meet us through her words on the page:

> I think the only way to live as a writer is to draw on one's real *familiar* life – to find the treasure in that . . . And the curious thing is that if we describe this which seems to us so intensely personal, other people take it to themselves and understand it as if it were their own.

Claire Harman, 2023

N. B. The texts of the stories in this collection have been taken from first book publication, with one exception, 'Je ne parle pas français', which was bowdlerised for inclusion in *Bliss and Other Stories*, so its earlier publication is used here. Information about date of composition and dates of first publication, in both magazine/periodical and book form, can be found at the end of each story.

The Tiredness of Rosabel

At the corner of Oxford Circus Rosabel bought a bunch of violets, and that was practically the reason why she had so little tea — for a scone and a boiled egg and a cup of cocoa at Lyons are not ample sufficiency after a hard day's work in a millinery establishment. As she swung on to the step of the Atlas bus, grabbed her skirt with one hand and clung to the railing with the other, Rosabel thought she would have sacrificed her soul for a good dinner — roast duck and green peas, chestnut stuffing, pudding with brandy sauce — something hot and strong and filling. She sat down next to a girl very much her own age who was reading *Anna Lombard* in a cheap, paper-covered edition, and the rain had tear-spattered the pages. Rosabel looked out of the windows; the street was blurred and misty, but light striking on the panes turned their dullness to opal and silver, and the jewellers' shops seen through this, were fairy palaces. Her feet were horribly wet, and she knew the bottom of her skirt and petticoat would be coated with black, greasy mud. There was a sickening smell of warm humanity — it seemed to be oozing out of everybody in the bus — and everybody had the same expression, sitting so still, staring in front of them. How many times had she read these advertisements — 'Sapolio Saves Time, Saves Labour' — 'Heinz's Tomato Sauce' — and the inane, annoying dialogue between doctor and judge concerning the superlative merits of 'Lamp-lough's Pyretic Saline'. She glanced at the book which the girl read so earnestly, mouthing the words in a way that Rosabel detested, licking her first finger and thumb each time that she turned the page. She could not see very clearly; it was something about a hot, voluptuous night, a band playing, and a girl with lovely, white shoulders. Oh, heavens! Rosabel stirred suddenly and unfastened the two top buttons of her coat . . . she felt almost stifled. Through her half-closed eyes the whole row of people on the opposite seat seemed to resolve into one fatuous, staring face . . .

And this was her corner. She stumbled a little on her way out and lurched against the girl next to her. 'I beg your pardon,' said Rosabel, but the girl did not even look up. Rosabel saw that she was smiling as she read.

Westbourne Grove looked as she had always imagined Venice to look at night, mysterious, dark, even the hansoms were like gondolas dodging up and down, and the lights trailing luridly – tongues of flame licking the wet street – magic fish swimming in the Grand Canal. She was more than glad to reach Richmond Road, but from the corner of the street until she came to No. 26 she thought of those four flights of stairs. Oh, why four flights! It was really criminal to expect people to live so high up. Every house ought to have a lift, something simple and inexpensive, or else an electric staircase like the one at Earl's Court – but four flights! When she stood in the hall and saw the first flight ahead of her and the stuffed albatross head on the landing, glimmering ghost-like in the light of the little gas jet, she almost cried. Well, they had to be faced; it was very like bicycling up a steep hill, but there was not the satisfaction of flying down the other side . . .

Her own room at last! She closed the door, lit the gas, took off her hat and coat, skirt, blouse, unhooked her old flannel dressing-gown from behind the door, pulled it on, then unlaced her boots – on consideration her stockings were not wet enough to change. She went over to the wash-stand. The jug had not been filled again today. There was just enough water to soak the sponge, and the enamel was coming off the basin – that was the second time she had scratched her chin.

It was just seven o'clock. If she pulled the blind up and put out the gas it was much more restful – Rosabel did not want to read. So she knelt down on the floor, pillowing her arms on the window-sill . . . just one little sheet of glass between her and the great wet world outside!

She began to think of all that had happened during the day. Would she ever forget that awful woman in the grey mackintosh who had wanted a trimmed motor-cap – 'something purple with something rosy each side' – or the girl who had tried on every hat in the shop and then said she would 'call in tomorrow and decide definitely'. Rosabel could not help smiling; the excuse was worn so thin . . .

But there had been one other – a girl with beautiful red hair and a white skin and eyes the colour of that green ribbon shot with gold they had got from Paris last week. Rosabel had seen her electric brougham at the door; a man had come in with her, quite a young man, and so well dressed.

'What is it exactly that I want, Harry?' she had said, as Rosabel took the pins out of her hat, untied her veil, and gave her a hand-mirror.

'You must have a black hat,' he had answered, 'a black hat with a feather that goes right round it and then round your neck and ties in a bow under your chin, and the ends tuck into your belt – a decent-sized feather.'

The girl glanced at Rosabel laughingly. 'Have you any hats like that?'

They had been very hard to please; Harry would demand the impossible, and Rosabel was almost in despair. Then she remembered the big, untouched box upstairs.

'Oh, one moment, Madam,' she had said. 'I think perhaps I can show you something that will please you better.' She had run up, breathlessly, cut the cords, scattered the tissue paper, and yes, there was the very hat – rather large, soft, with a great, curled feather, and a black velvet rose, nothing else. They had been charmed. The girl had put it on and then handed it to Rosabel.

'Let me see how it looks on you,' she said, frowning a little, very serious indeed.

Rosabel turned to the mirror and placed it on her brown hair, then faced them.

'Oh, Harry, isn't it adorable,' the girl cried, 'I must have that!' She smiled again at Rosabel. 'It suits you beautifully.'

A sudden, ridiculous feeling of anger had seized Rosabel. She longed to throw the lovely, perishable thing in the girl's face, and bent over the hat, flushing.

'It's exquisitely finished off inside, Madam,' she said. The girl swept out to her brougham, and left Harry to pay and bring the box with him.

'I shall go straight home and put it on before I come out to lunch with you,' Rosabel heard her say.

The man leaned over her as she made out the bill, then, as he counted the money into her hand – 'Ever been painted?' he said.

'No,' said Rosabel shortly, realising the swift change in his voice, the slight tinge of insolence, of familiarity.

'Oh, well you ought to be,' said Harry. 'You've got such a damned pretty little figure.'

Rosabel did not pay the slightest attention. How handsome he had been! She had thought of no one else all day; his face fascinated her; she could see clearly his fine, straight eyebrows, and his hair grew back from his forehead with just the slightest suspicion of crisp curl, his laughing, disdainful mouth. She saw again his slim hands counting the money into hers . . . Rosabel suddenly pushed the hair back from her face, her forehead was hot . . . if those slim hands could rest one moment . . . the luck of that girl!

Suppose they changed places. Rosabel would drive home with him, of course they were in love with each other, but not engaged, very nearly, and she would say – 'I won't be one moment.' He would wait in the brougham while her maid took the hat-box up the stairs, following Rosabel. Then the great, white and pink bedroom with roses everywhere in dull silver vases. She would sit down before the mirror and the little French maid would fasten her hat and find her a thin, fine veil and another pair of white suède gloves – a button had come off the gloves she had worn that morning. She had scented her furs and gloves and handkerchief, taken a big muff and run downstairs. The butler opened the door, Harry was waiting, they drove away together . . . *That* was life, thought Rosabel! On the way to the Carlton they stopped at Gerard's, Harry bought her great sprays of Parma violets, filled her hands with them.

'Oh, they are sweet!' she said, holding them against her face.

'It is as you always should be,' said Harry, 'with your hands full of violets.'

(Rosabel realised that her knees were getting stiff; she sat down on the floor and leaned her head against the wall.) Oh, that lunch! The table covered with flowers, a band hidden behind a grove of palms playing music that fired her blood like wine – the soup, and oysters, and pigeons, and creamed potatoes, and champagne, of course, and afterwards coffee and cigarettes. She would lean over the table fingering her glass with one hand, talking with that charming gaiety which Harry so appreciated. Afterwards a matinée, something that gripped them both, and then tea at the 'Cottage'.

'Sugar? Milk? Cream?' The little homely questions seemed to suggest a joyous intimacy. And then home again in the dusk, and the scent of the Parma violets seemed to drench the air with their sweetness.

'I'll call for you at nine,' he said as he left her.

The fire had been lighted in her boudoir, the curtains drawn, there were a great pile of letters waiting her – invitations for the Opera, dinners, balls, a week-end on the river, a motor tour – she glanced through them listlessly as she went upstairs to dress. A fire in her bedroom, too, and her beautiful, shining dress spread on the bed – white tulle over silver, silver shoes, silver scarf, a little silver fan. Rosabel knew that she was the most famous woman at the ball that night; men paid her homage, a foreign Prince desired to be presented to this English wonder. Yes, it was a voluptuous night, a band playing, and *her* lovely white shoulders . . .

But she became very tired. Harry took her home, and came in with her for just one moment. The fire was out in the drawing-room, but the sleepy maid waited for her in her boudoir. She took off her cloak, dismissed the servant, and went over to the fire-place, and stood peeling off her gloves; the firelight shone on her hair, Harry came across the room and caught her in his arms – 'Rosabel, Rosabel, Rosabel . . .' Oh, the haven of those arms, and she was very tired.

(The real Rosabel, the girl crouched on the floor in the dark, laughed aloud, and put her hand up to her hot mouth.)

Of course they rode in the park next morning, the engagement had been announced in the *Court Circular*, all the world knew, all the world was shaking hands with her . . .

They were married shortly afterwards at St George's, Hanover Square, and motored down to Harry's old ancestral home for the honeymoon; the peasants in the village curtseyed to them as they passed; under the folds of the rug he pressed her hands convulsively. And that night she wore again her white and silver frock. She was tired after the journey and went upstairs to bed . . . quite early . . .

The real Rosabel got up from the floor and undressed slowly, folding her clothes over the back of a chair. She slipped over her head her coarse, calico nightdress, and took the pins out of her hair – the soft, brown flood of it fell round her, warmly. Then she blew out the candle and groped her way into bed, pulling the blankets and grimy 'honeycomb' quilt closely round her neck, cuddling down in the darkness . . .

So she slept and dreamed, and smiled in her sleep, and once threw out her arm to feel for something which was not there, dreaming still.

And the night passed. Presently the cold fingers of dawn closed over her uncovered hand; grey light flooded the dull room. Rosabel shivered, drew a little gasping breath, sat up. And because her heritage was that tragic optimism, which is all too often the only inheritance of youth, still half asleep, she smiled, with a little nervous tremor round her mouth.

(written 1908, first published in *Something Childish and Other Stories*, 1924)

The Child-Who-Was-Tired

She was just beginning to walk along a little white road with tall black trees on either side, a little road that led to nowhere, and where nobody walked at all, when a hand gripped her shoulder, shook her, slapped her ear.

'Oh, oh, don't stop me,' cried the Child-Who-Was-Tired. 'Let me go.'

'Get up, you good-for-nothing brat,' said a voice; 'get up and light the oven or I'll shake every bone out of your body.'

With an immense effort she opened her eyes, and saw the Frau standing by, the baby bundled under one arm. The three other children who shared the same bed with the Child-Who-Was-Tired, accustomed to brawls, slept on peacefully. In a corner of the room the Man was fastening his braces.

'What do you mean by sleeping like this the whole night through – like a sack of potatoes? You've let the baby wet his bed twice.'

She did not answer, but tied her petticoat string, and buttoned on her plaid frock with cold, shaking fingers.

'There, that's enough. Take the baby into the kitchen with you, and heat that cold coffee on the spirit-lamp for the master, and give him the loaf of black bread out of the table drawer. Don't guzzle it yourself or I'll know.'

The Frau staggered across the room, flung herself on to her bed, drawing the pink bolster round her shoulders.

It was almost dark in the kitchen. She laid the baby on the wooden settle, covering him with a shawl, then poured the coffee from the earthenware jug into the saucepan, and set it on the spirit-lamp to boil.

'I'm sleepy,' nodded the Child-Who-Was-Tired, kneeling on the floor and splitting the damp pine logs into little chips. 'That's why I'm not awake.'

The oven took a long time to light. Perhaps it was cold, like herself, and sleepy . . . Perhaps it had been dreaming of a little white road with black trees on either side, a little road that led to nowhere.

Then the door was pulled violently open and the Man strode in.

'Here, what are you doing sitting on the floor?' he shouted. 'Give me my coffee. I've got to be off. Ugh! You haven't even washed over the table.'

She sprang to her feet, poured his coffee into an enamel cup and gave him bread and a knife, then, taking a wash rag from the sink, smeared over the black linoleumed table.

'Swine of a day – swine's life,' mumbled the Man, sitting by the table and staring out of the window at the bruised sky, which seemed to bulge heavily over the dull land. He stuffed his mouth with bread and then swilled it down with the coffee.

The Child drew a pail of water, turned up her sleeves, frowning the while at her arms, as if to scold them for being so thin, so much like little stunted twigs, and began to mop over the floor.

'Stop sousing about the water while I'm here,' grumbled the Man. 'Stop the baby snivelling; it's been going on like that all night.'

The Child gathered the baby into her lap and sat rocking him.

'Ts – ts – ts,' she said. 'He's cutting his eye teeth, that's what makes him cry so. *And* dribble – I never seen a baby dribble like this one.' She wiped his mouth and nose with a corner of her skirt. 'Some babies get their teeth without you knowing it,' she went on, 'and some take on this way all the time. I once heard of a baby that died, and they found all its teeth in its stomach.'

The Man got up, unhooked his cloak from the back of the door, and flung it round him.

'There's another coming,' said he.

'What – a tooth!' exclaimed the Child, startled for the first time that morning out of her dreadful heaviness, and thrusting her finger into the baby's mouth.

'No,' he said grimly, 'another baby. Now, get on with your work; it's time the others got up for school.' She stood a moment quite silently, hearing his heavy steps on the stone passage, then the gravel walk, and finally the slam of the front gate.

'Another baby! Hasn't she finished having them *yet*?' thought the Child. 'Two babies getting eye teeth – two babies to get up for in the night – two babies to carry about and wash their little piggy clothes!' She looked with horror at the one in her arms, who, seeming to understand the contemptuous loathing of her tired glance, doubled his fists, stiffened his body, and began violently screaming.

'Ts – ts – ts.' She laid him on the settle and went back to her floor-washing. He never ceased crying for a moment, but she got quite used to it and kept time with her broom. Oh, how tired she was! Oh, the heavy broom handle and the burning spot just at the back of her neck that ached so, and a funny little fluttering feeling just at the back of her waistband, as though something were going to break.

The clock struck six. She set the pan of milk in the oven, and went into the next room to wake and dress the three children. Anton and Hans lay together in attitudes of mutual amity which certainly never existed out of their sleeping hours. Lena was curled up, her knees under her chin, only a straight, standing-up pigtail of hair showing above the bolster.

'Get up,' cried the Child, speaking in a voice of immense authority, pulling off the bedclothes and giving the boys sundry pokes and digs. 'I've been calling you this last half-hour. It's late, and I'll tell on you if you don't get dressed this minute.'

Anton awoke sufficiently to turn over and kick Hans on a tender part, whereupon Hans pulled Lena's pigtail until she shrieked for her mother.

'Oh, do be quiet,' whispered the Child. 'Oh, do get up and dress. You know what will happen. There – I'll help you.'

But the warning came too late. The Frau got out of bed, walked in a determined fashion into the kitchen, returning with a bundle of twigs in her hand fastened together with a strong cord. One by one she laid the children across her knee and severely beat them, expending a final burst of energy on the Child-Who-Was-Tired, then returned to bed, with a comfortable sense of her maternal duties in good working order for the day. Very subdued, the three allowed themselves to be dressed and washed by the Child, who even laced the boys' boots, having found through experience that if left to themselves they hopped about for at least five minutes to find a comfortable ledge for their foot, and then spat on their hands and broke the bootlaces.

While she gave them their breakfast they became uproarious, and the baby would not cease crying. When she filled the tin kettle with milk, tied on the rubber teat, and, first moistening it herself, tried with little coaxing words to make him drink, he threw the bottle on to the floor and trembled all over.

'Eye teeth!' shouted Hans, hitting Anton over the head with his empty cup; 'he's getting the evil-eye teeth, I should say.'

'Smarty!' retorted Lena, poking out her tongue at him, and then, when he promptly did the same, crying at the top of her voice, 'Mother, Hans is making faces at me!'

'That's right,' said Hans; 'go on howling, and when you're in bed tonight I'll wait till you're asleep, and then I'll creep over and take a little tiny piece of your arm and twist and twist it until –' He leaned over the table making the most horrible faces at Lena, not noticing that Anton was standing behind his chair until the little boy bent over and spat on his brother's shaven head.

'Oh, weh! oh, weh!'

The Child-Who-Was-Tired pushed and pulled them apart, muffled them into their coats, and drove them out of the house.

'Hurry, hurry! the second bell's rung,' she urged, knowing perfectly well she was telling a story, and rather exulting in the fact. She washed up the breakfast things, then went down to the cellar to look out the potatoes and beetroot.

Such a funny, cold place the coal cellar! With potatoes banked on one corner, beetroot in an old candle box, two tubs of sauerkraut, and a twisted mass of dahlia roots – that looked as real as though they were fighting one another, thought the Child.

She gathered the potatoes into her skirt, choosing big ones with few eyes because they were easier to peel, and bending over the dull heap in the silent cellar, she began to nod.

'Here, you, what are you doing down there?' cried the Frau from the top of the stairs. 'The baby's fallen off the settle, and got a bump as big as an egg over his eye. Come up here, and I'll teach you!'

'It wasn't me – it wasn't me!' screamed the Child, beaten from one side of the hall to the other, so that the potatoes and beetroot rolled out of her skirt.

The Frau seemed to be as big as a giant, and there was a certain heaviness in all her movements that was terrifying to anyone so small.

'Sit in the corner, and peel and wash the vegetables, and keep the baby quiet while I do the washing.'

Whimpering she obeyed, but as to keeping the baby quiet, that was impossible. His face was hot, little beads of sweat stood all over his head, and he stiffened his body and cried. She held him on her knees, with a pan of cold water beside her for the cleaned vegetables and the 'ducks' bucket' for the peelings.

'Ts – ts – ts!' she crooned, scraping and boring; 'there's going to be another soon, and you can't both keep on crying. Why don't you go to sleep, baby? I would, if I were you. I'll tell you a dream. Once upon a time there was a little white road –'

She shook back her head, a great lump ached in her throat and then the tears ran down her face on to the vegetables.

'That's no good,' said the Child, shaking them away. 'Just stop crying until I've finished this, baby, and I'll walk you up and down.'

But by that time she had to peg out the washing for the Frau. A wind had sprung up. Standing on tiptoe in the yard, she almost felt she would be blown away. There was a bad smell coming from the ducks' coop, which was half full of manure water, but away in the meadow she saw the grass blowing like little green hairs. And she remembered having heard of a child who had once played for a whole day in just such a meadow with real sausages and beer for her dinner – and not a little bit of tiredness. Who had told her that story? She could not remember, and yet it was so plain.

The wet clothes flapped in her face as she pegged them; danced and jigged on the line, bulged out and twisted. She walked back to the house with lagging steps, looking longingly at the grass in the meadow.

'What must I do now, please?' she said.

'Make the beds and hang the baby's mattress out of the window, then get the wagon and take him for a little walk along the road. In front of the house, mind – where I can see you. Don't stand there, gaping! Then come in when I call you and help me cut up the salad.'

When she had made the beds the Child stood and looked at them. Gently she stroked the pillow with her hand, and then, just for one moment, let her head rest there. Again the smarting lump in her throat, the stupid tears that fell and kept on falling as she dressed the baby and dragged the little wagon up and down the road.

A man passed, driving a bullock wagon. He wore a long, queer feather in his hat, and whistled as he passed. Two girls with bundles on their shoulders came walking out of the village – one wore a red handkerchief about her head and one a blue. They were laughing and holding each other by the hand. Then the sun pushed by a heavy fold of grey cloud and spread a warm yellow light over everything.

'Perhaps,' thought the Child-Who-Was-Tired, 'if I walked far enough up this road I might come to a little white one, with tall black trees on either side – a little road –'

'Salad, salad!' cried the Frau's voice from the house.

Soon the children came home from school, dinner was eaten, the Man took the Frau's share of pudding as well as his own, and the three children seemed to smear themselves all over with whatever they ate. Then more dish-washing and more cleaning and baby-minding. So the afternoon dragged coldly through.

Old Frau Grathwohl came in with a fresh piece of pig's flesh for the Frau, and the Child listened to them gossiping together.

'Frau Manda went on her "journey to Rome" last night, and brought back a daughter. How are you feeling?'

'I was sick twice this morning,' said the Frau. 'My insides are all twisted up with having children too quickly.'

'I see you've got a new help,' commented old Mother Grathwohl.

'Oh, dear Lord' – the Frau lowered her voice – 'don't you know her? She's the free-born one – daughter of the waitress at the railway station. They found her mother trying to squeeze her head in the wash-hand jug, and the child's half silly.'

'Ts – ts – ts!' whispered the 'free-born' one to the baby.

As the day drew in the Child-Who-Was-Tired did not know how to fight her sleepiness any longer. She was afraid to sit down or stand still. As she sat at supper the Man and the Frau seemed to swell to an immense size as she watched them, and then become smaller than dolls, with little voices that seemed to come from outside the window. Looking at the baby, it suddenly had two heads, and then no head. Even his crying made her feel worse. When she thought of the nearness of bedtime she shook all over with excited joy. But as eight o'clock approached there was the sound of wheels on the road, and presently in came a party of friends to spend the evening.

Then it was:

'Put on the coffee.'

'Bring me the sugar tin.'

'Carry the chairs out of the bedroom.'

'Set the table.'

And, finally, the Frau sent her into the next room to keep the baby quiet.

There was a little piece of candle burning in the enamel bracket. As she walked up and down she saw her great big shadow on the wall like a grown-up person with a grown-up baby. Whatever would it look like when she carried two babies so!

'Ts – ts – ts! Once upon a time she was walking along a little white road, with oh! such great big black trees on either side.'

'Here, you!' called the Frau's voice, 'bring me my new jacket from behind the door.' And as she took it into the warm room one of the women said, 'She looks like an owl. Such children are seldom right in their heads.'

'Why don't you keep that baby quiet?' said the Man, who had just drunk enough beer to make him feel very brave and master of his house.

'If you don't keep that baby quiet you'll know why later on.'

They burst out laughing as she stumbled back into the bedroom.

'I don't believe Holy Mary could keep him quiet,' she murmured. 'Did Jesus cry like this when He was little? If I was not so tired perhaps I could do it; but the baby just knows that I want to go to sleep. And there is going to be another one.'

She flung the baby on the bed, and stood looking at him with terror.

From the next room there came the jingle of glasses and the warm sound of laughter.

And she suddenly had a beautiful, marvellous idea.

She laughed for the first time that day, and clapped her hands.

'Ts – ts – ts!' she said, 'lie there, silly one; you *will* go to sleep. You'll not cry any more or wake up in the night. Funny, little, ugly baby.'

He opened his eyes, and shrieked loudly at the sight of the Child-Who-Was-Tired. From the next room she heard the Frau call out to her.

'One moment – he is almost asleep,' she cried.

And then gently, smiling, on tiptoe, she brought the pink bolster from the Frau's bed and covered the baby's face with it, pressed with all her might as he struggled, 'like a duck with its head off, wriggling,' she thought.

She heaved a long sigh, then fell back on to the floor, and was walking along a little white road with tall black trees on either side, a little road that led to nowhere, and where nobody walked at all – nobody at all.

(first published 1910, first book publication
In a German Pension, 1911)

The Luft Bad

I think it must be the umbrellas which make us look ridiculous.

When I was admitted into the enclosure for the first time, and saw my fellow-bathers walking about very nearly 'in their nakeds', it struck me that the umbrellas gave a distinctly 'Little Black Sambo' touch.

Ridiculous dignity in holding over yourself a green cotton thing with a red parroquet handle when you are dressed in nothing larger than a handkerchief.

There are no trees in the 'Luft Bad'. It boasts a collection of plain, wooden cells, a bath shelter, two swings and two odd clubs – one, presumably the lost property of Hercules or the German army, and the other to be used with safety in the cradle.

And there in all weathers we take the air – walking, or sitting in little companies talking over each other's ailments and measurements and ills that flesh is heir to.

A high wooden wall compasses us all about; above it the pine trees look down a little superciliously, nudging each other in a way that is peculiarly trying to a *débutante*. Over the wall, on the right side, is the men's section. We hear them chopping down trees and sawing through planks, dashing heavy weights to the ground, and singing part songs. Yes, they take it far more seriously.

On the first day I was conscious of my legs, and went back into my cell three times to look at my watch, but when a woman with whom I had played chess for three weeks cut me dead, I took heart and joined a circle.

We lay curled on the ground while a Hungarian lady of immense proportions told us what a beautiful tomb she had bought for her second husband.

'A vault it is,' she said, 'with nice black railings. And so large that I can go down there and walk about. Both their photographs are there, with two very handsome wreaths sent me by my first husband's brother. There is an enlargement of a family group photograph, too,

and an illuminated address presented to my first husband on his marriage. I am often there; it makes such a pleasant excursion for a fine
Saturday afternoon.'

She suddenly lay down flat on her back, took in six long breaths,
and sat up again.

'The death agony was dreadful,' she said brightly; 'of the second, I
mean. The "first" was run into by a furniture wagon, and had fifty
marks stolen out of a new waistcoat pocket, but the "second" was
dying for sixty-seven hours. I never ceased crying once – not even to
put the children to bed.'

A young Russian, with a 'bang' curl on her forehead, turned to me.

'Can you do the "Salome" dance?' she asked. 'I can.'

'How delightful,' I said.

'Shall I do it now? Would you like to see me?'

She sprang to her feet, executed a series of amazing contortions for
the next ten minutes, and then paused, panting, twisting her long hair.

'Isn't that nice?' she said. 'And now I am perspiring so splendidly. I
shall go and take a bath.'

Opposite to me was the brownest woman I have ever seen, lying on
her back, her arms clasped over her head.

'How long have you been here today?' she was asked.

'Oh, I spend the day here now,' she answered. 'I am making my own
"cure", and living entirely on raw vegetables and nuts, and each day I
feel my spirit is stronger and purer. After all, what can you expect? The
majority of us are walking about with pig corpuscles and oxen frag-
ments in our brain. The wonder is the world is as good as it is. Now I
live on the simple, provided food' – she pointed to a little bag beside
her – 'a lettuce, a carrot, a potato, and some nuts are ample, rational
nourishment. I wash them under the tap and eat them raw, just as they
come from the harmless earth – fresh and uncontaminated.'

'Do you take nothing else all day?' I cried.

'Water. And perhaps a banana if I wake in the night.' She turned
round and leaned on one elbow. 'You overeat yourself dreadfully,' she
said; 'shamelessly! How can you expect the Flame of the Spirit to
burn brightly under layers of superfluous flesh?'

I wished she would not stare at me, and thought of going to look
at my watch again when a little girl wearing a string of coral beads
joined us.

'The poor Frau Hauptmann cannot join us today,' she said; 'she has come out in spots all over on account of her nerves. She was very excited yesterday after having written two postcards.'

'A delicate woman,' volunteered the Hungarian, 'but pleasant. Fancy, she has a separate plate for each of her front teeth! But she has no right to let her daughters wear such short sailor suits. They sit about on benches, crossing their legs in a most shameless manner. What are you going to do this afternoon, Fräulein Anna?'

'Oh,' said the Coral Necklace, 'the Herr Oberleutnant has asked me to go with him to Landsdorf. He must buy some eggs there to take home to his mother. He saves a penny on eight eggs by knowing the right peasants to bargain with.'

'Are you an American?' said the Vegetable Lady, turning to me.

'No.'

'Then you are an Englishwoman?'

'Well, hardly –'

'You must be one of the two; you cannot help it. I have seen you walking alone several times. You wear your –'

I got up and climbed on to the swing. The air was sweet and cool, rushing past my body. Above, white clouds trailed delicately through the blue sky. From the pine forest streamed a wild perfume, the branches swayed together, rhythmically, sonorously. I felt so light and free and happy – so childish! I wanted to poke my tongue out at the circle on the grass, who, drawing close together, were whispering meaningly.

'Perhaps you do not know,' cried a voice from one of the cells, 'to swing is very upsetting for the stomach? A friend of mine could keep nothing down for three weeks after exciting herself so.'

I went to the bath shelter and was hosed.

As I dressed, someone tapped on the wall.

'Do you know,' said a voice, 'there is a man who *lives* in the Luft Bad next door? He buries himself up to the armpits in mud and refuses to believe in the Trinity.'

The umbrellas are the saving grace of the Luft Bad. Now, when I go, I take my husband's 'storm' gamp and sit in a corner, hiding behind it.

Not that I am in the least ashamed of my legs.

(first published 1910, first book publication
In a German Pension, 1911)

A Birthday

Andreas Binzer woke slowly. He turned over on the narrow bed and stretched himself – yawned – opening his mouth as widely as possible and bringing his teeth together afterwards with a sharp 'click'. The sound of that click fascinated him; he repeated it quickly several times, with a snapping movement of the jaws. What teeth! he thought. Sound as a bell, every man jack of them. Never had one out, never had one stopped. That comes of no tomfoolery in eating, and a good regular brushing night and morning. He raised himself on his left elbow and waved his right arm over the side of the bed to feel for the chair where he put his watch and chain overnight. No chair was there – of course, he'd forgotten, there wasn't a chair in this wretched spare room. Had to put the confounded thing under his pillow. 'Half-past eight, Sunday, breakfast at nine – time for the bath' – his brain ticked to the watch. He sprang out of bed and went over to the window. The venetian blind was broken, hung fan-shaped over the upper pane . . . 'That blind must be mended. I'll get the office boy to drop in and fix it on his way home tomorrow – he's a good hand at blinds. Give him twopence and he'll do it as well as a carpenter . . . Anna could do it herself if she was all right. So would I, for the matter of that, but I don't like to trust myself on rickety step-ladders.' He looked up at the sky: it shone, strangely white, unflecked with cloud; he looked down at the row of garden strips and back yards. The fence of these gardens was built along the edge of a gully, spanned by an iron suspension bridge, and the people had a wretched habit of throwing their empty tins over the fence into the gully. Just like them, of course! Andreas started counting the tins, and decided, viciously, to write a letter to the papers about it and sign it – sign it in full.

The servant girl came out of their back door into the yard, carrying his boots. She threw one down on the ground, thrust her hand into the other, and stared at it, sucking in her cheeks. Suddenly she bent forward, spat on the toecap, and started polishing with a brush rooted out of her apron pocket . . . 'Slut of a girl! Heaven knows what infectious disease may be breeding now in that boot. Anna must get rid of that girl – even if she has to do without one for a bit – as soon as she's up and about again. The way she chucked one boot down and then spat upon the other! She didn't care whose boots she'd got hold of. *She* had no false notions of the respect due to the master of the house.' He turned away from the window and switched his bath towel from the wash-stand rail, sick at heart. 'I'm too sensitive for a man – that's what's the matter with me. Have been from the beginning, and will be to the end.'

There was a gentle knock at the door and his mother came in. She closed the door after her and leaned against it. Andreas noticed that her cap was crooked, and a long tail of hair hung over her shoulder. He went forward and kissed her.

'Good morning, mother; how's Anna?'

The old woman spoke quickly, clasping and unclasping her hands.

'Andreas, please go to Doctor Erb as soon as you are dressed.'

'Why,' he said, 'is she bad?'

Frau Binzer nodded, and Andreas, watching her, saw her face suddenly change; a fine network of wrinkles seemed to pull over it from under the skin surface.

'Sit down on the bed a moment,' he said. 'Been up all night?'

'Yes. No, I won't sit down, I must go back to her. Anna has been in pain all night. She wouldn't have you disturbed before because she said you looked so run down yesterday. You told her you had caught a cold and been very worried.'

Straightway Andreas felt that he was being accused.

'Well, she made me tell her, worried it out of me; you know the way she does.'

Again Frau Binzer nodded.

'Oh yes, I know. She says, is your cold better, and there's a warm undervest for you in the left-hand corner of the big drawer.'

Quite automatically Andreas cleared his throat twice.

'Yes,' he answered. 'Tell her my throat certainly feels looser. I suppose I'd better not disturb her?'

'No, and besides, *time,* Andreas.'

'I'll be ready in five minutes.'

They went into the passage. As Frau Binzer opened the door of the front bedroom, a long wail came from the room.

That shocked and terrified Andreas. He dashed into the bathroom, turned on both taps as far as they would go, cleaned his teeth and pared his nails while the water was running.

'Frightful business, frightful business,' he heard himself whispering. 'And I can't understand it. It isn't as though it were her first – it's her third. Old Schäfer told me, yesterday, his wife simply 'dropped' her fourth. Anna ought to have had a qualified nurse. Mother gives way to her. Mother spoils her. I wonder what she meant by saying I'd worried Anna yesterday. Nice remark to make to a husband at a time like this. Unstrung, I suppose – and my sensitiveness again.'

When he went into the kitchen for his boots, the servant girl was bent over the stove, cooking breakfast. 'Breathing into that, now, I suppose,' thought Andreas, and was very short with the servant girl. She did not notice. She was full of terrified joy and importance in the goings-on upstairs. She felt she was learning the secrets of life with every breath she drew. Had laid the table that morning saying, 'Boy,' as she put down the first dish, 'Girl,' as she placed the second – it had worked out with the saltspoon to 'Boy.' 'For two pins I'd tell the master that, to comfort him, like,' she decided. But the master gave her no opening.

'Put an extra cup and saucer on the table,' he said; 'the doctor may want some coffee.'

'The doctor, sir?' The servant girl whipped a spoon out of a pan, and spilled two drops of grease on the stove. 'Shall I fry something extra?' But the master had gone, slamming the door after him. He walked down the street – there was nobody about at all – dead and alive this place on a Sunday morning. As he crossed the suspension bridge a strong stench of fennel and decayed refuse streamed from the gully, and again Andreas began concocting a letter. He turned into the main road. The shutters were still up before the shops. Scraps of newspaper, hay and fruit skins strewed the pavement; the gutters were choked with the leavings of Saturday night. Two dogs sprawled in the middle of the road, scuffling and biting. Only the public-house at the corner was open; a young barman slopped water over the doorstep.

Fastidiously, his lips curling, Andreas picked his way through the water. 'Extraordinary how I am noticing things this morning. It's partly the effect of Sunday. I loathe a Sunday when Anna's tied by the

leg and the children are away. On Sunday a man has the right to expect
his family. Everything here's filthy, the whole place might be down
with the plague, and will be, too, if this street's not swept away. I'd like
to have a hand on the government ropes.' He braced his shoulders.
'Now for this doctor.'

'Doctor Erb is at breakfast,' the maid informed him. She showed
him into the waiting-room, a dark and musty place, with some ferns
under a glass-case by the window. 'He says he won't be a minute,
please, sir, and there is a paper on the table.'

'Unhealthy hole,' thought Binzer, walking over to the window and
drumming his fingers on the glass fern-shade. 'At breakfast, is he?
That's the mistake I made: turning out early on an empty stomach.'

A milk cart rattled down the street, the driver standing at the back,
cracking a whip; he wore an immense geranium flower stuck in the
lapel of his coat. Firm as a rock he stood, bending back a little in the
swaying cart. Andreas craned his neck to watch him all the way down
the road, even after he had gone, listening for the sharp sound of those
rattling cans.

'H'm, not much wrong with him,' he reflected. 'Wouldn't mind a
taste of that life myself. Up early, work all over by eleven o'clock,
nothing to do but loaf about all day until milking time.' Which he
knew was an exaggeration, but he wanted to pity himself.

The maid opened the door, and stood aside for Doctor Erb. Andreas
wheeled round; the two men shook hands.

'Well, Binzer,' said the doctor jovially, brushing some crumbs from
a pearl-coloured waistcoat, 'son and heir becoming importunate?'

Up went Binzer's spirits with a bound. Son and heir, by Jove! He
was glad to have to deal with a man again. And a sane fellow this, who
came across this sort of thing every day of the week.

'That's about the measure of it, Doctor,' he answered, smiling and
picking up his hat. 'Mother dragged me out of bed this morning with
imperative orders to bring you along.'

'Gig will be round in a minute. Drive back with me, won't you?
Extraordinary, sultry day; you're as red as a beetroot already.'

Andreas affected to laugh. The doctor had one annoying habit –
imagined he had the right to poke fun at everybody simply because he
was a doctor. 'The man's riddled with conceit, like all these professionals,' Andreas decided.

'What sort of night did Frau Binzer have?' asked the doctor. 'Ah, here's the gig. Tell me on the way up. Sit as near the middle as you can, will you, Binzer? Your weight tilts it over a bit one side – that's the worst of you successful business men.'

'Two stone heavier than I, if he's a pound,' thought Andreas. 'The man may be all right in his profession – but heaven preserve me.'

'Off you go, my beauty.' Doctor Erb flicked the little brown mare. 'Did your wife get any sleep last night?'

'No; I don't think she did,' answered Andreas shortly. 'To tell you the truth, I'm not satisfied that she hasn't a nurse.'

'Oh, your mother's worth a dozen nurses,' cried the doctor, with immense gusto. 'To tell you the truth, I'm not keen on nurses – too raw – raw as rump-steak. They wrestle for a baby as though they were wrestling with Death for the body of Patroclus ... Ever seen that picture by an English artist. Leighton? Wonderful thing – full of sinew!'

'There he goes again,' thought Andreas, 'airing off his knowledge to make a fool of me.'

'Now your mother – she's firm – she's capable. Does what she's told with a fund of sympathy. Look at these shops we're passing – they're festering sores. How on earth this government can tolerate –'

'They're not so bad – sound enough – only want a coat of paint.'

The doctor whistled a little tune and flicked the mare again.

'Well, I hope the young shaver won't give his mother too much trouble,' he said. 'Here we are.'

A skinny little boy, who had been sliding up and down the back seat of the gig, sprang out and held the horse's head. Andreas went straight into the dining-room and left the servant girl to take the doctor upstairs. He sat down, poured out some coffee, and bit through half a roll before helping himself to fish. Then he noticed there was no hot plate for the fish – the whole house was at sixes and sevens. He rang the bell, but the servant girl came in with a tray holding a bowl of soup and a hot plate.

'I've been keeping them on the stove,' she simpered.

'Ah, thanks, that's very kind of you.' As he swallowed the soup his heart warmed to this fool of a girl.

'Oh, it's a good thing Doctor Erb has come,' volunteered the servant girl, who was bursting for want of sympathy.

'H'm, h'm,' said Andreas.

She waited a moment, expectantly, rolling her eyes, then in full loathing of menkind went back to the kitchen and vowed herself to sterility.

Andreas cleared the soup bowl, and cleared the fish. As he ate, the room slowly darkened. A faint wind sprang up and beat the tree branches against the window. The dining-room looked over the breakwater of the harbour, and the sea swung heavily in rolling waves. Wind crept round the house, moaning drearily.

'We're in for a storm. That means I'm boxed up here all day. Well, there's one blessing; it'll clear the air.' He heard the servant girl rushing importantly round the house, slamming windows. Then he caught a glimpse of her in the garden, unpegging tea towels from the line across the lawn. She was a worker, there was no doubt about that. He took up a book, and wheeled his armchair over to the window. But it was useless. Too dark to read; he didn't believe in straining his eyes, and gas at ten o'clock in the morning seemed absurd. So he slipped down in the chair, leaned his elbows on the padded arms and gave himself up, for once, to idle dreaming. 'A boy? Yes, it was bound to be a boy this time . . .' 'What's your family, Binzer?' 'Oh, I've two girls and a boy!' A very nice little number. Of course he was the last man to have a favourite child, but a man needed a son. 'I'm working up the business for my son! Binzer & Son! It would mean living very tight for the next ten years, cutting expenses as fine as possible; and then —'

A tremendous gust of wind sprang upon the house, seized it, shook it, dropped, only to grip the more tightly. The waves swelled up along the breakwater and were whipped with broken foam. Over the white sky flew tattered streamers of grey cloud.

Andreas felt quite relieved to hear Doctor Erb coming down the stairs; he got up and lit the gas.

'Mind if I smoke in here?' asked Doctor Erb, lighting a cigarette before Andreas had time to answer. 'You don't smoke, do you? No time to indulge in pernicious little habits!'

'How is she now?' asked Andreas, loathing the man.

'Oh, well as can be expected, poor little soul. She begged me to come down and have a look at you. Said she knew you were worrying.' With laughing eyes the doctor looked at the breakfast-table. 'Managed to peck a bit, I see, eh?'

'Hoo-wih!' shouted the wind, shaking the window-sashes.

'Pity – this weather,' said Doctor Erb.

'Yes, it gets on Anna's nerves, and it's just nerve she wants.'

'Eh, what's that?' retorted the doctor. 'Nerve! Man alive! She's got twice the nerve of you and me rolled into one. Nerve! she's nothing but nerve. A woman who works as she does about the house and has three children in four years thrown in with the dusting, so to speak!'

He pitched his half-smoked cigarette into the fire-place and frowned at the window.

'Now *he's* accusing me,' thought Andreas. 'That's the second time this morning – first mother and now this man taking advantage of my sensitiveness.' He could not trust himself to speak, and rang the bell for the servant girl.

'Clear away the breakfast things,' he ordered. 'I can't have them messing about on the table till dinner!'

'Don't be hard on the girl,' coaxed Doctor Erb. 'She's got twice the work to do today.'

At that Binzer's anger blazed out.

'I'll trouble you, Doctor, not to interfere between me and my servants!' And he felt a fool at the same moment for not saying 'servant'.

Doctor Erb was not perturbed. He shook his head, thrust his hands into his pockets, and began balancing himself on toe and heel.

'You're jagged by the weather,' he said wryly, 'nothing else. A great pity – this storm. You know climate has an immense effect upon birth. A fine day perks a woman – gives her heart for her business. Good weather is as necessary to a confinement as it is to a washing day. Not bad – that last remark of mine – for a professional fossil, eh?'

Andreas made no reply.

'Well, I'll be getting back to my patient. Why don't you take a walk, and clear your head? That's the idea for you.'

'No,' he answered, 'I won't do that; it's too rough.'

He went back to his chair by the window. While the servant girl cleared away he pretended to read . . . then his dreams! It seemed years since he had had the time to himself to dream like that – he never had a breathing space. Saddled with work all day, and couldn't shake it off in the evening like other men. Besides, Anna was interested – they talked of practically nothing else together. Excellent mother she'd make for a boy; she had a grip of things.

Church bells started ringing through the windy air, now sounding
as though from very far away, then again as though all the churches in
the town had been suddenly transplanted into their street. They stirred
something in him, those bells, something vague and tender. Just about
that time Anna would call him from the hall. 'Andreas, come and have
your coat brushed. I'm ready.' Then off they would go, she hanging
on his arm, and looking up at him. She certainly was a little thing. He
remembered once saying when they were engaged, 'Just as high as my
heart,' and she had jumped on to a stool and pulled his head down,
laughing. A kid in those days, younger than her children in nature,
brighter, more 'go' and 'spirit' in her. The way she'd run down the
road to meet him after business! And the way she laughed when they
were looking for a house. By Jove! that laugh of hers! At the memory
he grinned, then grew suddenly grave. Marriage certainly changed a
woman far more than it did a man. Talk about sobering down. She had
lost all her go in two months! Well, once this boy business was over
she'd get stronger. He began to plan a little trip for them. He'd take her
away and they'd loaf about together somewhere. After all, dash it,
they were young still. She'd got into a groove; he'd have to force her
out of it, that's all.

He got up and went into the drawing-room, carefully shut the door
and took Anna's photograph from the top of the piano. She wore a
white dress with a big bow of some soft stuff under the chin, and
stood, a little stiffly, holding a sheaf of artificial poppies and corn in
her hands. Delicate she looked even then; her masses of hair gave her
that look. She seemed to droop under the heavy braids of it, and yet
she was smiling. Andreas caught his breath sharply. She was his wife –
that girl. Posh! it had only been taken four years ago. He held it close
to him, bent forward and kissed it. Then rubbed the glass with the
back of his hand. At that moment, fainter than he had heard in the passage, more terrifying, Andreas heard again that wailing cry. The wind
caught it up in mocking echo, blew it over the house-tops, down the
street, far away from him. He flung out his arms, 'I'm so damnably
helpless,' he said, and then, to the picture, 'Perhaps it's not as bad as it
sounds; perhaps it is just my sensitiveness.' In the half-light of the
drawing-room the smile seemed to deepen in Anna's portrait, and to
become secret, even cruel. 'No,' he reflected, 'that smile is not at all
her happiest expression – it was a mistake to let her have it taken

smiling like that. She doesn't look like my wife – like the mother of my son.' Yes, that was it, she did not look like the mother of a son who was going to be a partner in the firm. The picture got on his nerves; he held it in different lights, looked at it from a distance, sideways, spent, it seemed to Andreas afterwards, a whole lifetime trying to fit it in. The more he played with it the deeper grew his dislike of it. Thrice he carried it over to the fire-place and decided to chuck it behind the Japanese umbrella in the grate; then he thought it absurd to waste an expensive frame. There was no good in beating about the bush. Anna looked like a stranger – abnormal, a freak – it might be a picture taken just before or after death.

Suddenly he realised that the wind had dropped, that the whole house was still, terribly still. Cold and pale, with a disgusting feeling that spiders were creeping up his spine and across his face, he stood in the centre of the drawing-room, hearing Doctor Erb's footsteps descending the stairs.

He saw Doctor Erb come into the room; the room seemed to change into a great glass bowl that spun round, and Doctor Erb seemed to swim through this glass bowl towards him, like a goldfish in a pearl-coloured waistcoat.

'My beloved wife has passed away!' He wanted to shout it out before the doctor spoke.

'Well, she's hooked a boy this time!' said Doctor Erb. Andreas staggered forward.

'Look out. Keep on your pins,' said Doctor Erb, catching Binzer's arm, and murmuring, as he felt it, 'Flabby as butter.'

A glow spread all over Andreas. He was exultant.

'Well, by God! Nobody can accuse *me* of not knowing what suffering is,' he said.

(first published 1911, first book publication
In a German Pension, 1911)

The Swing of the Pendulum

The landlady knocked at the door. 'Come in,' said Viola.

'There is a letter for you,' said the landlady, 'a special letter' – she held the green envelope in a corner of her dingy apron.

'Thanks.' Viola, kneeling on the floor, poking at the little dusty stove, stretched out her hand. 'Any answer?'

'No; the messenger has gone.'

'Oh, all right!' She did not look the landlady in the face; she was ashamed of not having paid her rent, and wondered grimly, without any hope, if the woman would begin to bluster again.

'About this money owing to me –' said the landlady.

'Oh, the Lord – off she goes!' thought Viola, turning her back on the woman and making a grimace at the stove.

'It's settle – or it's go!' The landlady raised her voice; she began to bawl. 'I'm a lady, I am, and a respectable woman, I'll have you know. I'll have no lice in my house, sneaking their way into the furniture and eating up everything. It's cash – or out you go before twelve o'clock tomorrow.'

Viola felt rather than saw the woman's gesture. She shot out her arm in a stupid helpless way, as though a dirty pigeon had suddenly flown at her face. 'Filthy old beast! Ugh! And the smell of her – like stale cheese and damp washing.'

'Very well!' she answered shortly; 'it's cash down or I leave to-morrow. All right: don't shout.'

It was extraordinary – always before this woman came near her she trembled in her shoes – even the sound of those flat feet stumping up the stairs made her feel sick, but once they were face to face she felt immensely calm and indifferent, and could not understand why she even worried about money, nor why she sneaked out of the house on tiptoe, not even daring to shut the door after her in case the landlady should hear and shout something terrible, nor why she spent nights pacing up and down her room – drawing up sharply before the mirror and saying to a tragic reflection: 'Money, money, money!' When she was alone her poverty was like a huge dream-mountain on which her feet were fast rooted – aching with the ache of the size of the thing – but if it came to definite action, with no time for imaginings, her dream-mountain dwindled into a beastly 'hold-your-nose' affair, to be passed by as quickly as possible, with anger and a strong sense of superiority.

The landlady bounced out of the room, banging the door, so that it shook and rattled as though it had listened to the conversation and fully sympathised with the old hag.

Squatting on her heels, Viola opened the letter. It was from Casimir:

> I shall be with you at three o'clock this afternoon – and must be off again this evening. All news when we meet. I hope you are happier than I. – CASIMIR.

'Huh! how kind!' she sneered; 'how condescending. Too good of you, really!' She sprang to her feet, crumbling the letter in her hands. 'And how are you to know that I shall stick here awaiting your pleasure until three o'clock this afternoon?' But she knew she would; her rage was only half sincere. She longed to see Casimir, for she was confident that this time she would make him understand the situation . . . 'For, as it is, it's intolerable – intolerable!' she muttered.

It was ten o'clock in the morning of a grey day curiously lighted by pale flashes of sunshine. Searched by these flashes her room looked tumbled and grimed. She pulled down the window-blinds – but they gave a persistent, whitish glare which was just as bad. The only thing of life in the room was a jar of hyacinths given her by the landlady's daughter: it stood on the table exuding a sickly perfume from its plump petals; there were even rich buds unfolding, and the leaves shone like oil.

Viola went over to the wash-stand, poured some water into the enamel basin, and sponged her face and neck. She dipped her face into the water, opened her eyes, and shook her head from side to side – it was exhilarating. She did it three times. 'I suppose I could drown myself if I stayed under long enough,' she thought. 'I wonder how long it takes to become unconscious? . . . Often read of women drowning in a bucket. I wonder if any air enters by the ears – if the basin would have to be as deep as a bucket?' She experimented – gripped the wash-stand with both hands and slowly sank her head into the water, when again there was a knock on the door. Not the landlady this time – it must be Casimir. With her face and hair dripping, with her petticoat bodice unbuttoned, she ran and opened it.

A strange man stood against the lintel – seeing her, he opened his eyes very wide and smiled delightfully. 'Excuse me – does Fräulein Schäfer live here?'

'No; never heard of her.' His smile was so infectious, she wanted to smile too – and the water had made her feel so fresh and rosy.

The strange man appeared overwhelmed with astonishment. 'She doesn't?' he cried. 'She is out, you mean!'

'No, she's not living here,' answered Viola.

'But – pardon – one moment.' He moved from the door lintel, standing squarely in front of her. He unbuttoned his greatcoat and drew a slip of paper from the breast pocket, smoothing it in his gloved fingers before handing it to her.

'Yes, that's the address, right enough, but there must be a mistake in the number. So many lodging-houses in this street, you know, and so big.'

Drops of water fell from her hair on to the paper. She burst out laughing. 'Oh, *how* dreadful I must look – one moment!' She ran back to the wash-stand and caught up a towel. The door was still open . . . After all, there was nothing more to be said. Why on earth had she asked him to wait a moment? She folded the towel round her shoulders, and returned to the door, suddenly grave. 'I'm sorry; I know no such name?' in a sharp voice.

Said the strange man: 'Sorry, too. Have you been living here long?'

'Er – yes – a long time.' She began to close the door slowly.

'Well – good morning, thanks so much. Hope I haven't been a bother.'

'Good morning.'

She heard him walk down the passage and then pause – lighting a cigarette. Yes – a faint scent of delicious cigarette smoke penetrated her room. She sniffed at it, smiling again. Well, that had been a fascinating interlude! He looked so amazingly happy: his heavy clothes and big buttoned gloves; his beautifully brushed hair . . . and that smile . . . 'Jolly' was the word – just a well-fed boy with the world for his playground. People like that did one good – one felt 'made over' at the sight of them. *Sane* they were – so sane and solid. You could depend on them never having one mad impulse from the day they were born until the day they died. And Life was in league with them – jumped them on her knee – quite rightly too. At that moment she noticed Casimir's letter, crumpled up on the floor – the smile faded. Staring at the letter she began braiding her hair – a dull feeling of rage crept through her – she seemed to be braiding it into her brain, and binding it, tightly, above her head . . . Of course that had been the mistake all along. What had? Oh, Casimir's frightful seriousness. If she had been happy when they first met she never would have looked at him – but they had been like two patients in the same hospital ward – each finding comfort in the sickness of the other – sweet foundation for a love episode! Misfortune had knocked their heads together: they had looked at each other, stunned with the conflict and sympathised . . . 'I wish I could step outside the whole affair and just judge it – then I'd find a way out. I certainly was in love with Casimir . . . Oh, be sincere for once.' She flopped down on the bed and hid her face in the pillow. 'I was not in love. I wanted somebody to look after me – and keep me until my work began to sell – and he kept bothers with other men away. And what would have happened if he hadn't come along? I would have spent my wretched little pittance, and then – Yes, that was what decided me, thinking about that "then". He was the only solution. And I believed in him then. I thought his work had only to be recognised once, and he'd roll in wealth. I thought perhaps we might be poor for a month – but he said, if only he could have me, the stimulus . . . Funny, if it wasn't so damned tragic! Exactly the contrary has happened – he hasn't had a thing published for months – neither have I – but then I didn't expect to. Yes, the truth is, I'm hard and bitter, and I have neither faith nor love for unsuccessful men. I always end by despising them as I despise Casimir. I suppose it's the savage pride of the female who likes to think the man to whom she has given herself must be a very great chief indeed. But to stew in this disgusting house while Casimir scours the land in the hope of finding one editorial open door – it's humiliating. It's changed my whole nature. I wasn't born for poverty – I only flower among really jolly people, and people who never are worried.'

The figure of the strange man rose before her – would not be dismissed. 'That was the man for me, after all is said and done – a man without a care – who'd give me everything I want and with whom I'd always feel that sense of life and of being in touch with the world. I never wanted to fight – it was thrust on me. Really, there's a fount of happiness in me, that is drying up, little by little, in this hateful existence. I'll be dead if this goes on – and' – she stirred in the bed and flung out her arms – 'I want passion, and love, and adventure – I yearn for them. Why should I stay here and rot? – I am rotting!' she cried, comforting herself with the sound of her breaking voice. 'But if I tell Casimir all this when he comes this afternoon, and he says, "Go" – as he certainly will – that's another thing I loathe about him, – he's under my thumb – what should I do then – where should I go to?' There was nowhere. 'I don't want to work – or carve out my own path. I want ease and any amount of nursing in the lap of luxury. There is only one thing I'm fitted for, and that is to be a great courtesan.' But she did not know how to go about it. She was frightened to go into the streets – she heard of such awful things happening to those women – men with diseases – or men who didn't pay – besides, the idea of a strange man every night – no, that was out of the question. 'If I'd the clothes I would go to a really good hotel and find some wealthy man . . . like the strange man this morning. He would be ideal. Oh, if I only had his address – I am sure I would fascinate him. I'd keep him laughing all day – I'd make him give me unlimited money . . .' At the thought she grew warm and soft. She began to dream of a wonderful house, and of presses full of clothes and of perfumes. She saw herself stepping into carriages – looking at the strange man with a mysterious, voluptuous glance – she practised the glance, lying on the bed – and never another worry, just drugged with happiness. That was the life for her. Well, the thing to do was to let Casimir go on his wild-goose chase that evening, and while he was away – What! Also – please to remember – there was the rent to be paid before twelve next morning, and she hadn't the money for a square meal. At the thought of food she felt a sharp twinge in her stomach, a sensation as though there were a hand in her stomach, squeezing it dry. She was terribly hungry – all Casimir's fault – and that man had lived on the fat of the land ever since he was born. He looked as though he could order a magnificent dinner. Oh, why hadn't she played her cards better? – he'd been sent by Providence – and she'd snubbed him. 'If I had that time over again, I'd be safe by now.' And instead of the ordinary man who had spoken with her at the door her mind created a brilliant, laughing image, who would treat her like a queen . . . 'There's only one thing I could not stand – that he should be coarse or vulgar. Well, he wasn't – he was obviously a man of the world, and the way he apologised . . . I have enough faith in my own power and beauty to know I could make a man treat me just as I wanted to be treated.' . . . It floated into her dreams – that sweet scent of cigarette smoke. And then she remembered that she had heard nobody go down the stone stairs. Was it possible that the strange man was still there? . . . The thought was too absurd – Life didn't play tricks like that – and yet – she was quite conscious of his nearness. Very quietly she got up, unhooked from the back of the door a long white gown, buttoned it on – smiling slyly. She did not know what was going to happen. She only thought: 'Oh, what fun!' and that they were playing a delicious game – this strange man and she. Very gently she turned the door-handle, screwing up her face and biting her lip as the lock snapped back. Of course, there he was – leaning against the banister rail. He wheeled round as she slipped into the passage.

'Da,' she muttered, folding her gown tightly around her, 'I must go downstairs and fetch some wood. Brr! the cold!'

'There isn't any wood,' volunteered the strange man. She gave a little cry of astonishment, and then tossed her head.

'You, again,' she said scornfully, conscious the while of his merry eye, and the fresh, strong smell of his healthy body.

'The landlady shouted out there was no wood left. I just saw her go out to buy some.'

'Story – story!' she longed to cry. He came quite close to her, stood over her and whispered:

'Aren't you going to ask me to finish my cigarette in your room?'

She nodded. 'You may if you want to!'

In that moment together in the passage a miracle had happened. Her room was quite changed – it was full of sweet light and the scent of hyacinth flowers. Even the furniture appeared different – exciting. Quick as a flash she remembered childish parties when they had played charades, and one side had left the room and come in again to act a word – just what she was doing now. The strange man went over to the stove and sat down in her armchair. She did not want him to talk or come near her – it was enough to see him in the room, so secure and happy. How hungry she had been for the nearness of someone like that – who knew nothing at all about her – and made no demands – but just lived. Viola ran over to the table and put her arms round the jar of hyacinths.

'Beautiful! Beautiful!' she cried – burying her head in the flowers – and sniffing greedily at the scent. Over the leaves she looked at the man and laughed.

'You are a funny little thing,' said he lazily.

'Why? Because I love flowers?'

'I'd far rather you loved other things,' said the strange man slowly. She broke off a little pink petal and smiled at it.

'Let me send you some flowers,' said the strange man. 'I'll send you a roomful if you'd like them.'

His voice frightened her slightly. 'Oh no, thanks – this one is quite enough for me.'

'No, it isn't' – in a teasing voice.

'What a stupid remark!' thought Viola, and looking at him again he did not seem quite so jolly. She noticed that his eyes were set too closely together – and they were too small. Horrible thought, that he should prove stupid.

'What do you do all day?' she asked hastily.

'Nothing.'

'Nothing at all?'

'Why should I do anything?'

'Oh, don't imagine for one moment that I condemn such wisdom – only it sounds too good to be true!'

'What's that?' – he craned forward. 'What sounds too good to be true?' Yes – there was no denying it – he looked silly.

'I suppose the searching after Fräulein Schäfer doesn't occupy all your days.'

'Oh no' – he smiled broadly – 'that's very good! By Jove! no. I drive a good bit – are you keen on horses?'

She nodded. 'Love them.'

'You must come driving with me – I've got a fine pair of greys. Will you?'

'Pretty I'd look perched behind greys in my one and only hat,' thought she. Aloud: 'I'd love to.' Her easy acceptance pleased him.

'How about tomorrow?' he suggested. 'Suppose you have lunch with me tomorrow and I take you driving.'

After all – this was just a game. 'Yes, I'm not busy tomorrow,' she said.

A little pause – then the strange man patted his leg. 'Why don't you come and sit down?' he said.

She pretended not to see and swung on to the table. 'Oh, I'm all right here.'

'No, you're not' – again the teasing voice. 'Come and sit on my knee.'

'Oh no,' said Viola very heartily, suddenly busy with her hair.

'Why not?'

'I don't want to.'

'Oh, come along' – impatiently.

She shook her head from side to side. 'I wouldn't dream of such a thing.'

At that he got up and came over to her. 'Funny little pussy cat!' He put up one hand to touch her hair.

'Don't,' she said – and slipped off the table. 'I – I think it's time you went now.' She was quite frightened now – thinking only: 'This man must be got rid of as quickly as possible.'

'Oh, but you don't want me to go?'

'Yes, I do – I'm very busy.'

'Busy. What does the pussy cat do all day?'

'Lots and lots of things!' She wanted to push him out of the room and slam the door on him – idiot – fool – cruel disappointment.

'What's she frowning for?' he asked. 'Is she worried about anything?' Suddenly serious: 'I say – you know, are you in any financial difficulty? Do you want money? I'll give it to you if you like!'

'Money! Steady on the brake – don't lose your head!' – so she spoke to herself.

'I'll give you two hundred marks if you'll kiss me.'

'Oh, boo! What a condition! And I don't want to kiss you – I don't like kissing. Please go!'

'Yes – you do! – yes, you do.' He caught hold of her arms above the elbows. She struggled, and was quite amazed to realise how angry she felt.

'Let me go – immediately!' she cried – and he slipped one arm round her body, and drew her towards him – like a bar of iron across her back – that arm.

'Leave me alone, I tell you! Don't be mean! I didn't want this to happen when you came into my room. How dare you?'

'Well, kiss me and I'll go!'

It was too idiotic – dodging that stupid, smiling face.

'I won't kiss you! – you brute! – I won't!' Somehow she slipped out of his arms and ran to the wall – stood back against it – breathing quickly.

'Get out!' she stammered. 'Go on now, clear out!'

At that moment, when he was not touching her, she quite enjoyed herself. She thrilled at her own angry voice. 'To think I should talk to a man like that!' An angry flush spread over his face – his lips curled back, showing his teeth – just like a dog, thought Viola. He made a rush at her, and held her against the wall – pressed upon her with all the weight of his body. This time she could not get free.

'I won't kiss you. I won't. Stop doing that! Ugh! you're like a dog – you ought to find lovers round lamp-posts – you beast – you fiend!'

He did not answer. With an expression of the most absurd determination he pressed ever more heavily upon her. He did not even look at her – but rapped out in a sharp voice: 'Keep quiet – keep quiet.'

'Gar-r! Why are men so strong?' She began to cry. 'Go away – I don't want you, you dirty creature. I want to murder you. Oh, my God! if I had a knife.'

'Don't be silly – come and be good!' He dragged her towards the bed.

'Do you suppose I'm a light woman?' she snarled, and swooping over she fastened her teeth in his glove.

'Ach! don't do that – you are hurting me!'

She did not let go, but her heart said, 'Thank the Lord I thought of this.'

'Stop this minute – you vixen – you bitch.' He threw her away from him. She saw with joy that his eyes were full of tears. 'You've really hurt me,' he said in a choking voice.

'Of course I have. I meant to. That's nothing to what I'll do if you touch me again.'

The strange man picked up his hat. 'No, thanks,' he said grimly. 'But I'll not forget this – I'll go to your landlady.'

'Pooh!' She shrugged her shoulders and laughed. 'I'll tell her you forced your way in here and tried to assault me. Who will she believe? – with your bitten hand. You go and find your Schäfers.'

A sensation of glorious, intoxicating happiness flooded Viola. She rolled her eyes at him. 'If you don't go away this moment I'll bite you again,' she said, and the absurd words started her laughing. Even when the door was closed, hearing him descending the stairs, she laughed, and danced about the room.

What a morning! Oh, chalk it up. That was her first fight, and she'd won – she'd conquered that beast – all by herself. Her hands were still trembling. She pulled up the sleeve of her gown – great red marks on her arms. 'My ribs will be blue. I'll be blue all over,' she reflected. 'If only that beloved Casimir could have seen us.' And the feeling of rage and disgust against Casimir had totally disappeared. How could the poor darling help not having any money? It was her fault as much as his, and he, just like her, was apart from the world, fighting it, just as she had done. If only three o'clock would come. She saw herself running towards him and putting her arms round his neck. 'My blessed one! Of course we are bound to win. Do you love me still? Oh, I have been horrible lately.'

(first published in *In a German Pension*, 1911)

How Pearl Button was Kidnapped

Pearl Button swung on the little gate in front of the House of Boxes. It was the early afternoon of a sunshiny day with little winds playing hide-and-seek in it. They blew Pearl Button's pinafore frill into her mouth, and they blew the street dust all over the House of Boxes. Pearl watched it – like a cloud – like when mother peppered her fish and the top of the pepper-pot came off. She swung on the little gate, all alone, and she sang a small song. Two big women came walking down the street. One was dressed in red and the other was dressed in yellow and green. They had pink handkerchiefs over their heads, and both of them carried a big flax basket of ferns. They had no shoes and stockings on, and they came walking along, slowly, because they were so fat, and talking to each other and always smiling. Pearl stopped swinging, and when they saw her they stopped walking. They looked and looked at her and then they talked to each other, waving their arms and clapping their hands together. Pearl began to laugh.

The two women came up to her, keeping close to the hedge and looking in a frightened way towards the House of Boxes.

'Hallo, little girl!' said one.

Pearl said, 'Hallo!'

'You all alone by yourself?'

Pearl nodded.

'Where's your mother?'

'In the kitching, ironing-because-its-Tuesday.'

The women smiled at her and Pearl smiled back. 'Oh,' she said, 'haven't you got very white teeth indeed! Do it again.'

The dark women laughed, and again they talked to each other with funny words and wavings of the hands. 'What's your name?' they asked her.

'Pearl Button.'

'You coming with us, Pearl Button? We got beautiful things to show you,' whispered one of the women. So Pearl got down from the gate and she slipped out into the road. And she walked between the two dark women down the windy road, taking little running steps to keep up, and wondering what they had in their House of Boxes.

They walked a long way. 'You tired?' asked one of the women, bending down to Pearl. Pearl shook her head. They walked much further. 'You not tired?' asked the other woman. And Pearl shook her head again, but tears shook from her eyes at the same time and her lips trembled. One of the women gave over her flax basket of ferns and caught Pearl Button up in her arms, and walked with Pearl Button's head against her shoulder and her dusty little legs dangling. She was softer than a bed and she had a nice smell – a smell that made you bury your head and breathe and breathe it . . .

They set Pearl Button down in a log room full of other people the same colour as they were – and all these people came close to her and looked at her, nodding and laughing and throwing up their eyes. The woman who had carried Pearl took off her hair ribbon and shook her curls loose. There was a cry from the other women, and they crowded close and some of them ran a finger through Pearl's yellow curls, very gently, and one of them, a young one, lifted all Pearl's hair and kissed the back of her little white neck. Pearl felt shy but happy at the same time. There were some men on the floor, smoking, with rugs and feather mats round their shoulders. One of them made a funny face at her and he pulled a great big peach out of his pocket and set it on the floor, and flicked it with his finger as though it were a marble. It rolled right over to her. Pearl picked it up. 'Please can I eat it?' she asked. At that they all laughed and clapped their hands, and the man with the funny face made another at her and pulled a pear out of his pocket and sent it bobbling over the floor. Pearl laughed. The women sat on the floor and Pearl sat down too. The floor was very dusty. She carefully pulled up her pinafore and dress and sat on her petticoat as she had been taught to sit in dusty places, and she ate the fruit, the juice running all down her front.

'Oh!' she said in a very frightened voice to one of the women, 'I've spilled all the juice!'

'That doesn't matter at all,' said the woman, patting her cheek. A man came into the room with a long whip in his hand. He shouted something. They all got up, shouting, laughing, wrapping themselves up in rugs and blankets and feather mats. Pearl was carried again, this time into a great cart, and she sat on the lap of one of her women with

the driver beside her. It was a green cart with a red pony and a black
pony. It went very fast out of the town. The driver stood up and
waved the whip round his head. Pearl peered over the shoulder of her
woman. Other carts were behind like a procession. She waved at them.
Then the country came. First fields of short grass with sheep on them
and little bushes of white flowers and pink briar rose baskets – then big
trees on both sides of the road – and nothing to be seen except big
trees. Pearl tried to look through them but it was quite dark. Birds
were singing. She nestled closer in the big lap. The woman was warm
as a cat, and she moved up and down when she breathed, just like purr-
ing. Pearl played with a green ornament round her neck, and the
woman took the little hand and kissed each of her fingers and then
turned it over and kissed the dimples. Pearl had never been happy like
this before. On the top of a big hill they stopped. The driving man
turned to Pearl and said, 'Look, look!' and pointed with his whip.

And down at the bottom of the hill was something perfectly
different – a great big piece of blue water was creeping over the land.
She screamed and clutched at the big woman. 'What is it, what is it?'

'Why,' said the woman, 'it's the sea.'

'Will it hurt us – is it coming?'

'Ai-e, no, it doesn't come to us. It's very beautiful. You look again.'

Pearl looked. 'You're sure it can't come,' she said.

'Ai-e, no. It stays in its place,' said the big woman. Waves with
white tops came leaping over the blue. Pearl watched them break on a
long piece of land covered with garden-path shells. They drove round
a corner.

There were some little houses down close to the sea, with wood
fences round them and gardens inside. They comforted her. Pink and
red and blue washing hung over the fences, and as they came near
more people came out, and five yellow dogs with long thin tails. All
the people were fat and laughing, with little naked babies holding on
to them or rolling about in the gardens like puppies. Pearl was lifted
down and taken into a tiny house with only one room and a veranda.
There was a girl there with two pieces of black hair down to her feet.
She was setting the dinner on the floor. 'It *is* a funny place,' said Pearl,
watching the pretty girl while the woman unbuttoned her little drawers for her. She was very hungry. She ate meat and vegetables and fruit
and the woman gave her milk out of a green cup. And it was quite

silent except for the sea outside and the laughs of the two women watching her. 'Haven't you got any Houses of Boxes?' she said. 'Don't you all live in a row? Don't the men go to offices? Aren't there any nasty things?'

They took off her shoes and stockings, her pinafore and dress. She walked about in her petticoat and then she walked outside with the grass pushing between her toes. The two women came out with different sorts of baskets. They took her hands. Over a little paddock, through a fence, and then on warm sand with brown grass in it they went down to the sea. Pearl held back when the sand grew wet, but the women coaxed, 'Nothing to hurt, very beautiful. You come.' They dug in the sand and found some shells which they threw into the baskets. The sand was wet as mud pies. Pearl forgot her fright and began digging too. She got hot and wet, and suddenly over her feet broke a little line of foam. 'Oo, oo!' she shrieked, dabbling with her feet. 'Lovely, lovely!' She paddled in the shallow water. It was warm. She made a cup of her hands and caught some of it. But it stopped being blue in her hands. She was so excited that she rushed over to her woman and flung her little thin arms round the woman's neck, hugging her, kissing . . .

Suddenly the girl gave a frightful scream. The woman raised herself and Pearl slipped down on the sand and looked towards the land. Little men in blue coats – little blue men came running, running towards her with shouts and whistlings – a crowd of little blue men to carry her back to the House of Boxes.

(written 1910, first published 1912, first book publication
Something Childish and Other Stories, 1924)

The Woman at the Store

All that day the heat was terrible. The wind blew close to the ground; it rooted among the tussock grass, slithered along the road, so that the white pumice dust swirled in our faces, settled and sifted over us and was like a dry-skin itching for growth on our bodies. The horses stumbled along, coughing and chuffing. The pack-horse was sick – with a big open sore rubbed under the belly. Now and again she stopped short, threw back her head, looked at us as though she were going to cry, and whinnied. Hundreds of larks shrilled; the sky was slate colour, and the sound of the larks reminded me of slate pencils scraping over its surface. There was nothing to be seen but wave after wave of tussock grass, patched with purple orchids and manuka bushes covered with thick spider webs.

Jo rode ahead. He wore a blue galatea shirt, corduroy trousers and riding boots. A white handkerchief, spotted with red – it looked as though his nose had been bleeding on it – was knotted round his throat. Wisps of white hair straggled from under his wideawake – his moustache and eyebrows were called white – he slouched in the saddle, grunting. Not once that day had he sung

> 'I don't care, for don't you see,
> My wife's mother was in front of me!'

It was the first day we had been without it for a month, and now there seemed something uncanny in his silence. Jim rode beside me, white as a clown; his black eyes glittered and he kept shooting out his tongue and moistening his lips. He was dressed in a Jaeger vest and a pair of blue duck trousers, fastened round the waist with a plaited leather belt. We had hardly spoken since dawn. At noon we had lunched off fly biscuits and apricots by the side of a swampy creek.

'My stomach feels like the crop of a hen,' said Jo. 'Now then, Jim, you're the bright boy of the party – where's this 'ere store you kep' on talking about. "Oh yes," you says, "I know a fine store, with a paddock for the horses and a creek runnin' through, owned by a friend of mine who'll give yer a bottle of whisky before 'e shakes hands with yer." I'd like ter see that place – merely as a matter of curiosity – not that I'd ever doubt yer word – as yer know very well – *but . . .*'

Jim laughed. 'Don't forget there's a woman too, Jo, with blue eyes and yellow hair, who'll promise you something else before she shakes hands with you. Put that in your pipe and smoke it.'

'The heat's making you balmy,' said Jo. But he dug his knees into the horse. We shambled on. I half fell asleep and had a sort of uneasy dream that the horses were not moving forward at all – then that I was on a rocking-horse, and my old mother was scolding me for raising such a fearful dust from the drawing-room carpet. 'You've entirely worn off the pattern of the carpet,' I heard her saying, and she gave the reins a tug. I snivelled and woke to find Jim leaning over me, maliciously smiling.

'That was a case of all but,' said he. 'I just caught you. What's up? Been bye-bye?'

'No!' I raised my head. 'Thank the Lord we're arriving somewhere.'

We were on the brow of the hill, and below us there was a whare roofed with corrugated iron. It stood in a garden, rather far back from the road – a big paddock opposite, and a creek and a clump of young willow trees. A thin line of blue smoke stood up straight from the chimney of the whare; and as I looked a woman came out, followed by a child and a sheep dog – the woman carrying what appeared to me a black stick. She made gestures at us. The horses put on a final spurt, Jo took off his wideawake, shouted, threw out his chest, and began singing 'I don't care, for don't you see . . .' The sun pushed through the pale clouds and shed a vivid light over the scene. It gleamed on the woman's yellow hair, over her flapping pinafore and the rifle she was carrying. The child hid behind her, and the yellow dog, a mangy beast, scuttled back into the whare, his tail between his legs. We drew rein and dismounted.

'Hallo,' screamed the woman. 'I thought you was three 'awks. My kid comes runnin' in ter me. "Mumma," says she, "there's three brown things comin' over the 'ill," says she. An' I comes out smart, I can tell yer. "They'll be 'awks," I says to her. Oh, the 'awks about 'ere, yer wouldn't believe.'

The 'kid' gave us the benefit of one eye from behind the woman's pinafore – then retired again.

'Where's your old man?' asked Jim.

The woman blinked rapidly, screwing up her face.

'Away shearin'. Bin away a month. I suppose ye're not goin' to stop, are yer? There's a storm comin' up.'

'You bet we are,' said Jo. 'So you're on your lonely, missus?'

She stood, pleating the frills of her pinafore, and glancing from one to the other of us, like a hungry bird. I smiled at the thought of how Jim had pulled Jo's leg about her. Certainly her eyes were blue, and what hair she had was yellow, but ugly. She was a figure of fun. Looking at her, you felt there was nothing but sticks and wires under that pinafore – her front teeth were knocked out, she had red, pulpy hands and she wore on her feet a pair of dirty Bluchers.

'I'll go and turn out the horses,' said Jim. 'Got any embrocation? Poi's rubbed herself to hell!'

''Arf a mo!' The woman stood silent a moment, her nostrils expanding as she breathed. Then she shouted violently, 'I'd rather you didn't stop . . . You *can't,* and there's the end of it. I don't let out that paddock any more. You'll have to go on; I ain't got nothing!'

'Well, I'm blest!' said Jo heavily. He pulled me aside. 'Gone a bit off 'er dot,' he whispered. 'Too much alone, *you know,*' very significantly. 'Turn the sympathetic tap on 'er, she'll come round all right.'

But there was no need – she had come round by herself.

'Stop if yer like!' she muttered, shrugging her shoulders. To me – 'I'll give yer the embrocation if yer come along.'

'Right-o, I'll take it down to them.' We walked together up the garden path. It was planted on both sides with cabbages. They smelled like stale dish-water. Of flowers there were double poppies and sweet-williams. One little patch was divided off by pawa shells – presumably it belonged to the child – for she ran from her mother and began to grub in it with a broken clothes-peg. The yellow dog lay across the doorstep, biting fleas; the woman kicked him away.

'Gar-r, get away, you beast . . . the place ain't tidy. I 'aven't 'ad time ter fix things today – been ironing. Come right in.'

It was a large room, the walls plastered with old pages of English periodicals. Queen Victoria's Jubilee appeared to be the most recent number. A table with an ironing board and wash-tub on it, some wooden forms, a black horsehair sofa and some broken cane chairs pushed against the walls. The mantelpiece above the stove was draped in pink paper, further ornamented with dried grasses and ferns and a coloured print of Richard Seddon. There were four doors – one, judging from the smell, led into the 'Store', one on to the 'backyard', through a third I saw the bedroom. Flies buzzed in circles round the ceiling, and treacle papers and bundles of dried clover were pinned to the window curtains.

I was alone in the room; she had gone into the store for the embrocation. I heard her stamping about and muttering to herself: 'I got some, now where did I put that bottle? . . . It's behind the pickles . . . no, it ain't.' I cleared a place on the table and sat there, swinging my legs. Down in the paddock I could hear Jo singing and the sound of hammer strokes as Jim drove in the tent pegs. It was sunset. There is no twilight in our New Zealand days, but a curious half-hour when everything appears grotesque – it frightens – as though the savage spirit of the country walked abroad and sneered at what it saw. Sitting alone in the hideous room I grew afraid. The woman next door was a long time finding that stuff. What was she doing in there? Once I thought I heard her bang her hands down on the counter, and once she half moaned, turning it into a cough and clearing her throat. I wanted to shout 'Buck up!' but I kept silent.

'Good Lord, what a life!' I thought. 'Imagine being here day in, day out, with that rat of a child and a mangy dog. Imagine bothering about ironing. *Mad,* of course she's mad! Wonder how long she's been here – wonder if I could get her to talk.'

At that moment she poked her head round the door.

'Wot was it yer wanted?' she asked.

'Embrocation.'

'Oh, I forgot. I got it, it was in front of the pickle jars.'

She handed me the bottle.

'My, you do look tired, you do! Shall I knock yer up a few scones for supper! There's some tongue in the store, too, and I'll cook yer a cabbage if you fancy it.'

'Right-o.' I smiled at her. 'Come down to the paddock and bring the kid for tea.'

She shook her head, pursing up her mouth.

'Oh no. I don't fancy it. I'll send the kid down with the things and a billy of milk. Shall I knock up a few extry scones to take with yer ter-morrow?'

'Thanks.'

She came and stood by the door.

'How old is the kid?'

'Six – come next Christmas. I 'ad a bit of trouble with 'er one way an' another. I 'adn't any milk till a month after she was born and she sickened like a cow.'

'She's not like you – takes after her father?' Just as the woman had shouted her refusal at us before, she shouted at me then.

'No, she don't! She's the dead spit of me. Any fool could see that. Come on in now, Else, you stop messing in the dirt.'

I met Jo climbing over the paddock fence.

'What's the old bitch got in the store?' he asked.

'Don't know – didn't look.'

'Well, of all the fools. Jim's slanging you. What have you been doing all the time?'

'She couldn't find this stuff. Oh, my shakes, you are smart!'

Jo had washed, combed his wet hair in a line across his forehead, and buttoned a coat over his shirt. He grinned.

Jim snatched the embrocation from me. I went to the end of the paddock where the willows grew and bathed in the creek. The water was clear and soft as oil. Along the edges held by the grass and rushes white foam tumbled and bubbled. I lay in the water and looked up at the trees that were still a moment, then quivered lightly and again were still. The air smelled of rain. I forgot about the woman and the kid until I came back to the tent. Jim lay by the fire watching the billy boil.

I asked where Jo was, and if the kid had brought our supper.

'Pooh,' said Jim, rolling over and looking up at the sky. 'Didn't you see how Jo had been titivating? He said to me before he went up to the whare, "Dang it! she'll look better by night light – at any rate, my buck, she's female flesh!"'

'You had Jo about her looks – you had me too.'

'No – look here. I can't make it out. It's four years since I came past this way and I stopped here two days. The husband was a pal of mine once, down the West Coast – a fine, big chap, with a voice on him like a trombone. She's been barmaid down the Coast – as pretty as a wax doll. The coach used to come this way then once a fortnight, that was before they opened the railway up Napier way, and she had no end of a time! Told me once in a confidential moment that she knew one hundred and twenty-five different ways of kissing!'

'Oh, go on, Jim! She isn't the same woman!'

' 'Course she is . . . I can't make it out. What I think is the old man's cleared out and left her: that's all my eye about shearing. Sweet life! The only people who come through now are Maoris and sundowners!'

Through the dark we saw the gleam of the kid's pinafore. She trailed over to us with a basket in her hand, the milk billy in the other. I unpacked the basket, the child standing by.

'Come over here,' said Jim, snapping his fingers at her.

She went, the lamp from the inside of the tent cast a bright light over her. A mean, undersized brat, with whitish hair and weak eyes. She stood, legs wide apart and her stomach protruding.

'What do you do all day?' asked Jim.

She scraped out one ear with her little finger, looked at the result and said, 'Draw.'

'Huh! What do you draw? Leave your ears alone!'

'Pictures.'

'What on?'

'Bits of butter paper an' a pencil of my Mumma's.'

'Boh! What a lot of words at one time!' Jim rolled his eyes at her. 'Baa-lambs and moo-cows?'

'No, everything. I'll draw all of you when you're gone, and your horses and the tent, and that one' – she pointed to me – 'with no clothes on in the creek. I looked at her where she couldn't see me from.'

'Thanks very much. How ripping of you,' said Jim. 'Where's Dad?'

The kid pouted. 'I won't tell you because I don't like yer face!' She started operations on the other ear.

'Here,' I said. 'Take the basket, get along home and tell the other man supper's ready.'

'I don't want to.'

'I'll give you a box on the ear if you don't,' said Jim savagely.

'Hie! I'll tell Mumma. I'll tell Mumma.' The kid fled.

We ate until we were full, and had arrived at the smoke stage before Jo came back, very flushed and jaunty, a whisky bottle in his hand.

' 'Ave a drink – you two!' he shouted, carrying off matters with a high hand. ''Ere, shove along the cups.'

'One hundred and twenty-five different ways,' I murmured to Jim.

'What's that? Oh! stow it!' said Jo. 'Why 'ave you always got your knife into me. You gas like a kid at a Sunday School beano. She wants us to go there tonight and have a comfortable chat. I' – he waved his hand airily – 'I got 'er round.'

'Trust you for that,' laughed Jim. 'But did she tell you where the old man's got to?'

Jo looked up. 'Shearing! You 'eard 'er, you fool!'

The woman had fixed up the room, even to a light bouquet of sweet-williams on the table. She and I sat one side of the table, Jo and Jim the other. An oil lamp was set between us, the whisky bottle and glasses, and a jug of water. The kid knelt against one of the forms, drawing on butter paper; I wondered, grimly, if she was attempting the creek episode. But Jo had been right about night time. The woman's hair was tumbled – two red spots burned in her cheeks – her eyes shone – and we knew that they were kissing feet under the table. She had changed the blue pinafore for a white calico dressing-jacket and a black skirt – the kid was decorated to the extent of a blue sateen hair ribbon. In the stifling room, with the flies buzzing against the ceiling and dropping on to the table, we got slowly drunk.

'Now listen to me,' shouted the woman, banging her fist on the table. 'It's six years since I was married, and four miscarriages. I says to 'im, I says, what do you think I'm doin' up 'ere? If you was back at the Coast I'd 'ave you lynched for child murder. Over and over I tells 'im – you've broken my spirit and spoilt my looks, and wot for – that's wot I'm driving at.' She clutched her head with her hands and stared round at us. Speaking rapidly, 'Oh, some days – an' months of them – I 'ear them two words knockin' inside me all the time – "Wot for!" but sometimes I'll be cooking the spuds an' I lifts the lid off to give 'em a prong and I 'ears, quite suddin again, "Wot for!" Oh! I don't mean only the spuds and the kid – I mean – I mean,' she hiccoughed – 'you know what I mean, Mr Jo.'

'I know,' said Jo, scratching his head.

'Trouble with me is,' she leaned across the table, 'he left me too much alone. When the coach stopped coming, sometimes he'd go away days, sometimes he'd go away weeks, and leave me ter look after the store. Back 'e'd come – pleased as Punch. "Oh, 'allo," 'e'd say. "'Ow

are you gettin' on? Come and give us a kiss." Sometimes I'd turn a bit
nasty, and then 'e'd go off again, and if I took it all right, 'e'd wait till
'e could twist me round 'is finger, then 'e'd say, "Well, so long, I'm
off," and do you think I could keep 'im? – not me!'

'Mumma,' bleated the kid, 'I made a picture of them on the 'ill, an'
you an' me an' the dog down below.'

'Shut your mouth!' said the woman.

A vivid flash of lightning played over the room – we heard the
mutter of thunder.

'Good thing that's broke loose,' said Jo. 'I've 'ad it in me 'ead for
three days.'

'Where's your old man now?' asked Jim slowly.

The woman blubbered and dropped her head on to the table. 'Jim,
'e's gone shearin' and left me alone again,' she wailed.

''Ere, look out for the glasses,' said Jo. 'Cheer-o, 'ave another drop.
No good cryin' over spilt 'usbands! You, Jim, you blasted cuckoo!'

'Mr Jo,' said the woman, drying her eyes on her jacket frill, 'you're
a gent, an' if I was a secret woman I'd place any confidence in your
'ands. I don't mind if I do 'ave a glass on that.'

Every moment the lightning grew more vivid and the thunder
sounded nearer. Jim and I were silent – the kid never moved from
her bench. She poked her tongue out and blew on her paper as she
drew.

'It's the loneliness,' said the woman, addressing Jo – he made sheep's
eyes at her – 'and bein' shut up 'ere like a broody 'en.' He reached his
hand across the table and held hers, and though the position looked
most uncomfortable when they wanted to pass the water and whisky,
their hands stuck together as though glued. I pushed back my chair
and went over to the kid, who immediately sat flat down on her artistic achievements and made a face at me.

'You're not to look,' said she.

'Oh, come on, don't be nasty!' Jim came over to us, and we were
just drunk enough to wheedle the kid into showing us. And those
drawings of hers were extraordinary and repulsively vulgar. The cre-
ations of a lunatic with a lunatic's cleverness. There was no doubt
about it, the kid's mind was diseased. While she showed them to us,
she worked herself up into a mad excitement, laughing and trembling,
and shooting out her arms.

'Mumma,' she yelled. 'Now I'm going to draw them what you told me I never was to – now I am.'

The woman rushed from the table and beat the child's head with the flat of her hand.

'I'll smack you with yer clothes turned up if yer dare say that again,' she bawled.

Jo was too drunk to notice, but Jim caught her by the arm. The kid did not utter a cry. She drifted over to the window and began picking flies from the treacle paper.

We returned to the table – Jim and I sitting one side, the woman and Jo, touching shoulders, the other. We listened to the thunder, saying stupidly, 'That was a near one,' 'There it goes again,' and Jo, at a heavy hit, 'Now we're off,' 'Steady on the brake,' until rain began to fall, sharp as cannon shot on the iron roof.

'You'd better doss here for the night,' said the woman.

'That's right,' assented Jo, evidently in the know about this move.

'Bring up yer things from the tent. You two can doss in the store along with the kid – she's used to sleep in there and won't mind you.'

'Oh, Mumma, I never did,' interrupted the kid.

'Shut yer lies! An' Mr Jo can 'ave this room.'

It sounded a ridiculous arrangement, but it was useless to attempt to cross them, they were too far gone. While the woman sketched the plan of action, Jo sat, abnormally solemn and red, his eyes bulging, and pulling at his moustache.

'Give us a lantern,' said Jim, 'I'll go down to the paddock.' We two went together. Rain whipped in our faces, the land was light as though a bush fire was raging. We behaved like two children let loose in the thick of an adventure, laughed and shouted to each other, and came back to the whare to find the kid already bedded in the counter of the store. The woman brought us a lamp. Jo took his bundle from Jim, the door was shut.

'Good night all,' shouted Jo.

Jim and I sat on two sacks of potatoes. For the life of us we could not stop laughing. Strings of onions and half-hams dangled from the ceiling – wherever we looked there were advertisements for 'Camp Coffee' and tinned meats. We pointed at them, tried to read them aloud – overcome with laughter and hiccoughs. The kid in the counter stared at us. She threw off her blanket and scrambled to the floor, where she stood in her grey flannel nightgown rubbing one leg against the other. We paid no attention to her.

'Wot are you laughing at?' she said uneasily.

'You!' shouted Jim. 'The red tribe of you, my child.'

She flew into a rage and beat herself with her hands. 'I won't be laughed at, you curs – you.' He swooped down upon the child and swung her on to the counter.

'Go to sleep, Miss Smarty – or make a drawing – here's a pencil – you can use Mumma's account book.'

Through the rain we heard Jo creak over the boarding of the next room – the sound of a door being opened – then shut to.

'It's the loneliness,' whispered Jim.

'One hundred and twenty-five different ways – alas! my poor brother!'

The kid tore out a page and flung it at me.

'There you are,' she said. 'Now I done it ter spite Mumma for shutting me up 'ere with you two. I done the one she told me I never ought to. I done the one she told me she'd shoot me if I did. Don't care! Don't care!'

The kid had drawn the picture of the woman shooting at a man with a rook rifle and then digging a hole to bury him in.

She jumped off the counter and squirmed about on the floor biting her nails.

Jim and I sat till dawn with the drawing beside us. The rain ceased, the little kid fell asleep, breathing loudly. We got up, stole out of the whare, down into the paddock. White clouds floated over a pink sky – a chill wind blew; the air smelled of wet grass. Just as we swung into the saddle Jo came out of the whare – he motioned to us to ride on.

'I'll pick you up later,' he shouted.

A bend in the road, and the whole place disappeared.

(first published 1912, first book publication
Something Childish and Other Stories, 1924)

The Little Governess

Oh, dear, how she wished that it wasn't night-time. She'd have much rather travelled by day, much much rather. But the lady at the Governess Bureau had said: 'You had better take an evening boat and then if you get into a compartment for "Ladies Only" in the train you will be far safer than sleeping in a foreign hotel. Don't go out of the carriage; don't walk about the corridors and *be sure* to lock the lavatory door if you go there. The train arrives at Munich at eight o'clock, and Frau Arnholdt says that the Hotel Grunewald is only one minute away. A porter can take you there. She will arrive at six the same evening, so you will have a nice quiet day to rest after the journey and rub up your German. And when you want anything to eat I would advise you to pop into the nearest baker's and get a bun and some coffee. You haven't been abroad before, have you?' 'No.' 'Well, I always tell my girls that it's better to mistrust people at first rather than trust them, and it's safer to suspect people of evil intentions rather than good ones ... It sounds rather hard but we've got to be women of the world, haven't we?'

It had been nice in the Ladies' Cabin. The stewardess was so kind and changed her money for her and tucked up her feet. She lay on one of the hard pink-sprigged couches and watched the other passengers, friendly and natural, pinning their hats to the bolsters, taking off their boots and skirts, opening dressing-cases and arranging mysterious rustling little packages, tying their heads up in veils before lying down. *Thud, thud, thud,* went the steady screw of the steamer. The stewardess pulled a green shade over the light and sat down by the stove, her skirt turned back over her knees, a long piece of knitting on her lap. On a shelf above her head there was a water-bottle with a tight bunch of flowers stuck in it. 'I like travelling very much,' thought the little governess. She smiled and yielded to the warm rocking.

But when the boat stopped and she went up on deck, her dress-basket in one hand, her rug and umbrella in the other, a cold, strange wind flew under her hat. She looked up at the masts and spars of the ship, black against a green glittering sky, and down to the dark landing-stage where strange muffled figures lounged, waiting; she moved forward with the sleepy flock, all knowing where to go to and what to do except her, and she felt afraid. Just a little – just enough to wish – oh, to wish that it was daytime and that one of those women who had smiled at her in the glass, when they both did their hair in the Ladies' Cabin, was somewhere near now. 'Tickets, please. Show your tickets. Have your tickets ready.' She went down the gangway balancing herself carefully on her heels. Then a man in a black leather cap came forward and touched her on the arm. 'Where for, Miss?' He spoke English – he must be a guard or a stationmaster with a cap like that. She had scarcely answered when he pounced on her dress-basket. 'This way,' he shouted, in a rude, determined voice, and elbowing his way he strode past the people. 'But I don't want a porter.' What a horrible man! 'I don't want a porter. I want to carry it myself.' She had to run to keep up with him, and her anger, far stronger than she, ran before her and snatched the bag out of the wretch's hand. He paid no attention at all, but swung on down the long dark platform, and across a railway line. 'He is a robber.' She was sure he was a robber as she stepped between the silvery rails and felt the cinders crunch under her shoes. On the other side – oh, thank goodness! – there was a train with Munich written on it. The man stopped by the huge lighted carriages. 'Second class?' asked the insolent voice. 'Yes, a Ladies' compartment.' She was quite out of breath. She opened her little purse to find something small enough to give this horrible man while he tossed her dress-basket into the rack of an empty carriage that had a ticket, *Dames Seules,* gummed on the window. She got into the train and handed him twenty centimes. 'What's this?' shouted the man, glaring at the money and then at her, holding it up to his nose, sniffing at it as though he had never in his life seen, much less held, such a sum. 'It's a franc. You know that, don't you? It's a franc. That's my fare!' A franc! Did he imagine that she was going to give him a franc for playing a trick like that just because she was a girl and travelling alone at night? Never, never! She squeezed her purse in her hand and simply did not see him – she looked at a view of St Malo on the wall opposite and simply did not hear him. 'Ah, no. Ah, no. Four sous. You make a mistake. Here, take it. It's a franc I want.' He leapt on to the step of the train and threw the money on to her lap. Trembling with terror she screwed herself tight, tight, and put out an icy hand and took the money – stowed it away in her hand. 'That's all you're going to get,' she said. For a minute or two she felt his sharp eyes pricking her all over, while he nodded slowly, pulling down his mouth: 'Ve-ry well. *Trrrès bien.*' He shrugged his shoulders and disappeared into the dark. Oh, the relief! How simply terrible that had been! As she stood up to feel if the dress-basket was firm she caught sight of herself in the mirror, quite white, with big round eyes. She untied her 'motor veil' and unbuttoned her green cape. 'But it's all over now,' she said to the mirror face, feeling in some way that it was more frightened than she.

People began to assemble on the platform. They stood together in little groups talking; a strange light from the station lamps painted their faces almost green. A little boy in red clattered up with a huge tea-wagon and leaned against it, whistling and flicking his boots with a serviette. A woman in a black alpaca apron pushed a barrow with pillows for hire. Dreamy and vacant she looked – like a woman wheeling a perambulator – up and down, up and down – with a sleeping baby inside it. Wreaths of white smoke floated up from somewhere and hung below the roof like misty vines. 'How strange it all is,' thought the little governess, 'and the middle of the night, too.' She looked out from her safe corner, frightened no longer but proud that she had not given that franc. 'I can look after myself – of course I can. The great thing is not to –' Suddenly from the corridor there came a stamping of feet and men's voices, high and broken with snatches of loud laughter. They were coming her way. The little governess shrank into her corner as four young men in bowler hats passed, staring through the door and window. One of them, bursting with the joke, pointed to the notice *Dames Seules* and the four bent down the better to see the one little girl in the corner. Oh dear, they were in the carriage next door. She heard them tramping about, and then a sudden hush followed by a tall thin fellow with a tiny black moustache who flung her door open. 'If Mademoiselle cares to come in with us,' he said, in French. She saw the others crowding behind him, peeping under his arm and over his shoulder, and she sat very straight and still. 'If Mademoiselle will do us the honour,' mocked the tall man. One of them could be quiet no longer; his laughter went off in a loud crack. 'Mademoiselle is serious,' persisted the young man, bowing and grimacing. He took off his hat with a flourish, and she was alone again.

'*En voiture. En voi-ture!*' Someone ran up and down beside the train.

'I wish it wasn't night-time. I wish there was another woman in the carriage. I'm frightened of the men next door.' The little governess looked out to see her porter coming back again – the same man making for her carriage with his arms full of luggage. But – but what *was* he doing? He put his thumb nail under the label *Dames Seules* and tore it right off, and then stood aside squinting at her while an old man wrapped in a plaid cape climbed up the high step. 'But this is a ladies' compartment.' 'Oh no, Mademoiselle, you make a mistake. No, no, I assure you. Merci, Monsieur.' '*En voi-turre!*' A shrill whistle. The porter stepped off triumphant and the train started. For a moment or two big tears brimmed her eyes and through them she saw the old man unwinding a scarf from his neck and untying the flaps of his Jaeger cap. He looked very old. Ninety at least. He had a white moustache and big gold-rimmed spectacles with little blue eyes behind them and pink wrinkled cheeks. A nice face – and charming the way he bent forward and said in halting French: 'Do I disturb you, Mademoiselle? Would you rather I took all these things out of the rack and found another carriage?' What! that old man have to move all those heavy things just because she . . . 'No, it's quite all right. You don't disturb me at all.' 'Ah, a thousand thanks.' He sat down opposite her and unbuttoned the cape of his enormous coat and flung it off his shoulders.

The train seemed glad to have left the station. With a long leap it sprang into the dark. She rubbed a place in the window with her glove but she could see nothing – just a tree outspread like a black fan or a scatter of lights, or the line of a hill, solemn and huge. In the carriage next door the young men started singing '*Un, deux, trois.*' They sang the same song over and over at the tops of their voices.

'I never could have dared to go to sleep if I had been alone,' she decided. '*I couldn't* have put my feet up or even taken off my hat.' The singing gave her a queer little tremble in her stomach and, hugging herself to stop it, with her arms crossed under her cape, she felt really glad to have the old man in the carriage with her. Careful to see that he was not looking she peeped at him through her long lashes. He sat extremely upright, the chest thrown out, the chin well in, knees pressed together, reading a German paper. That was why he spoke French so funnily. He was a German. Something in the army, she supposed – a Colonel or a General – once, of course, not now; he was too old for that now. How spick and span he looked for an old man. He wore a pearl pin stuck in his black tie and a ring with a dark red stone on his little finger; the tip of a white silk handkerchief showed in the pocket of his double-breasted jacket. Somehow, altogether, he was really nice to look at. Most old men were so horrid. She couldn't bear them doddery – or they had a disgusting cough or something. But not having a beard – that made all the difference – and then his cheeks were so pink and his moustache so very white. Down went the German paper and the old man leaned forward with the same delightful courtesy: 'Do you speak German, Mademoiselle?' '*Ja, ein wenig, mehr als Französisch,*' said the little governess, blushing a deep pink colour that spread slowly over her cheeks and made her blue eyes look almost black. 'Ach, so!' The old man bowed graciously. 'Then perhaps you would care to look at some illustrated papers.' He slipped a rubber band from a little roll of them and handed them across. 'Thank you very much.' She was very fond of looking at pictures, but first she would take off her hat and gloves. So she stood up, unpinned the brown straw and put it neatly in the rack beside the dress-basket, stripped off her brown kid gloves, paired them in a tight roll and put them in the crown of the hat for safety, and then sat down again, more comfortably this time, her feet crossed, the papers on her lap. How kindly the old man in the corner watched her bare little hand turning over the big white pages, watched her lips moving as she pronounced the long words to herself, rested upon her hair that fairly blazed under the light. Alas! how tragic for a little governess to possess hair that made one think of tangerines and marigolds, of apricots and tortoise-shell cats and champagne! Perhaps that was what the old man was thinking as he gazed and gazed, and that not even the dark ugly clothes could disguise her soft beauty. Perhaps the flush that licked his cheeks and lips was a flush of rage that anyone so young and tender should have to travel alone and unprotected through the night. Who knows he was not murmuring in his sentimental German fashion: '*Ja, es ist eine Tragödie!* Would to God I were the child's grandpapa!'

'Thank you very much. They were very interesting.' She smiled prettily, handing back the papers. 'But you speak German extremely well,' said the old man. 'You have been in Germany before, of course?' 'Oh no, this is the first time' – a little pause, then – 'this is the first time that I have ever been abroad at all.' 'Really! I am surprised. You gave me the impression, if I may say so, that you were accustomed to trav-elling.' 'Oh, well – I have been about a good deal in England, and to Scotland, once.' 'So. I myself have been in England once, but I could not learn English.' He raised one hand and shook his head, laughing. 'No, it was too difficult for me . . . "Ow-do-you-do. Please vich is ze vay to Leicestaire Squaare."' She laughed too. 'Foreigners always say . . .' They had quite a little talk about it. 'But you will like Munich,' said the old man. 'Munich is a wonderful city. Museums, pictures, gal-leries, fine buildings and shops, concerts, theatres, restaurants – all are in Munich. I have travelled all over Europe many, many times in my life, but it is always to Munich that I return. You will enjoy yourself there.' 'I am not going to *stay* in Munich,' said the little governess, and she added shyly, 'I am going to a post as governess to a doctor's family in Augsburg.' 'Ah, that was it.' Augsburg he knew. Augsburg – well – was not beautiful. A solid manufacturing town. But if Germany was new to her he hoped she would find something interesting there too. 'I am sure I shall.' 'But what a pity not to see Munich before you go. You ought to take a little holiday on your way' – he smiled – 'and store up some pleasant memories.' 'I am afraid I could not do *that*,' said the little governess, shaking her head, suddenly important and serious. 'And also, if one is alone . . .' He quite understood. He bowed, serious too. They were silent after that. The train shattered on, baring its dark, flaming breast to the hills and to the valleys. It was warm in the car-riage. She seemed to lean against the dark rushing and to be carried away and away. Little sounds made themselves heard; steps in the cor-ridor, doors opening and shutting – a murmur of voices – whistling . . . Then the window was pricked with long needles of rain . . . But it did not matter . . . it was outside . . . and she had her umbrella . . . she pouted, sighed, opened and shut her hands once and fell fast asleep.

'Pardon! Pardon!' The sliding back of the carriage door woke her with a start. What had happened? Someone had come in and gone out again. The old man sat in his corner, more upright than ever, his hands in the pockets of his coat, frowning heavily. 'Ha! ha! ha!' came from the carriage next door. Still half asleep, she put her hands to her hair to make sure it wasn't a dream. 'Disgraceful!' muttered the old man more to himself than to her. 'Common, vulgar fellows! I am afraid they disturbed you, gracious Fräulein, blundering in here like that.'

No, not really. She was just going to wake up, and she took out her silver watch to look at the time. Half-past four. A cold blue light filled the window panes. Now when she rubbed a place she could see bright patches of fields, a clump of white houses like mushrooms, a road 'like a picture' with poplar trees on either side, a thread of river. How pretty it was! How pretty and how different! Even those pink clouds in the sky looked foreign. It was cold, but she pretended that it was far colder and rubbed her hands together and shivered, pulling at the collar of her coat because she was so happy.

The train began to slow down. The engine gave a long shrill whistle. They were coming to a town. Taller houses, pink and yellow, glided by, fast asleep behind their green eyelids, and guarded by the poplar trees that quivered in the blue air as if on tiptoe, listening. In one house a woman opened the shutters, flung a red and white mattress across the window frame and stood staring at the train. A pale woman with black hair and a white woollen shawl over her shoulders. More women appeared at the doors and at the windows of the sleeping houses. There came a flock of sheep. The shepherd wore a blue blouse and pointed wooden shoes. Look! look what flowers – and by the railway station too! Standard roses like bridesmaids' bouquets, white geraniums, waxy pink ones that you would *never* see out of a greenhouse at home. Slower and slower. A man with a watering-can was spraying the platform. 'A-a-a-ah!' Somebody came running and waving his arms. A huge fat woman waddled through the glass doors of the station with a tray of strawberries. Oh, she was thirsty! She was very thirsty! 'A-a-a-ah!' The same somebody ran back again. The train stopped.

The old man pulled his coat round him and got up, smiling at her. He murmured something she didn't quite catch, but she smiled back at him as he left the carriage. While he was away the little governess looked at herself again in the glass, shook and patted herself with the precise practical care of a girl who is old enough to travel by herself and has nobody else to assure her that she is 'quite all right behind.' Thirsty and thirsty! The air tasted of water. She let down the window and the fat woman with the strawberries passed as if on purpose, holding up the tray to her. '*Nein, dabke,*' said the little governess, looking at the big berries on their gleaming leaves. '*Wie viel?*' she asked as the fat woman moved away. 'Two marks fifty, Fräulein.' 'Good gracious!'

She came in from the window and sat down in the corner, very sobered for a minute. Half a crown! 'H-o-o-o-o-o-e-e-e!' shrieked the train, gathering itself together to be off again. She hoped the old man wouldn't be left behind. Oh, it was daylight – everything was lovely if only she hadn't been so thirsty. Where *was* the old man – oh, here he was – she dimpled at him as though he were an old accepted friend as he closed the door and, turning, took from under his cape a basket of the strawberries. 'If Fräulein would honour me by accepting these . . .' 'What, for me?' But she drew back and raised her hands as though he were about to put a wild little kitten on her lap.

'Certainly, for you,' said the old man. 'For myself it is twenty years since I was brave enough to eat strawberries.' 'Oh, thank you very much. *Danke bestens,*' she stammered, '*sie sind so sehr schön!*' 'Eat them and see,' said the old man, looking pleased and friendly. 'You won't have even one?' 'No, no, no.' Timidly and charmingly her hand hovered. They were so big and juicy she had to take two bites to them – the juice ran all down her fingers – and it was while she munched the berries that she first thought of the old man as a grandfather. What a perfect grandfather he would make! Just like one out of a book!

The sun came out, the pink clouds in the sky, the strawberry clouds were eaten by the blue. 'Are they good?' asked the old man. 'As good as they look?'

When she had eaten them she felt she had known him for years. She told him about Frau Arnholdt and how she had got the place. Did he know the Hotel Grunewald? Frau Arnholdt would not arrive until the evening. He listened, listened until he knew as much about the affair as she did, until he said – not looking at her – but smoothing the palms of his brown suède gloves together: 'I wonder if you would let me show you a little of Munich today. Nothing much – but just perhaps a picture gallery and the Englischer Garten. It seems such a pity that you should have to spend the day at the hotel, and also a little uncomfortable . . . in a strange place. *Nicht wahr?* You would be back there by the early afternoon or whenever you wish, of course, and you would give an old man a great deal of pleasure.'

It was not until long after she had said 'Yes' – because the moment she had said it and he had thanked her he began telling her about his travels in Turkey and attar of roses – that she wondered whether she had done wrong. After all, she really did not know him. But he was so

old and he had been so very kind – not to mention the strawberries . . .
And she couldn't have explained the reason why she said 'No,' and it
was her *last* day in a way, her last day to really enjoy herself in. 'Was I
wrong? Was I?' A drop of sunlight fell into her hands and lay there,
warm and quivering. 'If I might accompany you as far as the hotel,' he
suggested, 'and call for you again at about ten o'clock.' He took out his
pocket-book and handed her a card. 'Herr Regierungsrat . . .' He had
a title! Well, it was *bound* to be all right! So after that the little governess gave herself up to the excitement of being really abroad, to looking
out and reading the foreign advertisement signs, to being told about
the places they came to – having her attention and enjoyment looked
after by the charming old grandfather – until they reached Munich
and the Hauptbahnhof. 'Porter! Porter!' He found her a porter, disposed of his own luggage in a few words, guided her through the
bewildering crowd out of the station down the clean white steps into
the white road to the hotel. He explained who she was to the manager
as though all this had been bound to happen, and then for one moment
her little hand lost itself in the big brown suède ones. 'I will call for
you at ten o'clock.' He was gone.

'This way, Fräulein,' said a waiter, who had been dodging behind
the manager's back, all eyes and ears for the strange couple. She followed him up two flight of stairs into a dark bedroom. He dashed
down her dress-basket and pulled up a clattering, dusty blind. Ugh!
what an ugly, cold room – what enormous furniture! Fancy spending
the day in here! 'Is this the room Frau Arnholdt ordered?' asked the
little governess. The waiter had a curious way of staring as if there was
something *funny* about her. He pursed up his lips about to whistle, and
then changed his mind. '*Gewiss,*' he said. Well, why didn't he go? Why
did he stare so? '*Gehen Sie,*' said the little governess, with frigid English simplicity. His little eyes, like currants, nearly popped out of his
doughy cheeks. '*Gehen Sie sofort,*' she repeated icily. At the door he
turned. 'And the gentleman,' said he, 'shall I show the gentleman
upstairs when he comes?'

Over the white streets big white clouds fringed with silver – and sunshine everywhere. Fat, fat coachmen driving fat cabs; funny women
with little round hats cleaning the tramway lines; people laughing and
pushing against one another; trees on both sides of the streets and

everywhere you looked almost, immense fountains; a noise of laughing from the footpaths or the middle of the streets or the open
windows. And beside her, more beautifully brushed than ever, with a
rolled umbrella in one hand and yellow gloves instead of brown ones,
her grandfather who had asked her to spend the day. She wanted to
run, she wanted to hang on his arm, she wanted to cry every minute,
'Oh, I am so frightfully happy!' He guided her across the roads, stood
still while she 'looked', and his kind eyes beamed on her and he said
'just whatever you wish.' She ate two white sausages and two little
rolls of fresh bread at eleven o'clock in the morning and she drank
some beer, which he told her wasn't intoxicating, wasn't at all like
English beer, out of a glass like a flower vase. And then they took a cab
and really she must have seen thousands and thousands of wonderful
classical pictures in about a quarter of an hour! 'I shall have to think
them over when I am alone . . .' But when they came out of the picture gallery it was raining. The grandfather unfurled his umbrella and
held it over the little governess. They started to walk to the restaurant
for lunch. She, very close beside him so that he should have some of
the umbrella too. 'It goes easier,' he remarked in a detached way, 'if
you take my arm, Fräulein. And besides it is the custom in Germany.'
So she took his arm and walked beside him while he pointed out the
famous statues, so interested that he quite forgot to put down the
umbrella even when the rain was long over.

After lunch they went to a café to hear a gypsy band, but she did
not like that at all. Ugh! such horrible men were there with heads like
eggs and cuts on their faces, so she turned her chair and cupped her
burning cheeks in her hands and watched her old friend instead . . .
Then they went to the Englischer Garten.

'I wonder what the time is,' asked the little governess. 'My watch
has stopped. I forgot to wind it in the train last night. We've seen such
a lot of things that I feel it must be quite late.' 'Late!' He stopped in
front of her laughing and shaking his head in a way she had begun to
know. 'Then you have not really enjoyed yourself. Late! Why, we
have not had any ice-cream yet!' 'Oh, but I have enjoyed myself,' she
cried, distressed, 'more than I can possibly say. It has been wonderful!
Only Frau Arnholdt is to be at the hotel at six and I ought to be there
by five.' 'So you shall. After the ice-cream I shall put you into a cab
and you can go there comfortably.' She was happy again. The

chocolate ice-cream melted – melted in little sips a long way down. The shadows of the trees danced on the tablecloths, and she sat with her back safely turned to the ornamental clock that pointed to twenty-five minutes to seven. 'Really and truly,' said the little governess earnestly, 'this has been the happiest day of my life. I've never even imagined such a day.' In spite of the ice-cream her grateful baby heart glowed with love for the fairy grandfather.

So they walked out of the garden down a long alley. The day was nearly over. 'You see those big buildings opposite,' said the old man. 'The third storey – that is where I live. I and the old housekeeper who looks after me.' She was very interested. 'Now just before I find a cab for you, will you come and see my little "home" and let me give you a bottle of the attar of roses I told you about in the train? For remembrance?' She would love to. 'I've never seen a bachelor's flat in my life,' laughed the little governess.

The passage was quite dark. 'Ah, I suppose my old woman has gone out to buy me a chicken. One moment.' He opened a door and stood aside for her to pass, a little shy but curious, into a strange room. She did not know quite what to say. It wasn't pretty. In a way it was very ugly – but neat, and, she supposed, comfortable for such an old man. 'Well, what do you think of it?' He knelt down and took from a cupboard a round tray with two pink glasses and a tall pink bottle. 'Two little bedrooms beyond,' he said gaily, 'and a kitchen. It's enough, eh?' 'Oh, quite enough.' 'And if ever you should be in Munich and care to spend a day or two – why, there is always a little nest – a wing of a chicken, and a salad, and an old man delighted to be your host once more and many many times, dear little Fräulein!' He took the stopper out of the bottle and poured some wine into the two pink glasses. His hand shook and the wine spilled over the tray. It was very quiet in the room. She said: 'I think I ought to go now.' 'But you will have a tiny glass of wine with me – just one before you go?' said the old man. 'No, really no. I never drink wine. I – I have promised never to touch wine or anything like that.' And though he pleaded and though she felt dreadfully rude, especially when he seemed to take it to heart so, she was quite determined. 'No, *really,* please.' 'Well, will you just sit down on the sofa for five minutes and let me drink your health?' The little governess sat down on the edge of the red velvet couch and he sat down beside her and drank her health at a gulp. 'Have you really been happy today?' asked the old man, turning round, so close beside her that she felt his knee twitching against hers. Before she could answer he held her hands. 'And are you going to give me one little kiss before you go?' he asked, drawing her closer still.

It was a dream! It wasn't true! It wasn't the same old man at all. Ah, how horrible! The little governess stared at him in terror. 'No, no, no!' she stammered, struggling out of his hands. 'One little kiss. A kiss. What is it? Just a kiss, dear little Fräulein. A kiss.' He pushed his face forward, his lips smiling broadly; and how his little blue eyes gleamed behind the spectacles! 'Never – never. How can you!' She sprang up, but he was too quick and he held her against the wall, pressed against her his hard old body and his twitching knee, and though she shook her head from side to side, distracted, kissed her on the mouth. On the mouth! Where not a soul who wasn't a near relation had ever kissed her before . . .

She ran, ran down the street until she found a broad road with tram lines and a policeman standing in the middle like a clockwork doll. 'I want to get a tram to the Hauptbahnhof,' sobbed the little governess. 'Fräulein?' She wrung her hands at him. 'The Hauptbahnhof. There – there's one now,' and while he watched very much surprised, the little girl with her hat on one side, crying without a handkerchief, sprang on to the tram – not seeing the conductor's eyebrows, nor hearing the *hochwohlgebildete Dame* talking her over with a scandalised friend. She rocked herself and cried out loud and said 'Ah, ah!' pressing her hands to her mouth. 'She has been to the dentist,' shrilled a fat old woman, too stupid to be uncharitable. '*Na, sagen Sie 'mal,* what toothache! The child hasn't one left in her mouth.' While the tram swung and jangled through a world full of old men with twitching knees.

When the little governess reached the hall of the Hotel Grunewald the same waiter who had come into her room in the morning was standing by a table, polishing a tray of glasses. The sight of the little governess seemed to fill him out with some inexplicable important content. He was ready for her question; his answer came pat and suave. 'Yes, Fräulein, the lady has been here. I told her that you had arrived and gone out again immediately with a gentleman. She asked me when you were coming back again – but of course I could not say. And then she went to the manager.' He took up a glass from the table, held it up to the light, looked at it with one eye closed, and started polishing it with a corner of his apron. '. . . ?' 'Pardon, Fräulein? Ach, no, Fräulein. The manager could tell her nothing – nothing.' He shook his head and smiled at the brilliant glass. 'Where is the lady now?' asked the little governess, shuddering so violently that she had to hold her handkerchief up to her mouth. 'How should I know?' cried the waiter, and as he swooped past her to pounce upon a new arrival his heart beat so hard against his ribs that he nearly chuckled aloud. 'That's it! that's it!' he thought. 'That will show her.' And as he swung the new arrival's box on to his shoulders – hoop! – as though he were a giant and the box a feather, he minced over again the little governess's words, '*Gehen Sie. Gehen Sie sofort*. Shall I! Shall I!' he shouted to himself.

(written 1915, first published 1915, first book publication
Bliss and Other Stories, 1920)

An Indiscreet Journey

I

She is like St Anne. Yes, the concierge is the image of St Anne, with that black cloth over her head, the wisps of grey hair hanging, and the tiny smoking lamp in her hand. Really very beautiful, I thought, smiling at St Anne, who said severely: 'Six o'clock. You have only just got time. There is a bowl of milk on the writing-table.' I jumped out of my pyjamas and into a basin of cold water like any English lady in any French novel. The concierge, persuaded that I was on my way to prison cells and death by bayonets, opened the shutters and the cold clear light came through. A little steamer hooted on the river; a cart with two horses at a gallop flung past. The rapid swirling water; the tall black trees on the far side, grouped together like negroes conversing. Sinister, very, I thought, as I buttoned on my age-old Burberry. (That Burberry was very significant. It did not belong to me. I had borrowed it from a friend. My eye lighted upon it hanging in her little dark hall. The very thing! The perfect and adequate disguise – an old Burberry. Lions have been faced in a Burberry. Ladies have been rescued from open boats in mountainous seas wrapped in nothing else. An old Burberry seems to me the sign and the token of the undisputed venerable traveller, I decided, leaving my purple peg-top with the real seal collar and cuffs in exchange.)

'You will never get there,' said the concierge, watching me turn up the collar. 'Never! Never!' I ran down the echoing stairs – strange they sounded, like a piano flicked by a sleepy housemaid – and on to the Quai. 'Why so fast, *ma mignonne?*' said a lovely little boy in coloured socks, dancing in front of the electric lotus buds that curve over the entrance to the Métro. Alas! there was not even time to blow him a kiss. When I arrived at the big station I had only four minutes to spare, and the platform entrance was crowded and packed with soldiers, their yellow papers in one hand and big untidy bundles. The Commissaire of Police stood on one side, a Nameless Official on the other. Will he let me pass? Will he? He was an old man with a fat swollen face covered with big warts. Horn-rimmed spectacles squatted on his nose. Trembling, I made an effort. I conjured up my sweetest early-morning smile and handed it with the papers. But the delicate thing fluttered against the horn spectacles and fell. Nevertheless, he let me pass, and I ran, ran in and out among the soldiers and up the high steps into the yellow-painted carriage.

'Does one go direct to X.?' I asked the collector who dug at my ticket with a pair of forceps and handed it back again. 'No, Mademoiselle, you must change at X.Y.Z.'

'At – ?'

'X.Y.Z.'

Again I had not heard. 'At what time do we arrive there, if you please?'

'One o'clock.' But that was no good to me. I hadn't a watch. Oh, well – later.

Ah! the train had begun to move. The train was on my side. It swung out of the station, and soon we were passing the vegetable gardens, passing the tall, blind houses to let, passing the servants beating carpets. Up already and walking in the fields, rosy from the rivers and the red-fringed pools, the sun lighted upon the swinging train and stroked my muff and told me to take off that Burberry. I was not alone in the carriage. An old woman sat opposite, her skirt turned back over her knees, a bonnet of black lace on her head. In her fat hands, adorned with a wedding and two mourning rings, she held a letter. Slowly, slowly she sipped a sentence, and then looked up and out of the window, her lips trembling a little, and then another sentence, and again the old face turned to the light, tasting it . . . Two soldiers leaned out of the window, their heads nearly touching – one of them was whistling, the other had his coat fastened with some rusty safety-pins. And now there were soldiers everywhere working on the railway line, leaning against trucks or standing hands on hips, eyes fixed on the train as though they expected at least one camera at every window. And now we were passing big wooden sheds like rigged-up dancing halls or seaside pavilions, each flying a flag. In and out of them walked the Red Cross men; the wounded sat against the walls sunning themselves. At all the bridges, the crossings, the stations, a *petit soldat*, all boots and bayonet. Forlorn and desolate he looked, like a little comic picture waiting for the joke to be written underneath. Is there really such a thing as war? Are all these laughing voices really going to the war? These dark woods lighted so mysteriously by the white stems of the birch and the ash – these watery fields with the big birds flying over – these rivers green and blue in the light – have battles been fought in places like these?

What beautiful cemeteries we are passing! They flash gay in the sun. They seem to be full of cornflowers and poppies and daisies. How can there be so many flowers at this time of the year? But they are not flowers at all. They are bunches of ribbons tied on to the soldiers' graves.

I glanced up and caught the old woman's eye. She smiled and folded the letter. 'It is from my son – the first we have had since October. I am taking it to my daughter-in-law.'

'. . . ?'

'Yes, very good,' said the old woman, shaking down her skirt and putting her arm through the handle of her basket. 'He wants me to send him some handkerchiefs and a piece of stout string.'

What is the name of the station where I have to change? Perhaps I shall never know. I got up and leaned my arms across the window rail, my feet crossed. One cheek burned as in infancy on the way to the sea-side. When the war is over I shall have a barge and drift along these rivers with a white cat and a pot of mignonette to bear me company.

Down the side of the hill filed the troops, winking red and blue in the light. Far away, but plainly to be seen, some more flew by on bicycles. But really, *ma France adorée*, this uniform is ridiculous. Your soldiers are stamped upon your bosom like bright irreverent transfers.

The train slowed down, stopped . . . Everybody was getting out except me. A big boy, his sabots tied to his back with a piece of string, the inside of his tin wine cup stained a lovely impossible pink, looked very friendly. Does one change here perhaps for X.? Another whose képi had come out of a wet paper cracker swung my suit-case to earth. What darlings soldiers are! '*Merci bien, Monsieur, vous êtes tout à fait aimable* . . .' 'Not this way,' said a bayonet. 'Nor this,' said another. So I followed the crowd. 'Your passport, Mademoiselle . . .' '*We, Sir Edward Grey* . . .' I ran through the muddy square and into the buffet.

A green room with a stove jutting out and tables on each side. On the counter, beautiful with coloured bottles, a woman leans, her breasts in her folded arms. Through an open door I can see a kitchen, and the cook in a white coat breaking eggs into a bowl and tossing the shells into a corner. The blue and red coats of the men who are eating hang upon the walls. Their short swords and belts are piled upon chairs. Heavens! what a noise. The sunny air seemed all broken up and trembling with it. A little boy, very pale, swung from table to table, taking the orders, and poured me out a glass of purple coffee. *Ssssh,* came from the eggs. They were in a pan. The woman rushed from behind the counter and began to help the boy. *Toute de suite, tout' suite!* she chirruped to the loud impatient voices. There came a clatter of plates and the pop-pop of corks being drawn.

Suddenly in the doorway I saw someone with a pail of fish – brown speckled fish, like the fish one sees in a glass case, swimming through forests of beautiful pressed seaweed. He was an old man in a tattered jacket, standing humbly, waiting for someone to attend to him. A thin beard fell over his chest, his eyes under the tufted eyebrows were bent on the pail he carried. He looked as though he had escaped from some holy picture, and was entreating the soldiers' pardon for being there at all . . .

But what could I have done? I could not arrive at X. with two fishes hanging on a straw; and I am sure it is a penal offence in France to throw fish out of railway-carriage windows, I thought, miserably climbing into a smaller, shabbier train. Perhaps I might have taken them to – *ah, mon Dieu* – I had forgotten the name of my uncle and aunt again! Buffard, Buffon – what was it? Again I read the unfamiliar letter in the familiar handwriting.

My dear Niece,

Now that the weather is more settled, your uncle and I would be charmed if you would pay us a little visit. Telegraph me when you are coming. I shall meet you outside the station if I am free. Otherwise our good friend, Madame Grinçon, who lives in the little toll-house by the bridge, *juste en face de le gare*, will conduct you to our home. *Je vous embrasse bien tendrement.*

                                                        JULIE BOIFFARD.

A visiting card was enclosed: *M. Paul Boiffard.*
Boiffard – of course that was the name. *Ma tante Julie et mon oncle*

Paul – suddenly they were there with me, more real, more solid than any relations I had ever known. I saw *tante Julie* bridling, with the soup-tureen in her hands, and *oncle Paul* sitting at the table with a red and white napkin tied round his neck. Boiffard – Boiffard – I must remember the name. Supposing the Commissaire Militaire should ask me who the relations were I was going to and I muddled the name – Oh, how fatal! Buffard – no, Boiffard. And then for the first time, folding Aunt Julie's letter, I saw scrawled in a corner of the empty back page: *Venez vite, vite.* Strange impulsive woman! My heart began to beat . . .

'Ah, we are not far off now,' said the lady opposite. 'You are going to X, Mademoiselle?'

'*Oui, Madame.*'

'I also . . . You have been there before?'

'No, Madame. This is the first time.'

'Really, it is a strange time for a visit.'

I smiled faintly, and tried to keep my eyes off her hat. She was quite an ordinary little woman, but she wore a black velvet toque, with an incredibly surprised looking sea-gull camped on the very top of it. Its round eyes, fixed on me so inquiringly, were almost too much to bear. I had a dreadful impulse to shoo it away, or to lean forward and inform her of its presence . . .

'*Excusez-moi, Madame,* but perhaps you have not remarked there is an *espèce de* sea-gull *couché sur votre chapeau.*'

Could the bird be there on purpose? I must not laugh . . . I must not laugh. Had she ever looked at herself in a glass with that bird on her head?

'It is very difficult to get into X. at present, to pass the station,' she said, and she shook her head with the sea-gull at me. 'Ah, such an affair. One must sign one's name and state one's business.'

'Really, is it as bad as all that?'

'But naturally. You see the whole place is in the hands of the military, and' – she shrugged – 'they have to be strict. Many people do not get beyond the station at all. They arrive. They are put in the waiting-room, and there they remain.'

Did I or did I not detect in her voice a strange, insulting relish?

'I suppose such strictness is absolutely necessary,' I said coldly, stroking my muff.

'Necessary,' she cried. 'I should think so. Why, Mademoiselle, you cannot imagine what it would be like otherwise! You know what women are like about soldiers' – she raised a final hand – 'mad, completely mad. But –' and she gave a little laugh of triumph – 'they could not get into X. *Mon Dieu*, no! There is no question about that.'

'I don't suppose they even try,' said I.

'Don't you?' said the sea-gull.

Madame said nothing for a moment. 'Of course the authorities are very hard on the men. It means instant imprisonment, and then – off to the firing-line without a word.'

'What are *you* going to X. for?' said the sea-gull. 'What on earth are *you* doing here?'

'Are you making a long stay in X., Mademoiselle?'

She had won, she had won. I was terrified. A lamp-post swam past the train with the fatal name upon it. I could hardly breathe – the train had stopped. I smiled gaily at Madame and danced down the steps to the platform . . .

It was a hot little room, completely furnished, with two colonels seated at two tables. They were large grey-whiskered men with a touch of burnt red on their cheeks. Sumptuous and omnipotent they looked. One smoked what ladies love to call a heavy Egyptian cigarette, with a long creamy ash, the other toyed with a gilded pen. Their heads rolled on their tight collars, like big over-ripe fruits. I had a terrible feeling, as I handed my passport and ticket, that a soldier would step forward and tell me to kneel. I would have knelt without question.

'What's this?' said God I, querulously. He did not like my passport at all. The very sight of it seemed to annoy him. He waved a dissenting hand at it, with a '*Non, je ne peux pas manger ça*' air.

'But it won't do. It won't do at all, you know. Look, – read for yourself,' and he glanced with extreme distaste at my photograph, and then with even greater distaste his pebble eyes looked at me.

'Of course the photograph is deplorable,' I said, scarcely breathing with terror, 'but it has been viséd and viséd.'

He raised his big bulk and went over to God II.

'Courage!' I said to my muff and held it firmly, 'Courage!'

God II held up a finger to me, and I produced Aunt Julie's letter and her card. But he did not seem to feel the slightest interest in her. He stamped my passport idly, scribbled a word on my ticket, and I was on the platform again.

'That way – you pass out that way.'

Terribly pale, with a faint smile on his lips, his hand at salute, stood the little corporal. I gave no sign, I am sure I gave no sign. He stepped behind me.

'And then follow me as though you do not see me,' I heard him half whisper, half sing.

How fast he went, through the slippery mud towards a bridge. He had a postman's bag on his back, a paper parcel and the *Matin* in his hand. We seemed to dodge through a maze of policemen, and I could not keep up at all with the little corporal who began to whistle. From the toll-house 'our good friend, Madame Grinçon', her hands wrapped in a shawl, watched our coming, and against the toll-house there leaned a tiny faded cab. *Montez vite, vite!* said the little corporal, hurling my suit-case, the postman's bag, the paper parcel and the *Matin* on to the floor.

'A-ie! A-ie! Do not be so mad. Do not ride yourself. You will be seen,' wailed 'our good friend, Madame Grinçon'.

'*Ah, je m'en f . . .*' said the little corporal.

The driver jerked into activity. He lashed the bony horse and away we flew, both doors, which were the complete sides of the cab, flapping and banging.

'*Bon jour, mon amie.*'

'*Bon jour, mon ami.*'

And then we swooped down and clutched at the banging doors. They would not keep shut. They were fools of doors.

'Lean back, let me do it!' I cried. 'Policemen are as thick as violets everywhere.'

At the barracks the horse reared up and stopped. A crowd of laughing faces blotted the window.

'*Prends ça, mon vieux,*' said the little corporal, handing the paper parcel.

'It's all right,' called someone.

We waved, we were off again. By a river, down a strange white street, with little houses on either side, gay in the late sunlight.

'Jump out as soon as he stops again. The door will be open. Run straight inside. I will follow. The man is already paid. I know you will like the house. It is quite white. And the room is white too, and the people are –'

'White as snow.'

We looked at each other. We began to laugh. 'Now,' said the little corporal.

Out I flew and in at the door. There stood, presumably, my Aunt Julie. There in the background hovered, I supposed, my Uncle Paul.

'*Bon jour, Madame!*' '*Bon jour, Monsieur!*'

'It is all right, you are safe,' said my Aunt Julie. Heavens, how I loved her! And she opened the door of the white room and shut it upon us. Down went the suit-case, the postman's bag, the *Matin*. I threw my passport up into the air, and the little corporal caught it.

II

What an extraordinary thing. We had been there to lunch and to dinner each day; but now in the dusk and alone I could not find it. I clop-clopped in my borrowed *sabots* through the greasy mud, right to the end of the village, and there was not a sign of it. I could not even remember what it looked like, or if there was a name painted on the outside, or any bottles or tables showing at the window. Already the village houses were sealed for the night behind big wooden shutters. Strange and mysterious they looked in the ragged drifting light and thin rain, like a company of beggars perched on the hillside, their bosoms full of rich unlawful gold. There was nobody about but the soldiers. A group of wounded stood under a lamp-post, petting a mangy, shivering dog. Up the street came four big boys singing:

Dodo, mon homme, fais vit' dodo . . .

and swung off down the hill to their sheds behind the railway station. They seemed to take the last breath of the day with them. I began to walk slowly back.

'It must have been one of these houses. I remember it stood far back from the road – and there were no steps, not even a porch – one seemed to walk right through the window.' And then quite suddenly the waiting-boy came out of just such a place. He saw me and grinned cheerfully, and began to whistle through his teeth.

'*Bon soir, mon petit.*'

'*Bon soir, Madame.*' And he followed me up the café to our special table, right at the far end by the window, and marked by a bunch of violets that I had left in a glass there yesterday.

'You are two?' asked the waiting-boy, flicking the table with a red and white cloth. His long swinging steps echoed over the bare floor. He disappeared into the kitchen and came back to light the lamp that hung from the ceiling under a spreading shade, like a haymaker's hat. Warm light shone on the empty place that was really a barn, set out with dilapidated tables and chairs. Into the middle of the room a black stove jutted. At one side of it there was a table with a row of bottles on it, behind which Madame sat and took the money and made entries in a red book. Opposite her desk a door led into the kitchen. The walls were covered with a creamy paper patterned all over with green and swollen trees – hundreds and hundreds of trees reared their mushroom heads to the ceiling. I began to wonder who had chosen the paper and why. Did Madame think it was beautiful, or that it was a gay and lovely thing to eat one's dinner at all seasons in the middle of a forest . . . On either side of the clock there hung a picture: one, a young gentleman in black tights wooing a pear-shaped lady in yellow over the back of a garden seat, *Premier Rencontre*; two, the black and yellow in amorous confusion, *Triomphe d'Amour*.

The clock ticked to a soothing lilt, *C'est ça, c'est ça*. In the kitchen the waiting-boy was washing up. I heard the ghostly chatter of the dishes.

And years passed. Perhaps the war is long since over – there is no village outside at all – the streets are quiet under the grass. I have an idea this is the sort of thing one will do on the very last day of all – sit in an empty café and listen to a clock ticking until –

Madame came through the kitchen door, nodded to me and took her seat behind the table, her plump hands folded on the red book. *Ping* went the door. A handful of soldiers came in, took off their coats and began to play cards, chaffing and poking fun at the pretty waiting-boy, who threw up his little round head, rubbed his thick fringe out of his eyes and cheeked them back in his broken voice. Sometimes his voice boomed up from his throat, deep and harsh, and then in the middle of a sentence it broke and scattered in a funny squeaking. He seemed to enjoy it himself. You would not have been surprised if he had walked into the kitchen on his hands and brought back your dinner turning a catherine-wheel.

Ping went the door again. Two more men came in. They sat at the table nearest Madame, and she leaned to them with a birdlike movement, her head on one side. Oh, they had a grievance! The Lieutenant was a fool – nosing about – springing out at them – and they'd only been sewing on buttons. Yes, that was all – sewing on buttons, and up comes this young spark. 'Now then, what are you up to?' They mimicked the idiotic voice. Madame drew down her mouth, nodding sympathy. The waiting-boy served them with glasses. He took a bottle of some orange-coloured stuff and put it on the table edge. A shout from the card-players made him turn sharply, and crash! over went the bottle, spilling on the table, the floor – smash! to tinkling atoms. An amazed silence. Through it the drip-drip of the wine from the table on to the floor. It looked very strange dropping so slowly, as though the table were crying. Then there came a roar from the card-players. 'You'll catch it, my lad! That's the style! Now you've done it! . . . *Sept, huit, neuf.*' They started playing again. The waiting-boy never said a word. He stood, his head bent, his hands spread out, and then he knelt and gathered up the glass, piece by piece, and soaked the wine up with a cloth. Only when Madame cried cheerfully, 'You wait until *he* finds out,' did he raise his head.

'He can't say anything, if I pay for it,' he muttered, his face jerking, and he marched off into the kitchen with the soaking cloth.

'Il pleure de colère,' said Madame delightedly, patting her hair with her plump hands.

The café slowly filled. It grew very warm. Blue smoke mounted from the tables and hung about the haymaker's hat in misty wreaths. There was a suffocating smell of onion soup and boots and damp cloth. In the din the door sounded again. It opened to let in a weed of a fellow, who stood with his back against it, one hand shading his eyes.

'Hullo! you've got the bandage off?'

'How does it feel, *mon vieux*?'

'Let's have a look at them.'

But he made no reply. He shrugged and walked unsteadily to a table, sat down and leaned against the wall. Slowly his hand fell. In his white face his eyes showed, pink as a rabbit's. They brimmed and spilled, brimmed and spilled. He dragged a white cloth out of his pocket and wiped them.

'It's the smoke,' said someone. 'It's the smoke tickles them up for you.'

His comrades watched him a bit, watched his eyes fill again, again brim over. The water ran down his face, off his chin on to the table. He rubbed the place with his coat-sleeve, and then, as though forgetful, went on rubbing, rubbing with his hand across the table, staring in front of him. And then he started shaking his head to the movement of his hand. He gave a loud strange groan and dragged out the cloth again.

'*Huit, neuf, dix,*' said the card-players.

'*P'tit,* some more bread.'

'Two coffees.'

'*Un Picon!*'

The waiting-boy, quite recovered, but with scarlet cheeks, ran to and fro. A tremendous quarrel flared up among the card-players, raged for two minutes, and died in flickering laughter. 'Ooof!' groaned the man with the eyes, rocking and mopping. But nobody paid any attention to him except Madame. She made a little grimace at her two soldiers.

'*Mais vous savez, c'est un peu dégoûtant, ça,*' she said severely

'*Ah, oui, Madame,*' answered the soldiers, watching her bent head and pretty hands, as she arranged for the hundredth time a frill of lace on her lifted bosom.

'*V'là, Monsieur!*' cawed the waiting-boy over his shoulder to me. For some silly reason I pretended not to hear, and I leaned over the table smelling the violets, until the little corporal's hand closed over mine.

'Shall we have *un peu de charcuterie* to begin with?' he asked tenderly.

III

'In England,' said the blue-eyed soldier, 'you drink whisky with your meals. *N'est-ce pas, Mademoiselle?* A little glass of whisky neat before eating. Whisky and soda with your *bifteks,* and after, more whisky with hot water and lemon.'

'Is it true that?' asked his great friend who sat opposite, a big red-faced chap with a black beard and large moist eyes and hair that looked as though it had been cut with a sewing-machine.

'Well, not quite true,' said I.

'*Si, si*,' cried the blue-eyed soldier. 'I ought to know. I'm in business. English travellers come to my place, and it's always the same thing.'

'Bah, I can't stand whisky,' said the little corporal. 'It's too disgusting the morning after. Do you remember, *ma fille*, the whisky in that little bar at Montmartre?'

'*Souvenir tendre*,' sighed Blackbeard, putting two fingers in the breast of his coat and letting his head fall. He was very drunk.

'But I know something that you've never tasted,' said the blue-eyed soldier, pointing a finger at me; 'something really good.' *Cluck* he went with his tongue. '*E-patant!* And the curious thing is that you'd hardly know it from whisky except that it's' – he felt with his hand for the word – 'finer, sweeter perhaps, not so sharp, and it leaves you feeling gay as a rabbit next morning.'

'What is it called?'

'Mirabelle!' He rolled the word round his mouth, under his tongue. 'Ah-ha, that's the stuff.'

'I could eat another mushroom,' said Blackbeard. 'I would like another mushroom very much. I am sure I could eat another mushroom if Mademoiselle gave it to me out of her hand.'

'You ought to try it,' said the blue-eyed soldier, leaning both hands on the table and speaking so seriously that I began to wonder how much more sober he was than Blackbeard. 'You ought to try it, and tonight. I would like you to tell me if you don't think it's like whisky.'

'Perhaps they've got it here,' said the little corporal, and he called the waiting-boy. '*P'tit!*'

'*Non, Monsieur*,' said the boy, who never stopped smiling. He served us with dessert plates painted with blue parrots and horned beetles.

'What is the name for this in English?' said Blackbeard, pointing. I told him 'Parrot'.

'Ah, *mon Dieu!* . . . Pair-rot . . .' He put his arms round his plate. 'I love you, *ma petite* pair-rot. You are sweet, you are blonde, you are English. You do not know the difference between whisky and mirabelle.'

The little corporal and I looked at each other, laughing. He squeezed up his eyes when he laughed, so that you saw nothing but the long curly lashes.

'Well, I know a place where they do keep it,' said the blue-eyed soldier. '*Café des Amis*. We'll go there – I'll pay – I'll pay for the whole lot of us.' His gesture embraced thousands of pounds.

But with a loud whirring noise the clock on the wall struck half-past eight; and no soldier is allowed in a café after eight o'clock at night.

'It is fast,' said the blue-eyed soldier. The little corporal's watch said the same. So did the immense turnip that Blackbeard produced and carefully deposited on the head of one of the horned beetles.

'Ah, well, we'll take the risk,' said the blue-eyed soldier, and he thrust his arms into his immense cardboard coat. 'It's worth it,' he said. 'It's worth it. You just wait.'

Outside, stars shone between wispy clouds and the moon fluttered like a candle flame over a pointed spire. The shadows of the dark plume-like trees waved on the white houses. Not a soul to be seen. No sound to be heard but the *Hsh! Hsh!* of a far-away train, like a big beast shuffling in its sleep.

'You are cold,' whispered the little corporal. 'You are cold, *ma fille*.'

'No, really not.'

'But you are trembling.'

'Yes, but I'm not cold.'

'What are the women like in England?' asked Blackbeard. 'After the war is over I shall go to England. I shall find a little English woman and marry her – and her pair-rot.' He gave a loud choking laugh.

'Fool!' said the blue-eyed soldier, shaking him; and he leaned over to me. 'It is only after the second glass that you really taste it,' he whispered. 'The second little glass and then – ah! – then you know.'

Café des Amis gleamed in the moonlight. We glanced quickly up and down the road. We ran up the four wooden steps, and opened the ringing glass door into a low room lighted with a hanging lamp, where about ten people were dining. They were seated on two benches at a narrow table.

'Soldiers!' screamed a woman, leaping up from behind a white soup-tureen – a scrag of a woman in a black shawl. 'Soldiers! At this hour! Look at that clock, look at it.' And she pointed to the clock with the dripping ladle.

'It's fast,' said the blue-eyed soldier. 'It's fast, Madame. And don't make so much noise, I beg of you. We will drink and we will go.'

'Will you?' she cried, running round the table and planting herself in front of us. 'That's just what you won't do. Coming into an honest woman's house this hour of the night – making a scene – getting the police after you. Ah, no! Ah, no! It's a disgrace, that's what it is.'

'Sh!' said the little corporal, holding up his hand. Dead silence. In the silence we heard steps passing.

'The police,' whispered Blackbeard, winking at a pretty girl with rings in her ears, who smiled back at him, saucy. 'Sh!'

The faces lifted, listening. 'How beautiful they are!' I thought. 'They are like a family party having supper in the New Testament . . .' The steps died away.

'Serve you very well right if you had been caught,' scolded the angry woman. 'I'm sorry on your account that the police didn't come. You deserve it – you deserve it.'

'A little glass of mirabelle and we will go,' persisted the blue-eyed soldier.

Still scolding and muttering she took four glasses from the cupboard and a big bottle. 'But you're not going to drink in here. Don't you believe it.' The little corporal ran into the kitchen. 'Not there! Not there! Idiot!' she cried. 'Can't you see there's a window there, and a wall opposite where the police come every evening to . . .'

'Sh!' Another scare.

'You are mad and you will end in prison, – all four of you,' said the woman. She flounced out of the room. We tiptoed after her into a dark smelling scullery, full of pans of greasy water, of salad leaves and meat-bones.

'There now,' she said, putting down the glasses. 'Drink and go!'

'Ah, at last!' The blue-eyed soldier's happy voice trickled through the dark. 'What do you think? Isn't it just as I said? Hasn't it got a taste of excellent – *ex-cellent* whisky?'

(written 1915, first published in *Something Childish and Other Stories*, 1924)

The Wind Blows

Suddenly – dreadfully – she wakes up. What has happened? Something dreadful has happened. No – nothing has happened. It is only the wind shaking the house, rattling the windows, banging a piece of iron on the roof and making her bed tremble. Leaves flutter past the window, up and away; down in the avenue a whole newspaper wags in the air like a lost kite and falls, spiked on a pine tree. It is cold. Summer is over – it is autumn – everything is ugly. The carts rattle by, swinging from side to side; two Chinamen lollop along under their wooden yokes with the straining vegetable baskets – their pigtails and blue blouses fly out in the wind. A white dog on three legs yelps past the gate. It is all over! What is? Oh, everything! And she begins to plait her hair with shaking fingers, not daring to look in the glass. Mother is talking to grandmother in the hall.

'A perfect idiot! Imagine leaving anything out on the line in weather like this . . . Now my best little Teneriffe-work teacloth is simply in ribbons. *What* is that extraordinary smell? It's the porridge burning. Oh, heavens – this wind!'

She has a music lesson at ten o'clock. At the thought the minor movement of the Beethoven begins to play in her head, the trills long and terrible like little rolling drums . . . Marie Swainson runs into the garden next door to pick the 'chrysanths' before they are ruined. Her skirt flies up above her waist; she tries to beat it down, to tuck it between her legs while she stoops, but it is no use – up it flies. All the trees and bushes beat about her. She picks as quickly as she can, but she is quite distracted. She doesn't mind what she does – she pulls the plants up by the roots and bends and twists them, stamping her foot and swearing.

'For heaven's sake keep the front door shut! Go round to the back,' shouts someone. And then she hears Bogey:

'Mother, you're wanted on the telephone. Telephone, Mother. It's the butcher.'

How hideous life is – revolting, simply revolting . . . And now her hat-elastic's snapped. Of course it would. She'll wear her old tam and slip out the back way. But Mother has seen.

'Matilda. Matilda. Come back im-me-diately! What on earth have you got on your head? It looks like a tea-cosy. And why have you got that mane of hair on your forehead?'

'I can't come back, Mother. I'll be late for my lesson.'

'Come back immediately!'

She won't. She won't. She hates Mother. 'Go to hell,' she shouts, running down the road.

In waves, in clouds, in big round whirls the dust comes stinging, and with it little bits of straw and chaff and manure. There is a loud roaring sound from the trees in the gardens, and standing at the bottom of the road outside Mr Bullen's gate she can hear the sea sob: 'Ah! . . . Ah! . . . Ah-h!' But Mr Bullen's drawing-room is as quiet as a cave. The windows are closed, the blinds half pulled, and she is not late. The-girl-before-her has just started playing MacDowell's 'To an Iceberg'. Mr Bullen looks over at her and half smiles.

'Sit down,' he says. 'Sit over there in the sofa corner, little lady.'

How funny he is. He doesn't exactly laugh at you . . . but there is just something . . . Oh, how peaceful it is here. She likes this room. It smells of art serge and stale smoke and chrysanthemums . . . there is a big vase of them on the mantelpiece behind the pale photograph of Rubinstein . . . à mon ami Robert Bullen . . . Over the black glittering piano hangs 'Solitude' – a dark tragic woman draped in white, sitting on a rock, her knees crossed, her chin on her hands.

'No, no!' says Mr Bullen, and he leans over the other girl, puts his arms over her shoulders and plays the passage for her. The stupid – she's blushing! How ridiculous!

Now the-girl-before-her has gone; the front door slams. Mr Bullen comes back and walks up and down, very softly, waiting for her. What an extraordinary thing. Her fingers tremble so that she can't undo the knot in the music satchel. It's the wind . . . And her heart beats so hard she feels it must lift her blouse up and down. Mr Bullen does not say a word. The shabby red piano seat is long enough for two people to sit side by side. Mr Bullen sits down by her.

'Shall I begin with scales,' she asks, squeezing her hands together. 'I had some arpeggios, too.'

But he does not answer. She doesn't believe he even hears . . . and then suddenly his fresh hand with the ring on it reaches over and opens Beethoven.

'Let's have a little of the old master,' he says.

But why does he speak so kindly – so awfully kindly – and as though they had known each other for years and years and knew everything about each other.

He turns the page slowly. She watches his hand – it is a very nice hand and always looks as though it had just been washed.

'Here we are,' says Mr Bullen.

Oh, that kind voice – Oh, that minor movement. Here comes the little drums . . .

'Shall I take the repeat?'

'Yes, dear child.'

His voice is far, far too kind. The crotchets and quavers are dancing up and down the stave like little black boys on a fence. Why is he so . . . She will not cry – she has nothing to cry about . . .

'What is it, dear child?'

Mr Bullen takes her hands. His shoulder is there – just by her head. She leans on it ever so little, her cheek against the springy tweed.

'Life is so dreadful,' she murmurs, but she does not feel it's dreadful at all. He says something about 'waiting' and 'marking time' and 'that rare thing, a woman', but she does not hear. It is so comfortable . . . for ever . . .

Suddenly the door opens and in pops Marie Swainson, hours before her time.

'Take the allegretto a little faster,' says Mr Bullen, and gets up and begins to walk up and down again.

'Sit in the sofa corner, little lady,' he says to Marie.

The wind, the wind. It's frightening to be here in her room by herself. The bed, the mirror, the white jug and basin gleam like the sky outside. It's the bed that is frightening. There it lies, sound asleep . . . Does Mother imagine for one moment that she is going to darn all those stockings knotted up on the quilt like a coil of snakes? She's not. No, Mother. I do not see why I should . . . The wind – the wind! There's a funny smell of soot blowing down the chimney. Hasn't anyone written poems to the wind? . . . 'I bring fresh flowers to the leaves and showers.' . . . What nonsense.

'Is that you, Bogey?'

'Come for a walk round the esplanade, Matilda. I can't stand this any longer.'

'Right-o. I'll put on my ulster. Isn't it an awful day!' Bogey's ulster is just like hers. Hooking the collar she looks at herself in the glass. Her face is white, they have the same excited eyes and hot lips. Ah, they know those two in the glass. Goodbye, dears; we shall be back soon.

'This is better, isn't it?'

'Hook on,' says Bogey.

They cannot walk fast enough. Their heads bent, their legs just touching, they stride like one eager person through the town, down the asphalt zigzag where the fennel grows wild and on to the esplanade. It is dusky – just getting dusky. The wind is so strong that they have to fight their way through it, rocking like two old drunkards. All the poor little pahutu-kawas on the esplanade are bent to the ground.

'Come on! Come on! Let's get near.'

Over by the breakwater the sea is very high. They pull off their hats and her hair blows across her mouth, tasting of salt. The sea is so high that the waves do not break at all; they thump against the rough stone wall and suck up the weedy, dripping steps. A fine spray skims from the water right across the esplanade. They are covered with drops; the inside of her mouth tastes wet and cold.

Bogey's voice is breaking. When he speaks he rushes up and down the scale. It's funny – it makes you laugh – and yet it just suits the day. The wind carries their voices – away fly the sentences like little narrow ribbons.

'Quicker! Quicker!'

It is getting very dark. In the harbour the coal hulks show two lights – one high on a mast and one from the stern.

'Look, Bogey. Look over there.'

A big black steamer with a long loop of smoke streaming, with the portholes lighted, with lights everywhere, is putting out to sea. The wind does not stop her; she cuts through the waves, making for the open gate between the pointed rocks that leads to . . . It's the light that makes her look so awfully beautiful and mysterious . . . *They* are on board leaning over the rail arm in arm.

'. . . Who are they?'

'. . . Brother and sister.'

'Look, Bogey, there's the town. Doesn't it look small? There's the post-office clock chiming for the last time. There's the esplanade where we walked that windy day. Do you remember? I cried at my music lesson that day – how many years ago! Goodbye, little island, goodbye . . .'

Now the dark stretches a wing over the tumbling water. They can't see those two any more. Goodbye, goodbye. Don't forget . . . But the ship is gone, now.

The wind – the wind.

(first published in 1915, first book publication *Bliss and Other Stories*, 1920)

Late at Night

(Virginia is seated by the fire. Her outdoor things are thrown on a chair; her boots are faintly steaming in the fender.)

Virginia (*laying the letter down*): I don't like this letter at all – not at all. I wonder if he means it to be so snubbing – or if it's just his way. (*Reads.*) 'Many thanks for the socks. As I have had five pairs sent me lately, I am sure you will be pleased to hear I gave yours to a friend in my company.' No; it can't be my fancy. He must have meant it; it is a dreadful snub.

Oh, I wish I hadn't sent him that letter telling him to take care of himself. I'd give anything to have that letter back. I wrote it on a Sunday evening too – that was so fatal. I never ought to write letters on Sunday evenings – I always let myself go so. I can't think why Sunday evenings always have such a funny effect on me. I simply yearn to have someone to write to – or to love. Yes, that's it; they make me feel sad and full of love. Funny, isn't it!

I must start going to church again; it's fatal sitting in front of the fire and thinking. There are the hymns, too; one can let oneself go so safely in the hymns. (*She croons*) 'And then for those our Dearest and our Best' – (*but her eye lights on the next sentence in the letter*). 'It was most kind of you to have knitted them yourself.' Really! Really, that is too much! Men are abominably arrogant! He actually imagines that I knitted them myself. Why, I hardly know him; I've only spoken to him a few times. Why on earth should I knit him socks? He must think I am far gone to throw myself at his head like that. For it certainly is throwing oneself at a man's head to knit him socks – if he's almost a stranger. Buying him an odd pair is a different matter altogether. No; I shan't write to him again – that's definite. And, besides, what would be the use? I might get really keen on him and he'd never care a straw for me. Men don't.

I wonder why it is that after a certain point I always seem to repel people. Funny, isn't it! They like me at first; they think me

uncommon, or original; but then immediately I want to show them –
even give them a hint – that I like them, they seem to get frightened
and begin to disappear. I suppose I shall get embittered about it later
on. Perhaps they know somehow that I've got so much to give. Perhaps it's that that frightens them. Oh, I feel I've got such boundless,
boundless love to give to somebody – I would care for somebody so
utterly and so completely – watch over them – keep everything horrible away – and make them feel that if ever they wanted anything
done I lived to do it. If only I felt that somebody wanted me, that I was
of use to somebody, I should become a different person. Yes; that is
the secret of life for me – to feel loved, to feel wanted, to know that
somebody leaned on me for everything absolutely – for ever. And I
am strong, and far, far richer than most women. I am sure that most
women don't have this tremendous yearning to – express themselves.
I suppose that's it – to come into flower, almost. I'm all folded and shut
away in the dark and nobody cares. I suppose that is why I feel this
tremendous tenderness for plants and sick animals and birds – it's one
way of getting rid of this wealth, this burden of love. And then, of
course, they are so helpless – that's another thing. But I have a feeling
that if a man were really in love with you he'd be just as helpless too.
Yes, I am sure that men are very helpless . . .

I don't know why, I feel inclined to cry tonight. Certainly not
because of this letter; it isn't half important enough. But I keep wondering if things will ever change or if I shall go on like this until I am
old – just wanting and wanting. I'm not as young as I was even now.
I've got lines and my skin isn't a bit what it used to be. I never was really
pretty, not in the ordinary way, but I did have lovely skin and lovely
hair – and I walked well. I only caught sight of myself in a glass today –
stooping and shuffling along . . . I looked dowdy and elderly. Well, no;
perhaps not quite as bad as that; I always exaggerate about myself. But
I'm faddy about things now – that's a sign of age, I'm sure. The wind – I
can't bear being blown about in the wind now; and I hate having wet
feet. I never used to care about those things – I used almost to revel in
them – they made me feel so *one* with Nature in a way. But now I get
cross and I want to cry and I yearn for something to make me forget. I
suppose that's why women take to drink. Funny, isn't it!

The fire is going out. I'll burn this letter. What's it to me? Pooh! I
don't care. What is it to me? The five other women can send him socks!

And I don't suppose he was a bit what I imagined. I can just hear him saying, 'It was most kind of you, to have knitted them yourself.' He has a fascinating voice. I think it was his voice that attracted me to him – and his hands; they looked so strong – they were such man's hands. Oh, well, don't sentimentalise over it; burn it! . . . No, I can't now – the fire's gone out. I'll go to bed. I wonder if he really meant to be snubbing. Oh, I am tired. Often when I go to bed now I want to pull the clothes over my head – and just cry. Funny, isn't it!

(first published in 1917, first book publication
Something Childish and Other Stories, 1924)

Prelude

I

There was not an inch of room for Lottie and Kezia in the buggy. When Pat swung them on top of the luggage they wobbled; the grandmother's lap was full and Linda Burnell could not possibly have held a lump of a child on hers for any distance. Isabel, very superior, was perched beside the new handy-man on the driver's seat. Holdalls, bags and boxes were piled upon the floor. 'These are absolute necessities that I will not let out of my sight for one instant,' said Linda Burnell, her voice trembling with fatigue and excitement.

Lottie and Kezia stood on the patch of lawn just inside the gate all ready for the fray in their coats with brass anchor buttons and little round caps with battleship ribbons. Hand in hand, they stared with round solemn eyes, first at the absolute necessities and then at their mother.

'We shall simply have to leave them. That is all. We shall simply have to cast them off,' said Linda Burnell. A strange little laugh flew from her lips; she leaned back against the buttoned leather cushions and shut her eyes, her lips trembling with laughter. Happily at that moment Mrs Samuel Josephs, who had been watching the scene from behind her drawing-room blind, waddled down the garden path.

'Why nod leave the chudren with be for the afterdoon, Brs Burnell? They could go on the dray with the storeban when he comes in the eveding. Those thigs on the path have to go, dod't they?'

'Yes, everything outside the house is supposed to go,' said Linda Burnell, and she waved a white hand at the tables and chairs standing on their heads on the front lawn. How absurd they looked! Either they ought to be the other way up, or Lottie and Kezia ought to stand on their heads, too. And she longed to say: 'Stand on your heads, children, and wait for the storeman.' It seemed to her that would be so exquisitely funny that she could not attend to Mrs Samuel Josephs.

The fat creaking body leaned across the gate, and the big jelly of a face smiled. 'Dod't you worry, Brs Burnell. Loddie and Kezia can have tea with by chudren in the dursery, and I'll see theb on the dray afterwards.'

The grandmother considered. 'Yes, it really is quite the best plan. We are very obliged to you, Mrs Samuel Josephs. Children, say "thank you" to Mrs Samuel Josephs.'

Two subdued chirrups: 'Thank you, Mrs Samuel Josephs.'

'And be good little girls, and – come closer –' they advanced, 'don't forget to tell Mrs Samuel Josephs when you want to . . .'

'No, granma.'

'Dod't worry, Brs. Burnell.'

At the last moment Kezia let go Lottie's hand and darted towards the buggy.

'I want to kiss my granma goodbye again.'

But she was too late. The buggy rolled off up the road, Isabel bursting with pride, her nose turned up at all the world, Linda Burnell prostrated, and the grandmother rummaging among the very curious oddments she had had put in her black silk reticule at the last moment, for something to give her daughter. The buggy twinkled away in the sunlight and fine golden dust up the hill and over. Kezia bit her lip, but Lottie, carefully finding her handkerchief first, set up a wail.

'Mother! Granma!'

Mrs Samuel Josephs, like a huge warm black silk tea-cosy, enveloped her.

'It's all right, by dear. Be a brave child. You come and blay in the dursery!'

She put her arm round weeping Lottie and led her away. Kezia followed, making a face at Mrs Samuel Josephs' placket, which was undone as usual, with two long pink corset laces hanging out of it . . .

Lottie's weeping died down as she mounted the stairs, but the sight of her at the nursery door with swollen eyes and a blob of a nose gave great satisfaction to the S. J.'s, who sat on two benches before a long table covered with American cloth and set out with immense plates of bread and dripping and two brown jugs that faintly steamed.

'Hullo! You've been crying!'

'Ooh! Your eyes have gone right in.'

'Doesn't her nose look funny.'

'You're all red-and-patchy.'

Lottie was quite a success. She felt it and swelled, smiling timidly.

'Go and sid by Zaidee, ducky,' said Mrs Samuel Josephs, 'and Kezia, you sid ad the end by Boses.'

Moses grinned and gave her a nip as she sat down; but she pretended not to notice. She did hate boys.

'Which will you have?' asked Stanley, leaning across the table very politely, and smiling at her. 'Which will you have to begin with – strawberries and cream or bread and dripping?'

'Strawberries and cream, please,' said she.

'Ah-h-h-h.' How they all laughed and beat the table with their teaspoons. Wasn't that a take-in! Wasn't it now! Didn't he fox her! Good old Stan!

'Ma! She thought it was real.'

Even Mrs Samuel Josephs, pouring out the milk and water, could not help smiling. 'You bustn't tease theb on their last day,' she wheezed.

But Kezia bit a big piece out of her bread and dripping, and then stood the piece up on her plate. With the bite out it made a dear little sort of a gate. Pooh! She didn't care! A tear rolled down her cheek, but she wasn't crying. She couldn't have cried in front of those awful Samuel Josephs. She sat with her head bent, and as the tear dripped slowly down, she caught it with a neat little whisk of her tongue and ate it before any of them had seen.

II

After tea Kezia wandered back to their own house. Slowly she walked up the back steps, and through the scullery into the kitchen. Nothing was left in it but a lump of gritty yellow soap in one corner of the kitchen window-sill and a piece of flannel stained with a blue bag in another. The fire-place was choked up with rubbish. She poked among it but found nothing except a hair-tidy with a heart painted on it that had belonged to the servant girl. Even that she left lying, and she trailed through the narrow passage into the drawing-room. The Venetian blind was pulled down but not drawn close. Long pencil rays of sunlight shone through and the wavy shadow of a bush outside danced on the gold lines. Now it was still, now it began to flutter again, and now it came almost as far as her feet. Zoom! Zoom! a blue-bottle knocked against the ceiling; the carpet-tacks had little bits of red fluff sticking to them.

The dining-room window had a square of coloured glass at each corner. One was blue and one was yellow. Kezia bent down to have one more look at a blue lawn with blue arum lilies growing at the gate, and then at a yellow lawn with yellow lilies and a yellow fence. As she looked a little Chinese Lottie came out on to the lawn and began to dust the tables and chairs with a corner of her pinafore. Was that really Lottie? Kezia was not quite sure until she had looked through the ordinary window.

Upstairs in her father's and mother's room she found a pill box black and shiny outside and red in, holding a blob of cotton wool.

'I could keep a bird's egg in that,' she decided.

In the servant girl's room there was a stay-button stuck in a crack of the floor, and in another crack some beads and a long needle. She knew there was nothing in her grandmother's room; she had watched her pack. She went over to the window and leaned against it, pressing her hands against the pane.

Kezia liked to stand so before the window. She liked the feeling of the cold shining glass against her hot palms, and she liked to watch the funny white tops that came on her fingers when she pressed them hard against the pane. As she stood there, the day flickered out and dark came. With the dark crept the wind snuffling and howling. The windows of the empty house shook, a creaking came from the walls and floors, a piece of loose iron on the roof banged forlornly. Kezia was suddenly quite, quite still, with wide open eyes and knees pressed together. She was frightened. She wanted to call Lottie and to go on calling all the while she ran downstairs and out of the house. But IT was just behind her, waiting at the door, at the head of the stairs, at the bottom of the stairs, hiding in the passage, ready to dart out at the back door. But Lottie was at the back door, too.

'Kezia!' she called cheerfully. 'The storeman's here. Everything is on the dray and three horses, Kezia. Mrs Samuel Josephs has given us a big shawl to wear round us, and she says to button up your coat. She won't come out because of asthma.'

Lottie was very important.

'Now then, you kids,' called the storeman. He hooked his big thumbs under their arms and up they swung. Lottie arranged the shawl 'most beautifully' and the storeman tucked up their feet in a piece of old blanket.

'Lift up. Easy does it.'

They might have been a couple of young ponies. The storeman felt over the cords holding his load, unhooked the brake-chain from the wheel, and whistling, he swung up beside them.

'Keep close to me,' said Lottie, 'because otherwise you pull the shawl away from my side, Kezia.'

But Kezia edged up to the storeman. He towered beside her big as a giant and he smelled of nuts and new wooden boxes.

III

It was the first time that Lottie and Kezia had ever been out so late. Everything looked different – the painted wooden houses far smaller than they did by day, the gardens far bigger and wilder. Bright stars speckled the sky and the moon hung over the harbour dabbling the waves with gold. They could see the lighthouse shining on Quarantine Island, and the green lights on the old coal hulks.

'There comes the Picton boat,' said the storeman, pointing to a little steamer all hung with bright beads.

But when they reached the top of the hill and began to go down the other side the harbour disappeared, and although they were still in the town they were quite lost. Other carts rattled past. Everybody knew the storeman.

'Night, Fred.'

'Night O,' he shouted.

Kezia liked very much to hear him. Whenever a cart appeared in the distance she looked up and waited for his voice. He was an old friend; and she and her grandmother had often been to his place to buy grapes. The storeman lived alone in a cottage that had a glasshouse against one wall built by himself. All the glasshouse was spanned and arched over with one beautiful vine. He took her brown basket from her, lined it with three large leaves, and then he felt in his belt for a little horn knife, reached up and snapped off a big blue cluster and laid it on the leaves so tenderly that Kezia held her breath to watch. He was a very big man. He wore brown velvet trousers, and he had a long brown beard. But he never wore a collar, not even on Sunday. The back of his neck was burnt bright red.

'Where are we now?' Every few minutes one of the children asked him the question.

'Why, this is Hawk Street, or Charlotte Crescent.'

'Of course it is,' Lottie pricked up her ears at the last name; she always felt that Charlotte Crescent belonged specially to her. Very few people had streets with the same name as theirs.

'Look, Kezia, there is Charlotte Crescent. Doesn't it look different?' Now everything familiar was left behind. Now the big dray rattled into unknown country, along new roads with high clay banks on either side, up steep, steep hills, down into bushy valleys, through wide shallow rivers. Further and further. Lottie's head wagged; she drooped, she slipped half into Kezia's lap and lay there. But Kezia could not open her eyes wide enough. The wind blew and she shivered; but her cheeks and ears burned.

'Do stars ever blow about?' she asked.

'Not to notice,' said the storeman.

'We've got a nuncle and a naunt living near our new house,' said Kezia. 'They have got two children, Pip, the eldest is called, and the youngest's name is Rags. He's got a ram. He has to feed it with a nena-muel teapot and a glove top over the spout. He's going to show us. What is the difference between a ram and a sheep?'

'Well, a ram has horns and runs for you.'

Kezia considered. 'I don't want to see it frightfully,' she said. 'I hate rushing animals like dogs and parrots. I often dream that animals rush at me – even camels – and while they are rushing, their heads swell e-enormous.'

The storeman said nothing. Kezia peered up at him, screwing up her eyes. Then she put her finger out and stroked his sleeve; it felt hairy. 'Are we near?' she asked.

'Not far off, now,' answered the storeman. 'Getting tired?'

'Well, I'm not an atom bit sleepy,' said Kezia. 'But my eyes keep curling up in such a funny sort of way.' She gave a long sigh, and to stop her eyes from curling she shut them . . . When she opened them again they were clanking through a drive that cut through the garden like a whip-lash, looping suddenly an island of green, and behind the island, but out of sight until you came upon it, was the house. It was long and low built, with a pillared veranda and balcony all the way round. The soft white bulk of it lay stretched upon the green garden like a sleeping beast. And now one and now another of the windows leapt into light. Someone was walking through the empty rooms carrying a lamp. From the window downstairs the light of a fire flickered. A strange beautiful excitement seemed to stream from the house in quivering ripples.

'Where are we?' said Lottie, sitting up. Her reefer cap was all on one side and on her cheek there was the print of an anchor button she had pressed against while sleeping. Tenderly the storeman lifted her, set her cap straight, and pulled down her crumpled clothes. She stood blinking on the lowest veranda step watching Kezia, who seemed to come flying through the air to her feet.

'Ooh!' cried Kezia, flinging up her arms. The grandmother came out of the dark hall carrying a little lamp. She was smiling.

'You found your way in the dark?' said she.

'Perfectly well.'

But Lottie staggered on the lowest veranda step like a bird fallen out of the nest. If she stood still for a moment she fell asleep; if she leaned against anything her eyes closed. She could not walk another step.

'Kezia,' said the grandmother, 'can I trust you to carry the lamp?'

'Yes, my granma.'

The old woman bent down and gave the bright breathing thing into her hands and then she caught up drunken Lottie. 'This way.'

Through a square hall filled with bales and hundreds of parrots (but the parrots were only on the wall-paper) down a narrow passage where the parrots persisted in flying past Kezia with her lamp.

'Be very quiet,' warned the grandmother, putting down Lottie and opening the dining-room door. 'Poor little mother has got such a headache.'

Linda Burnell, in a long cane chair, with her feet on a hassock and a plaid over her knees, lay before a crackling fire. Burnell and Beryl sat at the table in the middle of the room eating a dish of fried chops and drinking tea out of a brown china teapot. Over the back of her mother's chair leaned Isabel. She had a comb in her fingers and in a gentle absorbed fashion she was combing the curls from her mother's forehead. Outside the pool of lamp and firelight the room stretched dark and bare to the hollow windows.

'Are those the children?' But Linda did not really care; she did not even open her eyes to see.

'Put down the lamp, Kezia,' said Aunt Beryl, 'or we shall have the house on fire before we are out of the packing cases. More tea, Stanley?'

'Well, you might just give me five-eighths of a cup,' said Burnell, leaning across the table. 'Have another chop, Beryl. Tip-top meat, isn't it? Not too lean and not too fat.' He turned to his wife. 'You're sure you won't change your mind, Linda darling?'

'The very thought of it is enough.' She raised one eyebrow in the way she had. The grandmother brought the children bread and milk and they sat up to table, flushed and sleepy behind the wavy steam.

'I had meat for my supper,' said Isabel, still combing gently. 'I had a whole chop for my supper, the bone and all and Worcester sauce. Didn't I, father?'

'Oh, don't boast, Isabel,' said Aunt Beryl.

Isabel looked astounded. 'I wasn't boasting, was I, Mummy? I never thought of boasting. I thought they would like to know. I only meant to tell them.'

'Very well. That's enough,' said Burnell. He pushed back his plate, took a tooth-pick out of his pocket and began picking his strong white teeth.

'You might see that Fred has a bite of something in the kitchen before he goes, will you, mother?'

'Yes, Stanley.' The old woman turned to go.

'Oh, hold on half a jiffy. I suppose nobody knows where my slippers were put? I suppose I shall not be able to get at them for a month or two – what?'

'Yes,' came from Linda. 'In the top of the canvas holdall marked "urgent necessities".'

'Well, you might get them for me, will you, mother?'

'Yes, Stanley.'

Burnell got up, stretched himself, and going over to the fire he turned his back to it and lifted up his coat-tails.

'By Jove, this is a pretty pickle. Eh, Beryl?'

Beryl, sipping tea, her elbows on the table, smiled over the cup at him. She wore an unfamiliar pink pinafore; the sleeves of her blouse were rolled up to her shoulders showing her lovely freckled arms, and she had let her hair fall down her back in a long pigtail.

'How long do you think it will take to get straight – couple of weeks – eh?' he chaffed.

'Good heavens, no,' said Beryl airily. 'The worst is over already. The servant girl and I have simply slaved all day, and ever since mother came she has worked like a horse, too. We have never sat down for a moment. We have had a day.'

Stanley scented a rebuke.

'Well, I suppose you did not expect me to rush away from the office and nail carpets – did you?'

'Certainly not,' laughed Beryl. She put down her cup and ran out of the dining-room.

'What the hell does she expect us to do?' asked Stanley. 'Sit down and fan herself with a palm-leaf fan while I have a gang of professionals to do the job? By Jove, if she can't do a hand's turn occasionally without shouting about it in return for . . .'

And he gloomed as the chops began to fight the tea in his sensitive stomach. But Linda put up a hand and dragged him down to the side of her long chair.

'This is a wretched time for you, old boy,' she said. Her cheeks were very white, but she smiled and curled her fingers into the big red hand she held. Burnell became quiet. Suddenly he began to whistle 'Pure as a lily, joyous and free' – a good sign.

'Think you're going to like it?' he asked.

'I don't want to tell you, but I think I ought to, mother,' said Isabel. 'Kezia is drinking tea out of Aunt Beryl's cup.'

IV

They were taken off to bed by the grandmother. She went first with a candle; the stairs rang to their climbing feet. Isabel and Lottie lay in a room to themselves, Kezia curled in her grandmother's soft bed.

'Aren't there going to be any sheets, my granma?'

'No, not tonight.'

'It's tickly,' said Kezia, 'but it's like Indians.' She dragged her

grandmother down to her and kissed her under the chin. 'Come to
bed soon and be my Indian brave.'

'What a silly you are,' said the old woman, tucking her in as she
loved to be tucked.

'Aren't you going to leave me a candle?'

'No. Sh – h. Go to sleep.'

'Well, can I have the door left open?'

She rolled herself up into a round but she did not go to sleep. From
all over the house came the sound of steps. The house itself creaked
and popped. Loud whispering voices came from downstairs. Once she
heard Aunt Beryl's rush of high laughter, and once she heard a loud
trumpeting from Burnell blowing his nose. Outside the window hundreds of black cats with yellow eyes sat in the sky watching her – but
she was not frightened. Lottie was saying to Isabel:

'I'm going to say my prayers in bed tonight.'

'No, you can't, Lottie.' Isabel was very firm. 'God only excuses you
saying your prayers in bed if you've got a temperature.' So Lottie
yielded:

> 'Gentle Jesus meek anmile,
> Look pon a little chile.
> Pity me, simple Lizzie,
> Suffer me to come to thee.'

And then they lay down back to back, their little behinds just
touching, and fell asleep.

Standing in a pool of moonlight Beryl Fairfield undressed herself. She
was tired, but she pretended to be more tired than she really was –
letting her clothes fall, pushing back with a languid gesture her warm,
heavy hair.

'Oh, how tired I am – very tired.'

She shut her eyes a moment, but her lips smiled. Her breath rose
and fell in her breast like two fanning wings. The window was wide
open; it was warm, and somewhere out there in the garden a young
man, dark and slender, with mocking eyes, tiptoed among the bushes,
and gathered the flowers into a big bouquet, and slipped under her
window and held it up to her. She saw herself bending forward. He

thrust his head among the bright waxy flowers, sly and laughing. 'No, no,' said Beryl. She turned from the window and dropped her night-gown over her head.

'How frightfully unreasonable Stanley is sometimes,' she thought, buttoning. And then, as she lay down, there came the old thought, the cruel thought – ah, if only she had money of her own.

A young man, immensely rich, has just arrived from England. He meets her quite by chance . . . The new governor is unmarried . . . There is a ball at Government house . . . Who is that exquisite creature in *eau-de-nil* satin? Beryl Fairfield . . .

'The thing that pleases me,' said Stanley, leaning against the side of the bed and giving himself a good scratch on his shoulders and back before turning in, 'is that I've got the place dirt cheap, Linda. I was talking about it to little Wally Bell today and he said he simply could not understand why they had accepted my figure. You see land about here is bound to become more and more valuable . . . in about ten years' time . . . of course we shall have to go very slow and cut down expenses as fine as possible. Not asleep – are you?'

'No, dear, I've heard every word,' said Linda.

He sprang into bed, leaned over her and blew out the candle.

'Good night, Mr Business Man,' said she, and she took hold of his head by the ears and gave him a quick kiss. Her faint far-away voice seemed to come from a deep well.

'Good night, darling.' He slipped his arm under her neck and drew her to him.

'Yes, clasp me,' said the faint voice from the deep well.

Pat the handy-man sprawled in his little room behind the kitchen. His sponge-bag, coat and trousers hung from the door-peg like a hanged man. From the edge of the blanket his twisted toes protruded, and on the floor beside him there was an empty cane bird-cage. He looked like a comic picture.

'Honk, honk,' came from the servant girl. She had adenoids.

Last to go to bed was the grandmother.

'What. Not asleep yet?'

'No, I'm waiting for you,' said Kezia. The old woman sighed and lay down beside her. Kezia thrust her head under her grandmother's arm and gave a little squeak. But the old woman only pressed her

faintly, and sighed again, took out her teeth, and put them in a glass of
water beside her on the floor.

In the garden some tiny owls, perched on the branches of a lace-
bark tree, called: 'More pork; more pork.' And far away in the bush
there sounded a harsh rapid chatter: 'Ha-ha-ha . . . Ha-ha-ha.'

V

Dawn came sharp and chill with red clouds on a faint green sky and
drops of water on every leaf and blade. A breeze blew over the garden,
dropping dew and dropping petals, shivered over the drenched paddocks, and was lost in the sombre bush. In the sky some tiny stars
floated for a moment and then they were gone – they were dissolved
like bubbles. And plain to be heard in the early quiet was the sound of
the creek in the paddock running over the brown stones, running in
and out of the sandy hollows, hiding under clumps of dark berry
bushes, spilling into a swamp of yellow water flowers and cresses.

And then at the first beam of sun the birds began. Big cheeky birds,
starlings and mynahs, whistled on the lawns, the little birds, the gold-
finches and linnets and fan-tails, flicked from bough to bough. A lovely
kingfisher perched on the paddock fence preening his rich beauty, and
a *tui* sang his three notes and laughed and sang them again.

'How loud the birds are,' said Linda in her dream. She was walking
with her father through a green paddock sprinkled with daisies. Suddenly he bent down and parted the grasses and showed her a tiny ball of
fluff just at her feet. 'Oh, papa, the darling.' She made a cup of her hands
and caught the tiny bird and stroked its head with her finger. It was quite
tame. But a funny thing happened. As she stroked it began to swell, it
ruffled and pouched, it grew bigger and bigger and its round eyes seemed
to smile knowingly at her. Now her arms were hardly wide enough to
hold it and she dropped it into her apron. It had become a baby with a
big naked head and a gaping bird-mouth, opening and shutting. Her
father broke into a loud clattering laugh and she woke to see Burnell
standing by the windows rattling the Venetian blind up to the very top.

'Hullo,' he said. 'Didn't wake you, did I? Nothing much wrong
with the weather this morning.'

He was enormously pleased. Weather like this set a final seal on his

bargain. He felt, somehow, that he had bought the lovely day, too –
got it chucked in dirt cheap with the house and ground. He dashed off
to his bath and Linda turned over and raised herself on one elbow to
see the room by daylight. All the furniture had found a place – all the
old paraphernalia, as she expressed it. Even the photographs were on
the mantelpiece and the medicine bottles on the shelf above the wash-
stand. Her clothes lay across a chair – her outdoor things, a purple
cape and a round hat with a plume in it. Looking at them she wished
that she was going away from this house, too. And she saw herself
driving away from them all in a little buggy, driving away from everybody and not even waving.

Back came Stanley girt with a towel, glowing and slapping his
thighs. He pitched the wet towel on top of her hat and cape, and
standing firm in the exact centre of a square of sunlight he began to do
his exercises. Deep breathing, bending and squatting like a frog and
shooting out his legs. He was so delighted with his firm, obedient
body that he hit himself on the chest and gave a loud 'Ah.' But this
amazing vigour seemed to set him worlds away from Linda. She lay on
the white tumbled bed and watched him as if from the clouds.

'Oh, damn! Oh, blast!' said Stanley, who had butted into a crisp
white shirt only to find that some idiot had fastened the neck-band
and he was caught. He stalked over to Linda waving his arms.

'You look like a big fat turkey,' said she.

'Fat. I like that,' said Stanley. 'I haven't a square inch of fat on me.
Feel that.'

'It's rock – it's iron,' mocked she.

'You'd be surprised,' said Stanley, as though this were intensely
interesting, 'at the number of chaps at the club who have got a corpor-
ation. Young chaps, you know – men of my age.' He began parting his
bushy ginger hair, his blue eyes fixed and round in the glass, his knees
bent, because the dressing-table was always – confound it – a bit too
low for him. 'Little Wally Bell, for instance,' and he straightened,
describing upon himself an enormous curve with the hairbrush. 'I
must say I've a perfect horror . . .'

'My dear, don't worry. You'll never be fat. You are far too energetic.'

'Yes, yes, I suppose that's true,' said he, comforted for the hundredth time, and taking a pearl penknife out of his pocket he began to
pare his nails.

'Breakfast, Stanley.' Beryl was at the door. 'Oh, Linda, mother says you are not to get up yet.' She popped her head in at the door. She had a big piece of syringa stuck through her hair.

'Everything we left on the veranda last night is simply sopping this morning. You should see poor dear mother wringing out the tables and the chairs. However, there is no harm done –' this with the faintest glance at Stanley.

'Have you told Pat to have the buggy round in time? It's a good six and a half miles to the office.'

'I can imagine what this early start for the office will be like,' thought Linda. 'It will be very high pressure indeed.'

'Pat, Pat.' She heard the servant girl calling. But Pat was evidently hard to find; the silly voice went baa – baaing through the garden.

Linda did not rest again until the final slam of the front door told her that Stanley was really gone.

Later she heard her children playing in the garden. Lottie's stolid, compact little voice cried: 'Ke – zia. Isa – bel.' She was always getting lost or losing people only to find them again, to her great surprise, round the next tree or the next corner. 'Oh, there you are after all.' They had been turned out after breakfast and told not to come back to the house until they were called. Isabel wheeled a neat pramload of prim dolls and Lottie was allowed for a great treat to walk beside her holding the doll's parasol over the face of the wax one.

'Where are you going to, Kezia?' asked Isabel, who longed to find some light and menial duty that Kezia might perform and so be roped in under her government.

'Oh, just away,' said Kezia . . .

Then she did not hear them any more. What a glare there was in the room. She hated blinds pulled up to the top at any time, but in the morning it was intolerable. She turned over to the wall and idly, with one finger, she traced a poppy on the wall-paper with a leaf and a stem and a fat bursting bud. In the quiet, and under her tracing finger, the poppy seemed to come alive. She could feel the sticky, silky petals, the stem, hairy like a gooseberry skin, the rough leaf and the tight glazed bud. Things had a habit of coming alive like that. Not only large substantial things like furniture but curtains and the patterns of stuffs and the fringes of quilts and cushions. How often she had seen the tassel fringe of her quilt change into a funny procession of dancers with priests attending . . . For there were some tassels that did not dance at all but walked stately, bent forward as if praying or chanting. How often the medicine bottles had turned into a row of little men with brown top-hats on; and the washstand jug had a way of sitting in the basin like a fat bird in a round nest.

'I dreamed about birds last night,' thought Linda. What was it? She had forgotten. But the strangest part of this coming alive of things was what they did. They listened, they seemed to swell out with some mysterious important content, and when they were full she felt that they smiled. But it was not for her, only, their sly secret smile; they were members of a secret society and they smiled among themselves. Sometimes, when she had fallen asleep in the daytime, she woke and could not lift a finger, could not even turn her eyes to left or right because THEY were there; sometimes when she went out of a room and left it empty, she knew as she clicked the door to that THEY were filling it. And there were times in the evenings when she was upstairs, perhaps, and everybody else was down, when she could hardly escape from them. Then she could not hurry, she could not hum a tune; if she tried to say ever so carelessly – 'Bother that old thimble' – THEY were not deceived. THEY knew how frightened she was; THEY saw how she turned her head away as she passed the mirror. What Linda always felt was that THEY wanted something of her, and she knew that if she gave herself up and was quiet, more than quiet, silent, motionless, something would really happen.

'It's very quiet now,' she thought. She opened her eyes wide, and she heard the silence spinning its soft endless web. How lightly she breathed; she scarcely had to breathe at all.

Yes, everything had come alive down to the minutest, tiniest particle, and she did not feel her bed, she floated, held up in the air. Only she seemed to be listening with her wide open watchful eyes, waiting for someone to come who just did not come, watching for something to happen that just did not happen.

VI

In the kitchen at the long deal table under the two windows old Mrs Fairfield was washing the breakfast dishes. The kitchen window looked out on to a big grass patch that led down to the vegetable garden and the rhubarb beds. On one side the grass patch was bordered by the scullery and wash-house and over this whitewashed lean-to there grew a knotted vine. She had noticed yesterday that a few tiny corkscrew tendrils had come right through some cracks in the scullery ceiling and all the windows of the lean-to had a thick frill of ruffled green.

'I am very fond of a grape vine,' declared Mrs Fairfield, 'but I do not think that the grapes will ripen here. It takes Australian sun.' And she remembered how Beryl when she was a baby had been picking some white grapes from the vine on the back veranda of their Tasmanian house and she had been stung on the leg by a huge red ant. She saw Beryl in a little plaid dress with red ribbon tie-ups on the shoulders screaming so dreadfully that half the street rushed in. And how the child's leg had swelled! 'T – t – t – t!' Mrs Fairfield caught her breath remembering. 'Poor child, how terrifying it was.' And she set her lips tight and went over to the stove for some more hot water. The water frothed up in the big soapy bowl with pink and blue bubbles on top of the foam. Old Mrs Fairfield's arms were bare to the elbow and stained a bright pink. She wore a grey foulard dress patterned with large purple pansies, a white linen apron and a high cap shaped like a jelly mould of white muslin. At her throat there was a silver crescent moon with five little owls seated on it, and round her neck she wore a watch-guard made of black beads.

It was hard to believe that she had not been in that kitchen for years; she was so much a part of it. She put the crocks away with a sure, precise touch, moving leisurely and ample from the stove to the dresser, looking into the pantry and the larder as though there were not an unfamiliar corner. When she had finished, everything in the kitchen had become part of a series of patterns. She stood in the middle of the room wiping her hands on a check cloth; a smile beamed on her lips; she thought it looked very nice, very satisfactory.

'Mother! Mother! Are you there?' called Beryl.

'Yes, dear. Do you want me?'

'No. I'm coming,' and Beryl rushed in, very flushed, dragging with her two big pictures.

'Mother, whatever can I do with these awful hideous Chinese paintings that Chung Wah gave Stanley when he went bankrupt? It's absurd to say that they are valuable, because they were hanging in Chung Wah's fruit shop for months before. I can't make out why

Stanley wants them kept. I'm sure he thinks them just as hideous as we do, but it's because of the frames,' she said spitefully. 'I suppose he thinks the frames might fetch something some day or other.'

'Why don't you hang them in the passage?' suggested Mrs Fairfield; 'they would not be much seen there.'

'I can't. There is no room. I've hung all the photographs of his office there before and after building, and the signed photos of his business friends, and that awful enlargement of Isabel lying on the mat in her singlet.' Her angry glance swept the placid kitchen. 'I know what I'll do. I'll hang them here. I will tell Stanley they got a little damp in the moving so I have put them in here for the time being.'

She dragged a chair forward, jumped on it, took a hammer and a big nail out of her pinafore pocket and banged away.

'There! That is enough! Hand me the picture, mother.'

'One moment, child.' Her mother was wiping over the carved ebony frame.

'Oh, mother, really you need not dust them. It would take years to dust all those little holes.' And she frowned at the top of her mother's head and bit her lip with impatience. Mother's deliberate way of doing things was simply maddening. It was old age, she supposed, loftily.

At last the two pictures were hung side by side. She jumped off the chair, stowing away the little hammer.

'They don't look so bad there, do they?' said she. 'And at any rate nobody need gaze at them except Pat and the servant girl – have I got a spider's web on my face, mother? I've been poking into that cupboard under the stairs and now something keeps tickling my nose.'

But before Mrs Fairfield had time to look Beryl had turned away. Someone tapped on the window: Linda was there, nodding and smiling. They heard the latch of the scullery door lift and she came in. She had no hat on; her hair stood upon her head in curling rings and she was wrapped up in an old cashmere shawl.

'I'm so hungry,' said Linda: 'where can I get something to eat, mother? This is the first time I've been in the kitchen. It says "mother" all over; everything is in pairs.'

'I will make you some tea,' said Mrs Fairfield, spreading a clean napkin over a corner of the table, 'and Beryl can have a cup with you.'

'Beryl, do you want half my gingerbread?' Linda waved the knife at her. 'Beryl, do you like the house now that we are here?'

'Oh yes, I like the house immensely and the garden is beautiful, but it feels very far away from everything to me. I can't imagine people coming out from town to see us in that dreadful jolting bus, and I am sure there is not anyone here to come and call. Of course it does not matter to you because –'

'But there's the buggy,' said Linda. 'Pat can drive you into town whenever you like.'

That was a consolation, certainly, but there was something at the back of Beryl's mind, something she did not even put into words for herself.

'Oh, well, at any rate it won't kill us,' she said dryly, putting down her empty cup and standing up and stretching. 'I am going to hang curtains.' And she ran away singing:

> How many thousand birds I see
> That sing aloud from every tree . . .

'. . . birds I see That sing aloud from every tree . . .' But when she reached the dining-room she stopped singing, her face changed; it became gloomy and sullen.

'One may as well rot here as anywhere else,' she muttered savagely, digging the stiff brass safety-pins into the red serge curtains.

The two left in the kitchen were quiet for a little. Linda leaned her cheek on her fingers and watched her mother. She thought her mother looked wonderfully beautiful with her back to the leafy window. There was something comforting in the sight of her that Linda felt she could never do without. She needed the sweet smell of her flesh, and the soft feel of her cheeks and her arms and shoulders still softer. She loved the way her hair curled, silver at her forehead, lighter at her neck, and bright brown still in the big coil under the muslin cap. Exquisite were her mother's hands, and the two rings she wore seemed to melt into her creamy skin. And she was always so fresh, so delicious. The old woman could bear nothing but linen next to her body and she bathed in cold water winter and summer.

'Isn't there anything for me to do?' asked Linda.

'No, darling. I wish you would go into the garden and give an eye to your children; but that I know you will not do.'

'Of course I will, but you know Isabel is much more grown-up than any of us.'

'Yes, but Kezia is not,' said Mrs Fairfield.

'Oh, Kezia has been tossed by a bull hours ago,' said Linda, winding herself up in her shawl again.

But no, Kezia had seen a bull through a hole in a knot of wood in the paling that separated the tennis lawn from the paddock. But she had not liked the bull frightfully, so she had walked away back through the orchard, up the grassy slope, along the path by the lace-bark tree and so into the spread tangled garden. She did not believe that she would ever not get lost in this garden. Twice she had found her way back to the big iron gates they had driven through the night before, and then had turned to walk up the drive that led to the house, but there were so many little paths on either side. On one side they all led into a tangle of tall dark trees and strange bushes with flat velvet leaves and feathery cream flowers that buzzed with flies when you shook them – this was the frightening side, and no garden at all. The little paths here were wet and clayey with tree roots spanned across them like the marks of big fowls' feet.

But on the other side of the drive there was a high box border and the paths had box edges and all of them led into a deeper and deeper tangle of flowers. The camellias were in bloom, white and crimson and pink and white striped with flashing leaves. You could not see a leaf on the syringa bushes for the white clusters. The roses were in flower – gentlemen's button-hole roses, little white ones, but far too full of insects to hold under anyone's nose, pink monthly roses with a ring of fallen petals round the bushes, cabbage roses on thick stalks, moss roses, always in bud, pink smooth beauties opening curl on curl, red ones so dark they seemed to turn back as they fell, and a certain exquisite cream kind with a slender red stem and bright scarlet leaves.

There were clumps of fairy bells, and all kinds of geraniums, and there were little trees of verbena and bluish lavender bushes and a bed of pelargoniums with velvet eyes and leaves like moths' wings. There was a bed of nothing but mignonette and another of nothing but pansies – borders of double and single daisies and all kinds of little tufty plants she had never seen before.

The red-hot pokers were taller than she; the Japanese sunflowers grew in a tiny jungle. She sat down on one of the box borders. By pressing hard at first it made a nice seat. But how dusty it was inside! Kezia bent down to look and sneezed and rubbed her nose.

And then she found herself at the top of the rolling grassy slope that led down to the orchard ... She looked down at the slope a moment; then she lay down on her back, gave a squeak and rolled over and over into the thick flowery orchard grass. As she lay waiting for things to stop spinning, she decided to go up to the house and ask the servant girl for an empty matchbox. She wanted to make a surprise for the grandmother ... First she would put a leaf inside with a big violet lying on it, then she would put a very small white picotee, perhaps, on each side of the violet, and then she would sprinkle some lavender on the top, but not to cover their heads.

She often made these surprises for the grandmother, and they were always most successful.

'Do you want a match, my granny?'

'Why, yes, child, I believe a match is just what I'm looking for.'

The grandmother slowly opened the box and came upon the picture inside.

'Good gracious, child! How you astonished me!'

'I can make her one every day here,' she thought, scrambling up the grass on her slippery shoes.

But on her way back to the house she came to that island that lay in the middle of the drive, dividing the drive into two arms that met in front of the house. The island was made of grass banked up high. Nothing grew on the top except one huge plant with thick, grey-green, thorny leaves, and out of the middle there sprang up a tall stout stem. Some of the leaves of the plant were so old that they curled up in the air no longer; they turned back, they were split and broken; some of them lay flat and withered on the ground.

Whatever could it be? She had never seen anything like it before. She stood and stared. And then she saw her mother coming down the path.

'Mother, what is it?' asked Kezia.

Linda looked up at the fat swelling plant with its cruel leaves and fleshy stem. High above them, as though becalmed in the air, and yet holding so fast to the earth it grew from, it might have had claws instead of roots. The curving leaves seemed to be hiding something; the blind stem cut into the air as if no wind could ever shake it.

'That is an aloe, Kezia,' said her mother.

'Does it ever have any flowers?'

'Yes, Kezia,' and Linda smiled down at her, and half shut her eyes. 'Once every hundred years.'

VII

On his way home from the office Stanley Burnell stopped the buggy at the Bodega, got out and bought a large bottle of oysters. At the China-man's shop next door he bought a pineapple in the pink of condition, and noticing a basket of fresh black cherries he told John to put him in a pound of those as well. The oysters and the pine he stowed away in the box under the front seat, but the cherries he kept in his hand.

Pat, the handy-man, leapt off the box and tucked him up again in the brown rug.

'Lift yer feet, Mr Burnell, while I give yer a fold under,' said he.

'Right! Right! First-rate!' said Stanley. 'You can make straight for home now.'

Pat gave the grey mare a touch and the buggy sprang forward.

'I believe this man is a first-rate chap,' thought Stanley. He liked the look of him sitting up there in his neat brown coat and brown bowler. He liked the way Pat had tucked him in, and he liked his eyes. There was nothing servile about him – and if there was one thing he hated more than another it was servility. And he looked as if he was pleased with his job – happy and contented already.

The grey mare went very well; Burnell was impatient to be out of the town. He wanted to be home. Ah, it was splendid to live in the country – to get right out of that hole of a town once the office was closed; and this drive in the fresh warm air, knowing all the while that his own house was at the other end, with its garden and paddocks, its three tip-top cows and enough fowls and ducks to keep them in poultry, was splendid too.

As they left the town finally and bowled away up the deserted road his heart beat hard for joy. He rooted in the bag and began to eat the cherries, three or four at a time, chucking the stones over the side of the buggy. They were delicious, so plump and cold, without a spot or a bruise on them.

Look at those two, now – black one side and white the other – perfect! A perfect little pair of Siamese twins. And he stuck them in his button-hole . . . By Jove, he wouldn't mind giving that chap up there a handful – but no, better not. Better wait until he had been with him a bit longer.

He began to plan what he would do with his Saturday afternoons and his Sundays. He wouldn't go to the club for lunch on Saturday. No, cut away from the office as soon as possible and get them to give him a couple of slices of cold meat and half a lettuce when he got home. And then he'd get a few chaps out from town to play tennis in the afternoon. Not too many – three at most. Beryl was a good player, too . . . He stretched out his right arm and slowly bent it, feeling the muscle . . . A bath, a good rub-down, a cigar on the veranda after dinner . . .

On Sunday morning they would go to church – children and all. Which reminded him that he must hire a pew, in the sun if possible and well forward so as to be out of the draught from the door. In fancy he heard himself intoning extremely well: 'When thou did overcome the *Sharpness* of Death Thou didst open the *King*dom of Heaven to *all* Believers.' And he saw the neat brass-edged card on the corner of the pew – Mr Stanley Burnell and family . . . The rest of the day he'd loaf about with Linda . . . Now they were walking about the garden; she was on his arm, and he was explaining to her at length what he intended doing at the office the week following. He heard her saying: 'My dear, I think that is most wise . . .' Talking things over with Linda was a wonderful help even though they were apt to drift away from the point.

Hang it all! They weren't getting along very fast. Pat had put the brake on again. Ugh! What a brute of a thing it was. He could feel it in the pit of his stomach.

A sort of panic overtook Burnell whenever he approached near home. Before he was well inside the gate he would shout to anyone within sight: 'Is everything all right?' And then he did not believe it was until he heard Linda say: 'Hullo! Are you home again?' That was the worst of living in the country – it took the deuce of a long time to get back . . . But now they weren't far off. They were on the top of the last hill; it was a gentle slope all the way now and not more than half a mile.

Pat trailed the whip over the mare's back and he coaxed her: 'Goop now. Goop now.'

It wanted a few minutes to sunset. Everything stood motionless bathed in bright, metallic light and from the paddocks on either side there streamed the milky scent of ripe grass. The iron gates were open. They dashed through and up the drive and round the island, stopping at the exact middle of the veranda.

'Did she satisfy yer, sir?' said Pat, getting off the box and grinning at his master.

'Very well indeed, Pat,' said Stanley.

Linda came out of the glass door; her voice rang in the shadowy quiet. 'Hullo! Are you home again?'

At the sound of her his heart beat so hard that he could hardly stop himself dashing up the steps and catching her in his arms.

'Yes, I'm home again. Is everything all right?'

Pat began to lead the buggy round to the side gate that opened into the courtyard.

'Here, half a moment,' said Burnell. 'Hand me those two parcels.' And he said to Linda, 'I've brought you back a bottle of oysters and a pineapple,' as though he had brought her back all the harvest of the earth.

They went into the hall; Linda carried the oysters in one hand and the pineapple in the other. Burnell shut the glass door, threw his hat down, put his arms round her and strained her to him, kissing the top of her head, her ears, her lips, her eyes.

'Oh, dear! Oh, dear!' said she. 'Wait a moment. Let me put down these silly things,' and she put the bottle of oysters and the pine on a little carved chair. 'What have you got in your button-hole – cherries?' She took them out and hung them over his ear.

'Don't do that, darling. They are for you.'

So she took them off his ear again. 'You don't mind if I save them. They'd spoil my appetite for dinner. Come and see your children. They are having tea.'

The lamp was lighted on the nursery table. Mrs Fairfield was cutting and spreading bread and butter. The three little girls sat up to table wearing large bibs embroidered with their names. They wiped their mouths as their father came in ready to be kissed. The windows were open; a jar of wild flowers stood on the mantelpiece, and the lamp made a big soft bubble of light on the ceiling.

'You seem pretty snug, mother,' said Burnell, blinking at the light. Isabel and Lottie sat one on either side of the table, Kezia at the bottom – the place at the top was empty.

'That's where my boy ought to sit,' thought Stanley. He tightened his arm round Linda's shoulder. By God, he was a perfect fool to feel as happy as this!

'We are, Stanley. We are very snug,' said Mrs Fairfield, cutting Kezia's bread into fingers.

'Like it better than town – eh, children?' asked Burnell.

'Oh, yes,' said the three little girls, and Isabel added as an after-thought: 'Thank you very much indeed, father dear.'

'Come upstairs,' said Linda. 'I'll bring your slippers.'

But the stairs were too narrow for them to go up arm in arm. It was quite dark in the room. He heard her ring tapping on the marble man-telpiece as she felt for the matches.

'I've got some, darling. I'll light the candles.'

But instead he came up behind her and again he put his arms round her and pressed her head into his shoulder.

'I'm so confoundedly happy,' he said.

'Are you?' She turned and put her hands on his breast and looked up at him.

'I don't know what has come over me,' he protested.

It was quite dark outside now and heavy dew was falling. When Linda shut the window the cold dew touched her finger tips. Far away a dog barked. 'I believe there is going to be a moon,' she said.

At the words, and with the cold wet dew on her fingers, she felt as though the moon had risen – that she was being strangely discovered in a flood of cold light. She shivered; she came away from the window and sat down upon the box ottoman beside Stanley.

In the dining-room, by the flicker of a wood fire, Beryl sat on a has-sock playing the guitar. She had bathed and changed all her clothes. Now she wore a white muslin dress with black spots on it and in her hair she had pinned a black silk rose.

> Nature has gone to her rest, love,
>   See, we are alone.
> Give me your hand to press, love,
>   Lightly within my own.

She played and sang half to herself, for she was watching herself playing and singing. The firelight gleamed on her shoes, on the ruddy belly of the guitar, and on her white fingers . . .

'If I were outside the window and looked in and saw myself I really would be rather struck,' thought she. Still more softly she played the accompaniment – not singing now but listening.

'. . . The first time that I ever saw you, little girl – oh, you had no idea that you were not alone – you were sitting with your little feet upon a hassock, playing the guitar. God, I can never forget . . .' Beryl flung up her head and began to sing again:

Even the moon is aweary . . .

But there came a loud bang at the door. The servant girl's crimson face popped through.

'Please, Miss Beryl, I've got to come and lay.'

'Certainly, Alice,' said Beryl, in a voice of ice. She put the guitar in a corner. Alice lunged in with a heavy black iron tray.

'Well, I have had a job with that oving,' said she. 'I can't get nothing to brown.'

'Really!' said Beryl.

But no, she could not stand that fool of a girl. She ran into the dark drawing-room and began walking up and down . . . Oh, she was restless, restless. There was a mirror over the mantel. She leaned her arms along and looked at her pale shadow in it. How beautiful she looked, but there was nobody to see, nobody.

'Why must you suffer so?' said the face in the mirror. 'You were not made for suffering . . . Smile!'

Beryl smiled, and really her smile *was* so adorable that she smiled again – but this time because she could not help it.

VIII

'Good morning, Mrs Jones.'

'Oh, good morning, Mrs Smith. I'm so glad to see you. Have you brought your children?'

'Yes, I've brought both my twins. I have had another baby since I saw you last, but she came so suddenly that I haven't had time to make her any clothes yet. So I left her . . . How is your husband?'

'Oh, he is very well, thank you. At least he had an awful cold but Queen Victoria – she's my godmother, you know – sent him a case of pineapples and that cured it im – mediately. Is that your new servant?'

'Yes, her name's Gwen. I've only had her two days. Oh, Gwen, this is my friend, Mrs Smith.'

'Good morning, Mrs Smith. Dinner won't be ready for about ten minutes.'

'I don't think you ought to introduce me to the servant. I think I ought to just begin talking to her.'

'Well, she's more of a lady-help than a servant and you do introduce lady-helps, I know, because Mrs Samuel Josephs had one.'

'Oh, well, it doesn't matter,' said the servant carelessly, beating up a chocolate custard with half a broken clothes peg. The dinner was baking beautifully on a concrete step. She began to lay the cloth on a pink garden seat. In front of each person she put two geranium leaf plates, a pine needle fork and a twig knife. There were three daisy heads on a laurel leaf for poached eggs, some slices of fuchsia petal cold beef, some lovely little rissoles made of earth and water and dandelion seeds, and the chocolate custard which she had decided to serve in the pawa shell she had cooked it in.

'You needn't trouble about my children,' said Mrs Smith graciously. 'If you'll just take this bottle and fill it at the tap – I mean at the dairy.'

'Oh, all right,' said Gwen, and she whispered to Mrs Jones: 'Shall I go and ask Alice for a little bit of real milk?'

But someone called from the front of the house and the luncheon party melted away, leaving the charming table, leaving the rissoles and the poached eggs to the ants and to an old snail who pushed his quivering horns over the edge of the garden seat and began to nibble a geranium plate.

'Come round to the front, children. Pip and Rags have come.'

The Trout boys were the cousins Kezia had mentioned to the storeman. They lived about a mile away in a house called Monkey Tree Cottage. Pip was tall for his age, with lank black hair and a white face, but Rags was very small and so thin that when he was undressed his shoulder blades stuck out like two little wings. They had a mongrel dog with pale blue eyes and a long tail turned up at the end who followed them everywhere; he was called Snooker. They spent half their time combing and brushing Snooker and dosing him with various awful mixtures concocted by Pip, and kept secretly by him in a broken jug covered with an old kettle lid. Even faithful little Rags was not allowed to know the full secret of these mixtures . . . Take some carbolic tooth powder and a pinch of sulphur powdered up fine, and perhaps a bit of starch to stiffen up Snooker's coat . . . But that was not all; Rags privately thought that the rest was gun-powder . . . And he never was allowed to help with the mixing because of the danger . . . 'Why, if a spot of this flew in your eye, you would be blinded for life,' Pip would say, stirring the mixture with an iron spoon. 'And there's always the chance – just the chance, mind you – of it exploding if you whack it hard enough . . . Two spoons of this in a kerosene tin will be enough to kill thousands of fleas.' But Snooker spent all his spare time biting and snuffling, and he stank abominably.

'It's because he is such a grand fighting dog,' Pip would say. 'All fighting dogs smell.'

The Trout boys had often spent the day with the Burnells in town, but now that they lived in this fine house and boncer garden they were inclined to be very friendly. Besides, both of them liked playing with girls – Pip, because he could fox them so, and because Lottie was so easily frightened, and Rags for a shameful reason. He adored dolls. How he would look at a doll as it lay asleep, speaking in a whisper and smiling timidly, and what a treat it was to him to be allowed to hold one . . .

'Curve your arms round her. Don't keep them stiff like that. You'll drop her,' Isabel would say sternly.

Now they were standing on the veranda and holding back Snooker, who wanted to go into the house but wasn't allowed to because Aunt Linda hated decent dogs.

'We came over in the bus with mum,' they said, 'and we're going to spend the afternoon with you. We brought over a batch of our gingerbread for Aunt Linda. Our Minnie made it. It's all over nuts.'

'I skinned the almonds,' said Pip. 'I just stuck my hand into a saucepan of boiling water and grabbed them out and gave them a kind of pinch and the nuts flew out of the skins, some of them as high as the ceiling. Didn't they, Rags?'

Rags nodded. 'When they make cakes at our place,' said Pip, 'we always stay in the kitchen, Rags and me, and I get the bowl and he gets the spoon and the egg-beater. Sponge cake's best. It's all frothy stuff, then.'

He ran down the veranda steps to the lawn, planted his hands on the grass, bent forward, and just did not stand on his head.

'That lawn's all bumpy,' he said. 'You have to have a flat place for standing on your head. I can walk round the monkey tree on my head at our place. Can't I, Rags?'

'Nearly,' said Rags faintly.

'Stand on your head on the veranda. That's quite flat,' said Kezia.

'No, smarty,' said Pip. 'You have to do it on something soft. Because if you give a jerk and fall over, something in your neck goes click, and it breaks off. Dad told me.'

'Oh, do let's play something,' said Kezia.

'Very well,' said Isabel quickly, 'we'll play hospitals. I will be the nurse and Pip can be the doctor and you and Lottie and Rags can be the sick people.'

Lottie didn't want to play that, because last time Pip had squeezed something down her throat and it hurt awfully.

'Pooh,' scoffed Pip. 'It was only the juice out of a bit of mandarin peel.'

'Well, let's play ladies,' said Isabel. 'Pip can be the father and you can be all our dear little children.'

'I hate playing ladies,' said Kezia. 'You always make us go to church hand in hand and come home and go to bed.'

Suddenly Pip took a filthy handkerchief out of his pocket. 'Snooker! Here, sir,' he called. But Snooker, as usual, tried to sneak away, his tail between his legs. Pip leapt on top of him, and pressed him between his knees.

'Keep his head firm, Rags,' he said, and he tied the handkerchief round Snooker's head with a funny knot sticking up at the top.

'Whatever is that for?' asked Lottie.

'It's to train his ears to grow more close to his head – see?' said Pip. 'All fighting dogs have ears that lie back. But Snooker's ears are a bit too soft.'

'I know,' said Kezia. 'They are always turning inside out. I hate that.'

Snooker lay down, made one feeble effort with his paw to get the handkerchief off, but finding he could not, trailed after the children, shivering with misery.

IX

Pat came swinging along; in his hand he held a little tomahawk that winked in the sun.

'Come with me,' he said to the children, 'and I'll show you how the kings of Ireland chop the head off a duck.'

They drew back – they didn't believe him, and besides, the Trout boys had never seen Pat before.

'Come on now,' he coaxed, smiling and holding out his hand to Kezia.

'Is it a real duck's head? One from the paddock?'

'It is,' said Pat. She put her hand in his hard dry one, and he stuck the tomahawk in his belt and held out the other to Rags. He loved little children.

'I'd better keep hold of Snooker's head if there's going to be any blood about,' said Pip, 'because the sight of blood makes him awfully wild.' He ran ahead dragging Snooker by the handkerchief.

'Do you think we ought to go?' whispered Isabel. 'We haven't asked or anything. Have we?'

At the bottom of the orchard a gate was set in the paling fence. On the other side a steep bank led down to a bridge that spanned the creek, and once up the bank on the other side you were on the fringe of the paddocks. A little old stable in the first paddock had been turned into a fowl-house. The fowls had strayed far away across the paddock down to a dumping ground in a hollow, but the ducks kept close to that part of the creek that flowed under the bridge.

Tall bushes overhung the stream with red leaves and yellow flowers and clusters of blackberries. At some places the stream was wide and shallow, but at others it tumbled into deep little pools with foam at the edges and quivering bubbles. It was in these pools that the big white ducks had made themselves at home, swimming and guzzling along the weedy banks.

Up and down they swam, preening their dazzling breasts, and other ducks with the same dazzling breasts and yellow bills swam upside down with them.

'There is the little Irish navy,' said Pat, 'and look at the old admiral there with the green neck and the grand little flagstaff on his tail.'

He pulled a handful of grain from his pocket and began to walk towards the fowl-house, lazy, his straw hat with the broken crown pulled over his eyes.

'Lid. Lid – lid – lid – lid –' he called.

'Qua. Qua – qua – qua – qua –' answered the ducks, making for land, and flapping and scrambling up the bank they streamed after him in a long waddling line. He coaxed them, pretending to throw the grain, shaking it in his hands and calling to them until they swept round him in a white ring.

From far away the fowls heard the clamour and they too came running across the paddock, their heads thrust forward, their wings spread, turning in their feet in the silly way fowls run and scolding as they came.

Then Pat scattered the grain and the greedy ducks began to gobble. Quickly he stooped, seized two, one under each arm, and strode across to the children. Their darting heads and round eyes frightened the children – all except Pip.

'Come on, sillies,' he cried, 'they can't bite. They haven't any teeth. They've only got those two little holes in their beaks for breathing through.'

'Will you hold one while I finish with the other?' asked Pat. Pip let go of Snooker. 'Won't I? Won't I? Give us one. I don't mind how much he kicks.'

He nearly sobbed with delight when Pat gave the white lump into his arms.

There was an old stump beside the door of the fowl-house. Pat grabbed the duck by the legs, laid it flat across the stump, and almost at the same moment down came the little tomahawk and the duck's head flew off the stump. Up the blood spurted over the white feathers and over his hand.

When the children saw the blood they were frightened no longer.

They crowded round him and began to scream. Even Isabel leapt about crying: 'The blood! The blood!' Pip forgot all about his duck. He simply threw it away from him and shouted, 'I saw it. I saw it,' and jumped round the wood block.

Rags, with cheeks as white as paper, ran up to the little head, put out a finger as if he wanted to touch it, shrank back again and then again put out a finger. He was shivering all over.

Even Lottie, frightened little Lottie, began to laugh and pointed at the duck and shrieked: 'Look, Kezia, look.'

'Watch it!' shouted Pat. He put down the body and it began to waddle – with only a long spurt of blood where the head had been; it began to pad away without a sound towards the steep bank that led to the stream . . . That was the crowning wonder.

'Do you see that? Do you see that?' yelled Pip. He ran among the little girls tugging at their pinafores.

'It's like a little engine. It's like a funny little railway engine,' squealed Isabel.

But Kezia suddenly rushed at Pat and flung her arms round his legs and butted her head as hard as she could against his knees.

'Put head back! Put head back!' she screamed.

When he stooped to move her she would not let go or take her head away. She held on as hard as she could and sobbed: 'Head back! Head back!' until it sounded like a loud strange hiccup.

'It's stopped. It's tumbled over. It's dead,' said Pip.

Pat dragged Kezia up into his arms. Her sun-bonnet had fallen back, but she would not let him look at her face. No, she pressed her face into a bone in his shoulder and clasped her arms round his neck.

The children stopped screaming as suddenly as they had begun. They stood round the dead duck. Rags was not frightened of the head any more. He knelt down and stroked it now.

'I don't think the head is quite dead yet,' he said. 'Do you think it would keep alive if I gave it something to drink?'

But Pip got very cross: 'Bah! You baby.' He whistled to Snooker and went off.

When Isabel went up to Lottie, Lottie snatched away.

'What are you always touching me for, Isabel?'

'There now,' said Pat to Kezia. 'There's the grand little girl.'

She put up her hands and touched his ears. She felt something.

Slowly she raised her quivering face and looked. Pat wore little round gold ear-rings. She never knew that men wore ear-rings. She was very much surprised.

'Do they come on and off?' she asked huskily.

X

Up in the house, in the warm tidy kitchen, Alice, the servant girl, was getting the afternoon tea. She was 'dressed'. She had on a black stuff dress that smelled under the arms, a white apron like a large sheet of paper, and a lace bow pinned on to her hair with two jetty pins. Also her comfortable carpet slippers were changed for a pair of black leather ones that pinched her corn on her little toe something dreadful . . .

It was warm in the kitchen. A blow-fly buzzed, a fan of whity steam came out of the kettle, and the lid kept up a rattling jig as the water bubbled. The clock ticked in the warm air, slow and deliberate, like the click of an old woman's knitting needle, and sometimes – for no reason at all, for there wasn't any breeze – the blind swung out and back, tapping the window.

Alice was making water-cress sandwiches. She had a lump of butter on the table, a barracouta loaf, and the cresses tumbled in a white cloth.

But propped against the butter dish there was a dirty, greasy little book, half unstitched, with curled edges, and while she mashed the butter she read:

> To dream of black-beetles drawing a hearse is bad. Signi-
> fies death of one you hold near or dear, either father,
> husband, brother, son, or intended. If beetles crawl back-
> wards as you watch them it means death from fire or from
> great height such as flight of stairs, scaffolding, etc.
>
> 'Spiders. To dream of spiders creeping over you is
> good. Signifies large sum of money in near future. Should
> party be in family way an easy confinement may be
> expected. But care should be taken in sixth month to
> avoid eating of probable present of shellfish . . .

*

How many thousand birds I see.

Oh, life. There was Miss Beryl. Alice dropped the knife and slipped the *Dream Book* under the butter dish. But she hadn't time to hide it quite, for Beryl ran into the kitchen and up to the table, and the first thing her eye lighted on were those greasy edges. Alice saw Miss Beryl's meaning little smile and the way she raised her eyebrows and screwed up her eyes as though she were not quite sure what that could be. She decided to answer if Miss Beryl should ask her: 'Nothing as belongs to you, Miss.' But she knew Miss Beryl would not ask her.

Alice was a mild creature in reality, but she had the most marvellous retorts ready for questions that she knew would never be put to her. The composing of them and the turning of them over and over in her mind comforted her just as much as if they'd been expressed. Really, they kept her alive in places where she'd been that chivvied she'd been afraid to go to bed at night with a box of matches on the chair in case she bit the tops off in her sleep, as you might say.

'Oh, Alice,' said Miss Beryl. 'There's one extra to tea, so heat a plate of yesterday's scones, please. And put on the Victoria sandwich as well as the coffee cake. And don't forget to put little doyleys under the plates — will you? You did yesterday, you know, and the tea looked so ugly and common. And, Alice, don't put that dreadful old pink and green cosy on the afternoon teapot again. That is only for the mornings. Really, I think it ought to be kept for the kitchen — it's so shabby, and quite smelly. Put on the Japanese one. You quite understand, don't you?'

Miss Beryl had finished.

That sing aloud from every tree . . .

she sang as she left the kitchen, very pleased with her firm handling of Alice.

Oh, Alice was wild. She wasn't one to mind being told, but there was something in the way Miss Beryl had of speaking to her that she couldn't stand. Oh, that she couldn't. It made her curl up inside, as you might say, and she fair trembled. But what Alice really hated Miss Beryl for was that she made her feel low. She talked to Alice in a special voice as though she wasn't quite all there; and she never lost her temper with her – never. Even when Alice dropped anything or forgot anything important Miss Beryl seemed to have expected it to happen.

'If you please, Mrs Burnell,' said an imaginary Alice, as she buttered the scones, 'I'd rather not take my orders from Miss Beryl. I may be only a common servant girl as doesn't know how to play the guitar, but . . .'

This last thrust pleased her so much that she quite recovered her temper.

'The only thing to do,' she heard, as she opened the dining-room door, 'is to cut the sleeves out entirely and just have a broad band of black velvet over the shoulders instead . . .'

XI

The white duck did not look as if it had ever had a head when Alice placed it in front of Stanley Burnell that night. It lay, in beautifully basted resignation, on a blue dish – its legs tied together with a piece of string and a wreath of little balls of stuffing round it.

It was hard to say which of the two, Alice or the duck, looked the better basted; they were both such a rich colour and they both had the same air of gloss and strain. But Alice was fiery red and the duck a Spanish mahogany.

Burnell ran his eye along the edge of the carving knife. He prided himself very much upon his carving, upon making a first-class job of it. He hated seeing a woman carve; they were always too slow and they never seemed to care what the meat looked like afterwards. Now he did; he took a real pride in cutting delicate shaves of cold beef, little wads of mutton, just the right thickness, and in dividing a chicken or a duck with nice precision . . .

'Is this the first of the home products?' he asked, knowing perfectly well that it was.

'Yes, the butcher did not come. We have found out that he only calls twice a week.'

But there was no need to apologise. It was a superb bird. It wasn't meat at all, but a kind of very superior jelly. 'My father would say,' said Burnell, 'this must have been one of those birds whose mother played to it in infancy upon the German flute. And the sweet strains of the dulcet instrument acted with such effect upon the infant mind . . .

Have some more, Beryl? You and I are the only ones in this house with a real feeling for food. I'm perfectly willing to state, in a court of law, if necessary, that I love good food.'

Tea was served in the drawing-room, and Beryl, who for some reason had been very charming to Stanley ever since he came home, suggested a game of crib. They sat at a little table near one of the open windows. Mrs Fairfield disappeared, and Linda lay in a rocking-chair, her arms above her head, rocking to and fro.

'You don't want the light – do you, Linda?' said Beryl. She moved the tall lamp so that she sat under its soft light.

How remote they looked, those two, from where Linda sat and rocked. The green table, the polished cards, Stanley's big hands and Beryl's tiny ones, all seemed to be part of one mysterious movement. Stanley himself, big and solid, in his dark suit, took his ease, and Beryl tossed her bright head and pouted. Round her throat she wore an unfamiliar velvet ribbon. It changed her, somehow – altered the shape of her face – but it was charming, Linda decided. The room smelled of lilies; there were two big jars of arums in the fire-place.

'Fifteen two – fifteen four – and a pair is six and a run of three is nine,' said Stanley, so deliberately, he might have been counting sheep.

'I've nothing but two pairs,' said Beryl, exaggerating her woe because she knew how he loved winning.

The cribbage pegs were like two little people going up the road together, turning round the sharp corner, and coming down the road again. They were pursuing each other. They did not so much want to get ahead as to keep near enough to talk – to keep near, perhaps that was all.

But no, there was always one who was impatient and hopped away as the other came up, and would not listen. Perhaps the white peg was frightened of the red one, or perhaps he was cruel and would not give the red one a chance to speak . . .

In the front of her dress Beryl wore a bunch of pansies, and once when the little pegs were side by side, she bent over and the pansies dropped out and covered them.

'What a shame,' said she, picking up the pansies. 'Just as they had a chance to fly into each other's arms.'

'Farewell, my girl,' laughed Stanley, and away the red peg hopped.

The drawing-room was long and narrow with glass doors that gave on to the veranda. It had a cream paper with a pattern of gilt roses, and the furniture, which had belonged to old Mrs Fairfield, was dark and plain. A little piano stood against the wall with yellow pleated silk let into the carved front. Above it hung an oil painting by Beryl of a large cluster of surprised-looking clematis. Each flower was the size of a small saucer, with a centre like an astonished eye fringed in black. But the room was not finished yet. Stanley had set his heart on a Chesterfield and two decent chairs. Linda liked it best as it was . . .

Two big moths flew in through the window and round and round the circle of lamplight.

'Fly away before it is too late. Fly out again.'

Round and round they flew; they seemed to bring the silence and the moonlight in with them on their silent wings . . .

'I've two kings,' said Stanley. 'Any good?'

'Quite good,' said Beryl.

Linda stopped rocking and got up. Stanley looked across. 'Anything the matter, darling?'

'No, nothing. I'm going to find mother.'

She went out of the room and standing at the foot of the stairs she called, but her mother's voice answered her from the veranda.

The moon that Lottie and Kezia had seen from the storeman's wagon was full, and the house, the garden, the old woman and Linda – all were bathed in dazzling light.

'I have been looking at the aloe,' said Mrs Fairfield. 'I believe it is going to flower this year. Look at the top there. Are those buds, or is it only an effect of light?'

As they stood on the steps, the high grassy bank on which the aloe rested rose up like a wave, and the aloe seemed to ride upon it like a ship with the oars lifted. Bright moonlight hung upon the lifted oars like water, and on the green wave glittered the dew.

'Do you feel it, too,' said Linda, and she spoke to her mother with the special voice that women use at night to each other as though they spoke in their sleep or from some hollow cave – 'Don't you feel that it is coming towards us?'

She dreamed that she was caught up out of the cold water into the ship with the lifted oars and the budding mast. Now the oars fell striking quickly, quickly. They rowed far away over the top of the garden trees, the paddocks and the dark bush beyond. Ah, she heard herself cry: 'Faster! Faster!' to those who were rowing.

How much more real this dream was than that they should go back to the house where the sleeping children lay and where Stanley and Beryl played cribbage.

'I believe those are buds,' said she. 'Let us go down into the garden, mother. I like that aloe. I like it more than anything here. And I am sure I shall remember it long after I've forgotten all the other things.'

She put her hand on her mother's arm and they walked down the steps, round the island and on to the main drive that led to the front gates.

Looking at it from below she could see the long sharp thorns that edged the aloe leaves, and at the sight of them her heart grew hard . . . She particularly liked the long sharp thorns . . . Nobody would dare to come near the ship or to follow after.

'Not even my Newfoundland dog,' thought she, 'that I'm so fond of in the daytime.'

For she really was fond of him; she loved and admired and respected him tremendously. Oh, better than anyone else in the world. She knew him through and through. He was the soul of truth and decency, and for all his practical experience he was awfully simple, easily pleased and easily hurt . . .

If only he wouldn't jump at her so, and bark so loudly, and watch her with such eager, loving eyes. He was too strong for her; she had always hated things that rush at her, from a child. There were times when he was frightening – really frightening. When she just had not screamed at the top of her voice: 'You are killing me.' And at those times she had longed to say the most coarse, hateful things . . .

'You know I'm very delicate. You know as well as I do that my heart is affected, and the doctor has told you I may die any moment. I have had three great lumps of children already . . .'

Yes, yes, it was true. Linda snatched her hand from mother's arm. For all her love and respect and admiration she hated him. And how tender he always was after times like those, how submissive, how thoughtful. He would do anything for her; he longed to serve her . . . Linda heard herself saying in a weak voice:

'Stanley, would you light a candle?'

And she heard his joyful voice answer: 'Of course I will, my darling.' And he leapt out of bed as though he were going to leap at the moon for her.

It had never been so plain to her as it was at this moment. There were all her feelings for him, sharp and defined, one as true as the other. And there was this other, this hatred, just as real as the rest. She could have done her feelings up in little packets and given them to Stanley. She longed to hand him that last one, for a surprise. She could see his eyes as he opened that . . .

She hugged her folded arms and began to laugh silently. How absurd life was – it was laughable, simply laughable. And why this mania of hers to keep alive at all? For it really was a mania, she thought, mocking and laughing.

'What am I guarding myself for so preciously? I shall go on having children and Stanley will go on making money and the children and the gardens will grow bigger and bigger, with whole fleets of aloes in them for me to choose from.'

She had been walking with her head bent, looking at nothing. Now she looked up and about her. They were standing by the red and white camellia trees. Beautiful were the rich dark leaves spangled with light and the round flowers that perch among them like red and white birds. Linda pulled a piece of verbena and crumpled it, and held her hands to her mother.

'Delicious,' said the old woman. 'Are you cold, child? Are you trembling? Yes, your hands are cold. We had better go back to the house.'

'What have you been thinking about?' said Linda. 'Tell me.'

'I haven't really been thinking of anything. I wondered as we passed the orchard what the fruit trees were like and whether we should be able to make much jam this autumn. There are splendid healthy currant bushes in the vegetable garden. I noticed them today. I should like to see those pantry shelves thoroughly well stocked with our own jam . . .'

XII

My darling Nan,

Don't think me a piggy wig because I haven't written before. I haven't had a moment, dear, and even now I feel so exhausted that I can hardly hold a pen.

Well, the dreadful deed is done. We have actually left the giddy whirl of town, and I can't see how we shall ever go back again, for my brother-in-law has bought this house 'lock, stock and barrel', to use his own words.

In a way, of course, it is an awful relief, for he has been threatening to take a place in the country ever since I've lived with them – and I must say the house and garden are awfully nice – a million times better than that awful cubby-hole in town.

But buried, my dear. Buried isn't the word.

We have got neighbours, but they are only farmers – big louts of boys who seem to be milking all day, and two dreadful females with rabbit teeth who brought us some scones when we were moving and said they would be pleased to help. But my sister who lives a mile away doesn't know a soul here, so I am sure we never shall. It's pretty certain nobody will ever come out from town to see us, because though there is a bus it's an awful old rattling thing with black leather sides that any decent person would rather die than ride in for six miles.

Such is life. It's a sad ending for poor little B. I'll get to be a most awful frump in a year or two and come and see you in a mackintosh and a sailor hat tied on with a white china silk motor veil. So pretty.

Stanley says that now we are settled – for after the most awful week of my life we really are settled – he is going to bring out a couple of men from the club on Saturday afternoons for tennis. In fact, two are promised as a great treat today. But, my dear, if you could see Stanley's men from the club . . . rather fattish, the type who look frightfully indecent without waistcoats – always with toes that turn in rather – so conspicuous when you are walking about a court in white shoes. And they are pulling up their trousers every minute – don't you know – and whacking at imaginary things with their rackets.

I used to play with them at the club last summer, and I am sure you will know the type when I tell you that after I'd been there about three times they all called me Miss Beryl. It's a weary world. Of course mother simply loves the place, but then I suppose when I am mother's age I shall be content to sit in the sun and shell peas into a basin. But I'm not – not – not.

What Linda thinks about the whole affair, per usual, I haven't the slightest idea. Mysterious as ever . . .

My dear, you know that white satin dress of mine. I have taken
the sleeves out entirely, put bands of black velvet across the shoulders and two big red poppies off my dear sister's *chapeau*. It is a
great success, though when I shall wear it I do not know.

Beryl sat writing this letter at a little table in her room. In a way, of
course, it was all perfectly true, but in another way it was all the greatest rubbish and she didn't believe a word of it. No, that wasn't true.
She felt all those things, but she didn't really feel them like that.

It was her other self who had written that letter. It not only bored,
it rather disgusted her real self.

'Flippant and silly,' said her real self. Yet she knew that she'd send it
and she'd always write that kind of twaddle to Nan Pym. In fact, it was
a very mild example of the kind of letter she generally wrote.

Beryl leaned her elbows on the table and read it through again. The
voice of the letter seemed to come up to her from the page. It was faint
already, like a voice heard over the telephone, high, gushing, with
something bitter in the sound. Oh, she detested it today.

'You've always got so much animation,' said Nan Pym. 'That's why
men are so keen on you.' And she had added, rather mournfully, for
men were not at all keen on Nan, who was a solid kind of girl, with fat
hips and a high colour – 'I can't understand how you can keep it up.
But it is your nature, I suppose.'

What rot. What nonsense. It wasn't her nature at all. Good heavens,
if she had ever been her real self with Nan Pym, Nannie would have
jumped out of the window with surprise . . . My dear, you know that
white satin of mine . . . Beryl slammed the letter-case to.

She jumped up and half unconsciously, half consciously she drifted
over to the looking-glass.

There stood a slim girl in white – a white serge skirt, a white silk
blouse, and a leather belt drawn in very tightly at her tiny waist.

Her face was heart-shaped, wide at the brows and with a pointed
chin – but not too pointed. Her eyes, her eyes were perhaps her best
feature; they were such a strange uncommon colour – greeny blue
with little gold points in them.

She had fine black eyebrows and long lashes – so long, that when
they lay on her cheeks you positively caught the light in them, someone or other had told her.

Her mouth was rather large. Too large? No, not really. Her under-lip protruded a little; she had a way of sucking it in that somebody else had told her was awfully fascinating.

Her nose was her least satisfactory feature. Not that it was really ugly. But it was not half as fine as Linda's. Linda really had a perfect little nose. Hers spread rather – not badly. And in all probability she exaggerated the spreadiness of it just because it was her nose, and she was so awfully critical of herself. She pinched it with a thumb and first finger and made a little face . . .

Lovely, lovely hair. And such a mass of it. It had the colour of fresh fallen leaves, brown and red with a glint of yellow. When she did it in a long plait she felt it on her backbone like a long snake. She loved to feel the weight of it dragging her head back, and she loved to feel it loose, covering her bare arms. 'Yes, my dear, there is no doubt about it, you really are a lovely little thing.'

At the words her bosom lifted; she took a long breath of delight, half closing her eyes.

But even as she looked the smile faded from her lips and eyes. Oh, God, there she was, back again, playing the same old game. False – false as ever. False as when she'd written to Nan Pym. False even when she was alone with herself, now.

What had that creature in the glass to do with her, and why was she staring? She dropped down to one side of her bed and buried her face in her arms.

'Oh,' she cried, 'I am so miserable – so frightfully miserable. I know that I'm silly and spiteful and vain; I'm always acting a part. I'm never my real self for a moment.' And plainly, plainly, she saw her false self running up and down the stairs, laughing a special trilling laugh if they had visitors, standing under the lamp if a man came to dinner, so that he should see the light on her hair, pouting and pretending to be a little girl when she was asked to play the guitar. Why? She even kept it up for Stanley's benefit. Only last night when he was reading the paper her false self had stood beside him and leaned against his shoulder on pur-pose. Hadn't she put her hand over his, pointing out something so that he should see how white her hand was beside his brown one.

How despicable! Despicable! Her heart was cold with rage. 'It's marvellous how you keep it up,' said she to the false self. But then it was only because she was so miserable – so miserable. If she had been happy and leading her own life, her false life would cease to be. She saw the real Beryl – a shadow . . . a shadow. Faint and unsubstantial she shone. What was there of her except the radiance? And for what tiny moments she was really she. Beryl could almost remember every one of them. At those times she had felt: 'Life is rich and mysterious and good, and I am rich and mysterious and good, too.' Shall I ever be that Beryl for ever? Shall I? How can I? And was there ever a time when I did not have a false self? . . . But just as she had got that far she heard the sound of little steps running along the passage; the door handle rattled. Kezia came in.

'Aunt Beryl, mother says will you please come down? Father is home with a man and lunch is ready.'

Botheration! How she had crumpled her skirt, kneeling in that idiotic way.

'Very well, Kezia.' She went over to the dressing-table and powdered her nose.

Kezia crossed too, and unscrewed a little pot of cream and sniffed it. Under her arm she carried a very dirty calico cat.

When Aunt Beryl ran out of the room she sat the cat up on the dressing-table and stuck the top of the cream jar over its ear.

'Now look at yourself,' said she sternly.

The calico cat was so overcome by the sight that it toppled over backwards and bumped and bumped on to the floor. And the top of the cream jar flew through the air and rolled like a penny in a round on the linoleum – and did not break.

But for Kezia it had broken the moment it flew through the air, and she picked it up, hot all over, and put it back on the dressing-table.

Then she tiptoed away, far too quickly and airily . . .

(first published in 1918, first book publication
Bliss and Other Stories, 1920)

A Dill Pickle

And then, after six years, she saw him again. He was seated at one of those little bamboo tables decorated with a Japanese vase of paper daffodils. There was a tall plate of fruit in front of him, and very carefully, in a way she recognised immediately as his 'special' way, he was peeling an orange.

He must have felt that shock of recognition in her, for he looked up and met her eyes. Incredible! He didn't know her! She smiled; he frowned. She came towards him. He closed his eyes an instant, but opening them his face lit up as though he had struck a match in a dark room. He laid down the orange and pushed back his chair, and she took her little warm hand out of her muff and gave it to him.

'Vera!' he exclaimed. 'How strange. Really, for a moment I didn't know you. Won't you sit down? You've had lunch? Won't you have some coffee?'

She hesitated, but of course she meant to.

'Yes, I'd like some coffee.' And she sat down opposite him.

'You've changed. You've changed very much,' he said, staring at her with that eager, lighted look. 'You look so well. I've never seen you look so well before.'

'Really?' She raised her veil and unbuttoned her high fur collar. 'I don't feel very well. I can't bear this weather, you know.'

'Ah, no. You hate the cold . . .'

'Loathe it.' She shuddered. 'And the worst of it is that the older one grows . . .'

He interrupted her. 'Excuse me,' and tapped on the table for the waitress. 'Please bring some coffee and cream.' To her: 'You are sure you won't eat anything? Some fruit, perhaps. The fruit here is very good.'

'No, thanks. Nothing.'

'Then that's settled.' And smiling just a hint too broadly he took up the orange again. 'You were saying – the older one grows –'

'The colder,' she laughed. But she was thinking how well she remembered that trick of his – the trick of interrupting her – and how it used to exasperate her six years ago. She used to feel then as though he, quite suddenly, in the middle of what she was saying, put his hand over her lips, turned from her, attended to something different, and then took his hand away, and with just the same slightly too broad smile, gave her his attention again . . . Now we are ready. That is settled.

'The colder!' He echoed her words, laughing too. 'Ah, ah. You still say the same things. And there is another thing about you that is not changed at all – your beautiful voice – your beautiful way of speaking.' Now he was very grave; he leaned towards her, and she smelled the warm, stinging scent of the orange peel. 'You have only to say one word and I would know your voice among all other voices. I don't know what it is – I've often wondered – that makes your voice such a – haunting memory . . . Do you remember that first afternoon we spent together at Kew Gardens? You were so surprised because I did not know the names of any flowers. I am still just as ignorant for all your telling me. But whenever it is very fine and warm, and I see some bright colours – it's awfully strange – I hear your voice saying: "Geranium, marigold and verbena." And I feel those three words are all I recall of some forgotten, heavenly language . . . You remember that afternoon?'

'Oh, yes, very well.' She drew a long, soft breath, as though the paper daffodils between them were almost too sweet to bear. Yet, what had remained in her mind of that particular afternoon was an absurd scene over the tea-table. A great many people taking tea in a Chinese pagoda, and he behaving like a maniac about the wasps – waving them away, flapping at them with his straw hat, serious and infuriated out of all proportion to the occasion. How delighted the sniggering tea drinkers had been. And how she had suffered.

But now, as he spoke, that memory faded. His was the truer. Yes, it had been a wonderful afternoon, full of geranium and marigold and verbena, and – warm sunshine. Her thoughts lingered over the last two words as though she sang them.

In the warmth, as it were, another memory unfolded. She saw herself sitting on a lawn. He lay beside her, and suddenly, after a long silence, he rolled over and put his head in her lap.

'I wish,' he said, in a low, troubled voice, 'I wish that I had taken poison and were about to die – here now!'

At that moment a little girl in a white dress, holding a long, dripping white lily, dodged from behind a bush, stared at them, and dodged back again. But he did not see. She leaned over him.

'Ah, why do you say that? I could not say that.'

But he gave a kind of soft moan, and taking her hand he held it to his cheek.

'Because I know I am going to love you too much – far too much. And I shall suffer so terribly, Vera, because you never, never will love me.'

He was certainly far better looking now than he had been then. He had lost all that dreamy vagueness and indecision. Now he had the air of a man who has found his place in life, and fills it with a confidence and an assurance which was, to say the least, impressive. He must have made money, too. His clothes were admirable, and at that moment he pulled a Russian cigarette-case out of his pocket.

'Won't you smoke?'

'Yes, I will.' She hovered over them. 'They look very good.'

'I think they are. I get them made for me by a little man in St James's Street. I don't smoke very much. I'm not like you – but when I do, they must be delicious, very fresh cigarettes. Smoking isn't a habit with me; it's a luxury – like perfume. Are you still so fond of perfumes? Ah, when I was in Russia . . .'

She broke in: 'You've really been to Russia?'

'Oh yes. I was there for over a year. Have you forgotten how we used to talk of going there?'

'No, I've not forgotten.'

He gave a strange half-laugh and leaned back in his chair. 'Isn't it curious. I have really carried out all those journeys that we planned. Yes, I have been to all those places that we talked of, and stayed in them long enough to – as you used to say – "air oneself" in them. In fact, I have spent the last three years of my life travelling all the time. Spain, Corsica, Siberia, Russia, Egypt. The only country left is China, and I mean to go there, too, when the war is over.'

As he spoke, so lightly, tapping the end of his cigarette against the ash-tray, she felt the strange beast that had slumbered so long within her bosom stir, stretch itself, yawn, prick up its ears, and suddenly bound to its feet, and fix its longing, hungry stare upon those far-away places. But all she said was, smiling gently: 'How I envy you.'

He accepted that. 'It has been,' he said, 'very wonderful – especially Russia. Russia was all that we had imagined, and far, far more. I even spent some days on a river boat on the Volga. Do you remember that boatman's song that you used to play?'

'Yes.' It began to play in her mind as she spoke.

'Do you ever play it now?'

'No, I've no piano.'

He was amazed at that. 'But what has become of your beautiful piano?'

She made a little grimace. 'Sold. Ages ago.'

'But you were so fond of music,' he wondered.

'I've no time for it now,' said she.

He let it go at that. 'That river life,' he went on, 'is something quite special. After a day or two you cannot realise that you have ever known another. And it is not necessary to know the language – the life of the boat creates a bond between you and the people that's more than sufficient. You eat with them, pass the day with them, and in the evening there is that endless singing.'

She shivered, hearing the boatman's song break out again loud and tragic, and seeing the boat floating on the darkening river with melancholy trees on either side . . . 'Yes, I should like that,' said she, stroking her muff.

'You'd like almost everything about Russian life,' he said warmly. 'It's so informal, so impulsive, so free without question. And then the peasants are so splendid. They are such human beings – yes, that is it. Even the man who drives your carriage has – has some real part in what is happening. I remember the evening a party of us, two friends of mine and the wife of one of them, went for a picnic by the Black Sea. We took supper and champagne and ate and drank on the grass. And while we were eating the coachman came up. "Have a dill pickle," he said. He wanted to share with us. That seemed to me so right, so – you know what I mean?'

And she seemed at that moment to be sitting on the grass beside the mysteriously Black Sea, black as velvet, and rippling against the banks in silent, velvet waves. She saw the carriage drawn up to one side of the road, and the little group on the grass, their faces and hands white in the moonlight. She saw the pale dress of the woman outspread and her folded parasol, lying on the grass like a huge pearl crochet-hook. Apart

from them, with his supper in a cloth on his knees, sat the coachman.
'Have a dill pickle,' said he, and although she was not certain what a
dill pickle was, she saw the greenish glass jar with a red chilli like a parrot's beak glimmering through. She sucked in her cheeks; the dill
pickle was terribly sour . . .

'Yes, I know perfectly what you mean,' she said.

In the pause that followed they looked at each other. In the past
when they had looked at each other like that they had felt such a
boundless understanding between them that their souls had, as it were,
put their arms round each other and dropped into the same sea, content to be drowned, like mournful lovers. But now, the surprising
thing was that it was he who held back. He who said:

'What a marvellous listener you are. When you look at me with
those wild eyes I feel that I could tell you things that I would never
breathe to another human being.'

Was there just a hint of mockery in his voice or was it her fancy?
She could not be sure.

'Before I met you,' he said, 'I had never spoken of myself to anybody. How well I remember one night, the night that I brought you
the little Christmas tree, telling you all about my childhood. And of
how I was so miserable that I ran away and lived under a cart in our
yard for two days without being discovered. And you listened, and
your eyes shone, and I felt that you had even made the little Christmas
tree listen too, as in a fairy story.'

But of that evening she had remembered a little pot of caviare. It
had cost seven and sixpence. He could not get over it. Think of it – a
tiny jar like that costing seven and sixpence. While she ate it he
watched her, delighted and shocked.

'No, really, that is eating money. You could not get seven shillings
into a little pot that size. Only think of the profit they must make . . .'
And he had begun some immensely complicated calculations . . . But
now goodbye to the caviare. The Christmas tree was on the table, and
the little boy lay under the cart with his head pillowed on the yard dog.

'The dog was called Bosun,' she cried delightedly.

But he did not follow. 'Which dog? Had you a dog? I don't remember a dog at all.'

'No, no. I mean the yard dog when you were a little boy.' He
laughed and snapped the cigarette-case to.

'Was he? Do you know I had forgotten that. It seems such ages ago. I cannot believe that it is only six years. After I had recognised you today – I had to take such a leap – I had to take a leap over my whole life to get back to that time. I was such a kid then.' He drummed on the table. 'I've often thought how I must have bored you. And now I understand so perfectly why you wrote to me as you did – although at the time that letter nearly finished my life. I found it again the other day, and I couldn't help laughing as I read it. It was so clever – such a true picture of me.' He glanced up. 'You're not going?'

She had buttoned her collar again and drawn down her veil.

'Yes, I am afraid I must,' she said, and managed a smile. Now she knew that he had been mocking.

'Ah no, please,' he pleaded. 'Don't go just for a moment,' and he caught up one of her gloves from the table and clutched at it as if that would hold her. 'I see so few people to talk to nowadays, that I have turned into a sort of barbarian,' he said. 'Have I said something to hurt you?'

'Not a bit,' she lied. But as she watched him draw her glove through his fingers, gently, gently, her anger really did die down, and besides, at the moment he looked more like himself of six years ago . . .

'What I really wanted then,' he said softly, 'was to be a sort of carpet – to make myself into a sort of carpet for you to walk on so that you need not be hurt by the sharp stones and the mud that you hated so. It was nothing more positive than that – nothing more selfish. Only I did desire, eventually, to turn into a magic carpet and carry you away to all those lands you longed to see.'

As he spoke she lifted her head as though she drank something; the strange beast in her bosom began to purr . . .

'I felt that you were more lonely than anybody else in the world,' he went on, 'and yet, perhaps, that you were the only person in the world who was really, truly alive. Born out of your time,' he murmured, stroking the glove, 'fated.'

Ah, God! What had she done! How had she dared to throw away her happiness like this. This was the only man who had ever understood her. Was it too late? Could it be too late? *She* was that glove that he held in his fingers . . .

'And then the fact that you had no friends and never had made friends with people. How I understood that, for neither had I. Is it just the same now?'

'Yes,' she breathed. 'Just the same. I am as alone as ever.'

'So am I,' he laughed gently, 'just the same.'

Suddenly with a quick gesture he handed her back the glove and scraped his chair on the floor. 'But what seemed to me so mysterious then is perfectly plain to me now. And to you, too, of course . . . It simply was that we were such egoists, so self-engrossed, so wrapped up in ourselves that we hadn't a corner in our hearts for anybody else. Do you know,' he cried, naïve and hearty, and dreadfully like another side of that old self again, 'I began studying a Mind System when I was in Russia, and I found that we were not peculiar at all. It's quite a well-known form of . . .'

She had gone. He sat there, thunder-struck, astounded beyond words . . . And then he asked the waitress for his bill.

'But the cream has not been touched,' he said. 'Please do not charge me for it.'

(first published in 1917, first book publication
Bliss and Other Stories, 1920)

Pictures

Eight o'clock in the morning. Miss Ada Moss lay in a black iron bedstead, staring up at the ceiling. Her room, a Bloomsbury top-floor back, smelled of soot and face powder and the paper of fried potatoes she brought in for supper the night before.

'Oh, dear,' thought Miss Moss, 'I am cold. I wonder why it is that I always wake up so cold in the mornings now. My knees and feet and my back – especially my back; it's like a sheet of ice. And I always was such a one for being warm in the old days. It's not as if I was skinny – I'm just the same full figure that I used to be. No, it's because I don't have a good hot dinner in the evenings.'

A pageant of Good Hot Dinners passed across the ceiling, each of them accompanied by a bottle of Nourishing Stout . . .

'Even if I were to get up now,' she thought, 'and have a sensible substantial breakfast . . .' A pageant of Sensible Substantial Breakfasts followed the dinners across the ceiling, shepherded by an enormous, white, uncut ham. Miss Moss shuddered and disappeared under the bedclothes. Suddenly, in bounced the landlady.

'There's a letter for you, Miss Moss.'

'Oh,' said Miss Moss, far too friendly, 'thank you very much, Mrs Pine. It's very good of you, I'm sure, to take the trouble.'

'No trouble at all,' said the landlady. 'I thought perhaps it was the letter you'd been expecting.'

'Why,' said Miss Moss brightly, 'yes, perhaps it is.' She put her head on one side and smiled vaguely at the letter. 'I shouldn't be surprised.'

The landlady's eyes popped. 'Well, I should, Miss Moss,' said she, 'and that's how it is. And I'll trouble you to open it, if you please. Many is the lady in my place as would have done it for you and have been within her rights. For things can't go on like this, Miss Moss, no indeed they can't. What with week in week out and first you've got it and then you haven't, and then it's another letter lost in the post or another manager down at Brighton but will be back on Tuesday for certain – I'm fair sick and tired and I won't stand it no more. Why should I, Miss Moss, I ask you, at a time like this, with prices flying up in the air and my poor dear lad in France? My sister Eliza was only saying to me yesterday – "Minnie," she says, "you're too soft-hearted. You could have let that room time and time again," says she, "and if people won't look after themselves in times like these, nobody else will," she says. "She may have had a College eddication and sung in West End concerts," says she, "but if your Lizzie says what's true," she says, "and she's washing her own wovens and drying them on the towel rail, it's easy to see where the finger's pointing. And it's high time you had done with it," says she.'

Miss Moss gave no sign of having heard this. She sat up in bed, tore open her letter and read:

Dear Madam,

Yours to hand. Am not producing at present, but have filed photo for future ref.

Yours truly,
Backwash Film Co.

This letter seemed to afford her peculiar satisfaction; she read it through twice before replying to the landlady.

'Well, Mrs Pine, I think you'll be sorry for what you said. This is from a manager, asking me to be there with evening dress at ten o'clock next Saturday morning.'

But the landlady was too quick for her. She pounced, secured the letter.

'Oh, is it! Is it indeed!' she cried.

'Give me back that letter. Give it back to me at once, you bad, wicked woman,' cried Miss Moss, who could not get out of bed because her nightdress was slit down the back. 'Give me back my private letter.' The landlady began slowly backing out of the room, holding the letter to her buttoned bodice.

'So it's come to this, has it?' said she. 'Well, Miss Moss, if I don't get my rent at eight o'clock tonight, we'll see who's a bad, wicked woman – that's all.' Here she nodded mysteriously. 'And I'll keep this letter.' Here her voice rose. 'It will be a pretty little bit of evidence!' And here it fell, sepulchral, '*My lady.*'

The door banged and Miss Moss was alone. She flung off the bedclothes, and sitting by the side of the bed, furious and shivering, she
stared at her fat white legs with their great knots of greeny-blue veins.

'Cockroach! That's what she is. She's a cockroach!' said Miss Moss.
'I could have her up for snatching my letter – I'm sure I could.' Still
keeping on her nightdress she began to drag on her clothes.

'Oh, if I could only pay that woman, I'd give her a piece of my
mind that she wouldn't forget. I'd tell her off proper.' She went over
to the chest of drawers for a safety-pin, and seeing herself in the glass
she gave a vague smile and shook her head. 'Well, old girl,' she murmured, 'you're up against it this time, and no mistake.' But the person
in the glass made an ugly face at her.

'You silly thing,' scolded Miss Moss. 'Now what's the good of crying: you'll only make your nose red. No, you get dressed and go out
and try your luck – that's what you've got to do.'

She unhooked her vanity bag from the bedpost, rooted in it, shook
it, turned it inside out.

'I'll have a nice cup of tea at an A B C to settle me before I go anywhere,' she decided. 'I've got one and thrippence – yes, just one and
three.'

Ten minutes later, a stout lady in blue serge, with a bunch of artificial 'parmas' at her bosom, a black hat covered with purple pansies,
white gloves, boots with white uppers, and a vanity bag containing
one and three, sang in a low contralto voice:

> Sweet-heart, remember when days are forlorn
> It al-ways is dar-kest before the dawn.

But the person in the glass made a face at her, and Miss Moss went
out. There were grey crabs all the way down the street slopping water
over grey stone steps. With his strange, hawking cry and the jangle of
the cans the milk-boy went his rounds. Outside Brittweiler's Swiss
House he made a splash, and an old brown cat without a tail appeared
from nowhere, and began greedily and silently drinking up the spill. It
gave Miss Moss a queer feeling to watch – a sinking, as you might say.

But when she came to the A B C she found the door propped open;
a man went in and out carrying trays of rolls, and there was nobody
inside except a waitress doing her hair and the cashier unlocking the

cash-boxes. She stood in the middle of the floor but neither of them saw her.

'My boy came home last night,' sang the waitress.

'Oh, I say – how topping for you!' gurgled the cashier.

'Yes, wasn't it,' sang the waitress. 'He brought me a sweet little brooch. Look, it's got "Dieppe" written on it.'

The cashier ran across to look and put her arm round the waitress's neck.

'Oh, I say – how topping for you.'

'Yes, isn't it,' said the waitress. 'O-oh, he is brahn. "Hullo," I said, "hullo, old mahogany."'

'Oh, I say,' gurgled the cashier, running back into her cage and nearly bumping into Miss Moss on the way. 'You are a *treat*!' Then the man with the rolls came in again, swerving past her.

'Can I have a cup of tea, Miss?' she asked.

But the waitress went on doing her hair. 'Oh,' she sang, 'we're not *open* yet.' She turned round and waved her comb at the cashier.

'*Are* we, dear?'

'Oh no,' said the cashier. Miss Moss went out.

'I'll go to Charing Cross. Yes, that's what I'll do,' she decided. 'But I won't have a cup of tea. No, I'll have a coffee. There's more of a tonic in coffee . . . Cheeky, those girls are! Her boy came home last night; he brought her a brooch with "Dieppe" written on it.' She began to cross the road . . .

'Look out, Fattie; don't go to sleep!' yelled a taxi-driver. She pretended not to hear.

'No, I won't go to Charing Cross,' she decided. 'I'll go straight to Kig and Kadgit. They're open at nine. If I get there early Mr Kadgit may have something by the morning's post . . . I'm very glad you turned up so early, Miss Moss. I've just heard from a manager who wants a lady to play . . . I think you'll just suit him. I'll give you a card to go and see him. It's three pounds a week and all found. If I were you I'd hop round as fast as I could. Lucky you turned up so early . . .'

But there was nobody at Kig and Kadgit's except the charwoman wiping over the 'lino' in the passage.

'Nobody here yet, Miss,' said the char.

'Oh, isn't Mr Kadgit here?' said Miss Moss, trying to dodge the pail and brush. 'Well, I'll just wait a moment, if I may.'

'You can't wait in the waiting-room, Miss. I 'aven't done it yet. Mr Kadgit's never 'ere before 'leven-thirty Saturdays. Sometimes 'e don't come at all.' And the char began crawling towards her.

'Dear me – how silly of me,' said Miss Moss. 'I forgot it was Saturday.'

'Mind your feet, *please*, Miss,' said the char. And Miss Moss was outside again.

That was one thing about Beit and Bithems; it was lively. You walked into the waiting-room, into a great buzz of conversation, and there was everybody; you knew almost everybody. The early ones sat on chairs and the later ones sat on the early ones' laps, while the gentlemen leaned negligently against the walls or preened themselves in front of the admiring ladies.

'Hello,' said Miss Moss, very gay. 'Here we are again!'

And young Mr Clayton, playing the banjo on his walking-stick, sang: 'Waiting for the Robert E. Lee.'

'Mr Bithem here yet?' asked Miss Moss, taking out an old dead powder-puff and powdering her nose mauve.

'Oh yes, dear,' cried the chorus. 'He's been here for ages. We've all been waiting here for more than an hour.'

'Dear me!' said Miss Moss. 'Anything doing, do you think?'

'Oh, a few jobs going for South Africa,' said young Mr Clayton. 'Hundred and fifty a week for two years, you know.'

'Oh!' cried the chorus. 'You *are* weird, Mr Clayton. Isn't he a *cure*? Isn't he a *scream*, dear? Oh, Mr Clayton, you do make me laugh. Isn't he a *comic*?'

A dark, mournful girl touched Miss Moss on the arm.

'I just missed a lovely job yesterday,' she said. 'Six weeks in the provinces and then the West End. The manager said I would have got it for certain if only I'd been robust enough. He said if my figure had been fuller, the part was made for me.' She stared at Miss Moss, and the dirty dark red rose under the brim of her hat looked, somehow, as though it shared the blow with her, and was crushed, too.

'Oh, dear, that was hard lines,' said Miss Moss, trying to appear indifferent. 'What was it – if I may ask?'

But the dark, mournful girl saw through her and a gleam of spite came into her heavy eyes.

'Oh, no good to you, my dear,' said she. 'He wanted someone

young, you know – a dark Spanish type – my style, but more figure, that was all.'

The inner door opened and Mr Bithem appeared in his shirt sleeves. He kept one hand on the door ready to whisk back again, and held up the other.

'Look here, ladies –' and then he paused, grinned his famous grin before he said – '*and bhoys.*' The waiting-room laughed so loudly at this that he had to hold both hands up. 'It's no good waiting this morning. Come back Monday; I'm expecting several calls on Monday.'

Miss Moss made a desperate rush forward. 'Mr Bithem, I wonder if you've heard from . . .'

'Now let me see,' said Mr Bithem slowly, staring; he had only seen Miss Moss four times a week for the past – how many weeks? 'Now, who are you?'

'Miss Ada Moss.'

'Oh yes, yes; of course, my dear. Not yet, my dear. Now I had a call for twenty-eight ladies today, but they had to be young and able to hop it a bit – see? And I had another call for sixteen – but they had to know something about sand-dancing. Look here, my dear, I'm up to the eyebrows this morning. Come back on Monday week; it's no good coming before that.' He gave her a whole grin to herself and patted her fat back. 'Hearts of oak, dear lady,' said Mr Bithem, 'hearts of oak!'

At the North-East Film Company the crowd was all the way up the stairs. Miss Moss found herself next to a fair little baby thing about thirty in a white lace hat with cherries round it.

'What a crowd!' said she. 'Anything special on?'

'*Didn't* you know, dear?' said the baby, opening her immense pale eyes. 'There was a call at nine-thirty for *attractive* girls. We've all been waiting for *hours*. Have you played for this company before?' Miss Moss put her head on one side. 'No, I don't think I have.'

'They're a lovely company to play for,' said the baby. 'A friend of mine has a friend who gets thirty pounds a day . . . Have you *arcted* much for the *fil*-lums?'

'Well, I'm not an actress by profession,' confessed Miss Moss. 'I'm a contralto singer. But things have been so bad lately that I've been doing a little.'

'It's *like* that, isn't it, dear?' said the baby.

'I had a splendid education at the College of Music,' said Miss Moss, 'and I got my silver medal for singing. I've often sung at West End concerts. But I thought, for a change, I'd try my luck . . .'

'Yes, it's *like* that, isn't it, dear?' said the baby.

At that moment a beautiful typist appeared at the top of the stairs.

'Are you all waiting for the North-East call?'

'Yes!' cried the chorus.

'Well, it's off. I've just had a 'phone through.'

'But look here! What about our expenses?' shouted a voice.

The typist looked down at them, and she couldn't help laughing.

'Oh, you weren't to have been *paid*. The North-East never *pay* their crowds.'

There was only a little round window at the Bitter Orange Company. No waiting-room – nobody at all except a girl, who came to the window when Miss Moss knocked, and said: 'Well?'

'Can I see the producer, please?' said Miss Moss pleasantly. The girl leaned on the window-bar, half shut her eyes and seemed to go to sleep for a moment. Miss Moss smiled at her. The girl not only frowned; she seemed to smell something vaguely unpleasant; she sniffed. Suddenly she moved away, came back with a paper and thrust it at Miss Moss.

'Fill up the form!' said she. And banged the window down.

'Can you aviate – high-dive – drive a car – buck-jump – shoot?' read Miss Moss. She walked along the street asking herself those questions. There was a high, cold wind blowing; it tugged at her, slapped her face, jeered; it knew she could not answer them. In the Square Gardens she found a little wire basket to drop the form into. And then she sat down on one of the benches to powder her nose. But the person in the pocket mirror made a hideous face at her, and that was too much for Miss Moss; she had a good cry. It cheered her wonderfully.

'Well, that's over,' she sighed. 'It's one comfort to be off my feet. And my nose will soon get cool in the air . . . It's very nice in here. Look at the sparrows. Cheep. Cheep. How close they come. I expect somebody feeds them. No, I've nothing for you, you cheeky little things . . .' She looked away from them. What was the big building opposite – the Café de Madrid? My goodness, what a smack that little child came down! Poor little mite! Never mind – up again . . . By eight o'clock tonight . . . Café de Madrid. 'I could just go in and sit there and have a coffee, that's all,' thought Miss Moss. 'It's such a place for artists too. I might just have a stroke of luck . . . A dark handsome gentleman in a fur coat comes in with a friend, and sits at my table, perhaps. "No, old chap, I've searched London for a contralto and I can't find a soul. You see, the music is difficult; have a look at it."' And Miss Moss heard herself saying: 'Excuse me, I happen to be a contralto, and I have sung that part many times . . . Extraordinary! "Come back to my studio and I'll try your voice now." . . . Ten pounds a week . . . Why should I feel nervous? It's not nervousness. Why shouldn't I go to the Café de Madrid? I'm a respectable woman – I'm a contralto singer. And I'm only trembling because I've had nothing to eat today . . . "A nice little piece of evidence, *my lady*." . . . Very well, Mrs Pine. Café de Madrid. They have concerts there in the evenings . . . "Why don't they begin?" The contralto has not arrived . . . "Excuse me, I happen to be a contralto; I have sung that music many times."'

It was almost dark in the café. Men, palms, red plush seats, white marble tables, waiters in aprons, Miss Moss walked through them all. Hardly had she sat down when a very stout gentleman wearing a very small hat that floated on the top of his head like a little yacht flopped into the chair opposite hers.

'Good evening!' said he.

Miss Moss said, in her cheerful way: 'Good evening!'

'Fine evening,' said the stout gentleman.

'Yes, very fine. Quite a treat, isn't it?' said she.

He crooked a sausage finger at the waiter – 'Bring me a large whisky' – and turned to Miss Moss. 'What's yours?'

'Well, I think I'll take a brandy if it's all the same.'

Five minutes later the stout gentleman leaned across the table and blew a puff of cigar smoke full in her face.

'That's a tempting bit o' ribbon!' said he.

Miss Moss blushed until a pulse at the top of her head that she never had felt before pounded away.

'I always was one for pink,' said she.

The stout gentleman considered her, drumming with her fingers on the table.

'I like 'em firm and well covered,' said he.

Miss Moss, to her surprise, gave a loud snigger.

Five minutes later the stout gentleman heaved himself up. 'Well, am I goin' your way, or are you comin' mine?' he asked.

'I'll come with you, if it's all the same,' said Miss Moss. And she sailed after the little yacht out of the café.

(written 1917, first published in 1919, first book publication
Bliss and Other Stories, 1920)

Je ne parle pas français

I do not know why I have such a fancy for this little café. It's dirty and sad, sad. It's not as if it had anything to distinguish it from a hundred others – it hasn't; or as if the same strange types came here every day, whom one could watch from one's corner and recognise and more or less (with a strong accent on the less) get the hang of.

But pray don't imagine that those brackets are a confession of my humility before the mystery of the human soul. Not at all; I don't believe in the human soul. I never have. I believe that people are like portmanteaux – packed with certain things, started going, thrown about, tossed away, dumped down, lost and found, half emptied suddenly, or squeezed fatter than ever, until finally the Ultimate Porter swings them on to the Ultimate Train and away they rattle . . .

Not but what these portmanteaux can be very fascinating. Oh, but very! I see myself standing in front of them, don't you know, like a Customs official.

'Have you anything to declare? Any wines, spirits, cigars, perfumes, silks?'

And the moment of hesitation as to whether I am going to be fooled just before I chalk that squiggle, and then the other moment of hesitation just after, as to whether I have been, are perhaps the two most thrilling instants in life. Yes, they are, to me.

But before I started that long and rather far-fetched and not frightfully original digression, what I meant to say quite simply was that there are no portmanteaux to be examined here because the clientele of this café, ladies and gentlemen, does not sit down. No, it stands at the counter, and it consists of a handful of workmen who come up from the river, all powdered over with white flour, lime or something, and a few soldiers, bringing with them thin, dark girls with silver rings in their ears and market baskets on their arms.

Madame is thin and dark, too, with white cheeks and white hands. In certain lights she looks quite transparent, shining out of her black shawl with an extraordinary effect. When she is not serving she sits on a stool with her face turned, always, to the window. Her dark-ringed eyes search among and follow after the people passing, but not as if she was looking for somebody. Perhaps, fifteen years ago, she was; but now the pose has become a habit. You can tell from her air of fatigue and hopelessness that she must have given them up for the last ten years, at least . . .

And then there is the waiter. Not pathetic – decidedly not comic. Never making one of those perfectly insignificant remarks which amaze you so coming from a waiter (as though the poor wretch were a sort of cross between a coffee-pot and a wine bottle and not expected to hold so much as a drop of anything else). He is grey, flat-footed and withered, with long, brittle nails that set your nerves on edge while he scrapes up your two sous. When he is not smearing over the table or flicking at a dead fly or two, he stands with one hand on the back of a chair, in his far too long apron, and over his other arm the three-cornered dip of dirty napkin, waiting to be photographed in connection with some wretched murder. 'Interior of Café where Body was Found.' You've seen him hundreds of times.

Do you believe that every place has its hour of the day when it really does come alive? That's not exactly what I mean. It's more like this. There does seem to be a moment when you realise that, quite by accident, you happen to have come on to the stage at exactly the moment you were expected. Everything is arranged for you – waiting for you. Ah, master of the situation! You fill with important breath. And at the same time you smile, secretly, slyly, because Life seems to be opposed to granting you these entrances, seems indeed to be engaged in snatching them from you and making them impossible, keeping you in the wings until it is too late, in fact . . . Just for once you've beaten the old hag.

I enjoyed one of these moments the first time I ever came in here. That's why I keep coming back, I suppose. Revisiting the scene of my triumph, or the scene of the crime where I had the old bitch by the throat for once and did what I pleased with her.

Query: Why am I so bitter against Life? And why do I see her as a rag-picker on the American cinema, shuffling along wrapped in a filthy shawl with her old claws crooked over a stick?

Answer: The direct result of the American cinema acting upon a weak mind.

Anyhow, the 'short winter afternoon was drawing to a close', as they say, and I was drifting along, either going home or not going home, when I found myself in here, walking over to this seat in the corner.

I hung up my English overcoat and grey felt hat on that same peg behind me, and after I had allowed the waiter time for at least twenty photographers to snap their fill of him, I ordered a coffee.

He poured me out a glass of the familiar, purplish stuff with a green wandering light playing over it, and shuffled off, and I sat pressing my hands against the glass because it was bitterly cold outside.

Suddenly I realised that quite apart from myself, I was smiling. Slowly I raised my head and saw myself in the mirror opposite. Yes, there I sat, leaning on the table, smiling my deep, sly smile, the glass of coffee with its vague plume of steam before me and beside it the ring of white saucer with two pieces of sugar.

I opened my eyes very wide. There I had been for all eternity, as it were, and now at last I was coming to life . . .

It was very quiet in the café. Outside, one could just see through the dusk that it had begun to snow. One could just see the shapes of horses and carts and people, soft and white, moving through the feathery air. The waiter disappeared and reappeared with an armful of straw. He strewed it over the floor from the door to the counter and round about the stove with humble, almost adoring gestures. One would not have been surprised if the door had opened and the Virgin Mary had come in, riding upon an ass, her meek hands folded over her big belly . . .

That's rather nice, don't you think, that bit about the Virgin? It comes from the pen so gently; it has such a 'dying fall'. I thought so at the time and decided to make a note of it. One never knows when a little tag like that may come in useful to round off a paragraph. So, taking care to move as little as possible because the 'spell' was still unbroken (you know that?), I reached over to the next table for a writing pad.

No paper or envelopes, of course. Only a morsel of pink blotting-paper, incredibly soft and limp and almost moist, like the tongue of a little dead kitten, which I've never felt.

I sat – but always underneath, in this state of expectation, rolling the little dead kitten's tongue round my finger and rolling the soft phrase round my mind while my eyes took in the girls' names and dirty jokes and drawings of bottles and cups that would not sit in the saucers, scattered over the writing pad.

They are always the same, you know. The girls always have the same names, the cups never sit in the saucers; all the hearts are stuck and tied up with ribbons.

But then, quite suddenly, at the bottom of the page, written in green ink, I fell on to that stupid, stale little phrase: *Je ne parle pas français.*

There! it had come – the moment – the *geste!* And although I was so ready, it caught me, it tumbled me over; I was simply overwhelmed. And the physical feeling was so curious, so particular. It was as if all of me, except my head and arms, all of me that was under the table, had simply dissolved, melted, turned into water. Just my head remained and two sticks of arms pressing on to the table. But, ah! the agony of that moment! How can I describe it? I didn't think of anything. I didn't even cry out to myself. Just for one moment I was not. I was Agony, Agony, Agony.

Then it passed, and the very second after I was thinking: 'Good God! Am I capable of feeling as strongly as that? But I was absolutely unconscious! I hadn't a phrase to meet it with! I was overcome! I was swept off my feet! I didn't even try, in the dimmest way, to put it down!'

And up I puffed and puffed, blowing off finally with: 'After all I must be first-rate. No second-rate mind could have experienced such an intensity of feeling so . . . purely.'

The waiter has touched a spill at the red stove and lighted a bubble of gas under a spreading shade. It is no use looking out of the window, Madame; it is quite dark now. Your white hands hover over your dark shawl. They are like two birds that have come home to roost. They are restless, restless . . . You tuck them, finally, under your warm little armpits.

Now the waiter has taken a long pole and clashed the curtains together. 'All gone', as children say.

And besides, I've no patience with people who can't let go of things, who will follow after and cry out. When a thing's gone, it's gone. It's over and done with. Let it go then! Ignore it, and comfort yourself, if you do want comforting, with the thought that you never do recover the same thing that you lose. It's always a new thing. The moment it leaves you it's changed. Why, that's even true of a hat you chase after; and I don't mean superficially – I mean profoundly speaking . . . I have made it a rule of my life never to regret and never to look back. Regret is an appalling waste of energy, and no one who intends to be a writer can afford to indulge in it. You can't get it into shape; you can't build on it; it's only good for wallowing in. Looking back, of course, is equally fatal to Art. It's keeping yourself poor. Art can't and won't stand poverty.

Je ne parle pas français. Je ne parle pas français. All the while I wrote that last page my other self has been chasing up and down out in the dark there. It left me just when I began to analyse my grand moment, dashed off distracted, like a lost dog who thinks at last, at last, he hears the familiar step again.

'Mouse! Mouse! Where are you? Are you near? Is that you leaning from the high window and stretching out your arms for the wings of the shutters? Are you this soft bundle moving towards me through the feathery snow? Are you this little girl pressing through the swing-doors of the restaurant? Is that your dark shadow bending forward in the cab? Where are you? Where are you? Which way must I turn? Which way shall I run? And every moment I stand here hesitating you are farther away again. Mouse! Mouse!'

Now the poor dog has come back into the café, his tail between his legs, quite exhausted.

'It was a . . . false . . . alarm. She's nowhere . . . to . . . be seen.'

'Lie down then! Lie down! Lie down!'

My name is Raoul Duquette. I am twenty-six years old and a Parisian, a true Parisian. About my family – it really doesn't matter. I have no family; I don't want any. I never think about my childhood. I've forgotten it.

In fact, there's only one memory that stands out at all. That is rather interesting because it seems to me now so very significant as regards myself from the literary point of view. It is this.

When I was about ten our laundress was an African woman, very big, very dark, with a check handkerchief over her frizzy hair. When she came to our house she always took particular notice of me, and after the clothes had been taken out of the basket she would lift me up into it and give me a rock while I held tight to the handles and screamed for joy and fright. I was tiny for my age, and pale, with a lovely little half-open mouth – I feel sure of that.

One day when I was standing at the door, watching her go, she turned round and beckoned to me, nodding and smiling in a strange secret way. I never thought of not following. She took me into a little outhouse at the end of the passage, caught me up in her arms and began kissing me. Ah, those kisses! Especially those kisses inside my ears that nearly deafened me.

And then with a soft growl she tore open her bodice and put me to her. When she set me down she took from her pocket a little round fried cake covered with sugar and I reeled along the passage back to our door.

As this performance was repeated once a week it is no wonder that I remember it so vividly. Besides, from that very first afternoon, my childhood was, to put it prettily, 'kissed away'. I became very languid, very caressing, and greedy beyond measure. And so quickened, so sharpened, I seemed to understand everybody and be able to do what I liked with everybody.

I suppose I was in a state of more or less physical excitement, and that was what appealed to them. For all Parisians are more than half – oh, well, enough of that. And enough of my childhood, too. Bury it under a laundry basket instead of a shower of roses and *passons oultre*.

I date myself from the moment that I became the tenant of a small bachelor flat on the fifth floor of a tall, not too shabby house, in a street that might or might not be discreet. Very useful, that . . . There I emerged, came out into the light and put out my two horns with a study and a bedroom and a kitchen on my back. And real furniture planted in the rooms. In the bedroom a wardrobe with a long glass, a big bed covered with a yellow puffed-up quilt, a bed table with a mar-bled top and a toilet set sprinkled with tiny apples. In my study – English writing table with drawers, writing chair with leather cushions, books, armchair. side table with paper-knife and lamp on it and some nude studies on the walls. I didn't use the kitchen except to throw old papers into.

Ah, I can see myself that first evening, after the furniture men had gone and I'd managed to get rid of my atrocious old concierge – walking about on tiptoe, arranging and standing in front of the glass with my hands in my pockets and saying to that radiant vision: 'I am a young man who has his own flat. I write for two newspapers. I am going in for serious literature. I am starting a career. The book that I shall bring out will simply stagger the critics. I am going to write about things that have never been touched before. I am going to make a name for myself as a writer about the submerged world. But not as others have done before me. Oh, no! Very naïvely, with a sort of tender humour and from the inside, as though it were all quite simple, quite natural. I see my way quite perfectly. Nobody has ever done it as I shall do it because none of the others have lived my experiences. I'm rich – I'm rich.'

All the same I had no more money than I have now. It's extraordinary how one can live without money ... I have quantities of good clothes, silk underwear, two evening suits, four pairs of patent leather boots with light uppers, all sorts of little things, like gloves and powder boxes and a manicure set, perfumes, very good soap, and nothing is paid for. If I find myself in need of right-down cash – well, there's always an African laundress and an outhouse, and I am very frank and *bon enfant* about plenty of sugar on the little fried cake afterwards ...

And here I should like to put something on record. Not from any strutting conceit, but rather with a mild sense of wonder. I've never yet made the first advances to any woman. It isn't as though I've known only one class of woman – not by any means. But from little prostitutes and kept women and elderly widows and shop girls and wives of respectable men, and even advanced modern literary ladies at the most select dinners and soirées (I've been there), I've met invariably with not only the same readiness, but with the same positive invitation. It surprised me at first. I used to look across the table and think 'Is that very distinguished young lady, discussing *le Kipling* with the gentleman with the brown beard, really pressing my foot?' And I was never really certain until I had pressed hers.

Curious, isn't it? Why should I be able to have any woman I want? I don't look at all like a maiden's dream ...

I am little and light with an olive skin, black eyes with long lashes, black silky hair cut short, tiny square teeth that show when I smile.

My hands are supple and small. A woman in a bread shop once said to me: 'You have the hands for making fine little pastries.' I confess, without my clothes I am rather charming. Plump, almost like a girl, with smooth shoulders, and I wear a thin gold bracelet above my left elbow.

But, wait! Isn't it strange I should have written all that about my body and so on? It's the result of my bad life, my submerged life. I am like a little woman in a café who has to introduce herself with a handful of photographs. 'Me in my chemise, coming out of an eggshell . . . Me upside down in a swing, with a frilly behind like a cauliflower . . .' You know the things.

If you think what I've written is merely superficial and impudent and cheap you're wrong. I'll admit it does sound so, but then it is not all. If it were, how could I have experienced what I did when I read that stale little phrase written in green ink, in the writing-pad? That proves there's more in me and that I really am important, doesn't it? Anything a fraction less than that moment of anguish I might have put on. But no! That was real.

'Waiter, a whisky.'

I hate whisky. Every time I take it into my mouth my stomach rises against it, and the stuff they keep here is sure to be particularly vile. I only ordered it because I am going to write about an Englishman. We French are incredibly old-fashioned and out of date still in some ways. I wonder I didn't ask him at the same time for a pair of tweed knickerbockers, a pipe, some long teeth and a set of ginger whiskers.

'Thanks, *mon vieux*. You haven't got perhaps a set of ginger whiskers?'

'No, monsieur,' he answers sadly. 'We don't sell American drinks.'

And having smeared a corner of the table he goes back to have another couple of dozen taken by artificial light.

Ugh! The smell of it! And the sickly sensation when one's throat contracts.

'It's bad stuff to get drunk on,' says Dick Harmon, turning his little glass in his fingers and smiling his slow, dreaming smile. So he gets drunk on it slowly and dreamily and at a certain moment begins to sing very low, very low, about a man who walks up and down trying to find a place where he can get some dinner.

Ah! how I loved that song, and how I loved the way he sang it, slowly, slowly, in a dark, soft voice

> There was a man
> Walked up and down
> To get a dinner in the town . . .

It seemed to hold, in its gravity and muffled measure, all those tall grey buildings, those fogs, those endless streets, those sharp shadows of policemen that mean England.

And then – the subject! The lean, starved creature walking up and down with every house barred against him because he had no 'home'. How extraordinarily English that is . . . I remember that it ended where he did at last 'find a place' and ordered a little cake of fish, but when he asked for bread the waiter cried contemptuously, in a loud voice: 'We don't serve bread with one fish ball.'

What more do you want? How profound those songs are! There is the whole psychology of a people; and how un-French – how un-French!

'Once more, Deeck, once more!' I would plead, clasping my hands and making a pretty mouth at him. He was perfectly content to sing it for ever.

There again. Even with Dick. It was he who made the first advances.

I met him at an evening party given by the editor of a new review. It was a very select, very fashionable affair. One or two of the older men were there and the ladies were extremely *comme il faut*. They sat on cubist sofas in full evening dress and allowed us to hand them thimbles of cherry brandy and to talk to them about their poetry. For, as far as I can remember, they were all poetesses.

It was impossible not to notice Dick. He was the only Englishman present, and instead of circulating gracefully round the room as we all did, he stayed in one place leaning against the wall, his hands in his pockets, that dreamy half smile on his lips, and replying in excellent French in his low, soft voice to anybody who spoke to him.

'Who is he?'

'An Englishman. From London. A writer. And he is making a special study of modern French literature.'

That was enough for me. My little book, *False Coins*, had just been published. I was a young, serious writer who was making a special study of modern English literature.

But I really had not time to fling my line before he said, giving himself a soft shake, coming right out of the water after the bait, as it were: 'Won't you come and see me at my hotel? Come about five o'clock and we can have a talk before going out to dinner.'

'Enchanted!'

I was so deeply, deeply flattered that I had to leave him then and there to preen and preen myself before the cubist sofas. What a catch! An Englishman, reserved, serious, making a special study of French literature . . .

That same night a copy of *False Coins* with a carefully cordial inscription was posted off, and a day or two later we did dine together and spent the evening talking.

Talking – but not only of literature. I discovered to my relief that it wasn't necessary to keep to the tendency of the modern novel, the need of a new form, or the reason why our young men appeared to be just missing it. Now and again, as if by accident, I threw in a card that seemed to have nothing to do with the game, just to see how he'd take it. But each time he gathered it into his hands with his dreamy look and smile unchanged. Perhaps he murmured: 'That's very curious.' But not as if it were curious at all.

That calm acceptance went to my head at last. It fascinated me. It led me on and on till I threw every card that I possessed at him and sat back and watched him arrange them in his hand.

'Very curious and interesting . . . '

By that time we were both fairly drunk, and he began to sing his song very soft, very low, about the man who walked up and down seeking his dinner.

But I was quite breathless at the thought of what I had done. I had shown somebody both sides of my life. Told him everything as sincerely and truthfully as I could. Taken immense pains to explain things about my submerged life that really were disgusting and never could possibly see the light of literary day. On the whole I had made myself out far worse than I was – more boastful, more cynical, more calculating.

And there sat the man I had confided in, singing to himself and smiling . . . It moved me so that real tears came into my eyes. I saw them glittering on my long silky lashes – so charming.

After that I took Dick about with me everywhere, and he came to my flat, and sat in the armchair, very indolent, playing with the paper-knife. I cannot think why his indolence and dreaminess always gave me the impression he had been to sea. And all his leisurely slow ways seemed to be allowing for the movement of the ship. This impression was so strong that often when we were together and he got up and left a little woman just when she did not expect him to get up and leave her, but quite the contrary, I would explain: 'He can't help it, Baby. He has to go back to his ship.' And I believed it far more than she did.

All the while we were together Dick never went with a woman. I sometimes wondered whether he wasn't completely innocent. Why didn't I ask him? Because I never did ask him anything about himself. But late one night he took out his pocket-book and a photograph dropped out of it. I picked it up and glanced at it before I gave it to him. It was of a woman. Not quite young. Dark, handsome, wild-looking, but so full in every line of a kind of haggard pride that even if Dick had not stretched out so quickly I wouldn't have looked longer.

'Out of my sight, you little perfumed fox-terrier of a Frenchman,' said she. (In my very worst moments my nose reminds me of a fox-terrier's.)

'That is my Mother,' said Dick, putting up the pocket-book.

But if he had not been Dick I should have been tempted to cross myself, just for fun.

This is how we parted. As we stood outside his hotel one night waiting for the concierge to release the catch of the outer door, he said, look-ing up at the sky: 'I hope it will be fine tomorrow. I am leaving for England in the morning.'

'You're not serious.'

'Perfectly. I have to get back. I've some work to do that I can't man-age here.'

'But – but have you made all your preparations?'

'Preparations?' He almost grinned. 'I've none to make.'

'But – enfin, Dick, England is not the other side of the boulevard.'

'It isn't much farther off,' said he. 'Only a few hours, you know.'
The door cracked open.

'Ah, I wish I'd known at the beginning of the evening!'

I felt hurt. I felt as a woman must feel when a man takes out his
watch and remembers an appointment that cannot possibly concern
her, except that its claim is the stronger. 'Why didn't you tell me?'

He put out his hand and stood, lightly swaying upon the step as
though the whole hotel were his ship, and the anchor weighed.

'I forgot. Truly I did. But you'll write, won't you? Good night, old
chap. I'll be over again one of these days.'

And then I stood on the shore alone, more like a little fox-terrier
than ever . . .

'But after all it was you who whistled to me, you who asked me to
come! What a spectacle I've cut wagging my tail and leaping round you,
only to be left like this while the boat sails off in its slow, dreamy way . . .
Curse these English! No, this is too insolent altogether. Who do you
imagine I am? A little paid guide to the night pleasures of Paris? . . . No,
monsieur. I am a young writer, very serious, and extremely interested in
modern English literature. And I have been insulted – insulted.'

Two days after came a long, charming letter from him, written in
French that was a shade too French, but saying how he missed me and
counted on our friendship, on keeping in touch.

I read it standing in front of the (unpaid for) wardrobe mirror. It was
early morning. I wore a blue kimono embroidered with white birds
and my hair was still wet; it lay on my forehead, wet and gleaming.

'Portrait of Madame Butterfly,' said I, 'on hearing of the arrival of
ce cher Pinkerton.'

According to the books I should have felt immensely relieved and
delighted. '. . . Going over to the window he drew apart the curtains
and looked out at the Paris trees, just breaking into buds and green . . .
Dick! Dick! My English friend!'

I didn't. I merely felt a little sick. Having been up for my first ride
in an aeroplane I didn't want to go up again, just now.

That passed, and months after, in the winter, Dick wrote that he was
coming back to Paris to stay indefinitely. Would I take rooms for him?
He was bringing a woman friend with him.

Of course I would. Away the little fox-terrier flew. It happened most usefully, too; for I owed much money at the hotel where I took my meals, and two English people requiring rooms for an indefinite time was an excellent sum on account.

Perhaps I did rather wonder, as I stood in the larger of the two rooms with Madame, saying 'Admirable,' what the woman friend would be like, but only vaguely. Either she would be very severe, flat back and front, or she would be tall, fair, dressed in mignonette green, name – Daisy, and smelling of rather sweetish lavender water.

You see, by this time, according to my rule of not looking back, I had almost forgotten Dick. I even got the tune of his song about the unfortunate man a little bit wrong when I tried to hum it . . .

I very nearly did not turn up at the station after all. I had arranged to, and had, in fact, dressed with particular care for the occasion. For I intended to take a new line with Dick this time. No more confidences and tears on eyelashes. No, thank you!

'Since you left Paris,' said I, knotting my black silver-spotted tie in the (also unpaid for) mirror over the mantelpiece, 'I have been very successful, you know. I have two more books in preparation, and then I have written a serial story, *Wrong Doors*, which is just on the point of publication and will bring me in a lot of money. And then my little book of poems,' I cried, seizing the clothes-brush and brushing the velvet collar of my new indigo-blue overcoat, 'my little book – *Left Umbrellas* – really did create,' and I laughed and waved the brush, 'an immense sensation!'

It was impossible not to believe this of the person who surveyed himself finally, from top to toe, drawing on his soft grey gloves. He was looking the part; he was the part.

That gave me an idea. I took out my notebook, and still in full view, jotted down a note or two . . . How can one look the part and not be the part? Or be the part and not look it? Isn't looking – being? Or being – looking? At any rate who is to say that it is not? . . .

This seemed to me extraordinarily profound at the time, and quite new. But I confess that something did whisper as, smiling, I put up the notebook: 'You – literary? you look as though you've taken down a bet on a racecourse!' But I didn't listen. I went out, shutting the door of the flat with a soft, quick pull so as not to warn the concierge of my departure, and ran down the stairs quick as a rabbit for the same reason.

But ah! the old spider. She was too quick for me. She let me run down the last little ladder of the web and then she pounced. 'One moment. One little moment, Monsieur,' she whispered, odiously confidential. 'Come in. Come in.' And she beckoned with a dripping soup ladle. I went to the door, but that was not good enough. Right inside and the door shut before she would speak.

There are two ways of managing your concierge if you haven't any money. One is – to take the high hand, make her your enemy, bluster, refuse to discuss anything; the other is – to keep in with her, butter her up to the two knots of the black rag tying up her jaws, pretend to confide in her, and rely on her to arrange with the gas man and to put off the landlord.

I had tried the second. But both are equally detestable and unsuccessful. At any rate whichever you're trying is the worse, the impossible one.

It was the landlord this time . . . Imitation of the landlord by the concierge threatening to toss me out . . . Imitation of the concierge by the concierge taming the wild bull . . . Imitation of the landlord rampant again, breathing in the concierge's face. I was the concierge. No, it was too nauseous. And all the while the black pot on the gas ring bubbling away, stewing out the hearts and livers of every tenant in the place.

'Ah!' I cried, staring at the clock on the mantelpiece, and then, realizing that it didn't go, striking my forehead as though the idea had nothing to do with it. 'Madame, I have a very important appointment with the director of my newspaper at nine-thirty. Perhaps tomorrow I shall be able to give you . . .'

Out, out. And down the métro and squeezed into a full carriage. The more the better. Everybody was one bolster the more between me and the concierge. I was radiant.

'Ah! pardon, Monsieur!' said the tall charming creature in black with a big full bosom and a great bunch of violets dropping from it. As the train swayed it thrust the bouquet right into my eyes. 'Ah! pardon, Monsieur!'

But I looked up at her, smiling mischievously.

'There is nothing I love more, Madame, than flowers on a balcony.'

At the very moment of speaking I caught sight of the huge man in a fur coat against whom my charmer was leaning. He poked his head over her shoulder and he went white to the nose; in fact his nose stood out a sort of cheese green.

'What was that you said to my wife?'

Gare Saint Lazare saved me. But you'll own that even as the author of *False Coins, Wrong Doors, Left Umbrellas*, and two in preparation, it was not too easy to go on my triumphant way.

At length, after countless trains had steamed into my mind, and countless Dick Harmons had come rolling towards me, the real train came. The little knot of us waiting at the barrier moved up close, craned forward, and broke into cries as though we were some kind of many-headed monster, and Paris behind us nothing but a great trap we had set to catch these sleepy innocents.

Into the trap they walked and were snatched and taken off to be devoured. Where was my prey?

'Good God!' My smile and my lifted hand fell together. For one terrible moment I thought this was the woman of the photograph, Dick's mother, walking towards me in Dick's coat and hat. In the effort – and you saw what an effort it was – to smile, his lips curled in just the same way and he made for me, haggard and wild and proud.

What had happened? What could have changed him like this? Should I mention it?

I waited for him and was even conscious of venturing a fox-terrier wag or two to see if he could possibly respond, in the way I said: 'Good evening, Dick! How are you, old chap? All right?'

'All right. All right.' He almost gasped. 'You've got the rooms?'

Twenty times, good God! I saw it all. Light broke on the dark waters and my sailor hadn't been drowned. I almost turned a somersault with amusement.

It was nervousness, of course. It was embarrassment. It was the famous English seriousness. What fun I was going to have! I could have hugged him.

'Yes, I've got the rooms,' I nearly shouted. 'But where is Madame?'

'She's been looking after the luggage,' he panted. 'Here she comes, now.'

Not this baby walking beside the old porter as though he were her nurse and had just lifted her out of her ugly perambulator while he trundled the boxes on it.

'And she's not Madame,' said Dick, drawling suddenly.

At that moment she caught sight of him and hailed him with her minute muff. She broke away from her nurse and ran up and said something, very quick, in English; but he replied in French: 'Oh, very well. I'll manage.'

But before he turned to the porter he indicated me with a vague wave and muttered something. We were introduced. She held out her hand in that strange boyish way Englishwomen do, and standing very straight in front of me with her chin raised and making – she too – the effort of her life to control her preposterous excitement, she said, wringing my hand (I'm sure she didn't know it was mine), *Je ne parle pas français*.

'But I'm sure you do,' I answered, so tender, so reassuring, I might have been a dentist about to draw her first little milk tooth.

'Of course she does.' Dick swerved back to us. 'Here, can't we get a cab or taxi or something? We don't want to stay in this cursed station all night. Do we?'

This was so rude that it took me a moment to recover; and he must have noticed, for he flung his arm round my shoulder in the old way, saying: 'Ah, forgive me, old chap. But we've had such a loathsome, hideous journey. We've taken years to come. Haven't we?' To her. But she did not answer. She bent her head and began stroking her grey muff; she walked beside us stroking her grey muff all the way.

'Have I been wrong?' thought I. 'Is this simply a case of frenzied impatience on their part? Are they merely "in need of a bed", as we say? Have they been suffering agonies on the journey? Sitting, perhaps, very close and warm under the same travelling rug?' and so on and so on while the driver strapped on the boxes. That done –

'Look here, Dick. I go home by métro. Here is the address of your hotel. Everything is arranged. Come and see me as soon as you can.'

Upon my life I thought he was going to faint. He went white to the lips.

'But you're coming back with us,' he cried. 'I thought it was all

settled. Of course you're coming back. You're not going to leave us.'
No, I gave it up. It was too difficult, too English for me.

'Certainly, certainly. Delighted. I only thought, perhaps . . . '

'You must come!' said Dick to the little fox-terrier. And again he
made that big awkward turn towards her.

'Get in, Mouse.'

And Mouse got in the black hole and sat stroking Mouse II and not
saying a word.

Away we jolted and rattled like three little dice that life had decided to
have a fling with.

I had insisted on taking the flap seat facing them because I would
not have missed for anything those occasional flashing glimpses I had
as we broke through the white circles of lamplight.

They revealed Dick, sitting far back in his corner, his coat collar
turned up, his hands thrust in his pockets, and his broad dark hat shading him as if it were a part of him – a sort of wing he hid under. They
showed her, sitting up very straight, her lovely little face more like a
drawing than a real face – every line was so full of meaning and so
sharp cut against the swimming dark.

For Mouse was beautiful. She was exquisite, but so fragile and fine
that each time I looked at her it was as if for the first time. She came
upon you with the same kind of shock that you feel when you have
been drinking tea out of a thin innocent cup and suddenly, at the bottom, you see a tiny creature, half butterfly, half woman, bowing to
you with her hands in her sleeves.

As far as I could make out she had dark hair and blue or black eyes.
Her long lashes and the two little feathers traced above were most
important.

She wore a long dark cloak such as one sees in old-fashioned pictures
of Englishwomen abroad. Where her arms came out of it there was
grey fur – fur round her neck, too, and her close-fitting cap was furry.

'Carrying out the mouse idea,' I decided.

Ah, but how intriguing it was – how intriguing! Their excitement
came nearer and nearer to me, while I ran out to meet it, bathed in it,
flung myself far out of my depth, until at last I was as hard put to it to
keep control as they.

But what I wanted to do was to behave in the most extraordinary fashion – like a clown. To start singing, with large extravagant gestures, to point out of the window and cry: 'We are now passing, ladies and gentlemen, one of the sights for which *notre Paris* is justly famous'; to jump out of the taxi while it was going, climb over the roof and dive in by another door; to hang out of the window and look for the hotel through the wrong end of a broken telescope, which was also a peculiarly ear-splitting trumpet.

I watched myself do all this, you understand, and even managed to applaud in a private way by putting my gloved hands gently together, while I said to Mouse: 'And is this your first visit to Paris?'

'Yes, I've not been here before.'

'Ah, then you have a great deal to see.'

And I was just going to touch lightly upon the objects of interest and the museums when we wrenched to a stop.

Do you know – it's very absurd – but as I pushed open the door for them and followed up the stairs to the bureau on the landing I felt somehow that this hotel was mine.

There was a vase of flowers on the window-sill of the bureau and I even went so far as to re-arrange a bud or two and to stand off and note the effect while the manageress welcomed them. And when she turned to me and handed me the keys (the *garçon* was hauling up the boxes) and said: 'Monsieur Duquette will show you your rooms' – I had a longing to tap Dick on the arm with a key and say, very confidentially: 'Look here, old chap. As a friend of mine I'll be only too willing to make a slight reduction . . .'

Up and up we climbed. Round and round. Past an occasional pair of boots (why is it one never sees an attractive pair of boots outside a door?). Higher and higher.

'I'm afraid they're rather high up,' I murmured idiotically. 'But I chose them because . . .'

They so obviously did not care why I chose them that I went no further. They accepted everything. They did not expect anything to be different. This was just part of what they were going through – that was how I analysed it.

'Arrived at last.' I ran from one side of the passage to the other, turning on the lights, explaining.

'This one I thought for you, Dick. The other is larger and it has a little dressing-room in the alcove.'

My 'proprietary' eye noted the clean towels and covers, and the bed linen embroidered in red cotton. I thought them rather charming rooms, sloping, full of angles, just the sort of rooms one would expect to find if one had not been to Paris before.

Dick dashed his hat down on the bed.

'Oughtn't I to help that chap with the boxes?' he asked – nobody.

'Yes, you ought,' replied Mouse, 'they're dreadfully heavy.'

And she turned to me with the first glimmer of a smile: 'Books, you know.' Oh, he darted such a strange look at her before he rushed out. And he not only helped, he must have torn the box off the *garçon's* back, for he staggered back, carrying one, dumped it down and then fetched in the other.

'That's yours, Dick,' said she.

'Well, you don't mind it standing here for the present, do you?' he asked, breathless, breathing hard (the box must have been tremendously heavy). He pulled out a handful of money. 'I suppose I ought to pay this chap.'

The *garçon*, standing by, seemed to think so too.

'And will you require anything further, Monsieur?'

'No! No!' said Dick impatiently.

But at that Mouse stepped forward. She said, too deliberately, not looking at Dick, with her quaint clipped English accent: 'Yes, I'd like some tea. Tea for three.'

And suddenly she raised her muff as though her hands were clasped inside it, and she was telling the pale, sweaty *garçon* by that action that she was at the end of her resources, that she cried out to him to save her with 'Tea. Immediately!'

This seemed to me so amazingly in the picture, so exactly the gesture and cry that one would expect (though I couldn't have imagined it) to be wrung out of an Englishwoman faced with a great crisis, that I was almost tempted to hold up my hand and protest.

'No! No! Enough. Enough. Let us leave off there. At the word – tea. For really, really, you've filled your greediest subscriber so full that he will burst if he has to swallow another word.'

It even pulled Dick up. Like someone who has been unconscious for a long long time he turned slowly to Mouse and slowly looked at her with his tired, haggard eyes, and murmured with the echo of his dreamy voice: 'Yes. That's a good idea.' And then: 'You must be tired, Mouse. Sit down.'

She sat down in a chair with lace tabs on the arms; he leaned against the bed, and I established myself on a straight-backed chair, crossed my legs and brushed some imaginary dust off the knees of my trousers. (The Parisian at his ease.)

There came a tiny pause. Then he said: 'Won't you take off your coat, Mouse?'

'No, thanks. Not just now.'

Were they going to ask me? Or should I hold up my hand and call out in a baby voice: 'It's my turn to be asked.'

No, I shouldn't. They didn't ask me.

The pause became a silence. A real silence.

'. . . Come, my Parisian fox-terrier! Amuse these sad English! It's no wonder they are such a nation for dogs.'

But, after all – why should I? It was not my 'job', as they would say. Nevertheless, I made a vivacious little bound at Mouse.

'What a pity it is that you did not arrive by daylight. There is such a charming view from these two windows. You know, the hotel is on a corner and each window looks down an immensely long, straight street.'

'Yes,' said she.

'Not that that sounds very charming,' I laughed. 'But there is so much animation – so many absurd little boys on bicycles and people hanging out of windows and – oh, well, you'll see for yourself in the morning . . . Very amusing. Very animated.'

'Oh, yes,' said she.

If the pale, sweaty *garçon* had not come in at that moment, carrying the tea-tray high on one hand as if the cups were cannon-balls and he a heavy weight lifter on the cinema . . .

He managed to lower it on to a round table.

'Bring the table over here,' said Mouse. The waiter seemed to be the only person she cared to speak to. She took her hands out of her muff, drew off her gloves and flung back the old-fashioned cape.

'Do you take milk and sugar?'

'No milk, thank you, and no sugar.'

I went over for mine like a little gentleman. She poured out another cup.

'That's for Dick.'

And the faithful fox-terrier carried it across to him and laid it at his feet, as it were.

'Oh, thanks,' said Dick.

And then I went back to my chair and she sank back in hers.

But Dick was off again. He stared wildly at the cup of tea for a moment, glanced round him, put it down on the bed-table, caught up his hat and stammered at full gallop: 'Oh, by the way, do you mind posting a letter for me? I want to get it off by tonight's post. I must. It's very urgent . . .' Feeling her eyes on him, he flung: 'It's to my mother.' To me: 'I won't be long. I've got everything I want. But it must go off tonight. You don't mind? It . . . it won't take any time.'

'Of course I'll post it. Delighted.'

'Won't you drink your tea first?' suggested Mouse softly.

. . . Tea? Tea? Yes, of course. Tea . . . A cup of tea on the bed-table . . . In his racing dream he flashed the brightest, most charming smile at his little hostess.

'No, thanks. Not just now.'

And still hoping it would not be any trouble to me he went out of the room and closed the door, and we heard him cross the passage.

I scalded myself with mine in my hurry to take the cup back to the table and to say as I stood there: 'You must forgive me if I am impertinent . . . if I am too frank. But Dick hasn't tried to disguise it – has he? There is something the matter. Can I help?'

(Soft music. Mouse gets up, walks the stage for a moment or so before she returns to her chair and pours him out, oh, such a brimming, such a burning cup that the tears come into the friend's eyes while he sips – while he drains it to the bitter dregs . . .)

I had time to do all this before she replied. First she looked in the teapot, filled it with hot water, and stirred it with a spoon.

'Yes, there is something the matter. No, I'm afraid you can't help, thank you.' Again I got that glimmer of a smile. 'I'm awfully sorry. It must be horrid for you.'

Horrid, indeed! Ah, why couldn't I tell her that it was months and months since I had been so entertained?

'But you are suffering,' I ventured softly, as though that was what I could not bear to see.

She didn't deny it. She nodded and bit her under-lip and I thought I saw her chin tremble.

'And there is really nothing I can do?' More softly still.

She shook her head, pushed back the table and jumped up.

'Oh, it will be all right soon,' she breathed, walking over to the dressing-table and standing with her back towards me. 'It will be all right. It can't go on like this.'

'But of course it can't.' I agreed, wondering whether it would look heartless if I lit a cigarette; I had a sudden longing to smoke.

In some way she saw my hand move to my breast pocket, half draw out my cigarette case and put it back again, for the next thing she said was: 'Matches . . . in . . . candlestick. I noticed them.'

And I heard from her voice that she was crying.

'Ah! thank you. Yes. Yes. I've found them.' I lighted my cigarette and walked up and down, smoking.

It was so quiet it might have been two o'clock in the morning. It was so quiet you heard the boards creak and pop as one does in a house in the country. I smoked the whole cigarette and stabbed the end into my saucer before Mouse turned round and came back to the table.

'Isn't Dick being rather a long time?'

'You are very tired. I expect you want to go to bed,' I said kindly. (And pray don't mind me if you do, said my mind.)

'But isn't he being a very long time?' she insisted.

I shrugged. 'He is, rather.'

Then I saw she looked at me strangely. She was listening.

'He's been gone ages,' she said, and she went with little light steps to the door, opened it, and crossed the passage into his room.

I waited. I listened too, now. I couldn't have borne to miss a word. She had left the door open. I stole across the room and looked after her. Dick's door was open, too. But – there wasn't a word to miss.

You know I had the mad idea that they were kissing in that quiet room – a long comfortable kiss. One of those kisses that not only puts one's grief to bed, but nurses it and warms it and tucks it up and keeps it fast enfolded until it is sleeping sound. Ah! how good that is.

It was over at last. I heard someone move and tiptoed away.

It was Mouse. She came back. She felt her way into the room carrying the letter for me. But it wasn't in an envelope; it was just a sheet of paper and she held it by the corner as though it was still wet.

Her head was bent so low – so tucked in her furry collar that I hadn't a notion – until she let the paper fall and almost fell herself on to the floor by the side of the bed, leaned her cheek against it, flung out her hands as though the last of her poor little weapons was gone and now she let herself be carried away, washed out into the deep water.

Flash! went my mind. Dick has shot himself, and then a succession of flashes while I rushed in, saw the body, head unharmed, small blue hole over temple, roused hotel, arranged funeral, attended funeral, closed cab, new morning coat . . .

I stooped down and picked up the paper and would you believe it – so ingrained is my Parisian sense of *comme il faut* – I murmured 'pardon' before I read it.

Mouse, my little Mouse,

It's no good. It's impossible. I can't see it through. Oh, I do love you. I do love you, Mouse, but I can't hurt her. People have been hurting her all her life. I simply dare not give her this final blow. You see, though she's stronger than both of us, she's so frail and proud. It would kill her – kill her, Mouse. And, oh God, I can't kill my mother! Not even for you. Not even for us. You do see that – don't you.

It all seemed so possible when we talked and planned, but the very moment the train started it was all over. I felt her drag me back to her – calling. I can hear her now as I write. And she's alone and she doesn't know. A man would have to be a devil to tell her and I'm not a devil, Mouse. She mustn't know. Oh, Mouse, somewhere, somewhere in you don't you agree? It's all so unspeakably awful that I don't know if I want to go or not. Do I? Or is Mother just dragging me? I don't know. My head is too tired. Mouse, Mouse – what will you do? But I can't think of that, either. I dare not. I'd break down. And I must not break down. All I've got to do is – just to tell you this and go. I couldn't have gone off without telling you. You'd have been frightened. And you must not be frightened. You won't – will you? I can't bear – but no more of that. And don't write. I should not have the courage to answer your letters and the sight of your spidery handwriting—

Forgive me. Don't love me any more. Yes. Love me. Love me. Dick.

What do you think of that? Wasn't that a rare find? My relief at his not having shot himself was mixed with a wonderful sense of elation. I was even – more than even with my 'that's very curious and interesting' Englishman . . .

She wept so strangely. With her eyes shut, with her face quite calm except for the quivering eyelids. The tears pearled down her cheeks and she let them fall.

But feeling my glance upon her she opened her eyes and saw me holding the letter.

'You've read it?'

Her voice was quite calm, but it was not her voice any more. It was like the voice you might imagine coming out of a tiny, cold sea-shell swept high and dry at last by the salt tide . . .

I nodded, quite overcome, you understand, and laid the letter down.

'It's incredible! incredible!' I whispered.

At that she got up from the floor, walked over to the wash-stand, dipped her handkerchief into the jug and sponged her eyes, saying: 'Oh, no. It's not incredible at all.' And still pressing the wet ball to her eyes she came back to me, to her chair with the lace tabs, and sank into it.

'I knew all along, of course,' said the cold, salty little voice. 'From the very moment that we started. I felt it all through me, but I still went on hoping –' and here she took the handkerchief down and gave me a final glimmer – 'as one so stupidly does, you know.'

'As one does.'

Silence.

'But what will you do? You'll go back? You'll see him?'

That made her sit right up and stare across at me.

'What an extraordinary idea!' she said, more coldly than ever. 'Of course I shall not dream of seeing him. As for going back – that is quite out of the question. I can't go back.'

'But . . .'

'It's impossible. For one thing all my friends think I am married.'

I put out my hand – 'Ah, my poor little friend.'

But she shrank away. (False move.)

Of course there was one question that had been at the back of my mind all this time. I hated it.

'Have you any money?'

'Yes, I have twenty pounds – here,' and she put her hand on her breast. I bowed. It was a great deal more than I had expected.

'And what are your plans?'

Yes, I know. My question was the most clumsy, the most idiotic one I could have put. She had been so tame, so confiding, letting me, at any rate spiritually speaking, hold her tiny quivering body in one hand and stroke her furry head – and now, I'd thrown her away. Oh, I could have kicked myself.

She stood up. 'I have no plans. But – it's very late. You must go now, please.'

How could I get her back? I wanted her back, I swear I was not acting then.

'Do feel that I am your friend,' I cried. 'You will let me come to-morrow, early? You will let me look after you a little – take care of you a little? You'll use me just as you think fit?'

I succeeded. She came out of her hole . . . timid . . . but she came out.

'Yes, you're very kind. Yes. Do come tomorrow. I shall be glad. It makes things rather difficult because –' and again I clasped her boyish hand – '*je ne parle pas français.*'

Not until I was half-way down the boulevard did it come over me – the full force of it.

Why, they were suffering . . . those two . . . really suffering. I have seen two people suffer as I don't suppose I ever shall again . . . And . . . 'Good night, my little cat,' said I, impudently, to the fattish old prostitute picking her way home through the slush . . . I didn't give her time to reply.

Of course you know what to expect. You anticipate, fully, what I am going to write. It wouldn't be me, otherwise.

I never went near the place again.

Yes, I still owe that considerable amount for lunches and dinners, but that's beside the mark. It's vulgar to mention it in the same breath with the fact that I never saw Mouse again.

Naturally, I intended to. Started out – got to the door – wrote and tore up letters – did all those things. But I simply could not make the final effort.

Even now I don't fully understand why. Of course I knew that I couldn't have kept it up. That had a great deal to do with it. But you would have thought, putting it at its lowest, curiosity couldn't have kept my fox-terrier nose away . . .

Je ne parle pas français. That was her swan song for me.

But how she makes me break my rule. Oh, you've seen for yourself, but I could give you countless examples.

. . . Evenings, when I sit in some gloomy café, and an automatic piano starts playing a 'mouse' tune (there are dozens of tunes that evoke just her) I begin to dream things like . . .

A little house on the edge of the sea, somewhere far, far away. A girl outside in a frock rather like Red Indian women wear, hailing a light, bare-foot boy who runs up from the beach.

'What have you got?'

'A fish.' I smile and give it to her.

. . . The same girl, the same boy, different costumes – sitting at an open window, eating fruit and leaning out and laughing.

'All the wild strawberries are for you, Mouse. I won't touch one.'

. . . A wet night. They are going home together under an umbrella. They stop on the door to press their wet cheeks together.

And so on and so on until some dirty old gallant comes up to my table and sits opposite and begins to grimace and yap. Until I hear myself saying: 'But I've got the little girl for you, *mon vieux*. So little . . . so tiny. And a virgin.' I kiss the tips of my fingers – 'A virgin' – and lay them upon my heart. 'I give you my word of honour as a gentleman, a writer, serious, young, and extremely interested in modern English literature.'

I must go. I must go. I reach down my coat and hat. Madame knows me. 'You haven't dined yet?' she smiles.

'No, not yet, Madame.'

I'd rather like to dine with her. Even to sleep with her afterwards. Would she be pale like that all over?

But no. She'd have large moles. They go with that kind of skin. And I can't bear them. They remind me somehow, disgustingly, of mushrooms.

(written 1918, first published by the Heron Press, 1920 [version used here], first book publication *Bliss and Other Stories*, 1920)

Bliss

Although Bertha Young was thirty she still had moments like this when she wanted to run instead of walk, to take dancing steps on and off the pavement, to bowl a hoop, to throw something up in the air and catch it again, or to stand still and laugh at – nothing – at nothing, simply.

What can you do if you are thirty and, turning the corner of your own street, you are overcome, suddenly, by a feeling of bliss – absolute bliss! – as though you'd suddenly swallowed a bright piece of that late afternoon sun and it burned in your bosom, sending out a little shower of sparks into every particle, into every finger and toe? . . .

Oh, is there no way you can express it without being 'drunk and disorderly'? How idiotic civilisation is! Why be given a body if you have to keep it shut up in a case like a rare, rare fiddle?

'No, that about the fiddle is not quite what I mean,' she thought, running up the steps and feeling in her bag for the key – she'd forgotten it, as usual – and rattling the letter-box. 'It's not what I mean, because – Thank you, Mary' – she went into the hall. 'Is nurse back?'

'Yes, M'm.'

'And has the fruit come?'

'Yes, M'm. Everything's come.'

'Bring the fruit up to the dining-room, will you? I'll arrange it before I go upstairs.'

It was dusky in the dining-room and quite chilly. But all the same Bertha threw off her coat; she could not bear the tight clasp of it another moment, and the cold air fell on her arms.

But in her bosom there was still that bright glowing place – that shower of little sparks coming from it. It was almost unbearable. She hardly dared to breathe for fear of fanning it higher, and yet she breathed deeply, deeply. She hardly dared to look into the cold mirror – but she did look, and it gave her back a woman, radiant, with smiling, trembling lips, with big, dark eyes and an air of listening, waiting for something . . . divine to happen . . . that she knew must happen . . . infallibly.

Mary brought in the fruit on a tray and with it a glass bowl, and a blue dish, very lovely, with a strange sheen on it as though it had been dipped in milk.

'Shall I turn on the light, M'm?'

'No, thank you. I can see quite well.'

There were tangerines and apples stained with strawberry pink. Some yellow pears, smooth as silk, some white grapes covered with a silver bloom and a big cluster of purple ones. These last she had bought to tone in with the new dining-room carpet. Yes, that did sound rather far-fetched and absurd, but it was really why she had bought them. She had thought in the shop: 'I must have some purple ones to bring the carpet up to the table.' And it had seemed quite sense at the time.

When she had finished with them and had made two pyramids of these bright round shapes, she stood away from the table to get the effect – and it really was most curious. For the dark table seemed to melt into the dusky light and the glass dish and the blue bowl to float in the air. This, of course, in her present mood, was so incredibly beautiful . . . She began to laugh.

'No, no. I'm getting hysterical.' And she seized her bag and coat and ran upstairs to the nursery.

Nurse sat at a low table giving Little B her supper after her bath. The baby had on a white flannel gown and a blue woollen jacket, and her dark, fine hair was brushed up into a funny little peak. She looked up when she saw her mother and began to jump.

'Now, my lovey, eat it up like a good girl,' said nurse, setting her lips in a way that Bertha knew, and that meant she had come into the nursery at another wrong moment.

'Has she been good, Nanny?'

'She's been a little sweet all the afternoon,' whispered Nanny. 'We went to the park and I sat down on a chair and took her out of the pram and a big dog came along and put its head on my knee and she clutched its ear, tugged it. Oh, you should have seen her.'

Bertha wanted to ask if it wasn't rather dangerous to let her clutch at a strange dog's ear. But she did not dare to. She stood watching them, her hands by her side, like the poor little girl in front of the rich little girl with the doll.

The baby looked up at her again, stared, and then smiled so charmingly that Bertha couldn't help crying:

'Oh, Nanny, do let me finish giving her her supper while you put the bath things away.'

'Well, M'm, she oughtn't to be changed hands while she's eating,' said Nanny, still whispering. 'It unsettles her; it's very likely to upset her.'

How absurd it was. Why have a baby if it has to be kept – not in a case like a rare, rare fiddle – but in another woman's arms?

'Oh, I must!' said she.

Very offended, Nanny handed her over.

'Now, don't excite her after her supper. You know you do, M'm. And I have such a time with her after!'

Thank heaven! Nanny went out of the room with the bath towels.

'Now I've got you to myself, my little precious,' said Bertha, as the baby leaned against her.

She ate delightfully, holding up her lips for the spoon and then waving her hands. Sometimes she wouldn't let the spoon go; and sometimes, just as Bertha had filled it, she waved it away to the four winds.

When the soup was finished Bertha turned round to the fire.

'You're nice – you're very nice!' said she, kissing her warm baby. 'I'm fond of you. I like you.'

And, indeed, she loved Little B so much – her neck as she bent forward, her exquisite toes as they shone transparent in the firelight – that all her feeling of bliss came back again, and again she didn't know how to express it – what to do with it.

'You're wanted on the telephone,' said Nanny, coming back in triumph and seizing *her* Little B.

Down she flew. It was Harry.

'Oh, is that you, Ber? Look here. I'll be late. I'll take a taxi and come along as quickly as I can, but get dinner put back ten minutes – will you? All right?'

'Yes, perfectly. Oh, Harry!'

'Yes?'

What had she to say? She'd nothing to say. She only wanted to get in touch with him for a moment. She couldn't absurdly cry: 'Hasn't it been a divine day!'

'What is it?' rapped out the little voice.

'Nothing. *Entendu*,' said Bertha, and hung up the receiver, thinking how much more than idiotic civilisation was.

They had people coming to dinner. The Norman Knights – a very sound couple – he was about to start a theatre, and she was awfully keen on interior decoration, a young man, Eddie Warren, who had just published a little book of poems and whom everybody was asking to dine, and a 'find' of Bertha's called Pearl Fulton. What Miss Fulton did, Bertha didn't know. They had met at the club and Bertha had fallen in love with her, as she always did fall in love with beautiful women who had something strange about them.

The provoking thing was that, though they had been about together and met a number of times and really talked, Bertha couldn't make her out. Up to a certain point Miss Fulton was rarely, wonderfully frank, but the certain point was there, and beyond that she would not go.

Was there anything beyond it? Harry said 'No.' Voted her dullish, and 'cold like all blonde women, with a touch, perhaps, of anaemia of the brain.' But Bertha wouldn't agree with him; not yet, at any rate.

'No, the way she has of sitting with her head a little on one side, and smiling, has something behind it, Harry, and I must find out what that something is.'

'Most likely it's a good stomach,' answered Harry.

He made a point of catching Bertha's heels with replies of that kind . . . 'liver frozen, my dear girl,' or 'pure flatulence,' or 'kidney disease,' . . . and so on. For some strange reason Bertha liked this, and almost admired it in him very much.

She went into the drawing-room and lighted the fire; then, picking up the cushions, one by one, that Mary had disposed so carefully, she threw them back on to the chairs and the couches. That made all the difference; the room came alive at once. As she was about to throw the last one she surprised herself by suddenly hugging it to her, passionately, passionately. But it did not put out the fire in her bosom. Oh, on the contrary!

The windows of the drawing-room opened on to a balcony

overlooking the garden. At the far end, against the wall, there was a tall, slender pear tree in fullest, richest bloom; it stood perfect, as though becalmed against the jade-green sky. Bertha couldn't help feeling, even from this distance, that it had not a single bud or a faded petal. Down below, in the garden beds, the red and yellow tulips, heavy with flowers, seemed to lean upon the dusk. A grey cat, dragging its belly, crept across the lawn, and a black one, its shadow, trailed after. The sight of them, so intent and so quick, gave Bertha a curious shiver.

'What creepy things cats are!' she stammered, and she turned away from the window and began walking up and down . . .

How strong the jonquils smelled in the warm room. Too strong? Oh, no. And yet, as though overcome, she flung down on a couch and pressed her hands to her eyes.

'I'm too happy – too happy!' she murmured.

And she seemed to see on her eyelids the lovely pear tree with its wide open blossoms as a symbol of her own life.

Really – really – she had everything. She was young. Harry and she were as much in love as ever, and they got on together splendidly and were really good pals. She had an adorable baby. They didn't have to worry about money. They had this absolutely satisfactory house and garden. And friends – modern, thrilling friends, writers and painters and poets or people keen on social questions – just the kind of friends they wanted. And then there were books, and there was music, and she had found a wonderful little dressmaker, and they were going abroad in the summer, and their new cook made the most superb omelettes . . .

'I'm absurd. Absurd!' She sat up; but she felt quite dizzy, quite drunk. It must have been the spring.

Yes, it was the spring. Now she was so tired she could not drag herself upstairs to dress.

A white dress, a string of jade beads, green shoes and stockings. It wasn't intentional. She had thought of this scheme hours before she stood at the drawing-room window.

Her petals rustled softly into the hall, and she kissed Mrs Norman Knight, who was taking off the most amusing orange coat with a procession of black monkeys round the hem and up the fronts.

'. . . Why! Why! Why is the middle-class so stodgy – so utterly without a sense of humour! My dear, it's only by a fluke that I am here at all – Norman being the protective fluke. For my darling monkeys so upset the train that it rose to a man and simply ate me with its eyes. Didn't laugh – wasn't amused – that I should have loved. No, just stared – and bored me through and through.'

'But the cream of it was,' said Norman, pressing a large tortoiseshell-rimmed monocle into his eye, 'you don't mind me telling this, Face, do you?' (In their home and among their friends they called each other Face and Mug.) 'The cream of it was when she, being full fed, turned to the woman beside her and said: "Haven't you ever seen a monkey before?"'

'Oh yes!' Mrs Norman Knight joined in the laughter. 'Wasn't that too absolutely creamy?'

And a funnier thing still was that now her coat was off she did look like a very intelligent monkey – who had even made that yellow silk dress out of scraped banana skins. And her amber ear-rings: they were like little dangling nuts.

'This is a sad, sad fall!' said Mug, pausing in front of Little B's per-ambulator. 'When the perambulator comes into the hall –' and he waved the rest of the quotation away.

The bell rang. It was lean, pale Eddie Warren (as usual) in a state of acute distress.

'It *is* the right house, *isn't* it?' he pleaded.

'Oh, I think so – I hope so,' said Bertha brightly.

'I have had such a *dreadful* experience with a taxi-man; he was *most* sinister. I couldn't get him to *stop*. The *more* I knocked and called the *faster* he went. And *in* the moonlight this *bizarre* figure with the *flattened* head *crouching* over the *lit-tle* wheel . . .'

He shuddered, taking off an immense white silk scarf. Bertha noticed that his socks were white, too – most charming.

'But how dreadful!' she cried.

'Yes, it really was,' said Eddie, following her into the drawing-room. 'I saw myself *driving* through Eternity in a *timeless* taxi.'

He knew the Norman Knights. In fact, he was going to write a play for N. K. when the theatre scheme came off.

'Well, Warren, how's the play?' said Norman Knight, dropping his monocle and giving his eye a moment in which to rise to the surface before it was screwed down again.

And Mrs Norman Knight: 'Oh, Mr Warren, what happy socks?'

'I *am* so glad you like them,' said he, staring at his feet. 'They seem to have got so *much* whiter since the moon rose.' And he turned his lean sorrowful young face to Bertha. 'There *is* a moon, you know.'

She wanted to cry: 'I am sure there is – often – often!'

He really was a most attractive person. But so was Face, crouched before the fire in her banana skins, and so was Mug, smoking a cigarette and saying as he flicked the ash: 'Why doth the bridegroom tarry?'

'There he is, now.'

Bang went the front door open and shut. Harry shouted: 'Hullo, you people. Down in five minutes.' And they heard him swarm up the stairs. Bertha couldn't help smiling; she knew how he loved doing things at high pressure. What, after all, did an extra five minutes matter? But he would pretend to himself that they mattered beyond measure. And then he would make a great point of coming into the drawing-room, extravagantly cool and collected.

Harry had such a zest for life. Oh, how she appreciated it in him. And his passion for fighting – for seeking in everything that came up against him another test of his power and of his courage – that, too, she understood. Even when it made him just occasionally, to other people, who didn't know him well, a little ridiculous perhaps ... For there were moments when he rushed into battle where no battle was ... She talked and laughed and positively forgot until he had come in (just as she had imagined) that Pearl Fulton had not turned up.

'I wonder if Miss Fulton has forgotten?'

'I expect so,' said Harry. 'Is she on the 'phone?'

'Ah! There's a taxi now.' And Bertha smiled with that little air of proprietorship that she always assumed while her women finds were new and mysterious. 'She lives in taxis.'

'She'll run to fat if she does,' said Harry coolly, ringing the bell for dinner. 'Frightful danger for blonde women.'

'Harry – don't,' warned Bertha, laughing up at him.

Came another tiny moment, while they waited, laughing and talking, just a trifle too much at their ease, a trifle too unaware. And then Miss Fulton, all in silver, with a silver fillet binding her pale blonde hair, came in smiling, her head a little on one side.

'Am I late?'

'No, not at all,' said Bertha. 'Come along.' And she took her arm and they moved into the dining-room.

What was there in the touch of that cool arm that could fan – fan – start blazing – blazing – the fire of bliss that Bertha did not know what to do with?

Miss Fulton did not look at her; but then she seldom did look at people directly. Her heavy eyelids lay upon her eyes and the strange half-smile came and went upon her lips as though she lived by listening rather than seeing. But Bertha knew, suddenly, as if the longest, most intimate look had passed between them – as if they had said to each other: 'You, too?' – that Pearl Fulton, stirring the beautiful red soup in the grey plate, was feeling just what she was feeling.

And the others? Face and Mug, Eddie and Harry, their spoons rising and falling – dabbing their lips with their napkins, crumbling bread, fiddling with the forks and glasses and talking.

'I met her at the Alpha show – the weirdest little person. She'd not only cut off her hair, but she seemed to have taken a dreadfully good snip off her legs and arms and her neck and her poor little nose as well.'

'Isn't she very *liée* with Michael Oat?'

'The man who wrote *Love in False Teeth*?'

'He wants to write a play for me. One act. One man. Decides to commit suicide. Gives all the reasons why he should and why he shouldn't. And just as he has made up his mind either to do it or not to do it – curtain. Not half a bad idea.'

'What's he going to call it – "Stomach Trouble"?'

'I *think* I've come across the *same* idea in a lit-tle French review, *quite* unknown in England.'

No, they didn't share it. They were dears – dears – and she loved having them there, at her table, and giving them delicious food and wine. In fact, she longed to tell them how delightful they were, and what a decorative group they made, how they seemed to set one another off and how they reminded her of a play by Tchekof!

Harry was enjoying his dinner. It was part of his – well, not his nature, exactly, and certainly not his pose – his – something or other – to talk about food and to glory in his 'shameless passion for the white flesh of the lobster' and 'the green of pistachio ices – green and cold like the eyelids of Egyptian dancers.'

When he looked up at her and said: 'Bertha, this is a very admirable *soufflé*!' she almost could have wept with child-like pleasure.

Oh, why did she feel so tender towards the whole world tonight? Everything was good – was right. All that happened seemed to fill again her brimming cup of bliss.

And still, in the back of her mind, there was the pear tree. It would be silver now, in the light of poor dear Eddie's moon, silver as Miss Fulton, who sat there turning a tangerine in her slender fingers that were so pale a light seemed to come from them.

What she simply couldn't make out – what was miraculous – was how she should have guessed Miss Fulton's mood so exactly and so instantly. For she never doubted for a moment that she was right, and yet what had she to go on? Less than nothing.

'I believe this does happen very, very rarely between women. Never between men,' thought Bertha. 'But while I am making the coffee in the drawing-room perhaps she will "give a sign".'

What she meant by that she did not know, and what would happen after that she could not imagine.

While she thought like this she saw herself talking and laughing. She had to talk because of her desire to laugh.

'I must laugh or die.'

But when she noticed Face's funny little habit of tucking something down the front of her bodice – as if she kept a tiny, secret hoard of nuts there, too – Bertha had to dig her nails into her hands – so as not to laugh too much.

It was over at last. And: 'Come and see my new coffee machine,' said Bertha.

'We only have a new coffee machine once a fortnight,' said Harry. Face took her arm this time; Miss Fulton bent her head and followed after.

The fire had died down in the drawing-room to a red, flickering 'nest of baby phoenixes', said Face.

'Don't turn up the light for a moment. It is so lovely.' And down she crouched by the fire again. She was always cold . . . 'without her little red flannel jacket, of course,' thought Bertha.

At that moment Miss Fulton 'gave the sign'.

'Have you a garden?' said the cool, sleepy voice.

This was so exquisite on her part that all Bertha could do was to obey. She crossed the room, pulled the curtains apart, and opened those long windows.

'There!' she breathed.

And the two women stood side by side looking at the slender, flowering tree. Although it was so still it seemed, like the flame of a candle, to stretch up, to point, to quiver in the bright air, to grow taller and taller as they gazed – almost to touch the rim of the round, silver moon.

How long did they stand there? Both, as it were, caught in that circle of unearthly light, understanding each other perfectly, creatures of another world, and wondering what they were to do in this one with all this blissful treasure that burned in their bosoms and dropped, in silver flowers, from their hair and hands?

For ever – for a moment? And did Miss Fulton murmur: 'Yes. Just *that*.' Or did Bertha dream it?

Then the light was snapped on and Face made the coffee and Harry said: 'My dear Mrs Knight, don't ask me about my baby. I never see her. I shan't feel the slightest interest in her until she has a lover,' and Mug took his eye out of the conservatory for a moment and then put it under glass again and Eddie Warren drank his coffee and set down the cup with a face of anguish as though he had drunk and seen the spider.

'What I want to do is to give the young men a show. I believe London is simply teeming with first-chop, unwritten plays. What I want to say to 'em is: "Here's the theatre. Fire ahead."'

'You know, my dear, I am going to decorate a room for the Jacob Nathans. Oh, I am so tempted to do a fried-fish scheme, with the backs of the chairs shaped like frying-pans and lovely chip potatoes embroidered all over the curtains.'

'The trouble with our young writing men is that they are still too romantic. You can't put out to sea without being seasick and wanting a basin. Well, why won't they have the courage of those basins?'

'A *dreadful* poem about a *girl* who was *violated* by a beggar *without* a nose in a lit-tle wood . . .'

Miss Fulton sank into the lowest, deepest chair and Harry handed round the cigarettes.

From the way he stood in front of her shaking the silver box and saying abruptly: 'Egyptian? Turkish? Virginian? They're all mixed up,' Bertha realised that she not only bored him; he really disliked her. And she decided from the way Miss Fulton said: 'No, thank you, I won't smoke,' that she felt it, too, and was hurt.

'Oh, Harry, don't dislike her. You are quite wrong about her. She's wonderful, wonderful. And, besides, how can you feel so differently about someone who means so much to me. I shall try to tell you when we are in bed tonight what has been happening. What she and I have shared.'

At those last words something strange and almost terrifying darted into Bertha's mind. And this something blind and smiling whispered to her: 'Soon these people will go. The house will be quiet – quiet. The lights will be out. And you and he will be alone together in the dark room – the warm bed . . .'

She jumped up from her chair and ran over to the piano.

'What a pity someone does not play!' she cried. 'What a pity somebody does not play.'

For the first time in her life Bertha Young desired her husband.

Oh, she'd loved him – she'd been in love with him, of course, in every other way, but just not in that way. And equally, of course, she'd understood that he was different. They'd discussed it so often. It had worried her dreadfully at first to find that she was so cold, but after a time it had not seemed to matter. They were so frank with each other – such good pals. That was the best of being modern.

But now – ardently! ardently! The word ached in her ardent body! Was this what that feeling of bliss had been leading up to? But then, then –

'My dear,' said Mrs Norman Knight, 'you know our shame. We are the victims of time and train. We live in Hampstead. It's been so nice.'

'I'll come with you into the hall,' said Bertha. 'I loved having you. But you must not miss the last train. That's so awful, isn't it?'

'Have a whisky, Knight, before you go?' called Harry.

'No, thanks, old chap.'

Bertha squeezed his hand for that as she shook it.

'Good night, goodbye,' she cried from the top step, feeling that this self of hers was taking leave of them for ever.

When she got back into the drawing-room the others were on the move.

'. . . Then you can come part of the way in my taxi.'

'I shall be *so* thankful *not* to have to face *another* drive *alone* after my *dreadful* experience.'

'You can get a taxi at the rank just at the end of the street. You won't have to walk more than a few yards.'

'That's a comfort. I'll go and put on my coat.'

Miss Fulton moved towards the hall and Bertha was following when Harry almost pushed past.

'Let me help you.'

Bertha knew that he was repenting his rudeness – she let him go. What a boy he was in some ways – so impulsive – so – simple.

And Eddie and she were left by the fire.

'I *wonder* if you have seen Bilks' *new* poem called *Table d'Hôte,*' said Eddie softly. 'It's *so* wonderful. In the last Anthology. Have you got a copy? I'd *so* like to *show* it to you. It begins with an *incredibly* beautiful line: "Why Must it Always be Tomato Soup?"'

'Yes,' said Bertha. And she moved noiselessly to a table opposite the drawing-room door and Eddie glided noiselessly after her. She picked up the little book and gave it to him; they had not made a sound.

While he looked it up she turned her head towards the hall. And she saw . . . Harry with Miss Fulton's coat in his arms and Miss Fulton with her back turned to him and her head bent. He tossed the coat away, put his hands on her shoulders and turned her violently to him. His lips said: 'I adore you,' and Miss Fulton laid her moonbeam fingers on his cheeks and smiled her sleepy smile. Harry's nostrils quivered; his lips curled back in a hideous grin while he whispered: 'Tomorrow,' and with her eyelids Miss Fulton said: 'Yes.'

'Here it is,' said Eddie. ' "Why Must it Always be Tomato Soup?" It's so *deeply* true, don't you feel? Tomato soup is so *dreadfully* eternal.'

'If you prefer,' said Harry's voice, very loud, from the hall, 'I can 'phone you a cab to come to the door.'

'Oh, no. It's not necessary,' said Miss Fulton, and she came up to Bertha and gave her the slender fingers to hold.

'Goodbye. Thank you so much.'

'Goodbye,' said Bertha.

Miss Fulton held her hand a moment longer.

'Your lovely pear tree!' she murmured.

And then she was gone, with Eddie following, like the black cat following the grey cat.

'I'll shut up shop,' said Harry, extravagantly cool and collected.

'Your lovely pear tree – pear tree – pear tree!'

Bertha simply ran over to the long windows.

'Oh, what is going to happen now?' she cried.

But the pear tree was as lovely as ever and as full of flower and as still.

(written 1918, first published in 1918, first book publication
Bliss and Other Stories, 1920)

Carnation

On those hot days Eve – curious Eve – always carried a flower. She snuffed it and snuffed it, twirled it in her fingers, laid it against her cheek, held it to her lips, tickled Katie's neck with it, and ended, finally, by pulling it to pieces and eating it, petal by petal.

'Roses are delicious, my dear Katie,' she would say, standing in the dim cloak-room, with a strange decoration of flowery hats on the hat pegs behind her – 'but carnations are simply divine! They taste like – like – ah well!' And away her little thin laugh flew, fluttering among those huge, strange flower heads on the wall behind her. (But how cruel her little thin laugh was! It had a long sharp beak and claws and two bead eyes, thought fanciful Katie.)

Today it was a carnation. She brought a carnation to the French class, a deep, deep red one, that looked as though it had been dipped in wine and left in the dark to dry. She held it on the desk before her, half shut her eyes and smiled.

'Isn't it a darling?' said she. But –

'*Un peu de silence, s'il vous plaît,*' came from M. Hugo. Oh, bother! It was too hot! Frightfully hot! Grilling simply!

The two square windows of the French Room were open at the bottom and the dark blinds drawn half-way down. Although no air came in, the blind cord swung out and back and the blind lifted. But really there was not a breath from the dazzle outside.

Even the girls, in the dusky room, in their pale blouses, with stiff butterfly-bow hair ribbons perched on their hair, seemed to give off a warm, weak light, and M. Hugo's white waistcoat gleamed like the belly of a shark.

Some of the girls were very red in the face and some were white. Vera Holland had pinned up her black curls *à la japonaise* with a penholder and a pink pencil; she looked charming. Francie Owen pushed her sleeves nearly up to the shoulders, and then she inked the little blue vein in her elbow, shut her arm together, and then looked to see the mark it made; she had a passion for inking herself; she always had a face drawn on her thumb nail, with black, forked hair. Sylvia Mann took off her collar and tie, took them off simply, and laid them on the desk beside her, as calm as if she were going to wash her hair in her bedroom at home. She *had* a nerve! Jennie Edwards tore a leaf out of her notebook and wrote 'Shall we ask old Hugo-Wugo to give us a thrippenny vanilla on the way home!!!' and passed it across to Connie Baker, who turned absolutely purple and nearly burst out crying. All of them lolled and gaped, staring at the round clock, which seemed to have grown paler, too; the hands scarcely crawled.

'*Un peu de silence, s'il vous plaît,*' came from M. Hugo. He held up a puffy hand. 'Ladies, as it is so 'ot we will take no more notes today, but I will read you' – and he paused and smiled a broad, gentle smile – 'a little French poetry.'

'Go – od God!' moaned Francie Owen.

M. Hugo's smile deepened. 'Well, Mees Owen, you need not attend. You can paint yourself. You can 'ave my red ink as well as your black one.'

How well they knew the little blue book with red edges that he tugged out of his coat-tail pocket! It had a green silk marker embroidered in forget-me-nots. They often giggled at it when he handed the book round. Poor old Hugo-Wugo! He adored reading poetry. He would begin, softly and calmly, and then gradually his voice would swell and vibrate and gather itself together, then it would be pleading and imploring and entreating, and then rising, rising triumphant, until it burst into light, as it were, and then – gradually again, it ebbed, it grew soft and warm and calm and died down into nothingness.

The great difficulty was, of course, if you felt at all feeble, not to get the most awful fit of the giggles. Not because it was funny, really, but because it made you feel uncomfortable, queer, silly, and somehow ashamed for old Hugo-Wugo. But – oh dear – if he was going to inflict it on them in this heat . . . !

'Courage, my pet,' said Eve, kissing the languid carnation.

He began, and most of the girls fell forward, over the desks, their heads on their arms, dead at the first shot. Only Eve and Katie sat upright and still. Katie did not know enough French to understand, but Eve sat listening, her eyebrows raised, her eyes half veiled, and a smile that was like the shadow of her cruel little laugh, like the wing shadows of that cruel little laugh fluttering over her lips. She made a warm, white cup of her fingers – the carnation inside. Oh, the scent! It floated across to Katie. It was too much. Katie turned away to the dazzling light outside the window.

Down below, she knew, there was a cobbled courtyard with stable buildings round it. That was why the French Room always smelled faintly of ammonia. It wasn't unpleasant; it was even part of the French language for Katie – something sharp and vivid and – and – biting!

Now she could hear a man clatter over the cobbles and the jing-jang of the pails he carried. And now *Hoo-hor-her! Hoo-hor-her!* as he worked the pump and a great gush of water followed. Now he was flinging the water over something, over the wheels of a carriage perhaps. And she saw the wheel, propped up, clear of the ground, spinning round, flashing scarlet and black, with great drops glancing off it. And all the while he worked the man kept up a high, bold whistling that skimmed over the noise of the water as a bird skims over the sea. He went away – he came back again leading a cluttering horse.

Hoo-hor-her! Hoo-hor-her! came from the pump. Now he dashed the water over the horse's legs and then swooped down and began brushing.

She *saw* him simply – in a faded shirt, his sleeves rolled up, his chest bare, all splashed with water – and as he whistled, loud and free, and as he moved, swooping and bending, Hugo-Wugo's voice began to warm, to deepen, to gather together, to swing, to rise – somehow or other to keep time with the man outside (Oh, the scent of Eve's carnation!) until they became one great rushing, rising, triumphant thing, bursting into light, and then –

The whole room broke into pieces.

'Thank you, ladies,' cried M. Hugo, bobbing at his high desk, over the wreckage.

And 'Keep it, dearest,' said Eve. '*Souvenir tendre*,' and she popped the carnation down the front of Katie's blouse.

(written 1918, first publication 1918, first book publication *Something Childish and Other Stories*, 1924)

Psychology

When she opened the door and saw him standing there she was more pleased than ever before, and he, too, as he followed her into the studio, seemed very, very happy to have come.

'Not busy?'

'No. Just going to have tea.'

'And you are not expecting anybody?'

'Nobody at all.'

'Ah! That's good.'

He laid aside his coat and hat gently, lingeringly, as though he had time and to spare for everything, or as though he were taking leave of them for ever, and came over to the fire and held out his hands to the quick, leaping flame.

Just for a moment both of them stood silent in that leaping light. Still, as it were, they tasted on their smiling lips the sweet shock of their greeting. Their secret selves whispered:

'Why should we speak? Isn't this enough?'

'More than enough. I never realised until this moment . . .'

'How good it is just to be with you . . .'

'Like this . . .'

'It's more than enough.'

But suddenly he turned and looked at her and she moved quickly away.

'Have a cigarette? I'll put the kettle on. Are you longing for tea?'

'No. Not longing.'

'Well, I am.'

'Oh, you.' He thumped the Armenian cushion and flung on to the *sommier*. 'You're a perfect little Chinee.'

'Yes, I am,' she laughed. 'I long for tea as strong men long for wine.'

She lighted the lamp under its broad orange shade, pulled the curtains and drew up the tea-table. Two birds sang in the kettle; the fire fluttered. He sat up clasping his knees. It was delightful – this business of having tea – and she always had delicious things to eat – little sharp sandwiches, short sweet almond fingers, and a dark, rich cake tasting of rum – but it was an interruption. He wanted it over, the table pushed away, their two chairs drawn up to the light, and the moment come when he took out his pipe, filled it, and said, pressing the tobacco tight into the bowl: 'I have been thinking over what you said last time and it seems to me . . .'

Yes, that was what he waited for and so did she. Yes, while she shook the teapot hot and dry over the spirit flame she saw those other two: him, leaning back, taking his ease among the cushions, and her, curled up *en escargot* in the blue shell armchair. The picture was so clear and so minute it might have been painted on the blue teapot lid. And yet she couldn't hurry. She could almost have cried: 'Give me time.' She must have time in which to grow calm. She wanted time in which to free herself from all these familiar things with which she lived so vividly. For all these gay things round her were part of her – her offspring – and they knew it and made the largest, most vehement claims. But now they must go. They must be swept away, shooed away – like children, sent up the shadowy stairs, packed into bed and commanded to go to sleep – at once – without a murmur!

For the special thrilling quality of their friendship was in their complete surrender. Like two open cities in the midst of some vast plain their two minds lay open to each other. And it wasn't as if he rode into hers like a conqueror, armed to the eyebrows and seeing nothing but a gay silken flutter – nor did she enter his like a queen walking soft on petals. No, they were eager, serious travellers, absorbed in understanding what was to be seen and discovering what was hidden – making the most of this extraordinary absolute chance which made it possible for him to be utterly truthful to her and for her to be utterly sincere with him.

And the best of it was they were both of them old enough to enjoy their adventure to the full without any stupid emotional complication. Passion would have ruined everything; they quite saw that. Besides, all that sort of thing was over and done with for both of them – he was thirty-one, she was thirty – they had had their experiences, and very rich and varied they had been, but now was the time for harvest – harvest. Weren't his novels to be very big novels indeed? And her plays. Who else had her exquisite sense of real English Comedy? . . .

Carefully she cut the cake into thick little wads and he reached across for a piece.

'Do realise how good it is,' she implored. 'Eat it imaginatively. Roll your eyes if you can and taste it on the breath. It's not a sandwich from the hatter's bag – it's the kind of cake that might have been mentioned in the Book of Genesis . . . And God said: "Let there be cake. And there was cake. And God saw that it was good."'

'You needn't entreat me,' said he. 'Really you needn't. It's a queer thing but I always do notice what I eat here and never anywhere else. I suppose it comes of living alone so long and always reading while I feed . . . my habit of looking upon food as just food . . . something that's there, at certain times . . . to be devoured . . . to be . . . not there.' He laughed. 'That shocks you. Doesn't it?'

'To the bone,' said she.

'But – look here –' He pushed away his cup and began to speak very fast. 'I simply haven't got any external life at all. I don't know the names of things a bit – trees and so on – and I never notice places or furniture or what people look like. One room is just like another to me – a place to sit and read or talk in – except,' and here he paused, smiled in a strange naïve way, and said, 'except this studio.' He looked round him and then at her; he laughed in his astonishment and pleasure. He was like a man who wakes up in a train to find that he has arrived, already, at the journey's end.

'Here's another queer thing. If I shut my eyes I can see this place down to every detail – every detail . . . Now I come to think of it – I've never realised this consciously before. Often when I am away from here I revisit it in spirit – wander about among your red chairs, stare at the bowl of fruit on the black table – and just touch, very lightly, that marvel of a sleeping boy's head.'

He looked at it as he spoke. It stood on the corner of the mantel-piece; the head to one side down-drooping, the lips parted, as though in his sleep the little boy listened to some sweet sound . . .

'I love that little boy,' he murmured. And then they both were silent.

A new silence came between them. Nothing in the least like the satisfactory pause that had followed their greetings – the 'Well, here we are together again, and there's no reason why we shouldn't go on from just where we left off last time.' That silence could be contained in the circle of warm, delightful fire and lamplight. How many times hadn't they flung something into it just for the fun of watching the ripples break on the easy shores. But into this unfamiliar pool the head of the little boy sleeping his timeless sleep dropped – and the ripples flowed away, away – boundlessly far – into deep glittering darkness.

And then both of them broke it. She said: 'I must make up the fire,' and he said: 'I have been trying a new . . .' Both of them escaped. She made up the fire and put the table back, the blue chair was wheeled forward, she curled up and he lay back among the cushions. Quickly! Quickly! They must stop it from happening again.

'Well, I read the book you left last time.'

'Oh, what do you think of it?'

They were off and all was as usual. But was it? Weren't they just a little too quick, too prompt with their replies, too ready to take each other up? Was this really anything more than a wonderfully good imitation of other occasions? His heart beat, her cheek burned, and the stupid thing was she could not discover where exactly they were or what exactly was happening. She hadn't time to glance back. And just as she had got so far it happened again. They faltered, wavered, broke down, were silent. Again they were conscious of the boundless, questioning dark. Again, there they were – two hunters, bending over their fire, but hearing suddenly from the jungle beyond a shake of wind and a loud, questioning cry . . .

She lifted her head. 'It's raining,' she murmured. And her voice was like his when he had said: 'I love that little boy.'

Well. Why didn't they just give way to it – yield – and see what will happen then? But no. Vague and troubled though they were, they knew enough to realise their precious friendship was in danger. She was the one who would be destroyed – not they – and they'd be no party to that.

He got up, knocked out his pipe, ran his hand through his hair and said: 'I have been wondering very much lately whether the novel of the future will be a psychological novel or not. How sure are you that psychology *qua* psychology has got anything to do with literature at all?'

'Do you mean you feel there's quite a chance that the mysterious non-existent creatures – the young writers of today – are trying simply to jump the psycho-analyst's claim?'

'Yes, I do. And I think it's because this generation is just wise enough to know that it is sick and to realise that its only chance of recovery is by going into its symptoms – making an exhaustive study of them – tracking them down – trying to get at the root of the trouble.'

'But oh,' she wailed. 'What a dreadfully dismal outlook.'

'Not at all,' said he. 'Look here . . .' On the talk went. And now it seemed they really had succeeded. She turned in her chair to look at him while she answered. Her smile said: 'We have won.' And he smiled back, confident: 'Absolutely.'

But the smile undid them. It lasted too long; it became a grin. They saw themselves as two little grinning puppets jigging away in nothingness.

'What have we been talking about?' thought he. He was so utterly bored he almost groaned.

'What a spectacle we have made of ourselves,' thought she. And she saw him laboriously – oh, laboriously – laying out the grounds and herself running after, putting here a tree and there a flowery shrub and here a handful of glittering fish in a pool. They were silent this time from sheer dismay.

The clock struck six merry little pings and the fire made a soft flutter. What fools they were – heavy, stodgy, elderly – with positively upholstered minds.

And now the silence put a spell upon them like solemn music. It was anguish – anguish for her to bear it and he would die – he'd die if it were broken . . . And yet he longed to break it. Not by speech. At any rate not by their ordinary maddening chatter. There was another way for them to speak to each other, and in the new way he wanted to murmur: 'Do you feel this too? Do you understand it at all?' . . .

Instead, to his horror, he heard himself say: 'I must be off; I'm meeting Brand at six.'

What devil made him say that instead of the other? She jumped – simply jumped out of her chair, and he heard her crying: 'You must rush, then. He's so punctual. Why didn't you say so before?'

'You've hurt me; you've hurt me! We've failed!' said her secret self while she handed him his hat and stick, smiling gaily. She wouldn't give him a moment for another word, but ran along the passage and opened the big outer door.

Could they leave each other like this? How could they? He stood on the step and she just inside holding the door. It was not raining now.

'You've hurt me – hurt me,' said her heart. 'Why don't you go? No, don't go. Stay. No – go!' And she looked out upon the night.

She saw the beautiful fall of the steps, the dark garden ringed with glittering ivy, on the other side of the road the huge bare willows and above them the sky big and bright with stars. But of course he would see nothing of all this. He was superior to it all. He – with his wonderful 'spiritual' vision!

She was right. He did see nothing at all. Misery! He'd missed it. It was too late to do anything now. Was it too late? Yes, it was. A cold snatch of hateful wind blew into the garden. Curse life! He heard her cry 'au revoir' and the door slammed.

Running back into the studio she behaved so strangely. She ran up and down lifting her arms and crying: 'Oh! Oh! How stupid! How imbecile! How stupid!' And then she flung herself down on the *sommier* thinking of nothing – just lying there in her rage. All was over. What was over? Oh – something was. And she'd never see him again – never. After a long long time (or perhaps ten minutes) had passed in that black gulf her bell rang a sharp quick jingle. It was he, of course. And equally, of course, she oughtn't to have paid the slightest attention to it but just let it go on ringing and ringing. She flew to answer.

On the doorstep there stood an elderly virgin, a pathetic creature who simply idolised her (heaven knows why) and had this habit of turning up and ringing the bell and then saying, when she opened the door: 'My dear, send me away!' She never did. As a rule she asked her in and let her admire everything and accepted the bunch of slightly soiled-looking flowers – more than graciously. But today . . .

'Oh, I am so sorry,' she cried. 'But I've got someone with me. We are working on some wood-cuts. I'm hopelessly busy all evening.'

'It doesn't matter. It doesn't matter at all, darling,' said the good friend. 'I was just passing and I thought I'd leave you some violets.' She fumbled down among the ribs of a large old umbrella. 'I put them down here. Such a good place to keep flowers out of the wind. Here they are,' she said, shaking out a little dead bunch.

For a moment she did not take the violets. But while she stood just inside, holding the door, a strange thing happened . . . Again she saw the beautiful fall of the steps, the dark garden ringed with glittering ivy, the willows, the big bright sky. Again she felt the silence that was like a question. But this time she did not hesitate. She moved forward. Very softly and gently, as though fearful of making a ripple in that boundless pool of quiet, she put her arms round her friend.

'My dear,' murmured her happy friend, quite overcome by this gratitude. 'They are really nothing. Just the simplest little thrippenny bunch.'

But as she spoke she was enfolded – more tenderly, more beautifully embraced, held by such a sweet pressure and for so long that the poor dear's mind positively reeled and she just had the strength to quaver: 'Then you really don't mind me too much?'

'Good night, my friend,' whispered the other. 'Come again soon.'

'Oh, I will. I will.'

This time she walked back to the studio slowly, and standing in the middle of the room with half-shut eyes she felt so light, so rested, as if she had woken up out of a childish sleep. Even the act of breathing was a joy . . .

The *sommier* was very untidy. All the cushions 'like furious mountains' as she said; she put them in order before going over to the writing-table.

'I have been thinking over our talk about the psychological novel,' she dashed off, 'it really is intensely interesting . . .' And so on and so on.

At the end she wrote: 'Good night, my friend. Come again soon.'

(written 1918, first published in *Bliss and Other Stories*, 1920)

The Man without a Temperament

He stood at the hall door turning the ring, turning the heavy signet ring upon his little finger while his glance travelled coolly, deliberately, over the round tables and basket chairs scattered about the glassed-in veranda. He pursed his lips – he might have been going to whistle – but he did not whistle – only turned the ring – turned the ring on his pink, freshly washed hands.

Over in the corner sat The Two Topknots, drinking a decoction they always drank at this hour – something whitish, greyish, in glasses, with little husks floating on the top – and rooting in a tin full of paper shavings for pieces of speckled biscuit, which they broke, dropped into the glasses and fished for with spoons. Their two coils of knitting, like two snakes, slumbered beside the tray.

The American Woman sat where she always sat against the glass wall, in the shadow of a great creeping thing with wide open purple eyes that pressed – that flattened itself against the glass, hungrily watching her. And she knoo it was there – she knoo it was looking at her just that way. She played up to it; she gave herself little airs. Sometimes she even pointed at it, crying: 'Isn't that the most terrible thing you've ever seen! Isn't that ghoulish!' It was on the other side of the veranda, after all . . . and besides it couldn't touch her, could it, Klaymongso? She was an American Woman, wasn't she, Klaymongso, and she'd just go right away to her Consul. Klaymongso, curled in her lap, with her torn antique brocade bag, a grubby handkerchief, and a pile of letters from home on top of him, sneezed for reply.

The other tables were empty. A glance passed between the American and the Topknots. She gave a foreign little shrug; they waved an understanding biscuit. But he saw nothing. Now he was still, now from his eyes you saw he listened. 'Hoo-e-zip-zoo-oo!' sounded the lift. The iron cage clanged open. Light dragging steps sounded across the hall, coming towards him. A hand, like a leaf, fell on his shoulder. A soft voice said: 'Let's go and sit over there – where we can see the drive. The trees are so lovely.' And he moved forward with the hand still on his shoulder, and the light, dragging steps beside his. He pulled out a chair and she sank into it, slowly, leaning her head against the back, her arms falling along the sides.

'Won't you bring the other up closer? It's such miles away.' But he did not move.

'Where's your shawl?' he asked.

'Oh!' She gave a little groan of dismay. 'How silly I am, I've left it upstairs on the bed. Never mind. Please don't go for it. I shan't want it, I know I shan't.'

'You'd better have it.' And he turned and swiftly crossed the veranda into the dim hall with its scarlet plush and gilt furniture – conjuror's furniture – its Notice of Services at the English Church, its green baize board with the unclaimed letters climbing the black lattice, huge 'Presentation' clock that struck the hours at the half-hours, bundles of sticks and umbrellas and sunshades in the clasp of a brown wooden bear, past the two crippled palms, two ancient beggars at the foot of the staircase, up the marble stairs three at a time, past the life-size group on the landing of two stout peasant children with their marble pinnies full of marble grapes, and along the corridor, with its piled-up wreckage of old tin boxes, leather trunks, canvas holdalls, to their room.

The servant girl was in their room, singing loudly while she emptied soapy water into a pail. The windows were open wide, the shutters put back, and the light glared in. She had thrown the carpets and the big white pillows over the balcony rails; the nets were looped up from the beds; on the writing-table there stood a pan of fluff and matchends. When she saw him her small, impudent eyes snapped and her singing changed to humming. But he gave no sign. His eyes searched the glaring room. Where the devil was the shawl!

'*Vous desirez, monsieur?*' mocked the servant girl.

No answer. He had seen it. He strode across the room, grabbed the grey cobweb and went out, banging the door. The servant girl's voice at its loudest and shrillest followed him along the corridor.

'Oh, there you are. What happened? What kept you? The tea's here, you see. I've just sent Antonio off for the hot water. Isn't it extraordinary? I must have told him about it sixty times at least, and still he doesn't bring it. Thank you. That's very nice. One does just feel the air when one bends forward.'

'Thanks.' He took his tea and sat down in the other chair. 'No, nothing to eat.'

'Oh do! Just one, you had so little at lunch and it's hours before dinner.'

Her shawl dropped off as she bent forward to hand him the biscuits. He took one and put it in his saucer.

'Oh, those trees along the drive,' she cried. 'I could look at them for ever. They are like the most exquisite huge ferns. And you see that one with the grey-silver bark and the clusters of cream-coloured flowers, I pulled down a head of them yesterday to smell, and the scent' – she shut her eyes at the memory and her voice thinned away, faint, airy – 'was like freshly ground nutmegs.' A little pause. She turned to him and smiled. 'You do know what nutmegs smell like – do you, Robert?'

And he smiled back at her. 'Now how am I going to prove to you that I do?'

Back came Antonio with not only the hot water – with letters on a salver and three rolls of paper.

'Oh, the post! Oh, how lovely! Oh, Robert, they mustn't be all for you! Have they just come, Antonio?' Her thin hands flew up and hovered over the letters that Antonio offered her, bending forward.

'Just this moment, Signora,' grinned Antonio. 'I took-a them from the postman myself. I made-a the postman give them for me.'

'Noble Antonio!' laughed she. 'There – those are mine, Robert; the rest are yours.'

Antonio wheeled sharply, stiffened, the grin went out of his face. His striped linen jacket and his flat gleaming fringe made him look like a wooden doll.

Mr Salesby put the letters into his pocket; the papers lay on the table. He turned the ring, turned the signet ring on his little finger and stared in front of him, blinking, vacant.

But she – with her teacup in one hand, the sheets of thin paper in the other, her head tilted back, her lips open, a brush of bright colour on her cheek-bones, sipped, sipped, drank . . . drank . . .

'From Lottie,' came her soft murmur. 'Poor dear . . . such trouble . . . left foot. She thought . . . neuritis . . . Doctor Blyth . . . flat foot . . . massage. So many robins this year . . . maid most satisfactory . . . Indian Colonel . . . every grain of rice separate . . . very heavy fall of snow.' And her wide lighted eyes looked up from the letter.

'Snow, Robert! Think of it!' And she touched the little dark violets pinned on her thin bosom and went back to the letter.

. . . Snow. Snow in London. Millie with the early morning cup of tea. 'There's been a terrible fall of snow in the night, sir.' 'Oh, has there, Millie?' The curtains ring apart, letting in the pale, reluctant light. He raises himself in the bed; he catches a glimpse of the solid houses opposite framed in white, of their window boxes full of great sprays of white coral . . . In the bathroom – overlooking the back garden. Snow – heavy snow over everything. The lawn is covered with a wavy pattern of cat's-paws; there is a thick, thick icing on the garden table; the withered pods of the laburnum tree are white tassels; only here and there in the ivy is a dark leaf showing . . . Warming his back at the dining-room fire, the paper drying over a chair. Millie with the bacon. 'Oh, if you please, sir, there's two little boys come as will do the steps and front for a shilling, shall I let them?' . . . And then flying lightly, lightly down the stairs – Jinnie. 'Oh, Robert, isn't it wonderful! Oh, what a pity it has to melt. Where's the pussy-wee?' 'I'll get him from Millie.' . . . 'Millie, you might just hand me up the kitten if you've got him down there.' 'Very good, sir.' He feels the little beating heart under his hand. 'Come on, old chap, your missus wants you.' 'Oh, Robert, do show him the snow – his first snow. Shall I open the window and give him a little piece on his paw to hold? . . .'

'Well, that's very satisfactory on the whole – very. Poor Lottie! Darling Anne! How I only wish I could send them something of this,' she cried, waving her letters at the brilliant, dazzling garden. 'More tea, Robert? Robert dear, more tea?'

'No, thanks, no. It was very good,' he drawled.

'Well, mine wasn't. Mine was just like chopped hay. Oh, here comes the Honeymoon Couple.'

Half striding, half running, carrying a basket between them and rods and lines, they came up the drive, up the shallow steps.

'My! have you been out fishing?' cried the American Woman.

They were out of breath, they panted: 'Yes, yes, we have been out in a little boat all day. We have caught seven. Four are good to eat. But three we shall give away. To the children.'

Mrs Salesby turned her chair to look; the Topknots laid the snakes down. They were a very dark young couple – black hair, olive skin, brilliant eyes and teeth. He was dressed 'English fashion' in a flannel jacket, white trousers and shoes. Round his neck he wore a silk scarf; his head, with his hair brushed back, was bare. And he kept mopping his forehead, rubbing his hands with a brilliant handkerchief. Her white skirt had a patch of wet; her neck and throat were stained a deep pink. When she lifted her arms big half-hoops of perspiration showed under her armpits; her hair clung in wet curls to her cheeks. She looked as though her young husband had been dipping her in the sea and fishing her out again to dry in the sun and then – in with her again – all day.

'Would Klaymongso like a fish?' they cried. Their laughing voices charged with excitement beat against the glassed-in veranda like birds and a strange, saltish smell came from the basket.

'You will sleep well tonight,' said a Topknot, picking her ear with a knitting needle while the other Topknot smiled and nodded.

The Honeymoon Couple looked at each other. A great wave seemed to go over them. They gasped, gulped, staggered a little and then came up laughing – laughing.

'We cannot go upstairs, we are too tired. We must have tea just as we are. Here – coffee. No – tea. No – coffee. Tea – coffee, Antonio!' Mrs Salesby turned.

'Robert! Robert!' Where was he? He wasn't there. Oh, there he was at the other end of the veranda, with his back turned, smoking a cigarette. 'Robert, shall we go for our little turn?'

'Right.' He stumped the cigarette into an ash-tray and sauntered over, his eyes on the ground. 'Will you be warm enough?'

'Oh, quite.'

'Sure?'

'Well,' she put her hand on his arm, 'perhaps' – and gave his arm the faintest pressure – 'it's not upstairs, it's only in the hall – perhaps you'd get me my cape. Hanging up.'

He came back with it and she bent her small head while he dropped it on her shoulders. Then, very stiff, he offered her his arm. She bowed sweetly to the people on the veranda while he just covered a yawn, and they went down the steps together.

'*Vous avez voo ça!*' said the American Woman.

'He is not a man,' said the Two Topknots, 'he is an ox. I say to my sister in the morning and at night when we are in bed, I tell her – *No man is he, but an ox!'*

Wheeling, tumbling, swooping, the laughter of the Honeymoon Couple dashed against the glass of the veranda.

The sun was still high. Every leaf, every flower in the garden lay open, motionless, as if exhausted, and a sweet, rich, rank smell filled the quivering air. Out of the thick, fleshy leaves of a cactus there rose an aloe stem loaded with pale flowers that looked as though they had been cut out of butter; light flashed upon the lifted spears of the palms; over a bed of scarlet waxen flowers some big black insects 'zoom-zoomed'; a great, gaudy creeper, orange splashed with jet, sprawled against a wall.

'I don't need my cape after all,' said she. 'It's really too warm.' So he took it off and carried it over his arm. 'Let us go down this path here. I feel so well today – marvellously better. Good heavens – look at those children! And to think it's November!'

In a corner of the garden there were two brimming tubs of water. Three little girls, having thoughtfully taken off their drawers and hung them on a bush, their skirts clasped to their waists, were standing in the tubs and tramping up and down. They screamed, their hair fell over their faces, they splashed one another. But suddenly, the smallest, who had a tub to herself, glanced up and saw who was looking. For a moment she seemed overcome with terror, then clumsily she struggled and strained out of her tub, and still holding her clothes above her waist, 'The Englishman! The Englishman!' she shrieked and fled away to hide. Shrieking and screaming the other two followed her. In a moment they were gone; in a moment there was nothing but the two brimming tubs and their little drawers on the bush.

'How – very – extraordinary!' said she. 'What made them so frightened? Surely they were much too young to . . .' She looked up at him. She thought he looked pale – but wonderfully handsome with that great tropical tree behind him with its long, spiked thorns.

For a moment he did not answer. Then he met her glance, and smiling his slow smile, '*Très* rum!' said he.

Très rum! Oh, she felt quite faint. Oh, why should she love him so much just because he said a thing like that. *Très* rum! That was Robert all over. Nobody else but Robert could ever say such a thing. To be so wonderful, so brilliant, so learned, and then to say in that queer, boyish voice . . . She could have wept.

'You know you're very absurd, sometimes,' said she.

'I am,' he answered. And they walked on.

But she was tired. She had had enough. She did not want to walk any more.

'Leave me here and go for a little constitutional, won't you? I'll be in one of these long chairs. What a good thing you've got my cape; you won't have to go upstairs for a rug. Thank you, Robert, I shall look at that delicious heliotrope . . . You won't be gone long?'

'No – no. You don't mind being left?'

'Silly! I want you to go. I can't expect you to drag after your invalid wife every minute . . . How long will you be?'

He took out his watch. 'It's just after half-past four. I'll be back at a quarter-past five.'

'Back at a quarter-past five,' she repeated, and she lay still in the long chair and folded her hands.

He turned away. Suddenly he was back again. 'Look here, would you like my watch?' And he dangled it before her.

'Oh!' She caught her breath. 'Very, very much.' And she clasped the watch, the warm watch, the darling watch in her fingers. 'Now go quickly.'

The gates of the Pension Villa Excelsior were open wide, jammed open against some bold geraniums. Stooping a little, staring straight ahead, walking swiftly, he passed through them and began climbing the hill that wound behind the town like a great rope looping the villas together. The dust lay thick. A carriage came bowling along driving towards the Excelsior. In it sat the General and the Countess; they had been for his daily airing. Mr Salesby stepped to one side but the dust beat up, thick, white, stifling like wool. The Countess just had time to nudge the General.

'There he goes,' she said spitefully.

But the General gave a loud caw and refused to look.

'It is the Englishman,' said the driver, turning round and smiling. And the Countess threw up her hands and nodded so amiably that he spat with satisfaction and gave the stumbling horse a cut.

On – on – past the finest villas in the town, magnificent palaces, palaces worth coming any distance to see, past the public gardens with the carved grottoes and statues and stone animals drinking at the fountain, into a poorer quarter. Here the road ran narrow and foul between

high lean houses, the ground floors of which were scooped and hollowed into stables and carpenters' shops. At a fountain ahead of him
two old hags were beating linen. As he passed them they squatted back
on their haunches, stared, and then their 'A-hak-kak-kak!' with the
slap, slap, of the stone on the linen sounded after him.

He reached the top of the hill; he turned a corner and the town was
hidden. Down he looked into a deep valley with a dried-up river bed
at the bottom. This side and that was covered with small dilapidated
houses that had broken stone verandas where the fruit lay drying,
tomato lanes in the garden and from the gates to the doors a trellis of
vines. The late sunlight, deep, golden, lay in the cup of the valley;
there was a smell of charcoal in the air. In the gardens the men were
cutting grapes. He watched a man standing in the greenish shade, raising up, holding a black cluster in one hand, taking the knife from his
belt, cutting, laying the bunch in a flat boat-shaped basket. The man
worked leisurely, silently, taking hundreds of years over the job. On
the hedges on the other side of the road there were grapes small as berries, growing wild, growing among the stones. He leaned against a
wall, filled his pipe, put a match to it . . .

Leaned across a gate, turned up the collar of his mackintosh. It was
going to rain. It didn't matter, he was prepared for it. You didn't expect
anything else in November. He looked over the bare field. From the
corner by the gate there came the smell of swedes, a great stack of
them, wet, rank coloured. Two men passed walking towards the straggling village. 'Good day!' 'Good day!' By Jove! he had to hurry if he
was going to catch that train home. Over the gate, across a field, over
the stile, into the lane, swinging along in the drifting rain and dusk . . .
Just home in time for a bath and a change before supper . . . In the
drawing-room; Jinnie is sitting pretty nearly in the fire. 'Oh, Robert,
I didn't hear you come in. Did you have a good time? How nice you
smell! A present?' 'Some bits of blackberry I picked for you. Pretty
colour.' 'Oh, lovely, Robert! Dennis and Beaty are coming to supper.'
Supper – cold beef, potatoes in their jackets, claret, household bread.
They are gay – everybody's laughing. 'Oh, we all know Robert,' says
Dennis, breathing on his eyeglasses and polishing them. 'By the way,
Dennis, I picked up a very jolly little edition of . . .'

★

A clock struck. He wheeled sharply. What time was it. Five? A quarter past? Back, back the way he came. As he passed through the gates he saw her on the look-out. She got up, waved and slowly she came to meet him, dragging the heavy cape. In her hand she carried a spray of heliotrope.

'You're late,' she cried gaily. 'You're three minutes late. Here's your watch, it's been very good while you were away. Did you have a nice time? Was it lovely? Tell me. Where did you go?'

'I say – put this *on*,' he said, taking the cape from her.

'Yes, I will. Yes, it's getting chilly. Shall we go up to our room?'

When they reached the lift she was coughing. He frowned.

'It's nothing. I haven't been out too late. Don't be cross.' She sat down on one of the red plush chairs while he rang and rang, and then, getting no answer, kept his finger on the bell.

'Oh, Robert, do you think you ought to?'

'Ought to what?'

The door of the *salon* opened. 'What is that? Who is making that noise?' sounded from within. Klaymongso began to yelp. 'Caw! Caw! Caw!' came from the General. A Topknot darted out with one hand to her ear, opened the staff door, 'Mr Queet! Mr Queet!' she bawled. That brought the manager up at a run.

'Is that you ringing the bell, Mr Salesby? Do you want the lift? Very good, sir. I'll take you up myself. Antonio wouldn't have been a minute, he was just taking off his apron –' And having ushered them in, the oily manager went to the door of the *salon*. 'Very sorry you should have been troubled, ladies and gentlemen.' Salesby stood in the cage, sucking in his cheeks, staring at the ceiling and turning the ring, turning the signet ring on his little finger . . .

Arrived in their room he went swiftly over to the washstand, shook the bottle, poured her out a dose and brought it across.

'Sit down. Drink it. And don't talk.' And he stood over her while she obeyed. Then he took the glass, rinsed it and put it back in its case. 'Would you like a cushion?'

'No, I'm quite all right. Come over here. Sit down by me just a minute, will you, Robert? Ah, that's very nice.' She turned and thrust the piece of heliotrope in the lapel of his coat. 'That,' she said, 'is most becoming.' And then she leaned her head against his shoulder and he put his arm round her.

'Robert –' her voice like a sigh – like a breath.

'Yes –'

They sat there for a long while. The sky flamed, paled; the two white beds were like two ships . . . At last he heard the servant girl running along the corridor with the hot-water cans, and gently he released her and turned on the light.

'Oh, what time is it? Oh, what a heavenly evening. Oh, Robert, I was thinking while you were away this afternoon . . .'

They were the last couple to enter the dining-room. The Countess was there with her lorgnette and her fan, the General was there with his special chair and the air cushion and the small rug over his knees. The American Woman was there showing Klaymongso a copy of the *Saturday Evening Post* . . . 'We're having a feast of reason and a flow of soul.' The Two Topknots were there feeling over the peaches and the pears in their dish of fruit and putting aside all they considered unripe or overripe to show to the manager, and the Honeymoon Couple leaned across the table, whispering, trying not to burst out laughing.

Mr Queet, in everyday clothes and white canvas shoes, served the soup, and Antonio, in full evening dress, handed it round.

'No,' said the American Woman, 'take it away, Antonio. We can't eat soup. We can't eat anything mushy, can we, Klaymongso?'

'Take them back and fill them to the rim!' said the Topknots, and they turned and watched while Antonio delivered the message.

'What is it? Rice? Is it cooked?' The Countess peered through her lorgnette. 'Mr Queet, the General can have some of this soup if it is cooked.'

'Very good, Countess.'

The Honeymoon Couple had their fish instead.

'Give me that one. That's the one I caught. No, it's not. Yes, it is. No, it's not. Well, it's looking at me with its eye, so it must be. Tee! Hee! Hee!' Their feet were locked together under the table.

'Robert, you're not eating again. Is anything the matter?'

'No. Off food, that's all.'

'Oh, what a bother. There are eggs and spinach coming. You don't like spinach, do you. I must tell them in future . . .'

An egg and mashed potatoes for the General.

'Mr Queet! Mr Queet!'

'Yes, Countess.'

'The General's egg's too hard again.'

'Caw! Caw! Caw!'

'Very sorry, Countess. Shall I have you another cooked, General?'

. . . They are the first to leave the dining-room. She rises, gathering her shawl and he stands aside, waiting for her to pass, turning the ring, turning the signet ring on his little finger. In the hall Mr Queet hovers. 'I thought you might not want to wait for the lift. Antonio's just serving the finger bowls. And I'm sorry the bell won't ring, it's out of order. I can't think what's happened.'

'Oh, I do hope . . .' from her.

'Get in,' says he.

Mr Queet steps after them and slams the door . . .

'. . . Robert, do you mind if I go to bed very soon? Won't you go down to the *salon* or out into the garden? Or perhaps you might smoke a cigar on the balcony. It's lovely out there. And I like cigar smoke. I always did. But if you'd rather . . .'

'No, I'll sit here.'

He takes a chair and sits on the balcony. He hears her moving about in the room, lightly, lightly, moving and rustling. Then she comes over to him. 'Good night, Robert.'

'Good night.' He takes her hand and kisses the palm. 'Don't catch cold.'

The sky is the colour of jade. There are a great many stars; an enormous white moon hangs over the garden. Far away lightning flutters – flutters like a wing – flutters like a broken bird that tries to fly and sinks again and again struggles.

The lights from the *salon* shine across the garden path and there is the sound of a piano. And once the American Woman, opening the French window to let Klaymongso into the garden, cries: 'Have you seen this moon?' But nobody answers.

He gets very cold sitting there, staring at the balcony rail. Finally he comes inside. The moon – the room is painted white with moonlight. The light trembles in the mirrors; the two beds seem to float. She is asleep. He sees her through the nets, half sitting, banked up with pillows, her white hands crossed on the sheet. Her white cheeks, her fair hair pressed against the pillow, are silvered over. He undresses quickly, stealthily and gets into bed. Lying there, his hands clasped behind his head . . .

. . . In his study. Late summer. The virginia creeper just on the turn . . .

'Well, my dear chap, that's the whole story. That's the long and the short of it. If she can't cut away for the next two years and give a decent climate a chance she don't stand a dog's – h'm – show. Better be frank about these things.' 'Oh, certainly . . .' 'And hang it all, old man, what's to prevent you going with her? It isn't as though you've got a regular job like us wage earners. You can do what you do wherever you are –' 'Two years.' 'Yes, I should give it two years. You'll have no trouble about letting this house, you know. As a matter of fact . . .'

. . . He is with her. 'Robert, the awful thing is – I suppose it's my illness – I simply feel I could not go alone. You see – you're everything. You're bread and wine, Robert, bread and wine. Oh, my darling – what am I saying? Of course I could, of course I won't take you away . . .'

He hears her stirring. Does she want something?

'Boogies?'

Good Lord! She is talking in her sleep. They haven't used that name for years.

'Boogies. Are you awake?'

'Yes, do you want anything?'

'Oh, I'm going to be a bother. I'm so sorry. Do you mind? There's a wretched mosquito inside my net – I can hear him singing. Would you catch him? I don't want to move because of my heart.'

'No, don't move. Stay where you are.' He switches on the light, lifts the net. 'Where is the little beggar? Have you spotted him?'

'Yes, there, over by the corner. Oh, I do feel such a fiend to have dragged you out of bed. Do you mind dreadfully?'

'No, of course not.' For a moment he hovers in his blue and white pyjamas. Then, 'got him,' he said.

'Oh, good. Was he a juicy one?'

'Beastly.' He went over to the washstand and dipped his fingers in water. 'Are you all right now? Shall I switch off the light?'

'Yes, please. No. Boogies! Come back here a moment. Sit down by me. Give me your hand.' She turns his signet ring. 'Why weren't you asleep? Boogies, listen. Come closer. I sometimes wonder – do you mind awfully being out here with me?'

He bends down. He kisses her. He tucks her in, he smooths the pillow.

'Rot!' he whispers.

(first published in 1920, first book publication
Bliss and Other Stories, 1920)

The Escape

It was his fault, wholly and solely his fault, that they had missed the train. What if the idiotic hotel people had refused to produce the bill? Wasn't that simply because he hadn't impressed upon the waiter at lunch that they must have it by two o'clock? Any other man would have sat there and refused to move until they handed it over. But no! His exquisite belief in human nature had allowed him to get up and expect one of those idiots to bring it to their room . . . And then, when the *voiture* did arrive, while they were still (Oh, heavens!) waiting for change, why hadn't he seen to the arrangement of the boxes so that they could, at least, have started the moment the money had come? Had he expected her to go outside, to stand under the awning in the heat and point with her parasol? Very amusing picture of English domestic life. Even when the driver had been told how fast he had to drive he had paid no attention whatsoever – just smiled. 'Oh,' she groaned, 'if she'd been a driver she couldn't have stopped smiling herself at the absurd, ridiculous way he was urged to hurry.' And she sat back and imitated his voice: '*Allez, vite, vite*' – and begged the driver's pardon for troubling him . . .

And then the station – unforgettable – with the sight of the jaunty little train shuffling away and those hideous children waving from the windows. 'Oh, why am I made to bear these things? Why am I exposed to them? . . .' The glare, the flies, while they waited, and he and the stationmaster put their heads together over the time-table, trying to find this other train, which, of course, they wouldn't catch. The people who'd gathered round, and the woman who'd held up that baby with that awful, awful head . . . 'Oh, to care as I care – to feel as I feel, and never to be saved anything – never to know for one moment what it was to . . . to . . .'

Her voice had changed. It was shaking now – crying now. She fumbled with her bag, and produced from its little maw a scented handkerchief. She put up her veil and, as though she were doing it for somebody else, pitifully, as though she were saying to somebody else: 'I know, my darling,' she pressed the handkerchief to her eyes.

The little bag, with its shiny, silvery jaws open, lay on her lap. He could see her powder-puff, her rouge stick, a bundle of letters, a phial of tiny black pills like seeds, a broken cigarette, a mirror, white ivory tablets with lists on them that had been heavily scored through. He thought: 'In Egypt she would be buried with those things.'

They had left the last of the houses, those small straggling houses with bits of broken pot flung among the flower-beds and half-naked hens scratching round the doorsteps. Now they were mounting a long steep road that wound round the hill and over into the next bay. The horses stumbled, pulling hard. Every five minutes, every two minutes the driver trailed the whip across them. His stout back was solid as wood; there were boils on his reddish neck, and he wore a new, a shining new straw hat . . .

There was a little wind, just enough wind to blow to satin the new leaves on the fruit trees, to stroke the fine grass, to turn to silver the smoky olives – just enough wind to start in front of the carriage a whirling, twirling snatch of dust that settled on their clothes like the finest ash. When she took out her powder-puff the powder came flying over them both.

'Oh, the dust,' she breathed, 'the disgusting, revolting dust.' And she put down her veil and lay back as if overcome.

'Why don't you put up your parasol?' he suggested. It was on the front seat, and he leaned forward to hand it to her. At that she suddenly sat upright and blazed again.

'Please leave my parasol alone! I don't want my parasol! And anyone who was not utterly insensitive would know that I'm far, far too exhausted to hold up a parasol. And with a wind like this tugging at it . . . Put it down at once,' she flashed, and then snatched the parasol from him, tossed it into the crumpled hood behind, and subsided, panting.

Another bend of the road, and down the hill there came a troop of little children, shrieking and giggling, little girls with sun-bleached hair, little boys in faded soldiers' caps. In their hands they carried flowers – any kind of flowers – grabbed by the head, and these they offered, running beside the carriage. Lilac, faded lilac, greeny-white snowballs, one arum lily, a handful of hyacinths. They thrust the

flowers and their impish faces into the carriage; one even threw into
her lap a bunch of marigolds. Poor little mice! He had his hand in his
trouser pocket before her. 'For heaven's sake don't give them anything.
Oh, how typical of you! Horrid little monkeys! Now they'll follow us
all the way. Don't encourage them; you *would* encourage beggars'; and
she hurled the bunch out of the carriage with, 'Well, do it when I'm
not there, please.'

He saw the queer shock on the children's faces. They stopped running, lagged behind, and then they began to shout something, and
went on shouting until the carriage had rounded yet another bend.

'Oh, how many more are there before the top of the hill is reached?
The horses haven't trotted once. Surely it isn't necessary for them to
walk the whole way.'

'We shall be there in a minute now,' he said, and took out his
cigarette-case. At that she turned round towards him. She clasped her
hands and held them against her breast; her dark eyes looked immense,
imploring, behind her veil; her nostrils quivered, she bit her lip, and
her head shook with a little nervous spasm. But when she spoke, her
voice was quite weak and very, very calm.

'I want to ask you something. I want to beg something of you,' she
said. 'I've asked you hundreds and hundreds of times before, but
you've forgotten. It's such a little thing, but if you knew what it meant
to me . . .' She pressed her hands together. 'But you can't know. No
human creature could know and be so cruel.' And then, slowly, deliberately, gazing at him with those huge, sombre eyes: 'I beg and implore
you for the last time that when we are driving together you won't
smoke. If you could imagine,' she said, 'the anguish I suffer when that
smoke comes floating across my face . . .'

'Very well,' he said. 'I won't. I forgot.' And he put the case back.

'Oh no,' said she, and almost began to laugh, and put the back of
her hand across her eyes. 'You couldn't have forgotten. Not that.'

The wind came, blowing stronger. They were at the top of the hill.
'Hoy-yip-yip-yip,' cried the driver. They swung down the road that
fell into a small valley, skirted the sea-coast at the bottom of it, and
then coiled over a gentle ridge on the other side. Now there were
houses again, blue-shuttered against the heat, with bright burning
gardens, with geranium carpets flung over the pinkish walls. The
coast-line was dark; on the edge of the sea a white silky fringe just

stirred. The carriage swung down the hill, bumped, shook. 'Yi-ip,' shouted the driver. She clutched the sides of the seat, she closed her eyes, and he knew she felt this was happening on purpose; this swinging and bumping, this was all done – and he was responsible for it, somehow – to spite her because she had asked if they couldn't go a little faster. But just as they reached the bottom of the valley there was one tremendous lurch. The carriage nearly overturned, and he saw her eyes blaze at him, and she positively hissed, 'I suppose you are enjoying this?'

They went on. They reached the bottom of the valley. Suddenly she stood up. '*Cocher! Cocher! Arrêtez-vous!*' She turned round and looked into the crumpled hood behind. 'I knew it,' she exclaimed. 'I knew it. I heard it fall, and so did you, at that last bump.'

'What? Where?'

'My parasol. It's gone. The parasol that belonged to my mother. The parasol that I prize more than – more than . . .' She was simply beside herself. The driver turned round, his gay, broad face smiling.

'I, too, heard something,' said he, simply and gaily. 'But I thought as Monsieur and Madame said nothing . . .'

'There. You hear that. Then you must have heard it too. So *that* accounts for the extraordinary smile on your face . . .'

'Look here,' he said, 'it can't be gone. If it fell out it will be there still. Stay where you are. I'll fetch it.'

But she saw through that. Oh, how she saw through it! 'No, thank you.' And she bent her spiteful, smiling eyes upon him, regardless of the driver. 'I'll go myself. I'll walk back and find it, and trust you not to follow. For' – knowing the driver did not understand, she spoke softly, gently – 'if I don't escape from you for a minute I shall go mad.'

She stepped out of the carriage. 'My bag.' He handed it to her.

'Madame prefers . . .'

But the driver had already swung down from his seat, and was seated on the parapet reading a small newspaper. The horses stood with hanging heads. It was still. The man in the carriage stretched himself out, folded his arms. He felt the sun beat on his knees. His head was sunk on his breast. 'Hish, hish,' sounded from the sea. The wind sighed in the valley and was quiet. He felt himself, lying there, a hollow man, a parched, withered man, as it were, of ashes. And the sea sounded, 'Hish, hish.'

It was then that he saw the tree, that he was conscious of its presence just inside a garden gate. It was an immense tree with a round, thick silver stem and a great arc of copper leaves that gave back the light and yet were sombre. There was something beyond the tree – a whiteness, a softness, an opaque mass, half hidden – with delicate pillars. As he looked at the tree he felt his breathing die away and he became part of the silence. It seemed to grow, it seemed to expand in the quivering heat until the great carved leaves hid the sky, and yet it was motionless. Then from within its depths or from beyond there came the sound of a woman's voice. A woman was singing. The warm untroubled voice floated upon the air, and it was all part of the silence as he was part of it. Suddenly, as the voice rose, soft, dreaming, gentle, he knew that it would come floating to him from the hidden leaves and his peace was shattered. What was happening to him? Something stirred in his breast. Something dark, something unbearable and dreadful pushed in his bosom, and like a great weed it floated, rocked . . . it was warm, stifling. He tried to struggle to tear at it, and at the same moment – all was over. Deep, deep, he sank into the silence, staring at the tree and waiting for the voice that came floating, falling, until he felt himself enfolded.

In the shaking corridor of the train. It was night. The train rushed and roared through the dark. He held on with both hands to the brass rail. The door of their carriage was open.

'Do not disturb yourself, Monsieur. He will come in and sit down when he wants to. He likes – he likes – it is his habit . . . *Oui, Madame, je suis un peu souffrante* . . . *Mes nerfs*. Oh, but my husband is never so happy as when he is travelling. He likes roughing it . . . My husband . . . My husband . . .'

The voices murmured, murmured. They were never still. But so great was his heavenly happiness as he stood there he wished he might live for ever.

(first published in 1920, first book publication
Bliss and Other Stories, 1920)

Bank Holiday

A stout man with a pink face wears dingy white flannel trousers, a blue coat with a pink handkerchief showing, and a straw hat much too small for him, perched at the back of his head. He plays the guitar. A little chap in white canvas shoes, his face hidden under a felt hat like a broken wing, breathes into a flute; and a tall thin fellow, with bursting over-ripe button boots, draws ribbons – long, twisted, streaming ribbons – of tune out of a fiddle. They stand, unsmiling, but not serious, in the broad sunlight opposite the fruit-shop; the pink spider of a hand beats the guitar, the little squat hand, with a brass-and-turquoise ring, forces the reluctant flute, and the fiddler's arm tries to saw the fiddle in two.

A crowd collects, eating oranges and bananas, tearing off the skins, dividing, sharing. One young girl has even a basket of strawberries, but she does not eat them. 'Aren't they *dear*!' She stares at the tiny pointed fruits as if she were afraid of them. The Australian soldier laughs. 'Here, go on, there's not more than a mouthful.' But he doesn't want her to eat them, either. He likes to watch her little frightened face, and her puzzled eyes lifted to his: 'Aren't they a *price*!' He pushes out his chest and grins. Old fat women in velvet bodices – old dusty pin-cushions – lean old hags like worn umbrellas with a quivering bonnet on top; young women, in muslins, with hats that might have grown on hedges, and high pointed shoes; men in khaki, sailors, shabby clerks, young Jews in fine cloth suits with padded shoulders and wide trousers, 'hospital boys' in blue – the sun discovers them – the loud, bold music holds them together in one big knot for a moment. The young ones are larking, pushing each other on and off the pavement, dodging, nudging; the old ones are talking: 'So I said to 'im, if you wants the doctor to yourself, fetch 'im, says I.'

'An' by the time they was cooked there wasn't so much as you could put in the palm of me 'and!'

The only ones who are quiet are the ragged children. They stand, as close up to the musicians as they can get, their hands behind their backs, their eyes big. Occasionally a leg hops, an arm wags. A tiny staggerer, overcome, turns round twice, sits down solemn, and then gets up again.

'Ain't it lovely?' whispers a small girl behind her hand.

And the music breaks into bright pieces, and joins together again, and again breaks, and is dissolved, and the crowd scatters, moving slowly up the hill.

At the corner of the road the stalls begin.

'Ticklers! Tuppence a tickler! 'Ool 'ave a tickler? Tickle 'em up, boys.' Little soft brooms on wire handles. They are eagerly bought by the soldiers.

'Buy a golliwog! Tuppence a golliwog!'

'Buy a jumping donkey! All alive-oh!'

'*Su*-perior chewing-gum. Buy something to do, boys.'

'Buy a rose. Give 'er a rose, boy. Roses, lady?'

'Fevvers! Fevvers!' They are hard to resist. Lovely, streaming feathers, emerald green, scarlet, bright blue, canary yellow. Even the babies wear feathers threaded through their bonnets.

And an old woman in a three-cornered paper hat cries as if it were her final parting advice, the only way of saving yourself or of bringing him to his senses: 'Buy a three-cornered 'at, my dear, an' put it on!'

It is a flying day, half sun, half wind. When the sun goes in a shadow flies over; when it comes out again it is fiery. The men and women feel it burning their backs, their breasts and their arms; they feel their bodies expanding, coming alive . . . so that they make large embracing gestures, lift up their arms, for nothing, swoop down on a girl, blurt into laughter.

Lemonade! A whole tank of it stands on a table covered with a cloth; and lemons like blunted fishes blob in the yellow water. It looks solid, like a jelly, in the thick glasses. Why can't they drink it without spilling it? Everybody spills it, and before the glass is handed back the last drops are thrown in a ring.

Round the ice-cream cart, with its striped awning and bright brass cover, the children cluster. Little tongues lick, lick round the cream trumpets, round the squares. The cover is lifted, the wooden spoon plunges in; one shuts one's eyes to feel it, silently scrunching.

'Let these little birds tell you your future!' She stands beside the cage, a shrivelled ageless Italian, clasping and unclasping her dark claws. Her face, a treasure of delicate carving, is tied in a green-and-gold scarf. And inside their prison the love-birds flutter towards the papers in the seed-tray.

'You have great strength of character. You will marry a red-haired man and have three children. Beware of a blonde woman. Look out! Look out! A motor-car driven by a fat chauffeur comes rushing down the hill. Inside there a blonde woman, pouting, leaning forward – rushing through your life – beware! beware!'

'Ladies and gentlemen, I am an auctioneer by profession, and if what I tell you is not the truth I am liable to have my licence taken away from me and a heavy imprisonment.' He holds the licence across his chest; the sweat pours down his face into his paper collar; his eyes look glazed. When he takes off his hat there is a deep pucker of angry flesh on his forehead. Nobody buys a watch.

Look out again! A huge barouche comes swinging down the hill with two old, old babies inside. She holds up a lace parasol; he sucks the knob of his cane, and the fat old bodies roll together as the cradle rocks, and the steaming horse leaves a trail of manure as it ambles down the hill.

Under a tree, Professor Leonard, in cap and gown, stands beside his banner. He is here 'for one day', from the London, Paris and Brussels Exhibition, to tell your fortune from your face. And he stands, smiling encouragement, like a clumsy dentist. When the big men, romping and swearing a moment before, hand across their sixpence, and stand before him, they are suddenly serious, dumb, timid, almost blushing as the Professor's quick hand notches the printed card. They are like little children caught playing in a forbidden garden by the owner, stepping from behind a tree.

The top of the hill is reached. How hot it is! How fine it is! The public-house is open and the crowd presses in. The mother sits on the pavement edge with her baby, and the father brings her out a glass of dark, brownish stuff, and then savagely elbows his way in again. A reek of beer floats from the public-house and a loud clatter and rattle of voices.

The wind has dropped and the sun burns more fiercely than ever. Outside the two swing-doors there is a thick mass of children like flies at the mouth of a sweet-jar.

And up, up the hill come the people, with ticklers and golliwogs and roses and feathers. Up, up they thrust into the light and heat, shouting, laughing, squealing, as though they were being pushed by something, far below, and by the sun, far ahead of them – drawn up into the full, bright, dazzling radiance to . . . what?

(first published in 1920, first book publication
The Garden Party and Other Stories, 1922)

The Young Girl

In her blue dress, with her cheeks lightly flushed, her blue, blue eyes, and her gold curls pinned up as though for the first time – pinned up to be out of the way for her flight – Mrs Raddick's daughter might have just dropped from this radiant heaven. Mrs Raddick's timid, faintly astonished, but deeply admiring glance looked as if she believed it, too; but the daughter didn't appear any too pleased – why should she? – to have alighted on the steps of the Casino. Indeed, she was bored – bored as though heaven had been full of casinos with snuffy old saints for *croupiers* and crowns to play with.

'You don't mind taking Hennie?' said Mrs Raddick. 'Sure you don't? There's the car, and you'll have tea and we'll be back here on this step – right here – in an hour. You see, I want her to go in. She's not been before, and it's worth seeing. I feel it wouldn't be fair to her.'

'Oh, shut up, mother,' said she wearily. 'Come along. Don't talk so much. And your bag's open; you'll be losing all your money again.'

'I'm sorry, darling,' said Mrs Raddick.

'Oh, *do* come in! I want to make money,' said the impatient voice. 'It's all jolly well for you – but I'm broke!'

'Here – take fifty francs, darling, take a hundred!' I saw Mrs Raddick pressing notes into her hand as they passed through the swing doors.

Hennie and I stood on the steps a minute, watching the people. He had a very broad, delighted smile.

'I say,' he cried, 'there's an English bulldog. Are they allowed to take dogs in there?'

'No, they're not.'

'He's a ripping chap, isn't he? I wish I had one. They're such fun. They frighten people so, and they're never fierce with their – the people they belong to.' Suddenly he squeezed my arm. 'I say, *do* look at that old woman. Who is she? Why does she look like that? Is she a gambler?'

The ancient, withered creature, wearing a green satin dress, a black

velvet cloak and a white hat with purple feathers, jerked slowly, slowly
up the steps as though she were being drawn up on wires. She stared
in front of her, she was laughing and nodding and cackling to herself;
her claws clutched round what looked like a dirty boot-bag.

But just at that moment there was Mrs Raddick again with – *her* –
and another lady hovering in the background. Mrs Raddick rushed at
me. She was brightly flushed, gay, a different creature. She was like a
woman who is saying 'goodbye' to her friends on the station platform, with not a minute to spare before the train starts.

'Oh, you're here, still. Isn't that lucky! You've not gone. Isn't that
fine! I've had the most dreadful time with – her,' and she waved to her
daughter, who stood absolutely still, disdainful, looking down, twiddling her foot on the step, miles away. 'They won't let her in. I swore
she was twenty-one. But they won't believe me. I showed the man my
purse; I didn't dare to do more. But it was no use. He simply scoffed . . .
And now I've just met Mrs MacEwen from New York, and she just
won thirteen thousand in the *Salle Privée* – and she wants me to go
back with her while the luck lasts. Of course I can't leave – her. But if
you'd –'

At that 'she' looked up; she simply withered her mother. 'Why
can't you leave me?' she said furiously. 'What utter rot! How dare you
make a scene like this? This is the last time I'll come out with you. You
really are too awful for words.' She looked her mother up and down.
'Calm yourself,' she said superbly.

Mrs Raddick was desperate, just desperate. She was 'wild' to go
back with Mrs MacEwen, but at the same time . . .

I seized my courage. 'Would you – do you care to come to tea
with – us?'

'Yes, yes, she'll be delighted. That's just what I wanted, isn't it, darling? Mrs MacEwen . . . I'll be back here in an hour . . . or less . . .
I'll –'

Mrs R. dashed up the steps. I saw her bag was open again.

So we three were left. But really it wasn't my fault. Hennie looked
crushed to the earth, too. When the car was there she wrapped her
dark coat round her – to escape contamination. Even her little feet
looked as though they scorned to carry her down the steps to us.

'I am so awfully sorry,' I murmured as the car started.

'Oh, I don't *mind*,' said she. 'I don't *want* to look twenty-one. Who would – if they were seventeen! It's' – and she gave a faint shudder – 'the stupidity I loathe, and being stared at by fat old men. Beasts!'

Hennie gave her a quick look and then peered out of the window.

We drew up before an immense palace of pink-and-white marble with orange trees outside the doors in gold-and-black tubs.

'Would you care to go in?' I suggested.

She hesitated, glanced, bit her lip, and resigned herself. 'Oh well, there seems nowhere else,' said she. 'Get out, Hennie.'

I went first – to find the table, of course – she followed. But the worst of it was having her little brother, who was only twelve, with us. That was the last, final straw – having that child, trailing at her heels.

There was one table. It had pink carnations and pink plates with little blue tea-napkins for sails.

'Shall we sit here?'

She put her hand wearily on the back of a white wicker chair.

'We may as well. Why not?' said she.

Hennie squeezed past her and wriggled on to a stool at the end. He felt awfully out of it. She didn't even take her gloves off. She lowered her eyes and drummed on the table. When a faint violin sounded she winced and bit her lip again. Silence.

The waitress appeared. I hardly dared to ask her. 'Tea – coffee? China tea – or iced tea with lemon?'

Really she didn't mind. It was all the same to her. She didn't really want anything. Hennie whispered, 'Chocolate!'

But just as the waitress turned away she cried out carelessly, 'Oh, you may as well bring me a chocolate too.'

While we waited she took out a little, gold powder-box with a mirror in the lid, shook the poor little puff as though she loathed it, and dabbed her lovely nose.

'Hennie,' she said, 'take those flowers away.' She pointed with her puff to the carnations, and I heard her murmur, 'I can't bear flowers on a table.' They had evidently been giving her intense pain, for she positively closed her eyes as I moved them away.

The waitress came back with the chocolate and the tea. She put the big, frothing cups before them and pushed across my clear glass. Hennie buried his nose, emerged, with, for one dreadful moment, a little trembling blob of cream on the tip. But he hastily wiped it off like a little gentleman. I wondered if I should dare draw her attention to her cup. She didn't notice it – didn't see it – until suddenly, quite by chance, she took a sip. I watched anxiously; she faintly shuddered.

'Dreadfully sweet!' said she.

A tiny boy with a head like a raisin and a chocolate body came round with a tray of pastries – row upon row of little freaks, little inspirations, little melting dreams. He offered them to her. 'Oh, I'm not at all hungry. Take them away.'

He offered them to Hennie. Hennie gave me a swift look – it must have been satisfactory – for he took a chocolate cream, a coffee éclair, a meringue stuffed with chestnut and a tiny horn filled with fresh strawberries. She could hardly bear to watch him. But just as the boy swerved away she held up her plate.

'Oh well, give me *one,*' said she.

The silver tongs dropped one, two, three – and a cherry tartlet. 'I don't know why you're giving me all these,' she said, and nearly smiled. 'I shan't eat them; I couldn't!'

I felt much more comfortable. I sipped my tea, leaned back, and even asked if I might smoke. At that she paused, the fork in her hand, opened her eyes and really did smile. 'Of course,' said she. 'I always expect people to.'

But at that moment a tragedy happened to Hennie. He speared his pastry horn too hard, and it flew in two, and one half spilled on the table. Ghastly affair! He turned crimson. Even his ears flared, and one ashamed hand crept across the table to take what was left of the body away.

'You *utter* little beast!' said she.

Good heavens! I had to fly to the rescue. I cried hastily, 'Will you be abroad long?'

But she had already forgotten Hennie. I was forgotten too. She was trying to remember something . . . She was miles away.

'I – don't – know,' she said slowly, from that far place.

'I suppose you prefer it to London. It's more – more –'

When I didn't go on she came back and looked at me, very puzzled. 'More – ?'

'*Enfin* – gayer,' I cried, waving my cigarette.

But that took a whole cake to consider. Even then, 'Oh well, that depends!' was all she could safely say.

Hennie had finished. He was still very warm.

I seized the butterfly list off the table. 'I say – what about an ice, Hennie? What about tangerine and ginger? No, something cooler. What about a fresh pineapple cream?'

Hennie strongly approved. The waitress had her eye on us. The order was taken when she looked up from her crumbs.

'Did you say tangerine and ginger? I like ginger. You can bring me one.' And then quickly, 'I wish that orchestra wouldn't play things from the year One. We were dancing to that all last Christmas. It's too sickening!'

But it was a charming air. Now that I noticed it, it warmed me.

'I think this is rather a nice place, don't you, Hennie?' I said.

Hennie said: 'Ripping!' He meant to say it very low, but it came out very high in a kind of squeak.

Nice? This place? Nice? For the first time she stared about her, try-ing to see what there was . . . She blinked; her lovely eyes wondered. A very good-looking elderly man stared back at her through a mon-ocle on a black ribbon. But him she simply couldn't see. There was a hole in the air where he was. She looked through and through him.

Finally the little flat spoons lay still on the glass plates. Hennie looked rather exhausted, but she pulled on her white gloves again. She had some trouble with her diamond wrist-watch; it got in her way. She tugged at it – tried to break the stupid little thing – it wouldn't break. Finally, she had to drag her glove over. I saw, after that, she couldn't stand this place a moment longer, and, indeed, she jumped up and turned away while I went through the vulgar act of paying for the tea.

And then we were outside again. It had grown dusky. The sky was sprinkled with small stars; the big lamps glowed. While we waited for the car to come up she stood on the step, just as before, twiddling her foot, looking down.

Hennie bounded forward to open the door and she got in and sank back with – oh – such a sigh!

'Tell him,' she gasped, 'to drive as fast as he can.'

Hennie grinned at his friend the chauffeur. '*Allie veet!*' said he. Then he composed himself and sat on the small seat facing us.

The gold powder-box came out again. Again the poor little puff was shaken; again there was that swift, deadly-secret glance between her and the mirror.

We tore through the black-and-gold town like a pair of scissors tearing through brocade. Hennie had great difficulty not to look as though he were hanging on to something.

And when we reached the Casino, of course Mrs Raddick wasn't there. There wasn't a sign of her on the steps – not a sign.

'Will you stay in the car while I go and look?'

But no – she wouldn't do that. Good heavens, no! Hennie could stay. She couldn't bear sitting in a car. She'd wait on the steps.

'But I scarcely like to leave you,' I murmured. 'I'd very much rather not leave you here.'

At that she threw back her coat; she turned and faced me; her lips parted. 'Good heavens – why! I – I don't mind it a bit. I – I like waiting.' And suddenly her cheeks crimsoned, her eyes grew dark – for a moment I thought she was going to cry. 'L – let me, please,' she stammered, in a warm, eager voice. 'I like it. I love waiting! Really – really I do! I'm always waiting – in all kinds of places . . .'

Her dark coat fell open, and her white throat – all her soft young body in the blue dress – was like a flower that is just emerging from its dark bud.

(first published in 1920, first book publication
The Garden Party and Other Stories, 1922)

The Stranger

It seemed to the little crowd on the wharf that she was never going to move again. There she lay, immense, motionless on the grey crinkled water, a loop of smoke above her, an immense flock of gulls screaming and diving after the galley droppings at the stern. You could just see little couples parading – little flies walking up and down the dish on the grey crinkled tablecloth. Other flies clustered and swarmed at the edge. Now there was a gleam of white on the lower deck – the cook's apron or the stewardess, perhaps. Now a tiny black spider raced up the ladder on to the bridge.

In the front of the crowd a strong-looking, middle-aged man, dressed very well, very snugly in a grey overcoat, grey silk scarf, thick gloves and dark felt hat, marched up and down twirling his folded umbrella. He seemed to be the leader of the little crowd on the wharf and at the same time to keep them together. He was something between the sheep-dog and the shepherd.

But what a fool – what a fool he had been not to bring any glasses! There wasn't a pair of glasses between the whole lot of them.

'Curious thing, Mr Scott, that none of us thought of glasses. We might have been able to stir 'em up a bit. We might have managed a little signalling. *Don't hesitate to land. Natives harmless.* Or: *A welcome awaits you. All is forgiven.* What? Eh?'

Mr Hammond's quick, eager glance, so nervous and yet so friendly and confiding, took in everybody on the wharf, roped in even those old chaps lounging against the gangways. They knew, every man-jack of them, that Mrs Hammond was on that boat, and he was so tremendously excited it never entered his head not to believe that this marvellous fact meant something to them too. It warmed his heart towards them. They were, he decided, as decent a crowd of people – Those old chaps over by the gangways, too – fine, solid old chaps. What chests – by Jove! And he squared his own, plunged his thick-gloved hands into his pockets, rocked from heel to toe.

'Yes, my wife's been in Europe for the last ten months. On a visit to our eldest girl, who was married last year. I brought her up here, as far as Crawford, myself. So I thought I'd better come and fetch her back. Yes, yes, yes.' The shrewd grey eyes narrowed again and searched anxiously, quickly, the motionless liner. Again his overcoat was unbuttoned. Out came the thin, butter-yellow watch again, and for the twentieth – fiftieth – hundredth time he made the calculation.

'Let me see, now. It was two fifteen when the doctor's launch went off. Two fifteen. It is now exactly twenty-eight minutes past four. That is to say, the doctor's been gone two hours and thirteen minutes. Two hours and thirteen minutes! Whee-ooh!' He gave a queer little half-whistle and snapped his watch to again. 'But I think we should have been told if there was anything up – don't you, Mr Gaven?'

'Oh yes, Mr Hammond! I don't think there's anything to – anything to worry about,' said Mr Gaven, knocking out his pipe against the heel of his shoe. 'At the same time –'

'Quite so! Quite so!' cried Mr Hammond. 'Dashed annoying!' He paced quickly up and down and came back again to his stand between Mr and Mrs Scott and Mr Gaven. 'It's getting quite dark, too,' and he waved his folded umbrella as though the dusk at least might have had the decency to keep off for a bit. But the dusk came slowly, spreading like a slow stain over the water. Little Jean Scott dragged at her mother's hand.

'I wan' my tea, mammy!' she wailed.

'I expect you do,' said Mr Hammond. 'I expect all these ladies want their tea.' And his kind, flushed, almost pitiful glance roped them all in again. He wondered whether Janey was having a final cup of tea in the saloon out there. He hoped so; he thought not. It would be just like her not to leave the deck. In that case perhaps the deck steward would bring her up a cup. If he'd been there he'd have got it for her – somehow. And for a moment he was on deck, standing over her, watching her little hand fold round the cup in the way she had, while she drank the only cup of tea to be got on board . . . But now he was back here, and the Lord only knew when that cursed Captain would stop hanging about in the stream. He took another turn, up and down, up and down. He walked as far as the cab-stand to make sure his driver hadn't disappeared; back he swerved again to the little flock huddled in the shelter of the banana crates. Little Jean Scott was still wanting her tea. Poor little beggar! He wished he had a bit of chocolate on him.

'Here, Jean!' he said. 'Like a lift up?' And easily, gently, he swung the little girl on to a higher barrel. The movement of holding her, steadying her, relieved him wonderfully, lightened his heart.

'Hold on,' he said, keeping an arm round her.

'Oh, don't worry about *Jean,* Mr Hammond!' said Mrs Scott.

'That's all right, Mrs Scott. No trouble. It's a pleasure. Jean's a little pal of mine, aren't you, Jean?'

'Yes, Mr Hammond,' said Jean, and she ran her finger down the dent of his felt hat.

But suddenly she caught him by the ear and gave a loud scream. 'Lo-ok, Mr Hammond! She's moving! Look, she's coming in!'

By Jove! So she was. At last! She was slowly, slowly turning round. A bell sounded far over the water and a great spout of steam gushed into the air. The gulls rose; they fluttered away like bits of white paper. And whether that deep throbbing was her engines or his heart Mr Hammond couldn't say. He had to nerve himself to bear it, whatever it was. At that moment old Captain Johnson, the harbour-master, came striding down the wharf, a leather portfolio under his arm.

'Jean'll be all right,' said Mr Scott. 'I'll hold her.' He was just in time. Mr Hammond had forgotten about Jean. He sprang away to greet old Captain Johnson.

'Well, Captain,' the eager, nervous voice rang out again, 'you've taken pity on us at last.'

'It's no good blaming me, Mr Hammond,' wheezed old Captain Johnson, staring at the liner. 'You got Mrs Hammond on board, ain't yer?'

'Yes, yes!' said Hammond, and he kept by the harbourmaster's side. 'Mrs Hammond's there. Hul-lo! We shan't be long now!'

With her telephone ring-ringing, the thrum of her screw filling the air, the big liner bore down on them, cutting sharp through the dark water so that big white shavings curled to either side. Hammond and the harbour-master kept in front of the rest. Hammond took off his hat; he raked the decks – they were crammed with passengers; he waved his hat and bawled a loud, strange 'Hul-lo!' across the water, and then turned round and burst out laughing and said something – nothing – to old Captain Johnson.

'Seen her?' asked the harbour-master.

'No, not yet. Steady – wait a bit!' And suddenly, between two great clumsy idiots – 'Get out of the way there!' he signed with his umbrella – he saw a hand raised – a white glove shaking a handkerchief. Another moment, and – thank God, thank God! – there she was. There was Janey. There was Mrs Hammond, yes, yes, yes – standing by the rail and smiling and nodding and waving her handkerchief.

'Well, that's first class – first class! Well, well, well!' He positively stamped. Like lightning he drew out his cigar-case and offered it to old Captain Johnson. 'Have a cigar, Captain! They're pretty good. Have a couple! Here' – and he pressed all the cigars in the case on the harbourmaster – 'I've a couple of boxes up at the hotel.'

'Thenks, Mr Hammond!' wheezed old Captain Johnson.

Hammond stuffed the cigar-case back. His hands were shaking, but he'd got hold of himself again. He was able to face Janey. There she was, leaning on the rail, talking to some woman and at the same time watching him, ready for him. It struck him, as the gulf of water closed, how small she looked on that huge ship. His heart was wrung with such a spasm that he could have cried out. How little she looked to have come all that long way and back by herself! Just like her, though. Just like Janey. She had the courage of a – And now the crew had come forward and parted the passengers; they had lowered the rails for the gangways.

The voices on shore and the voices on board flew to greet each other.

'All well?'

'All well.'

'How's mother?'

'Much better.'

'Hullo, Jean!'

'Hillo, Aun' Emily!'

'Had a good voyage?'

'Splendid!'

'Shan't be long now!'

'Not long now.'

The engines stopped. Slowly she edged to the wharf-side.

'Make way there – make way – make way!' And the wharf hands brought the heavy gangways along at a sweeping run. Hammond signed to Janey to stay where she was. The old harbour-master stepped

forward; he followed. As to 'ladies first,' or any rot like that, it never
entered his head.

'After you, Captain!' he cried genially. And, treading on the old
man's heels, he strode up the gangway on to the deck in a bee-line to
Janey, and Janey was clasped in his arms.

'Well, well, well! Yes, yes! Here we are at last!' he stammered. It
was all he could say. And Janey emerged, and her cool little voice – the
only voice in the world for him – said, 'Well, darling! Have you been
waiting long?'

No; not long. Or, at any rate, it didn't matter. It was over now. But
the point was, he had a cab waiting at the end of the wharf. Was she
ready to go off? Was her luggage ready? In that case they could cut off
sharp with her cabin luggage and let the rest go hang until tomorrow.
He bent over her and she looked up with her familiar half-smile. She
was just the same. Not a day changed. Just as he'd always known her.
She laid her small hand on his sleeve.

'How are the children, John?' she asked.

(Hang the children!) 'Perfectly well. Never better in their lives.'

'Haven't they sent me letters?'

'Yes, yes – of course! I've left them at the hotel for you to digest
later on.'

'We can't go quite so fast,' said she. 'I've got people to say goodbye
to – and then there's the Captain.' As his face fell she gave his arm a
small understanding squeeze. 'If the Captain comes off the bridge I
want you to thank him for having looked after your wife so beautifully.' Well, he'd got her. If she wanted another ten minutes – As he
gave way she was surrounded. The whole first-class seemed to want to
say goodbye to Janey.

'Goodbye, *dear* Mrs Hammond! And next time you're in Sydney I'll
expect you.'

'Darling Mrs Hammond! You won't forget to write to me, will
you?'

'Well, Mrs Hammond, what this boat would have been without
you!'

It was as plain as a pikestaff that she was by far the most popular
woman on board. And she took it all – just as usual. Absolutely composed. Just her little self – just Janey all over; standing there with her
veil thrown back. Hammond never noticed what his wife had on. It

was all the same to him whatever she wore. But today he did notice that she wore a black 'costume' – didn't they call it? – with white frills, trimmings he supposed they were, at the neck and sleeves. All this while Janey handed him round.

'John, dear!' And then: 'I want to introduce you to –'

Finally they did escape, and she led the way to her stateroom. To follow Janey down the passage that she knew so well – that was so strange to him; to part the green curtains after her and to step into the cabin that had been hers gave him exquisite happiness. But – confound it! – the stewardess was there on the floor, strapping up the rugs.

'That's the last, Mrs Hammond,' said the stewardess, rising and pulling down her cuffs.

He was introduced again, and then Janey and the stewardess disappeared into the passage. He heard whisperings. She was getting the tipping business over, he supposed. He sat down on the striped sofa and took his hat off. There were the rugs she had taken with her; they looked good as new. All her luggage looked fresh, perfect. The labels were written in her beautiful little clear hand – 'Mrs John Hammond.'

'Mrs John Hammond!' He gave a long sigh of content and leaned back, crossing his arms. The strain was over. He felt he could have sat there for ever sighing his relief – the relief at being rid of that horrible tug, pull, grip on his heart. The danger was over. That was the feeling. They were on dry land again.

But at that moment Janey's head came round the corner.

'Darling – do you mind? I just want to go and say goodbye to the doctor.'

Hammond started up. 'I'll come with you.'

'No, no!' she said. 'Don't bother. I'd rather not. I'll not be a minute.'

And before he could answer she was gone. He had half a mind to run after her; but instead he sat down again.

Would she really not be long? What was the time now? Out came the watch; he stared at nothing. That was rather queer of Janey, wasn't it? Why couldn't she have told the stewardess to say goodbye for her? Why did she have to go chasing after the ship's doctor? She could have sent a note from the hotel even if the affair had been urgent. Urgent? Did it – could it mean that she had been ill on the voyage – she was keeping something from him? That was it! He seized his hat. He was going off to find that fellow and to wring the truth out of him at all costs. He thought he'd noticed just something. She was just a touch too calm – too steady. From the very first moment –

The curtains rang. Janey was back. He jumped to his feet.

'Janey, have you been ill on this voyage? You have!'

'Ill?' Her airy little voice mocked him. She stepped over the rugs, came up close, touched his breast, and looked up at him.

'Darling,' she said, 'don't frighten me. Of course I haven't! Whatever makes you think I have? Do I look ill?'

But Hammond didn't see her. He only felt that she was looking at him and that there was no need to worry about anything. She was here to look after things. It was all right. Everything was.

The gentle pressure of her hand was so calming that he put his over hers to hold it there. And she said:

'Stand still. I want to look at you. I haven't seen you yet. You've had your beard beautifully trimmed, and you look – younger, I think, and decidedly thinner! Bachelor life agrees with you.'

'Agrees with me!' He groaned for love and caught her close again. And again, as always, he had the feeling he was holding something that never was quite his – his. Something too delicate, too precious, that would fly away once he let go.

'For God's sake let's get off to the hotel so that we can be by ourselves!' And he rang the bell hard for someone to look sharp with the luggage.

Walking down the wharf together she took his arm. He had her on his arm again. And the difference it made to get into the cab after Janey – to throw the red-and-yellow striped blanket round them both – to tell the driver to hurry because neither of them had had any tea. No more going without his tea or pouring out his own. She was back. He turned to her, squeezed her hand, and said gently, teasingly, in the 'special' voice he had for her: 'Glad to be home again, dearie?' She smiled; she didn't even bother to answer, but gently she drew his hand away as they came to the brighter streets.

'We've got the best room in the hotel,' he said. 'I wouldn't be put off with another. And I asked the chambermaid to put in a bit of a fire in case you felt chilly. She's a nice, attentive girl. And I thought now we were here we wouldn't bother to go home tomorrow, but spend the day looking round and leave the morning after. Does that suit you? There's no hurry, is there? The children will have you soon enough . . . I thought a day's sight-seeing might make a nice break in your journey – eh, Janey?'

'Have you taken the tickets for the day after?' she asked.

'I should think I have!' He unbuttoned his overcoat and took out his bulging pocket-book. 'Here we are! I reserved a first-class carriage to Salisbury. There it is – "Mr *and* Mrs John Hammond." I thought we might as well do ourselves comfortably, and we don't want other people butting in, do we? But if you'd like to stop here a bit longer – ?'

'Oh no!' said Janey quickly. 'Not for the world! The day after to-morrow, then. And the children –'

But they had reached the hotel. The manager was standing in the broad, brilliantly lighted porch. He came down to greet them. A porter ran from the hall for their boxes.

'Well, Mr Arnold, here's Mrs Hammond at last!'

The manager led them through the hall himself and pressed the elevator-bell. Hammond knew there were business pals of his sitting at the little hall tables having a drink before dinner. But he wasn't going to risk interruption; he looked neither to the right nor the left. They could think what they pleased. If they didn't understand, the more fools they – and he stepped out of the lift, unlocked the door of their room and shepherded Janey in. The door shut. Now, at last, they were alone together. He turned up the light. The curtains were drawn; the fire blazed. He flung his hat on to the huge bed and went towards her.

But – would you believe it! – again they were interrupted. This time it was the porter with the luggage. He made two journeys of it, leaving the door open in between, taking his time, whistling through his teeth in the corridor. Hammond paced up and down the room, tearing off his gloves, tearing off his scarf. Finally he flung his overcoat on to the bedside.

At last the fool was gone. The door clicked. Now they *were* alone. Said Hammond: 'I feel I'll never have you to myself again. These cursed people! Janey' – and he bent his flushed, eager gaze upon her – 'let's have dinner up here. If we go down to the restaurant we'll be interrupted, and then there's the confounded music' (the music he'd praised so highly, applauded so loudly last night!). 'We shan't be able to hear each other speak. Let's have something up here in front of the fire. It's too late for tea. I'll order a little supper, shall I? How does the idea strike you?'

'Do, darling!' said Janey. 'And while you're away – the children's letters –'

'Oh, later on will do!' said Hammond.

'But then we'd get it over,' said Janey. 'And I'd first have time to –'

'Oh, I needn't go down!' explained Hammond. 'I'll just ring and give the order . . . you don't want to send me away, do you?'

Janey shook her head and smiled.

'But you're thinking of something else. You're worrying about something,' said Hammond. 'What is it? Come and sit here – come and sit on my knee before the fire.'

'I'll just unpin my hat,' said Janey, and she went over to the dressing-table. 'A-ah!' She gave a little cry.

'What is it?'

'Nothing, darling. I've just found the children's letters. That's all right! They will keep. No hurry now!' She turned to him, clasping them. She tucked them into her frilled blouse. She cried quickly, gaily: 'Oh, how typical this dressing-table is of you!'

'Why? What's the matter with it?' said Hammond.

'If it were floating in eternity I should say "John!"' laughed Janey, staring at the big bottle of hair tonic, the wicker bottle of eau-de-Cologne, the two hairbrushes and a dozen new collars tied with pink tape. 'Is this all your luggage?'

'Hang my luggage!' said Hammond; but all the same he liked being laughed at by Janey. 'Let's talk. Let's get down to things. Tell me' – and as Janey perched on his knees he leaned back and drew her into the deep, ugly chair – 'tell me you're really glad to be back, Janey.'

'Yes, darling, I am glad,' she said.

But just as when he embraced her he felt she would fly away, so Hammond never knew – never knew for dead certain that she was as glad as he was. How could he know? Would he ever know? Would he always have this craving – this pang like hunger, somehow, to make Janey so much part of him that there wasn't any of her to escape? He wanted to blot out everybody, everything. He wished now he'd turned off the light. That might have brought her nearer. And now those letters from the children rustled in her blouse. He could have chucked them into the fire.

'Janey,' he whispered.

'Yes, dear?' She lay on his breast, but so lightly, so remotely. Their breathing rose and fell together.

'Janey!'

'What is it?'

'Turn to me,' he whispered. A slow, deep flush flowed into his forehead. 'Kiss me, Janey! You kiss me!'

It seemed to him there was a tiny pause – but long enough for him to suffer torture – before her lips touched his, firmly, lightly – kissing them as she always kissed him, as though the kiss – how could he describe it? – confirmed what they were saying, signed the contract. But that wasn't what he wanted; that wasn't at all what he thirsted for. He felt suddenly, horribly tired.

'If you knew,' he said, opening his eyes, 'what it's been like – waiting today. I thought the boat never would come in. There we were, hanging about. What kept you so long?'

She made no answer. She was looking away from him at the fire. The flames hurried – hurried over the coals, flickered, fell.

'Not asleep, are you?' said Hammond, and he jumped her up and down.

'No,' she said. And then: 'Don't do that, dear. No, I was thinking. As a matter of fact,' she said, 'one of the passengers died last night – a man. That's what held us up. We brought him in – I mean, he wasn't buried at sea. So, of course, the ship's doctor and the shore doctor –'

'What was it?' asked Hammond uneasily. He hated to hear of death. He hated this to have happened. It was, in some queer way, as though he and Janey had met a funeral on their way to the hotel.

'Oh, it wasn't anything in the least infectious!' said Janey. She was speaking scarcely above her breath. 'It was *heart*.' A pause. 'Poor fellow!' she said. 'Quite young.' And she watched the fire flicker and fall. 'He died in my arms,' said Janey.

The blow was so sudden that Hammond thought he would faint. He couldn't move; he couldn't breathe. He felt all his strength flowing – flowing into the big dark chair, and the big dark chair held him fast, gripped him, forced him to bear it.

'What?' he said dully. 'What's that you say?'

'The end was quite peaceful,' said the small voice. 'He just' – and Hammond saw her lift her gentle hand – 'breathed his life away at the end.' And her hand fell.

'Who – else was there?' Hammond managed to ask.

'Nobody. I was alone with him.'

Ah, my God, what was she saying! What was she doing to him! This would kill him! And all the while she spoke:

'I saw the change coming and I sent the steward for the doctor, but the doctor was too late. He couldn't have done anything, anyway.'

'But – why *you*, why *you*?' moaned Hammond.

At that Janey turned quickly, quickly searched his face.

'You don't *mind*, John, do you?' she asked. 'You don't – It's nothing to do with you and me.'

Somehow or other he managed to shake some sort of smile at her. Somehow or other he stammered: 'No – go – on, go on! I want you to tell me.'

'But, John darling –'

'Tell me, Janey!'

'There's nothing to tell,' she said, wondering. 'He was one of the first-class passengers. I saw he was very ill when he came on board . . . But he seemed to be so much better until yesterday. He had a severe attack in the afternoon – excitement – nervousness, I think, about arriving. And after that he never recovered.'

'But why didn't the stewardess –'

'Oh, my dear – the stewardess!' said Janey. 'What would he have felt? And besides . . . he might have wanted to leave a message . . . to –'

'Didn't he?' muttered Hammond. 'Didn't he say anything?'

'No, darling, not a word!' She shook her head softly. 'All the time I was with him he was too weak . . . he was too weak even to move a finger . . .'

Janey was silent. But her words, so light, so soft, so chill, seemed to hover in the air, to rain into his breast like snow.

The fire had gone red. Now it fell in with a sharp sound and the room was colder. Cold crept up his arms. The room was huge, immense, glittering. It filled his whole world. There was the great blind bed, with his coat flung across it like some headless man saying his prayers. There was the luggage, ready to be carried away again, anywhere, tossed into trains, carted on to boats.

. . . 'He was too weak. He was too weak to move a finger.' And yet he died in Janey's arms. She – who'd never – never once in all these years – never on one single solitary occasion –

No; he mustn't think of it. Madness lay in thinking of it. No, he wouldn't face it. He couldn't stand it. It was too much to bear!

And now Janey touched his tie with her fingers. She pinched the edges of the tie together.

'You're not – sorry I told you, John darling? It hasn't made you sad? It hasn't spoilt our evening – our being alone together?'

But at that he had to hide his face. He put his face into her bosom and his arms enfolded her.

Spoilt their evening! Spoilt their being alone together! They would never be alone together again.

(written 1920, first published in 1921, first book publication
The Garden Party and Other Stories, 1922)

Miss Brill

Although it was so brilliantly fine – the blue sky powdered with gold and the great spots of light like white wine splashed over the Jardins Publiques – Miss Brill was glad that she had decided on her fur. The air was motionless, but when you opened your mouth there was just a faint chill, like a chill from a glass of iced water before you sip, and now and again a leaf came drifting – from nowhere, from the sky. Miss Brill put up her hand and touched her fur. Dear little thing! It was nice to feel it again. She had taken it out of its box that afternoon, shaken out the moth-powder, given it a good brush, and rubbed the life back into the dim little eyes. 'What has been happening to me?' said the sad little eyes. Oh, how sweet it was to see them snap at her again from the red eiderdown! . . . But the nose, which was of some black composition, wasn't at all firm. It must have had a knock, somehow. Never mind – a little dab of black sealing-wax when the time came – when it was absolutely necessary . . . Little rogue! Yes, she really felt like that about it. Little rogue biting its tail just by her left ear. She could have taken it off and laid it on her lap and stroked it. She felt a tingling in her hands and arms, but that came from walking, she supposed. And when she breathed, something light and sad – no, not sad, exactly – something gentle seemed to move in her bosom.

There were a number of people out this afternoon, far more than last Sunday. And the band sounded louder and gayer. That was because the Season had begun. For although the band played all the year round on Sundays, out of season it was never the same. It was like someone playing with only the family to listen; it didn't care how it played if there weren't any strangers present. Wasn't the conductor wearing a new coat, too? She was sure it was new. He scraped with his foot and flapped his arms like a rooster about to crow, and the bandsmen sitting in the green rotunda blew out their cheeks and glared at the music. Now there came a little 'flutey' bit – very pretty! – a little chain of bright drops. She was sure it would be repeated. It was; she lifted her head and smiled.

Only two people shared her 'special' seat: a fine old man in a velvet coat, his hands clasped over a huge carved walking-stick, and a big old woman, sitting upright, with a roll of knitting on her embroidered apron. They did not speak. This was disappointing, for Miss Brill always looked forward to the conversation. She had become really quite expert, she thought, at listening as though she didn't listen, at sitting in other people's lives just for a minute while they talked round her.

She glanced, sideways, at the old couple. Perhaps they would go soon. Last Sunday, too, hadn't been as interesting as usual. An Englishman and his wife, he wearing a dreadful Panama hat and she button boots. And she'd gone on the whole time about how she ought to wear spectacles; she knew she needed them; but that it was no good getting any; they'd be sure to break and they'd never keep on. And he'd been so patient. He'd suggested everything – gold rims, the kind that curved round your ears, little pads inside the bridge. No, nothing would please her. 'They'll always be sliding down my nose!' Miss Brill had wanted to shake her.

The old people sat on the bench, still as statues. Never mind, there was always the crowd to watch. To and fro, in front of the flower-beds and the band rotunda, the couples and groups paraded, stopped to talk, to greet, to buy a handful of flowers from the old beggar who had his tray fixed to the railings. Little children ran among them, swooping and laughing; little boys with big white silk bows under their chins; little girls, little French dolls, dressed up in velvet and lace. And sometimes a tiny staggerer came suddenly rocking into the open from under the trees, stopped, stared, as suddenly sat down 'flop', until its small high-stepping mother, like a young hen, rushed scolding to its rescue. Other people sat on the benches and green chairs, but they were nearly always the same, Sunday after Sunday, and – Miss Brill had often noticed – there was something funny about nearly all of them. They were odd, silent, nearly all old, and from the way they stared they looked as though they'd just come from dark little rooms or even – even cupboards!

Behind the rotunda the slender trees with yellow leaves down drooping, and through them just a line of sea, and beyond the blue sky with gold-veined clouds.

Tum-tum-tum tiddle-um! tiddle-um! tum tiddley-um tum ta! blew the band.

Two young girls in red came by and two young soldiers in blue met them, and they laughed and paired and went off arm in arm. Two peasant women with funny straw hats passed, gravely, leading beautiful smoke-coloured donkeys. A cold, pale nun hurried by. A beautiful woman came along and dropped her bunch of violets, and a little boy ran after to hand them to her, and she took them and threw them away as if they'd been poisoned. Dear me! Miss Brill didn't know whether to admire that or not! And now an ermine toque and a gentleman in grey met just in front of her. He was tall, stiff, dignified, and she was wearing the ermine toque she'd bought when her hair was yellow. Now everything, her hair, her face, even her eyes, was the same colour as the shabby ermine, and her hand, in its cleaned glove, lifted to dab her lips, was a tiny yellowish paw. Oh, she was so pleased to see him – delighted! She rather thought they were going to meet that afternoon. She described where she'd been – everywhere, here, there, along by the sea. The day was so charming – didn't he agree? And wouldn't he, perhaps? . . . But he shook his head, lighted a cigarette, slowly breathed a great deep puff into her face and, even while she was still talking and laughing, flicked the match away and walked on. The ermine toque was alone; she smiled more brightly than ever. But even the band seemed to know what she was feeling and played more softly, played tenderly, and the drum beat 'The Brute! The Brute!' over and over. What would she do? What was going to happen now? But as Miss Brill wondered, the ermine toque turned, raised her hand as though she'd seen someone else, much nicer, just over there, and pattered away. And the band changed again and played more quickly, more gaily than ever, and the old couple on Miss Brill's seat got up and marched away, and such a funny old man with long whiskers hobbled along in time to the music and was nearly knocked over by four girls walking abreast.

Oh, how fascinating it was! How she enjoyed it! How she loved sitting here, watching it all! It was like a play. It was exactly like a play. Who could believe the sky at the back wasn't painted? But it wasn't till a little brown dog trotted on solemnly and then slowly trotted off, like a little 'theatre' dog, a little dog that had been drugged, that Miss Brill discovered what it was that made it so exciting. They were all on the stage. They weren't only the audience, not only looking on; they were acting. Even she had a part and came every Sunday. No doubt somebody would have noticed if she hadn't been there; she was part of the performance, after all. How strange she'd never thought of it like that before! And yet it explained why she made such a point of starting from home at just the same time each week – so as not to be late for the performance – and it also explained why she had quite a queer, shy feeling at telling her English pupils how she spent her Sunday afternoons. No wonder! Miss Brill nearly laughed out loud. She was on the stage. She thought of the old invalid gentleman to whom she read the newspaper four afternoons a week while he slept in the garden. She had got quite used to the frail head on the cotton pillow, the hollowed eyes, the open mouth and the high pinched nose. If he'd been dead she mightn't have noticed for weeks; she wouldn't have minded. But suddenly he knew he was having the paper read to him by an actress! 'An actress!' The old head lifted; two points of light quivered in the old eyes. 'An actress – are ye?' And Miss Brill smoothed the newspaper as though it were the manuscript of her part and said gently: 'Yes, I have been an actress for a long time.'

The band had been having a rest. Now they started again. And what they played was warm, sunny, yet there was just a faint chill – a something, what was it? – not sadness – no, not sadness – a something that made you want to sing. The tune lifted, lifted, the light shone; and it seemed to Miss Brill that in another moment all of them, all the whole company, would begin singing. The young ones, the laughing ones who were moving together, they would begin, and the men's voices, very resolute and brave, would join them. And then she too, she too, and the others on the benches – they would come in with a kind of accompaniment – something low, that scarcely rose or fell, something so beautiful – moving . . . And Miss Brill's eyes filled with tears and she looked smiling at all the other members of the company. Yes, we understand, we understand, she thought – though what they understood she didn't know.

Just at that moment a boy and a girl came and sat down where the old couple had been. They were beautifully dressed; they were in love. The hero and heroine, of course, just arrived from his father's yacht. And still soundlessly singing, still with that trembling smile, Miss Brill prepared to listen.

'No, not now,' said the girl. 'Not here, I can't.'

'But why? Because of that stupid old thing at the end there?' asked the boy. 'Why does she come here at all – who wants her? Why doesn't she keep her silly old mug at home?'

'It's her fu-fur which is so funny,' giggled the girl. 'It's exactly like a fried whiting.'

'Ah, be off with you!' said the boy in an angry whisper. Then: 'Tell me, ma petite chère –'

'No, not here,' said the girl. 'Not *yet*.'

On her way home she usually bought a slice of honey-cake at the baker's. It was her Sunday treat. Sometimes there was an almond in her slice, sometimes not. It made a great difference. If there was an almond it was like carrying home a tiny present – a surprise – something that might very well not have been there. She hurried on the almond Sundays and struck the match for the kettle in quite a dashing way.

But today she passed the baker's by, climbed the stairs, went into the little dark room – her room like a cupboard – and sat down on the red eiderdown. She sat there for a long time. The box that the fur came out of was on the bed. She unclasped the necklet quickly; quickly, without looking, laid it inside. But when she put the lid on she thought she heard something crying.

(written 1920, first published in 1920, first book publication
The Garden Party and Other Stories, 1922)

The Daughters of the Late Colonel

I

The week after was one of the busiest weeks of their lives. Even when they went to bed it was only their bodies that lay down and rested; their minds went on, thinking things out, talking things over, wondering, deciding, trying to remember where . . .

Constantia lay like a statue, her hands by her sides, her feet just overlapping each other, the sheet up to her chin. She stared at the ceiling.

'Do you think father would mind if we gave his top-hat to the porter?'

'The porter?' snapped Josephine. 'Why ever the porter? What a very extraordinary idea!'

'Because,' said Constantia slowly, 'he must often have to go to funerals. And I noticed at – at the cemetery that he only had a bowler.' She paused. 'I thought then how very much he'd appreciate a top-hat. We ought to give him a present, too. He was always very nice to father.'

'But,' cried Josephine, flouncing on her pillow and staring across the dark at Constantia, 'father's head!' And suddenly, for one awful moment, she nearly giggled. Not, of course, that she felt in the least like giggling. It must have been habit. Years ago, when they had stayed awake at night talking, their beds had simply heaved. And now the porter's head, disappearing, popped out, like a candle, under father's hat . . . The giggle mounted, mounted; she clenched her hands; she fought it down; she frowned fiercely at the dark and said 'Remember' terribly sternly.

'We can decide tomorrow,' she said.

Constantia had noticed nothing; she sighed.

'Do you think we ought to have our dressing-gowns dyed as well?'

'Black?' almost shrieked Josephine.

'Well, what else?' said Constantia. 'I was thinking – it doesn't seem quite sincere, in a way, to wear black out of doors and when we're fully dressed, and then when we're at home –'

'But nobody sees us,' said Josephine. She gave the bedclothes such a twitch that both her feet became uncovered and she had to creep up the pillows to get them well under again.

'Kate does,' said Constantia. 'And the postman very well might.'

Josephine thought of her dark-red slippers, which matched her dressing-gown, and of Constantia's favourite indefinite green ones which went with hers. Black! Two black dressing-gowns and two pairs of black woolly slippers, creeping off to the bathroom like black cats.

'I don't think it's absolutely necessary,' said she.

Silence. Then Constantia said, 'We shall have to post the papers with the notice in them tomorrow to catch the Ceylon mail . . . How many letters have we had up till now?'

'Twenty-three.'

Josephine had replied to them all, and twenty-three times when she came to 'We miss our dear father so much' she had broken down and had to use her handkerchief, and on some of them even to soak up a very light-blue tear with an edge of blotting-paper. Strange! She couldn't have put it on – but twenty-three times. Even now, though, when she said over to herself sadly 'We miss our dear father *so* much,' she could have cried if she'd wanted to.

'Have you got enough stamps?' came from Constantia.

'Oh, how can I tell?' said Josephine crossly. 'What's the good of asking me that now?'

'I was just wondering,' said Constantia mildly.

Silence again. There came a little rustle, a scurry, a hop.

'A mouse,' said Constantia.

'It can't be a mouse because there aren't any crumbs,' said Josephine.

'But it doesn't know there aren't,' said Constantia.

A spasm of pity squeezed her heart. Poor little thing! She wished she'd left a tiny piece of biscuit on the dressing-table. It was awful to think of it not finding anything. What would it do?

'I can't think how they manage to live at all,' she said slowly.

'Who?' demanded Josephine.

And Constantia said more loudly than she meant to, 'Mice.'

Josephine was furious. 'Oh, what nonsense, Con!' she said. 'What have mice got to do with it? You're asleep.'

'I don't think I am,' said Constantia. She shut her eyes to make sure. She was.

Josephine arched her spine, pulled up her knees, folded her arms so that her fists came under her ears, and pressed her cheek hard against the pillow.

II

Another thing which complicated matters was they had Nurse Andrews staying on with them that week. It was their own fault; they had asked her. It was Josephine's idea. On the morning – well, on the last morning, when the doctor had gone, Josephine had said to Constantia, 'Don't you think it would be rather nice if we asked Nurse Andrews to stay on for a week as our guest?'

'Very nice,' said Constantia.

'I thought,' went on Josephine quickly, 'I should just say this afternoon, after I've paid her, "My sister and I would be very pleased, after all you've done for us, Nurse Andrews, if you would stay on for a week as our guest." I'd have to put that in about being our guest in case –'

'Oh, but she could hardly expect to be paid!' cried Constantia.

'One never knows,' said Josephine sagely.

Nurse Andrews had, of course, jumped at the idea. But it was a bother. It meant they had to have regular sit-down meals at the proper times, whereas if they'd been alone they could just have asked Kate if she wouldn't have minded bringing them a tray wherever they were. And meal-times now that the strain was over were rather a trial.

Nurse Andrews was simply fearful about butter. Really they couldn't help feeling that about butter, at least, she took advantage of their kindness. And she had that maddening habit of asking for just an inch more bread to finish what she had on her plate, and then, at the last mouthful, absent-mindedly – of course it wasn't absent-mindedly – taking another helping. Josephine got very red when this happened, and she fastened her small, bead-like eyes on the tablecloth as if she saw a minute strange insect creeping through the web of it. But Constantia's long, pale face lengthened and set, and she gazed away – away – far over the desert, to where that line of camels unwound like a thread of wool . . .

'When I was with Lady Tukes,' said Nurse Andrews, 'she had such a dainty little contrayvance for the buttah. It was a silvah Cupid balanced on the – on the bordah of a glass dish, holding a tayny fork. And when you wanted some buttah you simply pressed his foot and he bent down and speared you a piece. It was quite a gayme.'

Josephine could hardly bear that. But 'I think those things are very extravagant' was all she said.

'But whey?' asked Nurse Andrews, beaming through her eyeglasses. 'No one, surely, would take more buttah than one wanted – would one?'

'Ring, Con,' cried Josephine. She couldn't trust herself to reply.

And proud young Kate, the enchanted princess, came in to see what the old tabbies wanted now. She snatched away their plates of mock something or other and slapped down a white, terrified blancmange.

'Jam, please, Kate,' said Josephine kindly.

Kate knelt and burst open the sideboard, lifted the lid of the jam-pot, saw it was empty, put it on the table, and stalked off.

'I'm afraid,' said Nurse Andrews a moment later, 'there isn't any.'

'Oh, what a bother!' said Josephine. She bit her lip. 'What had we better do?'

Constantia looked dubious. 'We can't disturb Kate again,' she said softly.

Nurse Andrews waited, smiling at them both. Her eyes wandered, spying at everything behind her eyeglasses. Constantia in despair went back to her camels. Josephine frowned heavily – concentrated. If it hadn't been for this idiotic woman she and Con would, of course, have eaten their blancmange without. Suddenly the idea came.

'I know,' she said. 'Marmalade. There's some marmalade in the sideboard. Get it, Con.'

'I hope,' laughed Nurse Andrews – and her laugh was like a spoon tinkling against a medicine-glass – 'I hope it's not very bittah marmalayde.'

III

But, after all, it was not long now, and then she'd be gone for good. And there was no getting over the fact that she had been very kind to father. She had nursed him day and night at the end. Indeed, both Constantia and Josephine felt privately she had rather overdone the not leaving him at the very last. For when they had gone in to say goodbye Nurse Andrews had sat beside his bed the whole time, holding his wrist and pretending to look at her watch. It couldn't have been necessary. It was so tactless, too. Supposing father had wanted to say something – something private to them. Not that he had. Oh, far from it! He lay there, purple, a dark, angry purple in the face, and never even looked at them when they came in. Then, as they were standing there, wondering what to do, he had suddenly opened one eye. Oh, what a difference it would have made, what a difference to their memory of him, how much easier to tell people about it, if he had only opened both! But no – one eye only. It glared at them a moment and then . . . went out.

IV

It had made it very awkward for them when Mr Farolles, of St John's, called the same afternoon.

'The end was quite peaceful, I trust?' were the first words he said as he glided towards them through the dark drawing-room.

'Quite,' said Josephine faintly. They both hung their heads. Both of them felt certain that eye wasn't at all a peaceful eye.

'Won't you sit down?' said Josephine.

'Thank you, Miss Pinner,' said Mr Farolles gratefully. He folded his coat-tails and began to lower himself into father's armchair but just as he touched it he almost sprang up and slid into the next chair instead.

He coughed. Josephine clasped her hands; Constantia looked vague.

'I want you to feel, Miss Pinner,' said Mr Farolles, 'and you, Miss Constantia, that I'm trying to be helpful. I want to be helpful to you both, if you will let me. These are the times,' said Mr Farolles, very simply and earnestly, 'when God means us to be helpful to one another.'

'Thank you very much, Mr Farolles,' said Josephine and Constantia.

'Not at all,' said Mr Farolles gently. He drew his kid gloves through his fingers and leaned forward. 'And if either of you would like a little Communion, either or both of you, here *and* now, you have only to tell me. A little Communion is often very help – a great comfort,' he added tenderly.

But the idea of a little Communion terrified them. What! In the drawing-room by themselves – with no – no altar or anything! The piano would be much too high, thought Constantia, and Mr Farolles could not possibly lean over it with the chalice. And Kate would be sure to come bursting in and interrupt them, thought Josephine. And supposing the bell rang in the middle? It might be somebody important – about their mourning. Would they get up reverently and go out, or would they have to wait . . . in torture?

'Perhaps you will send round a note by your good Kate if you would care for it later,' said Mr Farolles.

'Oh yes, thank you very much!' they both said.

Mr Farolles got up and took his black straw hat from the round table.

'And about the funeral,' he said softly. 'I may arrange that – as your dear father's old friend and yours, Miss Pinner – and Miss Constantia?'

Josephine and Constantia got up too.

'I should like it to be quite simple,' said Josephine firmly, 'and not too expensive. At the same time, I should like –'

'A good one that will last,' thought dreamy Constantia, as if Josephine were buying a nightgown. But, of course, Josephine didn't say that. 'One suitable to our father's position.' She was very nervous.

'I'll run round to our good friend Mr Knight,' said Mr Farolles soothingly. 'I will ask him to come and see you. I am sure you will find him very helpful indeed.'

V

Well, at any rate, all that part of it was over, though neither of them could possibly believe that father was never coming back. Josephine had had a moment of absolute terror at the cemetery, while the coffin was lowered, to think that she and Constantia had done this thing without asking his permission. What would father say when he found out? For he was bound to find out sooner or later. He always did. 'Buried. You two girls had me *buried*!' She heard his stick thumping. Oh, what would they say? What possible excuse could they make? It sounded such an appallingly heartless thing to do. Such a wicked advantage to take of a person because he happened to be helpless at the moment. The other people seemed to treat it all as a matter of course. They were strangers; they couldn't be expected to understand that father was the very last person for such a thing to happen to. No, the entire blame for it all would fall on her and Constantia. And the expense, she thought, stepping into the tight-buttoned cab. When she had to show him the bills. What would he say then?

She heard him absolutely roaring. 'And do you expect me to pay for this gimcrack excursion of yours?'

'Oh,' groaned poor Josephine aloud, 'we shouldn't have done it, Con!'

And Constantia, pale as a lemon in all that blackness, said in a frightened whisper, 'Done what, Jug?'

'Let them bu-bury father like that,' said Josephine, breaking down and crying into her new, queer-smelling mourning handkerchief.

'But what else could we have done?' asked Constantia wonder-ingly. 'We couldn't have kept him, Jug – we couldn't have kept him unburied. At any rate, not in a flat that size.'

Josephine blew her nose; the cab was dreadfully stuffy.

'I don't know,' she said forlornly. 'It is all so dreadful. I feel we ought to have tried to, just for a time at least. To make perfectly sure. One thing's certain' – and her tears sprang out again – 'father will never forgive us for this – never!'

VI

Father would never forgive them. That was what they felt more than ever when, two mornings later, they went into his room to go through his things. They had discussed it quite calmly. It was even down on Josephine's list of things to be done. *Go through father's things and settle about them.* But that was a very different matter from saying after breakfast:

'Well, are you ready, Con?'

'Yes, Jug – when you are.'

'Then I think we'd better get it over.'

It was dark in the hall. It had been a rule for years never to disturb father in the morning, whatever happened. And now they were going to open the door without knocking even . . . Constantia's eyes were enormous at the idea; Josephine felt weak in the knees.

'You – you go first,' she gasped, pushing Constantia.

But Constantia said, as she always had said on those occasions, 'No, Jug, that's not fair. You're eldest.'

Josephine was just going to say – what at other times she wouldn't have owned to for the world – what she kept for her very last weapon, 'But you're tallest,' when they noticed that the kitchen door was open, and there stood Kate . . .

'Very stiff,' said Josephine, grasping the door-handle and doing her best to turn it. As if anything ever deceived Kate!

It couldn't be helped. That girl was . . . Then the door was shut behind them, but – but they weren't in father's room at all. They might have suddenly walked through the wall by mistake into a different flat altogether. Was the door just behind them? They were too frightened to look. Josephine knew that if it was it was holding itself tight shut; Constantia felt that, like the doors in dreams, it hadn't any handle at all. It was the coldness which made it so awful. Or the whiteness – which? Everything was covered. The blinds were down, a cloth hung over the mirror, a sheet hid the bed; a huge fan of white paper filled the fire-place. Constantia timidly put out her hand; she almost expected a snowflake to fall. Josephine felt a queer tingling in her nose, as if her nose was freezing. Then a cab klop-klopped over the cobbles below, and the quiet seemed to shake into little pieces.

'I had better pull up a blind,' said Josephine bravely.

'Yes, it might be a good idea,' whispered Constantia.

They only gave the blind a touch, but it flew up and the cord flew after, rolling round the blind-stick, and the little tassel tapped as if trying to get free. That was too much for Constantia.

'Don't you think – don't you think we might put it off for another day?' she whispered.

'Why?' snapped Josephine, feeling, as usual, much better now that she knew for certain that Constantia was terrified. 'It's got to be done. But I do wish you wouldn't whisper, Con.'

'I didn't know I was whispering,' whispered Constantia.

'And why do you keep on staring at the bed?' said Josephine, raising her voice almost defiantly. 'There's nothing *on* the bed.'

'Oh, Jug, don't say so!' said poor Connie. 'At any rate, not so loudly.'

Josephine felt herself that she had gone too far. She took a wide swerve over to the chest of drawers, put out her hand, but quickly drew it back again.

'Connie!' she gasped, and she wheeled round and leaned with her back against the chest of drawers.

'Oh, Jug – what?'

Josephine could only glare. She had the most extraordinary feeling that she had just escaped something simply awful. But how could she explain to Constantia that father was in the chest of drawers? He was in the top drawer with his handkerchiefs and neckties, or in the next with his shirts and pyjamas, or in the lowest of all with his suits. He was watching there, hidden away – just behind the door-handle – ready to spring.

She pulled a funny old-fashioned face at Constantia, just as she used to in the old days when she was going to cry.

'I can't open,' she nearly wailed.

'No, don't, Jug,' whispered Constantia earnestly. 'It's much better not to. Don't let's open anything. At any rate, not for a long time.'

'But – but it seems so weak,' said Josephine, breaking down.

'But why not be weak for once, Jug?' argued Constantia, whispering quite fiercely. 'If it is weak.' And her pale stare flew from the locked writing-table – so safe – to the huge glittering wardrobe, and she began to breathe in a queer, panting way. 'Why shouldn't we be weak for once in our lives, Jug? It's quite excusable. Let's be weak – be weak, Jug. It's much nicer to be weak than to be strong.'

And then she did one of those amazingly bold things that she'd done about twice before in their lives: she marched over to the wardrobe, turned the key, and took it out of the lock. Took it out of the lock and held it up to Josephine, showing Josephine by her extraordinary smile that she knew what she'd done – she'd risked deliberately father being in there among his overcoats.

If the huge wardrobe had lurched forward, had crashed down on Constantia, Josephine wouldn't have been surprised. On the contrary, she would have thought it the only suitable thing to happen. But nothing happened. Only the room seemed quieter than ever, and bigger flakes of cold air fell on Josephine's shoulders and knees. She began to shiver.

'Come, Jug,' said Constantia, still with that awful callous smile; and Josephine followed just as she had that last time, when Constantia had pushed Benny into the round pond.

VII

But the strain told on them when they were back in the dining-room. They sat down, very shaky, and looked at each other.

'I don't feel I can settle to anything,' said Josephine, 'until I've had something. Do you think we could ask Kate for two cups of hot water?'

'I really don't see why we shouldn't,' said Constantia carefully. She was quite normal again. 'I won't ring. I'll go to the kitchen door and ask her.'

'Yes, do,' said Josephine, sinking down into a chair. 'Tell her, just two cups, Con, nothing else – on a tray.'

'She needn't even put the jug on, need she?' said Constantia, as though Kate might very well complain if the jug had been there.

'Oh no, certainly not! The jug's not at all necessary. She can pour it direct out of the kettle,' cried Josephine, feeling that would be a labour-saving indeed.

Their cold lips quivered at the greenish brims. Josephine curved her small red hands round the cup; Constantia sat up and blew on the wavy steam, making it flutter from one side to the other.

'Speaking of Benny,' said Josephine.

And though Benny hadn't been mentioned Constantia immediately looked as though he had.

'He'll expect us to send him something of father's, of course. But it's so difficult to know what to send to Ceylon.'

'You mean things get unstuck so on the voyage,' murmured Constantia.

'No, lost,' said Josephine sharply. 'You know there's no post. Only runners.'

Both paused to watch a black man in white linen drawers running through the pale fields for dear life, with a large brown-paper parcel in his hands. Josephine's black man was tiny; he scurried along glistening like an ant. But there was something blind and tireless about

Constantia's tall, thin fellow, which made him, she decided, a very unpleasant person indeed . . . On the veranda, dressed all in white and wearing a cork helmet, stood Benny. His right hand shook up and down, as father's did when he was impatient. And behind him, not in the least interested, sat Hilda, the unknown sister-in-law. She swung in a cane rocker and flicked over the leaves of the *Tatler*.

'I think his watch would be the most suitable present,' said Josephine.

Constantia looked up; she seemed surprised.

'Oh, would you trust a gold watch to a native?'

'But, of course, I'd disguise it,' said Josephine. 'No one would know it was a watch.' She liked the idea of having to make a parcel such a curious shape that no one could possibly guess what it was. She even thought for a moment of hiding the watch in a narrow cardboard corset-box that she'd kept by her for a long time, waiting for it to come in for something. It was such beautiful, firm cardboard. But, no, it wouldn't be appropriate for this occasion. It had lettering on it: *Medium Women's* 28. *Extra Firm Busks*. It would be almost too much of a surprise for Benny to open that and find father's watch inside.

'And, of course, it isn't as though it would be going – ticking, I mean,' said Constantia, who was still thinking of the native love of jewellery. 'At least,' she added, 'it would be very strange if after all that time it was.'

VIII

Josephine made no reply. She had flown off on one of her tangents. She had suddenly thought of Cyril. Wasn't it more usual for the only grandson to have the watch? And then dear Cyril was so appreciative and a gold watch meant so much to a young man. Benny, in all prob-ability, had quite got out of the habit of watches; men so seldom wore waistcoats in those hot climates. Whereas Cyril in London wore them from year's end to year's end. And it would be so nice for her and Constantia, when he came to tea, to know it was there. 'I see you've got on grandfather's watch, Cyril.' It would be somehow so satisfactory.

Dear boy! What a blow his sweet, sympathetic little note had been! Of course they quite understood; but it was most unfortunate.

'It would have been such a point, having him,' said Josephine.

'And he would have enjoyed it so,' said Constantia, not thinking what she was saying.

However, as soon as he got back he was coming to tea with his aunties. Cyril to tea was one of their rare treats.

'Now, Cyril, you mustn't be frightened of our cakes. Your Auntie Con and I bought them at Buzzard's this morning. We know what a man's appetite is. So don't be ashamed of making a good tea.'

Josephine cut recklessly into the rich dark cake that stood for her winter gloves or the soling and heeling of Constantia's only respectable shoes. But Cyril was most unmanlike in appetite.

'I say, Aunt Josephine, I simply can't. I've only just had lunch, you know.'

'Oh, Cyril, that can't be true! It's after four,' cried Josephine. Constantia sat with her knife poised over the chocolate-roll.

'It is, all the same,' said Cyril. 'I had to meet a man at Victoria, and he kept me hanging about till . . . there was only time to get lunch and to come on here. And he gave me – phew' – Cyril put his hand to his forehead – 'a terrific blow-out,' he said.

It was disappointing – today of all days. But still he couldn't be expected to know.

'But you'll have a meringue, won't you, Cyril?' said Aunt Josephine. 'These meringues were bought specially for you. Your dear father was so fond of them. We were sure you are, too.'

'I *am*, Aunt Josephine,' cried Cyril ardently. 'Do you mind if I take half to begin with?'

'Not at all, dear boy; but we mustn't let you off with that.'

'Is your dear father still so fond of meringues?' asked Auntie Con gently. She winced faintly as she broke through the shell of hers.

'Well, I don't quite know, Auntie Con,' said Cyril breezily.

At that they both looked up.

'Don't know?' almost snapped Josephine. 'Don't know a thing like that about your own father, Cyril?'

'Surely,' said Auntie Con softly.

Cyril tried to laugh it off. 'Oh, well,' he said, 'it's such a long time since –' He faltered. He stopped. Their faces were too much for him.

'Even *so*,' said Josephine.

And Auntie Con looked.

Cyril put down his teacup. 'Wait a bit,' he cried. 'Wait a bit, Aunt Josephine. What am I thinking of?'

He looked up. They were beginning to brighten. Cyril slapped his knee.

'Of course,' he said, 'it was meringues. How could I have forgotten? Yes, Aunt Josephine, you're perfectly right. Father's most frightfully keen on meringues.'

They didn't only beam. Aunt Josephine went scarlet with pleasure; Auntie Con gave a deep, deep sigh.

'And now, Cyril, you must come and see father,' said Josephine. 'He knows you were coming today.'

'Right,' said Cyril, very firmly and heartily. He got up from his chair; suddenly he glanced at the clock.

'I say, Auntie Con, isn't your clock a bit slow? I've got to meet a man at – at Paddington just after five. I'm afraid I shan't be able to stay very long with grandfather.'

'Oh, he won't expect you to stay *very* long!' said Aunt Josephine.

Constantia was still gazing at the clock. She couldn't make up her mind if it was fast or slow. It was one or the other, she felt almost certain of that. At any rate, it had been.

Cyril still lingered. 'Aren't you coming along, Auntie Con?'

'Of course,' said Josephine, 'we shall all go. Come on, Con.'

IX

They knocked at the door, and Cyril followed his aunts into grandfather's hot, sweetish room.

'Come on,' said Grandfather Pinner. 'Don't hang about. What is it? What've you been up to?'

He was sitting in front of a roaring fire, clasping his stick. He had a thick rug over his knees. On his lap there lay a beautiful pale yellow silk handkerchief.

'It's Cyril, father,' said Josephine shyly. And she took Cyril's hand and led him forward.

'Good afternoon, grandfather,' said Cyril, trying to take his hand out of Aunt Josephine's. Grandfather Pinner shot his eyes at Cyril in the way he was famous for. Where was Auntie Con? She stood on the other side of Aunt Josephine; her long arms hung down in front of her; her hands were clasped. She never took her eyes off grandfather.

'Well,' said Grandfather Pinner, beginning to thump, 'what have you got to tell me?'

What had he, what had he got to tell him? Cyril felt himself smiling like a perfect imbecile. The room was stifling, too.

But Aunt Josephine came to his rescue. She cried brightly, 'Cyril says his father is still very fond of meringues, father dear.'

'Eh?' said Grandfather Pinner, curving his hand like a purple meringue-shell over one ear.

Josephine repeated, 'Cyril says his father is still very fond of meringues.'

'Can't hear,' said old Colonel Pinner. And he waved Josephine away with his stick, then pointed with his stick to Cyril. 'Tell me what she's trying to say,' he said.

(My God!) 'Must I?' said Cyril, blushing and staring at Aunt Josephine.

'Do, dear,' she smiled. 'It will please him so much.'

'Come on, out with it!' cried Colonel Pinner testily, beginning to thump again.

And Cyril leaned forward and yelled, 'Father's still very fond of meringues.'

At that Grandfather Pinner jumped as though he had been shot.

'Don't shout!' he cried. 'What's the matter with the boy? *Meringues!* What about 'em?'

'Oh, Aunt Josephine, must we go on?' groaned Cyril desperately.

'It's quite all right, dear boy,' said Aunt Josephine, as though he and she were at the dentist's together. 'He'll understand in a minute.' And she whispered to Cyril, 'He's getting a bit deaf, you know.' Then she leaned forward and really bawled at Grandfather Pinner, 'Cyril only wanted to tell you, father dear, that *his* father is still very fond of meringues.'

Colonel Pinner heard that time, heard and brooded, looking Cyril up and down.

'What an esstrordinary thing!' said old Grandfather Pinner. 'What an esstrordinary thing to come all this way here to tell me!'

And Cyril felt it *was*.

'Yes, I shall send Cyril the watch,' said Josephine.

'That would be very nice,' said Constantia. 'I seem to remember last time he came there was some little trouble about the time.'

X

They were interrupted by Kate bursting through the door in her usual fashion, as though she had discovered some secret panel in the wall.

'Fried or boiled?' asked the bold voice.

Fried or boiled? Josephine and Constantia were quite bewildered for the moment. They could hardly take it in.

'Fried or boiled what, Kate?' asked Josephine, trying to begin to concentrate.

Kate gave a loud sniff. 'Fish.'

'Well, why didn't you say so immediately?' Josephine reproached her gently. 'How could you expect us to understand, Kate? There are a great many things in this world, you know, which are fried or boiled.' And after such a display of courage she said quite brightly to Constantia, 'Which do you prefer, Con?'

'I think it might be nice to have it fried,' said Constantia. 'On the other hand, of course, boiled fish is very nice. I think I prefer both equally well . . . Unless you . . . In that case –'

'I shall fry it,' said Kate, and she bounced back, leaving their door open and slamming the door of her kitchen.

Josephine gazed at Constantia; she raised her pale eyebrows until they rippled away into her pale hair. She got up. She said in a very lofty, imposing way, 'Do you mind following me into the drawing-room, Constantia? I've something of great importance to discuss with you.'

For it was always to the drawing-room they retired when they wanted to talk over Kate.

Josephine closed the door meaningly. 'Sit down, Constantia,' she said, still very grand. She might have been receiving Constantia for the first time. And Con looked round vaguely for a chair, as though she felt indeed quite a stranger.

'Now the question is,' said Josephine, bending forward, 'whether we shall keep her or not.'

'That is the question,' agreed Constantia.

'And this time,' said Josephine firmly, 'we must come to a definite decision.'

Constantia looked for a moment as though she might begin going over all the other times, but she pulled herself together and said, 'Yes, Jug.'

'You see, Con,' explained Josephine, 'everything is so changed now.' Constantia looked up quickly. 'I mean,' went on Josephine, 'we're not dependent on Kate as we were.' And she blushed faintly. 'There's not father to cook for.'

'That is perfectly true,' agreed Constantia. 'Father certainly doesn't want any cooking now whatever else –'

Josephine broke in sharply, 'You're not sleepy, are you, Con?'

'Sleepy, Jug?' Constantia was wide-eyed.

'Well, concentrate more,' said Josephine sharply, and she returned to the subject. 'What it comes to is, if we did' – and this she barely breathed, glancing at the door – 'give Kate notice' – she raised her voice again – 'we could manage our own food.'

'Why not?' cried Constantia. She couldn't help smiling. The idea was so exciting. She clasped her hands. 'What should we live on, Jug?'

'Oh, eggs in various forms!' said Jug, lofty again. 'And, besides, there are all the cooked foods.'

'But I've always heard,' said Constantia, 'they are considered so very expensive.'

'Not if one buys them in moderation,' said Josephine. But she tore herself away from this fascinating bypath and dragged Constantia after her.

'What we've got to decide now, however, is whether we really do trust Kate or not.'

Constantia leaned back. Her flat little laugh flew from her lips.

'Isn't it curious, Jug,' said she, 'that just on this one subject I've never been able to quite make up my mind?'

XI

She never had. The whole difficulty was to prove anything. How did one prove things, how could one? Suppose Kate had stood in front of her and deliberately made a face. Mightn't she very well have been in pain? Wasn't it impossible, at any rate, to ask Kate if she was making a face at her? If Kate answered 'No' – and, of course, she would say 'No' – what a position! How undignified! Then, again, Constantia suspected, she was almost certain that Kate went to her chest of draw- ers when she and Josephine were out, not to take things but to spy. Many times she had come back to find her amethyst cross in the most unlikely places, under her lace ties or on top of her evening Bertha. More than once she had laid a trap for Kate. She had arranged things in a special order and then called Josephine to witness.

'You see, Jug?'

'Quite, Con.'

'Now we shall be able to tell.'

But, oh dear, when she did go to look, she was as far off from a proof as ever! If anything was displaced, it might so very well have happened as she closed the drawer; a jolt might have done it so easily.

'You come, Jug, and decide. I really can't. It's too difficult.'

But after a pause and a long glare Josephine would sigh, 'Now you've put the doubt into my mind, Con, I'm sure I can't tell myself.'

'Well, we can't postpone it again,' said Josephine. 'If we postpone it this time –'

XII

But at that moment in the street below a barrel-organ struck up. Jose- phine and Constantia sprang to their feet together.

'Run, Con,' said Josephine. 'Run quickly. There's sixpence on the –'

Then they remembered. It didn't matter. They would never have to stop the organ-grinder again. Never again would she and Constantia be told to make that monkey take his noise somewhere else. Never would sound that loud, strange bellow when father thought they were not hurrying enough. The organ-grinder might play there all day and the stick would not thump.

> It never will thump again,
> It never will thump again,

played the barrel-organ.

What was Constantia thinking? She had such a strange smile; she looked different. She couldn't be going to cry.

'Jug, Jug,' said Constantia softly, pressing her hands together. 'Do you know what day it is? It's Saturday. It's a week today, a whole week.'

> A week since father died,
> A week since father died,

cried the barrel-organ. And Josephine, too, forgot to be practical and sensible; she smiled faintly, strangely. On the Indian carpet there fell a square of sunlight, pale red; it came and went and came – and stayed, deepened – until it shone almost golden.

'The sun's out,' said Josephine, as though it really mattered.

A perfect fountain of bubbling notes shook from the barrel-organ, round, bright notes, carelessly scattered.

Constantia lifted her big, cold hands as if to catch them, and then her hands fell again. She walked over to the mantelpiece to her favourite Buddha. And the stone and gilt image, whose smile always gave her such a queer feeling, almost a pain and yet a pleasant pain, seemed today to be more than smiling. He knew something; he had a secret. 'I know something that you don't know,' said her Buddha. Oh, what was it, what could it be? And yet she had always felt there was ... something.

The sunlight pressed through the windows, thieved its way in, flashed its light over the furniture and the photographs. Josephine watched it. When it came to mother's photograph, the enlargement over the piano, it lingered as though puzzled to find so little remained of mother, except the ear-rings shaped like tiny pagodas and a black feather boa. Why did the photographs of dead people always fade so? wondered Josephine. As soon as a person was dead their photograph died too. But, of course, this one of mother was very old. It was thirty-five years old. Josephine remembered standing on a chair and pointing out that feather boa to Constantia and telling her that it was a snake that had killed their mother in Ceylon ... Would everything have been different if mother hadn't died? She didn't see why. Aunt Florence had lived with them until they had left school, and they had moved three times and had their yearly holiday and . . . and there'd been changes of servants, of course.

Some little sparrows, young sparrows they sounded, chirped on the window-ledge. *Yeep – eyeep – yeep*. But Josephine felt they were not sparrows, not on the window-ledge. It was inside her, that queer little crying noise. *Yeep – eyeep – yeep*. Ah, what was it crying, so weak and forlorn?

If mother had lived, might they have married? But there had been nobody for them to marry. There had been father's Anglo-Indian friends before he quarrelled with them. But after that she and Constantia never met a single man except clergymen. How did one meet men? Or even if they'd met them, how could they have got to know men well enough to be more than strangers? One read of people having adventures, being followed, and so on. But nobody had ever followed Constantia and her. Oh yes, there had been one year at Eastbourne a mysterious man at their boarding-house who had put a note on the jug of hot water outside their bedroom door! But by the time Connie had found it the steam had made the writing too faint to read; they couldn't even make out to which of them it was addressed. And he had left next day. And that was all. The rest had been looking after father and at the same time keeping out of father's way. But now? But now? The thieving sun touched Josephine gently. She lifted her face. She was drawn over to the window by gentle beams . . .

Until the barrel-organ stopped playing Constantia stayed before the Buddha, wondering, but not as usual, not vaguely. This time her wonder was like longing. She remembered the times she had come in here, crept out of bed in her nightgown when the moon was full, and lain on the floor with her arms outstretched, as though she was crucified. Why? The big, pale moon had made her do it. The horrible dancing figures on the carved screen had leered at her and she hadn't minded. She remembered too how, whenever they were at the seaside, she had gone off by herself and got as close to the sea as she could, and sung something, something she had made up, while she gazed all over that restless water. There had been this other life, running out, bringing things home in bags, getting things on approval, discussing them with Jug, and taking them back to get more things on approval, and arranging father's trays and trying not to annoy father. But it all seemed to have happened in a kind of tunnel. It wasn't real. It was only when she came out of the tunnel into the moonlight or by the sea or into a thunderstorm that she really felt herself. What did it mean? What was it she was always wanting? What did it all lead to? Now? Now?

She turned away from the Buddha with one of her vague gestures. She went over to where Josephine was standing. She wanted to say something to Josephine, something frightfully important, about – about the future and what . . .

'Don't you think perhaps –' she began.

But Josephine interrupted her. 'I was wondering if now –' she murmured. They stopped; they waited for each other.

'Go on, Con,' said Josephine.

'No, no, Jug; after you,' said Constantia.

'No, say what you were going to say. You began,' said Josephine.

'I . . . I'd rather hear what you were going to say first,' said Constantia.

'Don't be absurd, Con.'

'Really, Jug.'

'Connie!'

'Oh, *Jug*!'

A pause. Then Constantia said faintly, 'I can't say what I was going to say, Jug, because I've forgotten what it was . . . that I was going to say.'

Josephine was silent for a moment. She stared at a big cloud where the sun had been. Then she replied shortly, 'I've forgotten too.'

(written 1920, first published in 1921, first book publication
The Garden Party and Other Stories, 1922)

Life of Ma Parker

When the literary gentleman, whose flat old Ma Parker cleaned every Tuesday, opened the door to her that morning, he asked after her grandson. Ma Parker stood on the doormat inside the dark little hall, and she stretched out her hand to help her gentleman shut the door before she replied. 'We buried 'im yesterday, sir,' she said quietly.

'Oh, dear me! I'm sorry to hear that,' said the literary gentleman in a shocked tone. He was in the middle of his breakfast. He wore a very shabby dressing-gown and carried a crumpled newspaper in one hand. But he felt awkward. He could hardly go back to the warm sitting-room without saying something – something more. Then because these people set such store by funerals he said kindly, 'I hope the funeral went off all right.'

'Beg parding, sir?' said old Ma Parker huskily.

Poor old bird! She did look dashed. 'I hope the funeral was a – a – success,' said he. Ma Parker gave no answer. She bent her head and hobbled off to the kitchen, clasping the old fish bag that held her cleaning things and an apron and a pair of felt shoes. The literary gentleman raised his eyebrows and went back to his breakfast.

'Overcome, I suppose,' he said aloud, helping himself to the marmalade.

Ma Parker drew the two jetty spears out of her toque and hung it behind the door. She unhooked her worn jacket and hung that up too. Then she tied her apron and sat down to take off her boots. To take off her boots or to put them on was an agony to her, but it had been an agony for years. In fact, she was so accustomed to the pain that her face was drawn and screwed up ready for the twinge before she'd so much as untied the laces. That over, she sat back with a sigh and softly rubbed her knees . . .

'Gran! Gran!' Her little grandson stood on her lap in his button boots. He'd just come in from playing in the street.

'Look what a state you've made your gran's skirt into – you wicked boy!'

But he put his arms round her neck and rubbed his cheek against hers.

'Gran, gi' us a penny!' he coaxed.

'Be off with you; Gran ain't got no pennies.'

'Yes, you 'ave.'

'No, I ain't.'

'Yes, you 'ave. Gi' us one!'

Already she was feeling for the old, squashed, black leather purse.

'Well, what'll you give your gran?'

He gave a shy little laugh and pressed closer. She felt his eyelid quivering against her cheek. 'I ain't got nothing,' he murmured . . .

The old woman sprang up, seized the iron kettle off the gas stove and took it over to the sink. The noise of the water drumming in the kettle deadened her pain, it seemed. She filled the pail, too, and the washing-up bowl.

It would take a whole book to describe the state of that kitchen. During the week the literary gentleman 'did' for himself. That is to say, he emptied the tea-leaves now and again into a jam jar set aside for that purpose, and if he ran out of clean forks he wiped over one or two on the roller towel. Otherwise, as he explained to his friends, his 'system' was quite simple, and he couldn't understand why people made all this fuss about housekeeping.

'You simply dirty everything you've got, get a hag in once a week to clean up, and the thing's done.'

The result looked like a gigantic dustbin. Even the floor was littered with toast crusts, envelopes, cigarette ends. But Ma Parker bore him no grudge. She pitied the poor young gentleman for having no one to look after him. Out of the smudgy little window you could see an immense expanse of sad-looking sky, and whenever there were clouds they looked very worn, old clouds, frayed at the edges, with holes in them, or dark stains like tea.

While the water was heating, Ma Parker began sweeping the floor. 'Yes,' she thought, as the broom knocked, 'what with one thing and another I've had my share. I've had a hard life.'

Even the neighbours said that of her. Many a time, hobbling home with her fish bag, she heard them, waiting at the corner, or leaning over the area railings, say among themselves, 'She's had a hard life, has Ma Parker.' And it was so true she wasn't in the least proud of it. It was just as if you were to say she lived in the basement-back at Number 27. A hard life! . . .

At sixteen she'd left Stratford and come up to London as kitching-maid. Yes, she was born in Stratford-on-Avon. Shakespeare, sir? No, people were always arsking her about him. But she'd never heard his name until she saw it on the theatres.

Nothing remained of Stratford except that 'sitting in the fire-place of a evening you could see the stars through the chimley,' and 'Mother always 'ad 'er side of bacon 'anging from the ceiling.' And there was something – a bush, there was – at the front door, that smelled ever so nice. But the bush was very vague. She'd only remembered it once or twice in the hospital, when she'd been taken bad.

That was a dreadful place – her first place. She was never allowed out. She never went upstairs except for prayers morning and evening. It was a fair cellar. And the cook was a cruel woman. She used to snatch away her letters from home before she'd read them, and throw them in the range because they made her dreamy . . . And the beedles! Would you believe it? – until she came to London she'd never seen a black beedle. Here Ma always gave a little laugh, as though – not to have seen a black beedle! Well! It was as if to say you'd never seen your own feet.

When that family was sold up she went as 'help' to a doctor's house, and after two years there, on the run from morning till night, she married her husband. He was a baker.

'A baker, Mrs Parker!' the literary gentleman would say. For occasionally he laid aside his tomes and lent an ear, at least, to this product called Life. 'It must be rather nice to be married to a baker!'

Mrs Parker didn't look so sure.

'Such a clean trade,' said the gentleman.

Mrs Parker didn't look convinced.

'And didn't you like handing the new loaves to the customers?'

'Well, sir,' said Mrs Parker, 'I wasn't in the shop above a great deal. We had thirteen little ones and buried seven of them. If it wasn't the 'ospital it was the infirmary, you might say!'

'You might, *indeed*, Mrs Parker!' said the gentleman, shuddering, and taking up his pen again.

Yes, seven had gone, and while the six were still small her

husband was taken ill with consumption. It was flour on the lungs, the doctor told her at the time . . . Her husband sat up in bed with his shirt pulled over his head, and the doctor's finger drew a circle on his back.

'Now, if we were to cut him open *here*, Mrs Parker,' said the doctor, 'you'd find his lungs chock-a-block with white powder. Breathe, my good fellow!' And Mrs Parker never knew for certain whether she saw or whether she fancied she saw a great fan of white dust come out of her poor dear husband's lips . . .

But the struggle she'd had to bring up those six little children and keep herself to herself. Terrible it had been! Then, just when they were old enough to go to school her husband's sister came to stop with them to help things along, and she hadn't been there more than two months when she fell down a flight of steps and hurt her spine. And for five years Ma Parker had another baby – and such a one for crying! – to look after. Then young Maudie went wrong and took her sister Alice with her; the two boys emigrimated, and young Jim went to India with the army, and Ethel, the youngest, married a good-for-nothing little waiter who died of ulcers the year little Lennie was born. And now little Lennie – my grandson . . .

The piles of dirty cups, dirty dishes, were washed and dried. The ink-black knives were cleaned with a piece of potato and finished off with a piece of cork. The table was scrubbed, and the dresser and the sink that had sardine tails swimming in it . . .

He'd never been a strong child – never from the first. He'd been one of those fair babies that everybody took for a girl. Silvery fair curls he had, blue eyes, and a little freckle like a diamond on one side of his nose. The trouble she and Ethel had had to rear that child! The things out of the newspapers they tried him with! Every Sunday morning Ethel would read aloud while Ma Parker did her washing.

> 'DEAR SIR, – Just a line to let you know my little Myrtil was laid out for dead . . . After four bottils . . . gained 8 lbs. in 9 weeks, *and is still putting it on*.'

And then the egg-cup of ink would come off the dresser and the letter would be written, and Ma would buy a postal order on her way to work next morning. But it was no use. Nothing made little Lennie put it on. Taking him to the cemetery, even, never gave him a colour; a nice shake-up in the bus never improved his appetite.

But he was gran's boy from the first . . .

'Whose boy are you?' said old Ma Parker, straightening up from the stove and going over to the smudgy window. And a little voice, so warm, so close, it half stifled her – it seemed to be in her breast under her heart – laughed out, and said, 'I'm gran's boy!'

At that moment there was a sound of steps, and the literary gentleman appeared, dressed for walking.

'Oh, Mrs Parker, I'm going out.'

'Very good, sir.'

'And you'll find your half-crown in the tray of the inkstand.'

'Thank you, sir.'

'Oh, by the way, Mrs Parker,' said the literary gentleman quickly, 'you didn't throw away any cocoa last time you were here – did you?'

'No, sir.'

'*Very* strange. I could have sworn I left a teaspoonful of cocoa in the tin.' He broke off. He said softly and firmly, 'You'll always tell me when you throw things away – won't you, Mrs Parker?' And he walked off very well pleased with himself, convinced, in fact, he'd shown Mrs Parker that under his apparent carelessness he was as vigilant as a woman.

The door banged. She took her brushes and cloths into the bedroom. But when she began to make the bed, smoothing, tucking, patting, the thought of little Lennie was unbearable. Why did he have to suffer so? That's what she couldn't understand. Why should a little angel child have to arsk for his breath and fight for it? There was no sense in making a child suffer like that.

. . . From Lennie's little box of a chest there came a sound as though something was boiling. There was a great lump of something bubbling in his chest that he couldn't get rid of. When he coughed, the sweat sprang out on his head; his eyes bulged, his hands waved, and the great lump bubbled as a potato knocks in a saucepan. But what was more awful than all was when he didn't cough he sat against the pillow and never spoke or answered, or even made as if he heard. Only he looked offended.

'It's not your poor old gran's doing it, my lovey,' said old Ma Parker, patting back the damp hair from his scarlet ears. But Lennie moved his head and edged away. Dreadfully offended with her he looked – and solemn. He bent his head and looked at her sideways as though he couldn't have believed it of his gran.

But at the last . . . Ma Parker threw the counterpane over the bed. No, she simply couldn't think about it. It was too much – she'd had too much in her life to bear. She'd borne it up till now, she'd kept herself to herself, and never once had she been seen to cry. Never by a living soul. Not even her own children had seen Ma break down. She'd kept a proud face always. But now! Lennie gone – what had she? She had nothing. He was all she'd got from life, and now he was took too. Why must it all have happened to me? she wondered. 'What have I done?' said old Ma Parker. 'What have I done?'

As she said those words she suddenly let fall her brush. She found herself in the kitchen. Her misery was so terrible that she pinned on her hat, put on her jacket and walked out of the flat like a person in a dream. She did not know what she was doing. She was like a person so dazed by the horror of what has happened that he walks away – anywhere, as though by walking away he could escape . . .

It was cold in the street. There was a wind like ice. People went flitting by, very fast; the men walked like scissors; the women trod like cats. And nobody knew – nobody cared. Even if she broke down, if at last, after all these years, she were to cry, she'd find herself in the lock-up as like as not.

But at the thought of crying it was as though little Lennie leapt in his gran's arms. Ah, that's what she wants to do, my dove. Gran wants to cry. If she could only cry now, cry for a long time, over everything, beginning with her first place and the cruel cook, going on to the doctor's, and then the seven little ones, death of her husband, the children's leaving her, and all the years of misery that led up to Lennie. But to have a proper cry over all these things would take a long time. All the same, the time for it had come. She must do it. She couldn't put it off any longer; she couldn't wait any more . . . Where could she go?

'She's had a hard life, has Ma Parker.' Yes, a hard life, indeed! Her chin began to tremble; there was no time to lose. But where? Where?

She couldn't go home; Ethel was there. It would frighten Ethel out of her life. She couldn't sit on a bench anywhere; people would come arsking her questions. She couldn't possibly go back to the gentleman's flat; she had no right to cry in strangers' houses. If she sat on some steps a policeman would speak to her.

Oh, wasn't there anywhere where she could hide and keep herself to herself and stay as long as she liked, not disturbing anybody, and nobody worrying her? Wasn't there anywhere in the world where she could have her cry out – at last?

Ma Parker stood, looking up and down. The icy wind blew out her apron into a balloon. And now it began to rain. There was nowhere.

(first published in 1921, first book publication
The Garden Party and Other Stories, 1922)

At The Bay

I

Very early morning. The sun was not yet risen, and the whole of Crescent Bay was hidden under a white sea-mist. The big bush-covered hills at the back were smothered. You could not see where they ended and the paddocks and bungalows began. The sandy road was gone and the paddocks and bungalows the other side of it; there were no white dunes covered with reddish grass beyond them; there was nothing to mark which was beach and where was the sea. A heavy dew had fallen. The grass was blue. Big drops hung on the bushes and just did not fall; the silvery, fluffy toi-toi was limp on its long stalks, and all the marigolds and the pinks in the bungalow gardens were bowed to the earth with wetness. Drenched were the cold fuchsias, round pearls of dew lay on the flat nasturtium leaves. It looked as though the sea had beaten up softly in the darkness, as though one immense wave had come rippling, rippling – how far? Perhaps if you had waked up in the middle of the night you might have seen a big fish flicking in at the window and gone again . . .

Ah-Aah! sounded the sleepy sea. And from the bush there came the sound of little streams flowing, quickly, lightly, slipping between the smooth stones, gushing into ferny basins and out again; and there was the splashing of big drops on large leaves, and something else – what was it? – a faint stirring and shaking, the snapping of a twig and then such silence that it seemed someone was listening.

Round the corner of Crescent Bay, between the piled-up masses of broken rock, a flock of sheep came pattering. They were huddled together, a small, tossing, woolly mass, and their thin, stick-like legs trotted along quickly as if the cold and the quiet had frightened them. Behind them an old sheep-dog, his soaking paws covered with sand, ran along with his nose to the ground, but carelessly, as if thinking of something else. And then in the rocky gateway the shepherd himself appeared. He was a lean, upright old man, in a frieze coat that was covered with a web of tiny drops, velvet trousers tied under the knee, and a wideawake with a folded blue handkerchief round the brim. One hand was crammed into his belt, the other grasped a beautifully smooth yellow stick. And as he walked, taking his time, he kept up a very soft light whistling, an airy, far-away fluting that sounded mournful and tender. The old dog cut an ancient caper or two and then drew up sharp, ashamed of his levity, and walked a few dignified paces by his master's side. The sheep ran forward in little pattering rushes; they began to bleat, and ghostly flocks and herds answered them from under the sea. 'Baa! Baaa!' For a time they seemed to be always on the same piece of ground. There ahead was stretched the sandy road with shallow puddles; the same soaking bushes showed on either side the same shadowy palings. Then something immense came into view; an enormous shock-haired giant with his arms stretched out. It was the big gum tree outside Mrs Stubbs's shop, and as they passed by there was a strong whiff of eucalyptus. And now big spots of light gleamed in the mist. The shepherd stopped whistling; he rubbed his red nose and wet beard on his wet sleeve and, screwing up his eyes, glanced in the direction of the sea. The sun was rising. It was marvellous how quickly the mist thinned, sped away, dissolved from the shallow plain, rolled up from the bush and was gone as if in a hurry to escape; big twists and curls jostled and shouldered each other as the silvery beams broadened. The far-away sky – a bright, pure blue – was reflected in the puddles, and the drops, swimming along the telegraph poles, flashed into points of light. Now the leaping, glittering sea was so bright it made one's eyes ache to look at it. The shepherd drew a pipe, the bowl as small as an acorn, out of his breast-pocket, fumbled for a chunk of speckled tobacco, pared off a few shavings and stuffed the bowl. He was a grave, fine-looking old man. As he lit up and the blue smoke wreathed his head, the dog, watching, looked proud of him.

'Baa! Baaa!' The sheep spread out into a fan. They were just clear of the summer colony before the first sleeper turned over and lifted a drowsy head; their cry sounded in the dreams of little children . . . who lifted their arms to drag down, to cuddle the darling little woolly lambs of sleep. Then the first inhabitant appeared; it was the Burnells' cat Florrie, sitting on the gatepost, far too early as usual, looking for their milk-girl. When she saw the old sheep-dog she sprang up quickly, arched her back, drew in her tabby head, and seemed to give a little fastidious shiver. 'Ugh! What a coarse, revolting creature!' said Florrie. But the old sheep-dog, not looking up, waggled past, flinging out his legs from side to side. Only one of his ears twitched to prove that he saw, and thought her a silly young female.

The breeze of morning lifted in the bush and the smell of leaves and wet black earth mingled with the sharp smell of the sea. Myriads of birds were singing. A goldfinch flew over the shepherd's head and, perching on the tiptop of a spray, it turned to the sun, ruffling its small breast feathers. And now they had passed the fisherman's hut, passed the charred-looking little *whare* where Leila the milk-girl lived with her old Gran. The sheep strayed over a yellow swamp and Wag, the sheep-dog, padded after, rounded them up and headed them for the steeper, narrower rocky pass that led out of Crescent Bay and towards Daylight Cove. 'Baa! Baaa!' Faint the cry came as they rocked along the fast-drying road. The shepherd put away his pipe, dropping it into his breast-pocket so that the little bowl hung over. And straightway the soft airy whistling began again. Wag ran out along a ledge of rock after something that smelled, and ran back again disgusted. Then pushing, nudging, hurrying, the sheep rounded the bend and the shepherd followed after out of sight.

II

A few moments later the back door of one of the bungalows opened, and a figure in a broad-striped bathing-suit flung down the paddock, cleared the stile, rushed through the tussock grass into the hollow, staggered up the sandy hillock, and raced for dear life over the big porous stones, over the cold, wet pebbles, on to the hard sand that gleamed like oil. Splish-Splosh! Splish-Splosh! The water bubbled round his legs as Stanley Burnell waded out exulting. First man in as usual! He'd beaten them all again. And he swooped down to souse his head and neck.

'Hail, brother! All hail, Thou Mighty One!' A velvety bass voice came booming over the water.

Great Scott! Damnation take it! Stanley lifted up to see a dark head bobbing far out and an arm lifted. It was Jonathan Trout – there before him! 'Glorious morning!' sang the voice.

'Yes, very fine!' said Stanley briefly. Why the dickens didn't the fellow stick to his part of the sea? Why should he come barging over to this exact spot? Stanley gave a kick, a lunge and struck out, swimming overarm. But Jonathan was a match for him. Up he came, his black hair sleek on his forehead, his short beard sleek.

'I had an extraordinary dream last night!' he shouted.

What was the matter with the man? This mania for conversation irritated Stanley beyond words. And it was always the same — always some piffle about a dream he'd had, or some cranky idea he'd got hold of, or some rot he'd been reading. Stanley turned over on his back and kicked with his legs till he was a living water-spout. But even then . . . 'I dreamed I was hanging over a terrifically high cliff, shouting to someone below.' You would be! thought Stanley. He could stick no more of it. He stopped splashing. 'Look here, Trout,' he said, 'I'm in rather a hurry this morning.'

'You're WHAT?' Jonathan was so surprised — or pretended to be — that he sank under the water, then reappeared again blowing.

'All I mean is,' said Stanley, 'I've no time to — to — to fool about. I want to get this over. I'm in a hurry. I've work to do this morning — see?'

Jonathan was gone before Stanley had finished. 'Pass, friend!' said the bass voice gently, and he slid away through the water with scarcely a ripple . . . But curse the fellow! He'd ruined Stanley's bathe. What an unpractical idiot the man was! Stanley struck out to sea again, and then as quickly swam in again, and away he rushed up the beach. He felt cheated.

Jonathan stayed a little longer in the water. He floated, gently moving his hands like fins, and letting the sea rock his long, skinny body. It was curious, but in spite of everything he was fond of Stanley Burnell. True, he had a fiendish desire to tease him sometimes, to poke fun at him, but at bottom he was sorry for the fellow. There was something pathetic in his determination to make a job of everything. You couldn't help feeling he'd be caught out one day, and then what an almighty cropper he'd come! At that moment an immense wave lifted Jonathan, rode past him, and broke along the beach with a joyful sound. What a beauty! And now there came another. That was the way to live — carelessly, recklessly, spending oneself. He got on to his feet and began to wade towards the shore, pressing his toes into the firm, wrinkled sand. To take things easy, not to fight against the ebb and flow of life, but to give way to it – that was what was needed. It was this tension that was all wrong. To live – to live! And the perfect morning, so fresh and fair, basking in the light, as though laughing at its own beauty, seemed to whisper, 'Why not?'

But now he was out of the water Jonathan turned blue with cold. He ached all over; it was as though someone was wringing the blood out of him. And stalking up the beach, shivering, all his muscles tight, he too felt his bathe was spoilt. He'd stayed in too long.

III

Beryl was alone in the living-room when Stanley appeared, wearing a blue serge suit, a stiff collar and a spotted tie. He looked almost uncannily clean and brushed; he was going to town for the day. Dropping into his chair, he pulled out his watch and put it beside his plate.

'I've just got twenty-five minutes,' he said. 'You might go and see if the porridge is ready, Beryl?'

'Mother's just gone for it,' said Beryl. She sat down at the table and poured out his tea.

'Thanks!' Stanley took a sip. 'Hallo!' he said in an astonished voice, 'you've forgotten the sugar.'

'Oh, sorry!' But even then Beryl didn't help him; she pushed the basin across. What did this mean? As Stanley helped himself his blue eyes widened; they seemed to quiver. He shot a quick glance at his sister-in-law and leaned back.

'Nothing wrong, is there?' he asked carelessly, fingering his collar.

Beryl's head was bent; she turned her plate in her fingers.

'Nothing,' said her light voice. Then she too looked up, and smiled at Stanley. 'Why should there be?'

'O-oh! No reason at all as far as I know. I thought you seemed rather –'

At that moment the door opened and the three little girls appeared, each carrying a porridge plate. They were dressed alike in blue jerseys and knickers; their brown legs were bare, and each had her hair plaited and pinned up in what was called a horse's tail. Behind them came Mrs Fairfield with the tray.

'Carefully, children,' she warned. But they were taking the very greatest care. They loved being allowed to carry things. 'Have you said good morning to your father?'

'Yes, grandma.' They settled themselves on the bench opposite Stanley and Beryl.

'Good morning, Stanley!' Old Mrs Fairfield gave him his plate.

'Morning, mother! How's the boy?'

'Splendid! He only woke up once last night. What a perfect morning!' The old woman paused, her hand on the loaf of bread, to gaze out of the open door into the garden. The sea sounded. Through the wide-open window streamed the sun on to the yellow varnished walls and bare floor. Everything on the table flashed and glittered. In the middle there was an old salad bowl filled with yellow and red nasturtiums. She smiled, and a look of deep content shone in her eyes.

'You might *cut* me a slice of that bread, mother,' said Stanley. 'I've only twelve and a half minutes before the coach passes. Has anyone given my shoes to the servant girl?'

'Yes, they're ready for you.' Mrs Fairfield was quite unruffled.

'Oh, Kezia! Why are you such a messy child!' cried Beryl despairingly.

'Me, Aunt Beryl?' Kezia stared at her. What had she done now? She had only dug a river down the middle of her porridge, filled it, and was eating the banks away. But she did that every single morning, and no one had said a word up till now.

'Why can't you eat your food properly like Isabel and Lottie?' How unfair grown-ups are!

'But Lottie always makes a floating island, don't you, Lottie?'

'I don't,' said Isabel smartly. 'I just sprinkle mine with sugar and put on the milk and finish it. Only babies play with their food.'

Stanley pushed back his chair and got up.

'Would you get me those shoes, mother? And, Beryl, if you've finished, I wish you'd cut down to the gate and stop the coach. Run in to your mother, Isabel, and ask her where my bowler hat's been put. Wait a minute – have you children been playing with my stick?'

'No, father!'

'But I put it here,' Stanley began to bluster. 'I remember distinctly putting it in this corner. Now, who's had it? There's no time to lose. Look sharp! The stick's got to be found.'

Even Alice, the servant girl, was drawn into the chase. 'You haven't been using it to poke the kitchen fire with by any chance?'

Stanley dashed into the bedroom where Linda was lying. 'Most extraordinary thing. I can't keep a single possession to myself. They've made away with my stick, now!'

'Stick, dear? What stick?' Linda's vagueness on these occasions could not be real, Stanley decided. Would nobody sympathise with him?

'Coach! Coach, Stanley!' Beryl's voice cried from the gate.

Stanley waved his arm to Linda. 'No time to say goodbye!' he cried. And he meant that as a punishment to her.

He snatched his bowler hat, dashed out of the house, and swung down the garden path. Yes, the coach was there waiting, and Beryl, leaning over the open gate, was laughing up at somebody or other just as if nothing had happened. The heartlessness of women! The way they took it for granted it was your job to slave away for them while they didn't even take the trouble to see that your walking-stick wasn't lost. Kelly trailed his whip across the horses.

'Goodbye, Stanley,' called Beryl, sweetly and gaily. It was easy enough to say goodbye! And there she stood, idle, shading her eyes with her hand. The worst of it was Stanley had to shout goodbye too, for the sake of appearances. Then he saw her turn, give a little skip and run back to the house. She was glad to be rid of him!

Yes, she was thankful. Into the living-room she ran and called 'He's gone!' Linda cried from her room: 'Beryl! Has Stanley gone?' Old Mrs Fairfield appeared, carrying the boy in his little flannel coatee.

'Gone?'

'Gone!'

Oh, the relief, the difference it made to have the man out of the house. Their very voices were changed as they called to one another; they sounded warm and loving and as if they shared a secret. Beryl went over to the table. 'Have another cup of tea, mother. It's still hot.' She wanted, somehow, to celebrate the fact that they could do what they liked now. There was no man to disturb them; the whole perfect day was theirs.

'No, thank you, child,' said old Mrs Fairfield, but the way at that moment she tossed the boy up and said 'a-goos-a-goos-a-ga!' to him meant that she felt the same. The little girls ran into the paddock like chickens let out of a coop.

Even Alice, the servant girl, washing up the dishes in the kitchen, caught the infection and used the precious tank water in a perfectly reckless fashion.

'Oh, these men!' said she, and she plunged the teapot into the bowl and held it under the water even after it had stopped bubbling, as if it too was a man and drowning was too good for them.

IV

'Wait for me, Isa-bel! Kezia, wait for me!'

There was poor little Lottie, left behind again, because she found it so fearfully hard to get over the stile by herself. When she stood on the first step her knees began to wobble; she grasped the post. Then you had to put one leg over. But which leg? She never could decide. And when she did finally put one leg over with a sort of stamp of despair – then the feeling was awful. She was half in the paddock still and half in the tussock grass. She clutched the post desperately and lifted up her voice. 'Wait for me!'

'No, don't you wait for her, Kezia!' said Isabel. 'She's such a little silly. She's always making a fuss. Come on!' And she tugged Kezia's jersey. 'You can use my bucket if you come with me,' she said kindly. 'It's bigger than yours.' But Kezia couldn't leave Lottie all by herself. She ran back to her. By this time Lottie was very red in the face and breathing heavily.

'Here, put your other foot over,' said Kezia.

'Where?'

Lottie looked down at Kezia as if from a mountain height.

'Here where my hand is.' Kezia patted the place.

'Oh, *there* do you mean?' Lottie gave a deep sigh and put the second foot over.

'Now – sort of turn round and sit down and slide,' said Kezia.

'But there's nothing to sit down *on*, Kezia,' said Lottie.

She managed it at last, and once it was over she shook herself and began to beam.

'I'm getting better at climbing over stiles, aren't I, Kezia?'

Lottie's was a very hopeful nature.

The pink and the blue sun-bonnet followed Isabel's bright red sun-bonnet up that sliding, slipping hill. At the top they paused to decide where to go and to have a good stare at who was there already. Seen from behind, standing against the skyline, gesticulating largely with their spades, they looked like minute puzzled explorers.

The whole family of Samuel Josephs was there already with their lady-help, who sat on a camp-stool and kept order with a whistle that she wore tied round her neck, and a small cane with which she directed operations. The Samuel Josephs never played by themselves or managed their own game. If they did, it ended in the boys pouring water down the girls' necks or the girls trying to put little black crabs into the boys' pockets. So Mrs S. J. and the poor lady-help drew up what she called a 'brogramme' every morning to keep them 'abused and out of bischief.' It was all competitions or races or round games. Everything began with a piercing blast of the lady-help's whistle and ended with another. There were even prizes – large, rather dirty paper parcels which the lady-help with a sour little smile drew out of a bulging string kit. The Samuel Josephs fought fearfully for the prizes and cheated and pinched one another's arms – they were all expert pinchers. The only time the Burnell children ever played with them Kezia had got a prize, and when she undid three bits of paper she found a very small rusty button-hook. She couldn't understand why they made such a fuss . . .

But they never played with the Samuel Josephs now or even went to their parties. The Samuel Josephs were always giving children's parties at the Bay and there was always the same food. A big washhand basin of very brown fruit salad, buns cut into four and a washhand jug full of something the lady-help called 'Limmonadear.' And you went away in the evening with half the frill torn off your frock or something spilled all down the front of your openwork pinafore, leaving the Samuel Josephs leaping like savages on their lawn. No! They were too awful.

On the other side of the beach, close down to the water, two little boys, their knickers rolled up, twinkled like spiders. One was digging, the other pattered in and out of the water, filling a small bucket. They were the Trout boys, Pip and Rags. But Pip was so busy digging and Rags was so busy helping that they didn't see their little cousins until they were quite close.

'Look!' said Pip. 'Look what I've discovered.' And he showed them an old, wet, squashed-looking boot. The three little girls stared.

'Whatever are you going to do with it?' asked Kezia.

'Keep it, of course!' Pip was very scornful. 'It's a find – see?'

Yes, Kezia saw that. All the same . . .

'There's lots of things buried in the sand,' explained Pip. 'They get chucked up from wrecks. Treasure. Why – you might find –'

'But why does Rags have to keep on pouring water in?' asked Lottie.

'Oh, that's to moisten it,' said Pip, 'to make the work a bit easier. Keep it up, Rags.'

And good little Rags ran up and down, pouring in the water that turned brown like cocoa.

'Here, shall I show you what I found yesterday?' said Pip mysteriously, and he stuck his spade into the sand. 'Promise not to tell.'

They promised.

'Say, cross my heart straight dinkum.'

The little girls said it.

Pip took something out of his pocket, rubbed it a long time on the front of his jersey, then breathed on it and rubbed it again.

'Now turn round!' he ordered.

They turned round.

'All look the same way! Keep still! Now!'

And his hand opened; he held up to the light something that flashed, that winked, that was a most lovely green.

'It's a nemeral,' said Pip solemnly.

'Is it really, Pip?' Even Isabel was impressed.

The lovely green thing seemed to dance in Pip's fingers. Aunt Beryl had a nemeral in a ring, but it was a very small one. This one was as big as a star and far more beautiful.

V

As the morning lengthened whole parties appeared over the sand-hills and came down on the beach to bathe. It was understood that at eleven o'clock the women and children of the summer colony had the sea to themselves. First the women undressed, pulled on their bathing dresses and covered their heads in hideous caps like sponge-bags; then the children were unbuttoned. The beach was strewn with little heaps of

clothes and shoes; the big summer hats, with stones on them to keep
them from blowing away, looked like immense shells. It was strange
that even the sea seemed to sound differently when all those leaping,
laughing figures ran into the waves. Old Mrs Fairfield, in a lilac cotton
dress and a black hat tied under the chin, gathered her little brood and
got them ready. The little Trout boys whipped their shirts over their
heads, and away the five sped, while their grandma sat with one hand
in her knitting-bag ready to draw out the ball of wool when she was
satisfied they were safely in.

The firm compact little girls were not half so brave as the tender,
delicate-looking little boys. Pips and Rags, shivering, crouching
down, slapping the water, never hesitated. But Isabel, who could swim
twelve strokes, and Kezia, who could nearly swim eight, only followed on the strict understanding they were not to be splashed. As for
Lottie, she didn't follow at all. She liked to be left to go in her own
way, please. And that way was to sit down at the edge of the water, her
legs straight, her knees pressed together, and to make vague motions
with her arms as if she expected to be wafted out to sea. But when a
bigger wave than usual, an old whiskery one, came lolloping along in
her direction, she scrambled to her feet with a face of horror and flew
up the beach again.

'Here, mother, keep these for me, will you?'

Two rings and a thin gold chain were dropped into Mrs Fairfield's lap.

'Yes, dear. But aren't you going to bathe here?'

'No-o,' Beryl drawled. She sounded vague. 'I'm undressing further
along. I'm going to bathe with Mrs Harry Kember.'

'Very well.' But Mrs Fairfield's lips set. She disapproved of Mrs
Harry Kember. Beryl knew it.

Poor old mother, she smiled, as she skimmed over the stones. Poor
old mother! Old! Oh, what joy, what bliss it was to be young . . .

'You looked very pleased,' said Mrs Harry Kember. She sat hunched
up on the stones, her arms round her knees, smoking.

'It's such a lovely day,' said Beryl, smiling down at her.

'Oh, my *dear*!' Mrs Harry Kember's voice sounded as though she
knew better than that. But then her voice always sounded as though
she knew something more about you than you did yourself. She was a
long, strange-looking woman with narrow hands and feet. Her face,
too, was long and narrow and exhausted-looking; even her fair curled

fringe looked burnt out and withered. She was the only woman at the Bay who smoked, and she smoked incessantly, keeping the cigarette between her lips while she talked, and only taking it out when the ash was so long you could not understand why it did not fall. When she was not playing bridge – she played bridge every day of her life – she spent her time lying in the full glare of the sun. She could stand any amount of it; she never had enough. All the same, it did not seem to warm her. Parched, withered, cold, she lay stretched on the stones like a piece of tossed-up driftwood. The women at the Bay thought she was very, very fast. Her lack of vanity, her slang, the way she treated men as though she was one of them, and the fact that she didn't care twopence about her house and called the servant Gladys 'Glad-eyes', was disgraceful. Standing on the veranda steps Mrs Kember would call in her indifferent, tired voice, 'I say, Glad-eyes, you might heave me a handkerchief if I've got one, will you?' And Glad-eyes, a red bow in her hair instead of a cap, and white shoes, came running with an impudent smile. It was an absolute scandal! True, she had no children, and her husband . . . Here the voices were always raised; they became fervent. How can he have married her? How can he, how can he? It must have been money, of course, but even then!

Mrs Kember's husband was at least ten years younger than she was, and so incredibly handsome that he looked like a mask or a most perfect illustration in an American novel rather than a man. Black hair, dark blue eyes, red lips, a slow sleepy smile, a fine tennis player, a perfect dancer, and with it all a mystery. Harry Kember was like a man walking in his sleep. Men couldn't stand him, they couldn't get a word out of the chap; he ignored his wife just as she ignored him. How did he live? Of course there were stories, but such stories! They simply couldn't be told. The women he'd been seen with, the places he'd been seen in . . . but nothing was ever certain, nothing definite. Some of the women at the Bay privately thought he'd commit a murder one day. Yes, even while they talked to Mrs Kember and took in the awful concoction she was wearing, they saw her, stretched as she lay on the beach; but cold, bloody, and still with a cigarette stuck in the corner of her mouth.

Mrs Kember rose, yawned, unsnapped her belt buckle, and tugged at the tape of her blouse. And Beryl stepped out of her skirt and shed her jersey, and stood up in her short white petticoat, and her camisole with ribbon bows on the shoulders.

'Mercy on us,' said Mrs Harry Kember, 'what a little beauty you are!'

'Don't!' said Beryl softly; but, drawing off one stocking and then the other, she felt a little beauty.

'My dear – why not?' said Mrs Harry Kember, stamping on her own petticoat. Really – her underclothes! A pair of blue cotton knickers and a linen bodice that reminded one somehow of a pillow-case . . . 'And you don't wear stays, do you?' She touched Beryl's waist, and Beryl sprang away with a small affected cry. Then 'Never!' she said firmly.

'Lucky little creature,' sighed Mrs Kember, unfastening her own.

Beryl turned her back and began the complicated movements of someone who is trying to take off her clothes and to pull on her bathing-dress all at one and the same time.

'Oh, my dear – don't mind me,' said Mrs Harry Kember. 'Why be shy? I shan't eat you. I shan't be shocked like those other ninnies.' And she gave her strange neighing laugh and grimaced at the other women.

But Beryl was shy. She never undressed in front of anybody. Was that silly? Mrs Harry Kember made her feel it was silly, even something to be ashamed of. Why be shy indeed! She glanced quickly at her friend standing so boldly in her torn chemise and lighting a fresh cigarette; and a quick, bold, evil feeling started up in her breast. Laughing recklessly, she drew on the limp, sandy-feeling bathing-dress that was not quite dry and fastened the twisted buttons.

'That's better,' said Mrs Harry Kember. They began to go down the beach together. 'Really, it's a sin for you to wear clothes, my dear. Somebody's got to tell you some day.'

The water was quite warm. It was that marvellous transparent blue, flecked with silver, but the sand at the bottom looked gold; when you kicked with your toes there rose a little puff of gold-dust. Now the waves just reached her breast. Beryl stood, her arms outstretched, gazing out, and as each wave came she gave the slightest little jump, so that it seemed it was the wave which lifted her so gently.

'I believe in pretty girls having a good time,' said Mrs Harry Kember. 'Why not? Don't you make a mistake, my dear. Enjoy yourself.' And suddenly she turned turtle, disappeared, and swam away quickly, quickly, like a rat. Then she flicked round and began swimming back.

She was going to say something else. Beryl felt that she was being poisoned by this cold woman, but she longed to hear. But oh, how strange, how horrible! As Mrs Harry Kember came up close she looked, in her black waterproof bathing-cap, with her sleepy face lifted above the water, just her chin touching, like a horrible caricature of her husband.

VI

In a steamer chair, under a manuka tree that grew in the middle of the front grass patch, Linda Burnell dreamed the morning away. She did nothing. She looked up at the dark, close, dry leaves of the manuka, at the chinks of blue between, and now and again a tiny yellowish flower dropped on her. Pretty – yes, if you held one of those flowers on the palm of your hand and looked at it closely, it was an exquisite small thing. Each pale yellow petal shone as if each was the careful work of a loving hand. The tiny tongue in the centre gave it the shape of a bell. And when you turned it over the outside was a deep bronze colour. But as soon as they flowered, they fell and were scattered. You brushed them off your frock as you talked; the horrid little things got caught in one's hair. Why, then, flower at all? Who takes the trouble – or the joy – to make all these things that are wasted, wasted ... It was uncanny.

On the grass beside her, lying between two pillows, was the boy. Sound asleep he lay, his head turned away from his mother. His fine dark hair looked more like a shadow than like real hair, but his ear was a bright, deep coral. Linda clasped her hands above her head and crossed her feet. It was very pleasant to know that all these bungalows were empty, that everybody was down on the beach, out of sight, out of hearing. She had the garden to herself; she was alone.

Dazzling white the picotees shone; the golden-eyed marigolds glittered; the nasturtiums wreathed the veranda poles in green and gold flame. If only one had time to look at these flowers long enough, time to get over the sense of novelty and strangeness, time to know them! But as soon as one paused to part the petals, to discover the under-side of the leaf, along came Life and one was swept away. And, lying in her cane chair, Linda felt so light; she felt like a leaf. Along came Life like a wind and she was seized and shaken; she had to go. Oh dear, would it always be so? Was there no escape?

. . . Now she sat on the veranda of their Tasmanian home, leaning against her father's knee. And he promised, 'As soon as you and I are old enough, Linny, we'll cut off somewhere, we'll escape. Two boys together. I have a fancy I'd like to sail up a river in China.' Linda saw that river, very wide, covered with little rafts and boats. She saw the yellow hats of the boatmen and she heard their high, thin voices as they called . . .

'Yes, papa.'

But just then a very broad young man with bright ginger hair walked slowly past their house, and slowly, solemnly even, uncovered. Linda's father pulled her ear teasingly, in the way he had.

'Linny's beau,' he whispered.

'Oh, papa, fancy being married to Stanley Burnell!'

Well, she was married to him. And what was more she loved him. Not the Stanley whom every one saw, not the everyday one; but a timid, sensitive, innocent Stanley who knelt down every night to say his prayers, and who longed to be good. Stanley was simple. If he believed in people – as he believed in her, for instance – it was with his whole heart. He could not be disloyal; he could not tell a lie. And how terribly he suffered if he thought anyone – she – was not being dead straight, dead sincere with him! 'This is too subtle for me!' He flung out the words, but his open, quivering, distraught look was like the look of a trapped beast.

But the trouble was – here Linda felt almost inclined to laugh, though heaven knows it was no laughing matter – she saw *her* Stanley so seldom. There were glimpses, moments, breathing spaces of calm, but all the rest of the time it was like living in a house that couldn't be cured of the habit of catching fire, or a ship that got wrecked every day. And it was always Stanley who was in the thick of the danger. Her whole time was spent in rescuing him, and restoring him, and calming him down, and listening to his story. And what was left of her time was spent in the dread of having children.

Linda frowned; she sat up quickly in her steamer chair and clasped her ankles. Yes, that was her real grudge against life; that was what she could not understand. That was the question she asked and asked, and listened in vain for the answer. It was all very well to say it was the common lot of women to bear children. It wasn't true. She, for one, could prove that wrong. She was broken, made weak, her courage was gone, through child-bearing. And what made it doubly hard to bear was, she did not love her children. It was useless pretending. Even if she had had the strength she never would have nursed and played with the little girls. No, it was as though a cold breath had chilled her through and through on each of those awful journeys; she had no warmth left to give them. As to the boy – well, thank heaven, mother had taken him; he was mother's, or Beryl's, or anybody's who wanted him. She had hardly held him in her arms. She was so indifferent about him, that as he lay there . . . Linda glanced down.

The boy had turned over. He lay facing her, and he was no longer asleep. His dark-blue, baby eyes were open; he looked as though he was peeping at his mother. And suddenly his face dimpled; it broke into a wide, toothless smile, a perfect beam, no less.

'I'm here!' that happy smile seemed to say. 'Why don't you like me?'

There was something so quaint, so unexpected about that smile that Linda smiled herself. But she checked herself and said to the boy coldly, 'I don't like babies.'

'Don't like babies?' The boy couldn't believe her. 'Don't like *me*?' He waved his arms foolishly at his mother.

Linda dropped off her chair on to the grass.

'Why do you keep on smiling?' she said severely. 'If you knew what I was thinking about, you wouldn't.'

But he only squeezed up his eyes, slyly, and rolled his head on the pillow. He didn't believe a word she said.

'We know all about that!' smiled the boy.

Linda was so astonished at the confidence of this little creature . . . Ah no, be sincere. That was not what she felt; it was something far different, it was something so new, so . . . The tears danced in her eyes; she breathed in a small whisper to the boy, 'Hallo, my funny!'

But by now the boy had forgotten his mother. He was serious again. Something pink, something soft waved in front of him. He made a grab at it and it immediately disappeared. But when he lay back, another, like the first, appeared. This time he determined to catch it. He made a tremendous effort and rolled right over.

VII

The tide was out; the beach was deserted; lazily flopped the warm sea. The sun beat down, beat down hot and fiery on the fine sand, baking the grey and blue and black and white-veined pebbles. It sucked up the little drop of water that lay in the hollow of the curved shells; it bleached the pink convolvulus that threaded through and through the sand-hills. Nothing seemed to move but the small sand-hoppers. Pit-pit-pit! They were never still.

Over there on the weed-hung rocks that looked at low tide like shaggy beasts come down to the water to drink, the sunlight seemed to spin like a silver coin dropped into each of the small rock pools. They danced, they quivered, and minute ripples laved the porous shores. Looking down, bending over, each pool was like a lake with pink and blue houses clustered on the shores; and oh! the vast mountainous country behind those houses – the ravines, the passes, the dangerous creeks and fearful tracks that led to the water's edge. Underneath waved the sea-forest – pink thread-like trees, velvet anemones, and orange berry-spotted weeds. Now a stone on the bottom moved, rocked, and there was a glimpse of a black feeler; now a thread-like creature wavered by and was lost. Something was happening to the pink, waving trees; they were changing to a cold moonlight blue. And now there sounded the faintest 'plop.' Who made that sound? What was going on down there? And how strong, how damp the seaweed smelled in the hot sun . . .

The green blinds were drawn in the bungalows of the summer colony. Over the verandas, prone on the paddock, flung over the fences, there were exhausted-looking bathing-dresses and rough striped towels. Each back window seemed to have a pair of sand-shoes on the sill and some lumps of rock or a bucket or a collection of pawa shells. The bush quivered in a haze of heat; the sandy road was empty except for the Trouts' dog Snooker, who lay stretched in the very middle of it. His blue eye was turned up, his legs stuck out stiffly, and he gave an occasional desperate sounding puff, as much as to say he had decided to make an end of it and was only waiting for some kind cart to come along.

'What are you looking at, my grandma? Why do you keep stopping and sort of staring at the wall?'

Kezia and her grandmother were taking their siesta together. The little girl, wearing only her short drawers and her under-bodice, her arms and legs bare, lay on one of the puffed-up pillows of her grandma's bed, and the old woman, in a white ruffled dressing-gown, sat in a rocker at the window, with a long piece of pink knitting in her lap. This room that they shared, like the other rooms of the bungalow, was of light varnished wood and the floor was bare. The furniture was of the shabbiest, the simplest. The dressing-table, for instance, was a packing-case in a sprigged muslin petticoat, and the mirror above was very strange; it was as though a little piece of forked lightning was imprisoned in it. On the table there stood a jar of sea-pinks, pressed so tightly together they looked more like a velvet pin-cushion, and a special shell which Kezia had given her grandma for a pin-tray, and another even more special which she had thought would make a very nice place for a watch to curl up in.

'Tell me, grandma,' said Kezia.

The old woman sighed, whipped the wool twice round her thumb, and drew the bone needle through. She was casting on.

'I was thinking of your Uncle William, darling,' she said quietly.

'My Australian Uncle William?' said Kezia. She had another.

'Yes, of course.'

'The one I never saw?'

'That was the one.'

'Well, what happened to him?' Kezia knew perfectly well, but she wanted to be told again.

'He went to the mines, and he got a sunstroke there and died,' said old Mrs Fairfield.

Kezia blinked and considered the picture again . . . A little man fallen over like a tin soldier by the side of a big black hole.

'Does it make you sad to think about him, grandma?' She hated her grandma to be sad.

It was the old woman's turn to consider. Did it make her sad? To look back, back. To stare down the years, as Kezia had seen her doing. To look after *them* as a woman does, long after *they* were out of sight. Did it make her sad? No, life was like that.

'No, Kezia.'

'But why?' asked Kezia. She lifted one bare arm and began to draw things in the air. 'Why did Uncle William have to die? He wasn't old.'

Mrs Fairfield began counting the stitches in threes. 'It just happened,' she said in an absorbed voice.

'Does everybody have to die?' asked Kezia.

'Everybody!'

'*Me?*' Kezia sounded fearfully incredulous.

'Some day, my darling.'

'But, grandma.' Kezia waved her left leg and waggled the toes. They felt sandy. 'What if I just won't?'

The old woman sighed again and drew a long thread from the ball.

'We're not asked, Kezia,' she said sadly. 'It happens to all of us sooner or later.'

Kezia lay still thinking this over. She didn't want to die. It meant she would have to leave here, leave everywhere, for ever, leave – leave her grandma. She rolled over quickly.

'Grandma,' she said in a startled voice.

'What, my pet!'

'*You're* not to die.' Kezia was very decided.

'Ah, Kezia' – her grandma looked up and smiled and shook her head – 'don't let's talk about it.'

'But you're not to. You couldn't leave me. You couldn't not be there.' This was awful. 'Promise me you won't ever do it, grandma,' pleaded Kezia.

The old woman went on knitting.

'Promise me! Say never!'

But still her grandma was silent.

Kezia rolled off the bed; she couldn't bear it any longer, and lightly she leapt on to her grandma's knees, clasped her hands round the old woman's throat and began kissing her, under the chin, behind the ear, and blowing down her neck.

'Say never . . . say never . . . say never –' She gasped between the kisses. And then she began, very softly and lightly, to tickle her grandma.

'Kezia!' The old woman dropped her knitting. She swung back in the rocker. She began to tickle Kezia. 'Say never, say never, say never,' gurgled Kezia, while they lay there laughing in each other's arms. 'Come, that's enough, my squirrel! That's enough, my wild pony!' said old Mrs Fairfield, setting her cap straight. 'Pick up my knitting.'

Both of them had forgotten what the 'never' was about.

VIII

The sun was still full on the garden when the back door of the Burnells' shut with a bang and a very gay figure walked down the path to the gate. It was Alice, the servant girl, dressed for her afternoon out. She wore a white cotton dress with such large red spots on it, and so many that they made you shudder, white shoes and a leghorn turned up under the brim with poppies. Of course she wore gloves, white ones, stained at the fastenings with iron-mould, and in one hand she carried a very dashed-looking sunshade which she referred to as her *perishall*.

Beryl, sitting in the window, fanning her freshly washed hair, thought she had never seen such a guy. If Alice had only blacked her face with a piece of cork before she started out the picture would have been complete. And where did a girl like that go to in a place like this? The heart-shaped Fijian fan beat scornfully at that lovely bright mane. She supposed Alice had picked up some horrible common larrikin and they'd go off into the bush together. Pity to make herself so conspicuous; they'd have hard work to hide with Alice in that rig-out.

But no, Beryl was unfair. Alice was going to tea with Mrs Stubbs, who'd sent her an 'invite' by the little boy who called for orders. She had taken ever such a liking to Mrs Stubbs ever since the first time she went to the shop to get something for her mosquitoes.

'Dear heart!' Mrs Stubbs had clapped her hand to her side. 'I never seen anyone so eaten. You might have been attacked by canningbals.'

Alice did wish there'd been a bit of life on the road though. Made her feel so queer, having nobody behind her. Made her feel all weak in the spine. She couldn't believe that someone wasn't watching her. And yet it was silly to turn round; it gave you away. She pulled up her gloves, hummed to herself and said to the distant gum tree, 'Shan't be long now.' But that was hardly company.

Mrs Stubbs's shop was perched on a little hillock just off the road. It had two big windows for eyes, a broad veranda for a hat, and the sign on the roof, scrawled MRS STUBBS'S, was like a little card stuck rakishly in the hat crown.

On the veranda there hung a long string of bathing-dresses, clinging together as though they'd just been rescued from the sea rather than waiting to go in, and beside them there hung a cluster of sand-shoes so extraordinarily mixed that to get at one pair you had to tear apart and forcibly separate at least fifty. Even then it was the rarest thing to find the left that belonged to the right. So many people had lost patience and gone off with one shoe that fitted and one that was a little too big . . . Mrs Stubbs prided herself on keeping something of everything. The two windows, arranged in the form of precarious pyramids, were crammed so tight, piled so high, that it seemed only a conjuror could prevent them from toppling over. In the left-hand corner of one window, glued to the pane by four gelatine lozenges, there was – and there had been from time immemorial – a notice:

LOST! HANSOME GOLE BROOCH
SOLID GOLD
ON OR NEAR BEACH
REWARD OFFERED

Alice pressed open the door. The bell jangled, the red serge curtains parted, and Mrs Stubbs appeared. With her broad smile and the long bacon knife in her hand she looked like a friendly brigand. Alice was welcomed so warmly that she found it quite difficult to keep up her 'manners'. They consisted of persistent little coughs and hems, pulls at her gloves, tweaks at her skirt, and a curious difficulty in seeing what was set before her or understanding what was said.

Tea was laid on the parlour table – ham, sardines, a whole pound of butter, and such a large johnny cake that it looked like an advertisement for somebody's baking powder. But the Primus stove roared so loudly that it was useless to try to talk above it. Alice sat down on the edge of a basket-chair while Mrs Stubbs pumped the stove still higher. Suddenly Mrs Stubbs whipped the cushion off a chair and disclosed a large brown paper parcel.

'I've just had some new photers taken, my dear,' she shouted cheerfully to Alice. 'Tell me what you think of them.'

In a very dainty, refined way Alice wet her finger and put the tissue back from the first one. Life! How many there were! There were three dozzing at least. And she held hers up to the light.

Mrs Stubbs sat in an armchair, leaning very much to one side. There was a look of mild astonishment on her large face, and well there might be. For though the armchair stood on a carpet, to the left of it, miraculously skirting the carpet border, there was a dashing waterfall. On her right stood a Grecian pillar with a giant fern tree on either side of it, and in the background towered a gaunt mountain, pale with snow.

'It is a nice style, isn't it?' shouted Mrs Stubbs; and Alice had just screamed 'Sweetly' when the roaring of the Primus stove died down, fizzled out, ceased, and she said 'Pretty' in a silence that was frightening.

'Draw up your chair, my dear,' said Mrs Stubbs, beginning to pour out. 'Yes,' she said thoughtfully, as she handed the tea, 'but I don't care about the size. I'm having an enlarge-mint. All very well for Christmas cards, but I never was the one for small photers myself. You get no comfort out of them. To say the truth, I find them dis'eartening.'

Alice quite saw what she meant.

'Size,' said Mrs Stubbs. 'Give me size. That was what my poor dear husband was always saying. He couldn't stand anything small. Gave him the creeps. And, strange as it may seem, my dear' – here Mrs Stubbs creaked and seemed to expand herself at the memory – 'it was dropsy that carried him off at the larst. Many's the time they drawn one and a half pints from 'im at the 'ospital ... It seemed like a judgmint.'

Alice burned to know exactly what it was that was drawn from him. She ventured, 'I suppose it was water.'

But Mrs Stubbs fixed Alice with her eyes and replied meaningly, 'It was *liquid,* my dear.'

Liquid! Alice jumped away from the word like a cat and came back to it, nosing and wary.

'That's 'im!' said Mrs Stubbs, and she pointed dramatically to the life-size head and shoulders of a burly man with a dead white rose in the button-hole of his coat that made you think of a curl of cold mutton fat. Just below, in silver letters on a red cardboard ground, were the words, 'Be not afraid, it is I.'

'It's ever such a fine face,' said Alice faintly.

The pale-blue bow on the top of Mrs Stubbs's fair frizzy hair quivered. She arched her plump neck. What a neck she had! It was bright pink where it began and then it changed to warm apricot, and that faded to the colour of a brown egg and then to a deep creamy.

'All the same, my dear,' she said surprisingly, 'freedom's best!' Her soft, fat chuckle sounded like a purr. 'Freedom's best,' said Mrs Stubbs again.

Freedom! Alice gave a loud, silly little titter. She felt awkward. Her mind flew back to her own kitching. Ever so queer! She wanted to be back in it again.

IX

A strange company assembled in the Burnells' washhouse after tea. Round the table there sat a bull, a rooster, a donkey that kept forgetting it was a donkey, a sheep and a bee. The washhouse was the perfect place for such a meeting because they could make as much noise as they liked and nobody ever interrupted. It was a small tin shed standing apart from the bungalow. Against the wall there was a deep trough and in the corner a copper with a basket of clothes-pegs on top of it. The little window, spun over with cobwebs, had a piece of candle and a mouse-trap on the dusty sill. There were clotheslines criss-crossed overhead and, hanging from a peg on the wall, a very big, a huge, rusty horseshoe. The table was in the middle with a form at either side.

'You can't be a bee, Kezia. A bee's not an animal. It's a ninseck.'

'Oh, but I do want to be a bee frightfully,' wailed Kezia . . . A tiny bee, all yellow-furry, with striped legs. She drew her legs up under her and leaned over the table. She felt she was a bee.

'A ninseck must be an animal,' she said stoutly. 'It makes a noise. It's not like a fish.'

'I'm a bull, I'm a bull!' cried Pip. And he gave such a tremendous bellow — how did he make that noise? — that Lottie looked quite alarmed.

'I'll be a sheep,' said little Rags. 'A whole lot of sheep went past this morning.'

'How do you know?'

'Dad heard them. Baa!' He sounded like the little lamb that trots behind and seems to wait to be carried.

'Cock-a-doodle-do!' shrilled Isabel. With her red cheeks and bright eyes she looked like a rooster.

'What'll I be?' Lottie asked everybody, and she sat there smiling, waiting for them to decide for her. It had to be an easy one.

'Be a donkey, Lottie.' It was Kezia's suggestion. 'Heehaw! You can't forget that.'

'Hee-haw!' said Lottie solemnly. 'When do I have to say it?'

'I'll explain, I'll explain,' said the bull. It was he who had the cards. He waved them round his head. 'All be quiet! All listen!' And he waited for them. 'Look here, Lottie.' He turned up a card. 'It's got two spots on it – see? Now, if you put that card in the middle and some-body else has one with two spots as well, you say "Hee-haw," and the card's yours.'

'Mine?' Lottie was round-eyed. 'To keep?'

'No, silly. Just for the game, see? Just while we're playing.' The bull was very cross with her.

'Oh, Lottie, you *are* a little silly,' said the proud rooster.

Lottie looked at both of them. Then she hung her head; her lip quivered. 'I don't not want to play,' she whispered. The others glanced at one another like conspirators. All of them knew what that meant. She would go away and be discovered somewhere standing with her pinny thrown over her head, in a corner, or against a wall, or even behind a chair.

'Yes, you *do,* Lottie. It's quite easy,' said Kezia.

And Isabel, repentant, said exactly like a grown-up, 'Watch *me,* Lottie, and you'll soon learn.'

'Cheer up, Lot,' said Pip. 'There, I know what I'll do. I'll give you the first one. It's mine, really, but I'll give it to you. Here you are.' And he slammed the card down in front of Lottie.

Lottie revived at that. But now she was in another difficulty. 'I haven't got a hanky,' she said; 'I want one badly, too.'

'Here, Lottie, you can use mine.' Rags dipped into his sailor blouse and brought up a very wet-looking one, knotted together. 'Be very careful,' he warned her. 'Only use that corner. Don't undo it. I've got a little star-fish inside I'm going to try and tame.'

'Oh, come on, you girls,' said the bull. 'And mind – you're not to look at your cards. You've got to keep your hands under the table till I say "Go."'

Smack went the cards round the table. They tried with all their might to see, but Pip was too quick for them. It was very exciting, sitting there in the washhouse; it was all they could do not to burst into a little chorus of animals before Pip had finished dealing.

'Now, Lottie, you begin.'

Timidly Lottie stretched out a hand, took the top card off her pack, had a good look at it – it was plain she was counting the spots – and put it down.

'No, Lottie, you can't do that. You mustn't look first. You must turn it the other way over.'

'But then everybody will see it the same time as me,' said Lottie.

The game proceeded. Mooe-ooo-er! The bull was terrible. He charged over the table and seemed to eat the cards up.

Bss-ss! said the bee.

Cock-a-doodle-do! Isabel stood up in her excitement and moved her elbows like wings.

Baa! Little Rags put down the King of Diamonds and Lottie put down the one they called the King of Spain. She had hardly any cards left.

'Why don't you call out, Lottie?'

'I've forgotten what I am,' said the donkey woefully.

'Well, change! Be a dog instead! Bow-wow!'

'Oh yes. That's *much* easier.' Lottie smiled again. But when she and Kezia both had one Kezia waited on purpose. The others made signs to Lottie and pointed. Lottie turned very red; she looked bewildered, and at last she said, 'Heehaw! Ke-zia.'

'Ss! Wait a minute!' They were in the very thick of it when the bull stopped them, holding up his hand. 'What's that? What's that noise?'

'What noise? What do you mean?' asked the rooster.

'Ss! Shut up! Listen!' They were mouse-still. 'I thought I heard a – a sort of knocking,' said the bull.

'What was it like?' asked the sheep faintly.

No answer.

The bee gave a shudder. 'Whatever did we shut the door for?' she said softly. Oh, why, why had they shut the door?

While they were playing, the day had faded; the gorgeous sunset had blazed and died. And now the quick dark came racing over the sea, over the sand-hills, up the paddock. You were frightened to look in the corners of the washhouse, and yet you had to look with all your might. And somewhere, far away, grandma was lighting a lamp. The blinds were being pulled down; the kitchen fire leapt in the tins on the mantelpiece.

'It would be awful now,' said the bull, 'if a spider was to fall from the ceiling on to the table, wouldn't it?'

'Spiders don't fall from ceilings.'

'Yes, they do. Our Min told us she'd seen a spider as big as a saucer, with long hairs on it like a gooseberry.'

Quickly all the little heads were jerked up; all the little bodies drew together, pressed together.

'Why doesn't somebody come and call us?' cried the rooster.

Oh, those grown-ups, laughing and snug, sitting in the lamplight, drinking out of cups! They'd forgotten about them. No, not really forgotten. That was what their smile meant. They had decided to leave them there all by themselves.

Suddenly Lottie gave such a piercing scream that all of them jumped off the forms, all of them screamed too. 'A face – a face looking!' shrieked Lottie.

It was true, it was real. Pressed against the window was a pale face, black eyes, a black beard.

'Grandma! Mother! Somebody!'

But they had not got to the door, tumbling over one another, before it opened for Uncle Jonathan. He had come to take the little boys home.

X

He had meant to be there before, but in the front garden he had come upon Linda walking up and down the grass, stopping to pick off a dead pink or give a top-heavy carnation something to lean against, or to take a deep breath of something, and then walking on again, with her little air of remoteness. Over her white frock she wore a yellow, pink-fringed shawl from the Chinaman's shop.

'Hallo, Jonathan!' called Linda. And Jonathan whipped off his shabby panama, pressed it against his breast, dropped on one knee, and kissed Linda's hand.

'Greeting, my Fair One! Greeting, my Celestial Peach Blossom!' boomed the bass voice gently. 'Where are the other noble dames?'

'Beryl's out playing bridge and mother's giving the boy his bath . . . Have you come to borrow something?'

The Trouts were for ever running out of things and sending across to the Burnells' at the last moment.

But Jonathan only answered, 'A little love, a little kindness'; and he walked by his sister-in-law's side.

Linda dropped into Beryl's hammock under the manuka tree and Jonathan stretched himself on the grass beside her, pulled a long stalk and began chewing it. They knew each other well. The voices of children cried from the other gardens. A fisherman's light cart shook along the sandy road, and from far away they heard a dog barking; it was muffled as though the dog had its head in a sack. If you listened you could just hear the soft swish of the sea at full tide sweeping the pebbles. The sun was sinking.

'And so you go back to the office on Monday, do you, Jonathan?' asked Linda.

'On Monday the cage door opens and clangs to upon the victim for another eleven months and a week,' answered Jonathan.

Linda swung a little. 'It must be awful,' she said slowly.

'Would ye have me laugh, my fair sister? Would ye have me weep?'

Linda was so accustomed to Jonathan's way of talking that she paid no attention to it.

'I suppose,' she said vaguely, 'one gets used to it. One gets used to anything.'

'Does one? Hum!' The 'Hum' was so deep it seemed to boom from underneath the ground. 'I wonder how it's done,' brooded Jonathan; 'I've never managed it.'

Looking at him as he lay there, Linda thought again how attractive he was. It was strange to think that he was only an ordinary clerk, that Stanley earned twice as much money as he. What was the matter with Jonathan? He had no ambition; she supposed that was it. And yet one felt he was gifted, exceptional. He was passionately fond of music; every spare penny he had went on books. He was always full of new ideas, schemes, plans. But nothing came of it all. The new fire blazed in Jonathan; you almost heard it roaring softly as he explained, described and dilated on the new thing; but a moment later it had fallen in and there was nothing but ashes, and Jonathan went about with a look like hunger in his black eyes. At these times he exaggerated his absurd manner of speaking, and he sang in church – he was the leader of the choir – with such fearful dramatic intensity that the meanest hymn put on an unholy splendour.

'It seems to me just as imbecile, just as infernal, to have to go to the office on Monday,' said Jonathan, 'as it always has done and always will do. To spend all the best years of one's life sitting on a stool from nine to five, scratching in somebody's ledger! It's a queer use to make of one's . . . one and only life, isn't it? Or do I fondly dream?' He rolled over on the grass and looked up at Linda. 'Tell me, what is the difference between my life and that of an ordinary prisoner. The only difference I can see is that I put myself in jail and nobody's ever going to let me out. That's a more intolerable situation than the other. For if I'd been – pushed in, against my will – kicking, even – once the door was locked, or at any rate in five years or so, I might have accepted the fact and begun to take an interest in the flight of flies or counting the warder's steps along the passage with particular attention to variations of tread and so on. But as it is, I'm like an insect that's flown into a room of its own accord. I dash against the walls, dash against the windows, flop against the ceiling, do everything on God's earth, in fact, except fly out again. And all the while I'm thinking, like that moth, or that butterfly, or whatever it is, "The shortness of life! The shortness of life!" I've only one night or one day, and there's this vast dangerous garden, waiting out there, undiscovered, unexplored.'

'But, if you feel like that, why –' began Linda quickly.

'*Ah!*' cried Jonathan. And that 'Ah!' was somehow almost exultant. 'There you have me. Why? Why indeed? There's the maddening, mysterious question. Why don't I fly out again? There's the window or the door or whatever it was I came in by. It's not hopelessly shut – is it? Why don't I find it and be off? Answer me that, little sister.' But he gave her no time to answer.

'I'm exactly like that insect again. For some reason' – Jonathan paused between the words – 'it's not allowed, it's forbidden, it's against the insect law, to stop banging and flopping and crawling up the pane even for an instant. Why don't I leave the office? Why don't I seriously consider, this moment, for instance, what it is that prevents me leaving? It's not as though I'm tremendously tied. I've two boys to provide for, but, after all, they're boys. I could cut off to sea, or get a job up-country, or –' Suddenly he smiled at Linda and said in a changed voice, as if he were confiding a secret, 'Weak . . . weak. No stamina. No anchor. No guiding principle, let us call it.' But then the dark velvety voice rolled out:

> Would ye hear the story
> How it unfolds itself . . .

and they were silent.

The sun had set. In the western sky there were great masses of crushed-up rose-coloured clouds. Broad beams of light shone through the clouds and beyond them as if they would cover the whole sky. Overhead the blue faded; it turned a pale gold, and the bush outlined against it gleamed dark and brilliant like metal. Sometimes when those beams of light show in the sky they are very awful. They remind you that up there sits Jehovah, the jealous God, the Almighty, Whose eye is upon you, ever watchful, never weary. You remember that at His coming the whole earth will shake into one ruined graveyard; the cold, bright angels will drive you this way and that, and there will be no time to explain what could be explained so simply . . . But tonight it seemed to Linda there was something infinitely joyful and loving in those silver beams. And now no sound came from the sea. It breathed softly as if it would draw that tender, joyful beauty into its own bosom.

'It's all wrong, it's all wrong,' came the shadowy voice of Jonathan. 'It's not the scene, it's not the setting for . . . three stools, three desks, three inkpots and a wire blind.'

Linda knew that he would never change, but she said, 'Is it too late, even now?'

'I'm old – I'm old,' intoned Jonathan. He bent towards her, he passed his hand over his head. 'Look!' His black hair was speckled all over with silver, like the breast plumage of a black fowl.

Linda was surprised. She had no idea that he was grey. And yet, as he stood up beside her and sighed and stretched, she saw him, for the first time, not resolute, not gallant, not careless, but touched already with age. He looked very tall on the darkening grass, and the thought crossed her mind, 'He is like a weed.'

Jonathan stooped again and kissed her fingers.

'Heaven reward thy sweet patience, lady mine,' he murmured. 'I must go seek those heirs to my fame and fortune . . .' He was gone.

XI

Light shone in the windows of the bungalow. Two square patches of gold fell upon the pinks and the peaked marigolds. Florrie, the cat, came out on to the veranda and sat on the top step, her white paws close together, her tail curled round. She looked content, as though she had been waiting for this moment all day.

'Thank goodness, it's getting late,' said Florrie. 'Thank goodness, the long day is over.' Her greengage eyes opened.

Presently there sounded the rumble of the coach, the crack of Kelly's whip. It came near enough for one to hear the voices of the men from town, talking loudly together. It stopped at the Burnells' gate.

Stanley was half-way up the path before he saw Linda. 'Is that you, darling?'

'Yes, Stanley.'

He leapt across the flower-bed and seized her in his arms. She was enfolded in that familiar, eager, strong embrace.

'Forgive me, darling, forgive me,' stammered Stanley, and he put his hand under her chin and lifted her face to him.

'Forgive you?' smiled Linda. 'But whatever for?'

'Good God! You can't have forgotten,' cried Stanley Burnell. 'I've thought of nothing else all day. I've had the hell of a day. I made up my mind to dash out and telegraph, and then I thought the wire mightn't reach you before I did. I've been in tortures, Linda.'

'But, Stanley,' said Linda, 'what must I forgive you for?'

'Linda!' – Stanley was very hurt – 'didn't you realise – you must have realised – I went away without saying goodbye to you this morning? I can't imagine how I can have done such a thing. My confounded temper, of course. But – well' – and he sighed and took her in his arms again – 'I've suffered for it enough today.'

'What's that you've got in your hand?' asked Linda. 'New gloves? Let me see.'

'Oh, just a cheap pair of wash-leather ones,' said Stanley humbly. 'I noticed Bell was wearing some in the coach this morning, so, as I was passing the shop, I dashed in and got myself a pair. What are you smiling at? You don't think it was wrong of me, do you?'

'On the *con*-trary, darling,' said Linda, 'I think it was most sensible.'

She pulled one of the large, pale gloves on her own fingers and looked at her hand, turning it this way and that. She was still smiling.

Stanley wanted to say, 'I was thinking of you the whole time I bought them.' It was true, but for some reason he couldn't say it. 'Let's go in,' said he.

XII

Why does one feel so different at night? Why is it so exciting to be awake when everybody else is asleep? Late – it is very late! And yet every moment you feel more and more wakeful, as though you were slowly, almost with every breath, waking up into a new, wonderful, far more thrilling and exciting world than the daylight one. And what is this queer sensation that you're a conspirator? Lightly, stealthily you move about your room. You take something off the dressing-table and put it down again without a sound. And everything, even the bedpost, knows you, responds, shares your secret . . .

You're not very fond of your room by day. You never think about it. You're in and out, the door opens and slams, the cupboard creaks. You sit down on the side of your bed, change your shoes and dash out again. A dive down to the glass, two pins in your hair, powder your nose and off again. But now – it's suddenly dear to you. It's a darling little funny room. It's yours. Oh, what a joy it is to own things! Mine – my own!

'My very own for ever?'

'Yes.' Their lips met.

No, of course, that had nothing to do with it. That was all nonsense and rubbish. But, in spite of herself, Beryl saw so plainly two people standing in the middle of her room. Her arms were round his neck; he held her. And now he whispered, 'My beauty, my little beauty!' She jumped off her bed, ran over to the window and knelt on the window-seat, with her elbows on the sill. But the beautiful night, the garden, every bush, every leaf, even the white palings, even the stars, were conspirators too. So bright was the moon that the flowers were bright as by day; the shadow of the nasturtiums, exquisite lily-like leaves and wide-open flowers, lay across the silvery veranda. The manuka tree, bent by the southerly winds, was like a bird on one leg stretching out a wing.

But when Beryl looked at the bush, it seemed to her the bush was sad.

'We are dumb trees, reaching up in the night, imploring we know not what,' said the sorrowful bush.

It is true when you are by yourself and you think about life, it is always sad. All that excitement and so on has a way of suddenly leaving you, and it's as though, in the silence, somebody called your name, and you heard your name for the first time. 'Beryl!'

'Yes, I'm here. I'm Beryl. Who wants me?'

'Beryl!'

'Let me come.'

It is lonely living by oneself. Of course, there are relations, friends, heaps of them; but that's not what she means. She wants someone who will find the Beryl they none of them know, who will expect her to be that Beryl always. She wants a lover.

'Take me away from all these other people, my love. Let us go far away. Let us live our life, all new, all ours, from the very beginning. Let us make our fire. Let us sit down to eat together. Let us have long talks at night.'

And the thought was almost, 'Save me, my love. Save me!'

. . . 'Oh, go on! Don't be a prude, my dear. You enjoy yourself while you're young. That's my advice.' And a high rush of silly laughter joined Mrs Harry Kember's loud, indifferent neigh.

You see, it's so frightfully difficult when you've nobody. You're so at the mercy of things. You can't just be rude. And you've always this horror of seeming inexperienced and stuffy like the other ninnies at the Bay. And – and it's fascinating to know you've power over people. Yes, that is fascinating . . .

Oh why, oh why doesn't 'he' come soon?

If I go on living here, thought Beryl, anything may happen to me.

'But how do you know he is coming at all?' mocked a small voice within her.

But Beryl dismissed it. She couldn't be left. Other people, perhaps, but not she. It wasn't possible to think that Beryl Fairfield never married, that lovely, fascinating girl.

'Do you remember Beryl Fairfield?'

'Remember her! As if I could forget her! It was one summer at the Bay that I saw her. She was standing on the beach in a blue' – no, pink – 'muslin frock, holding on a big cream' – no, black – 'straw hat. But it's years ago now.'

'She's as lovely as ever, more so if anything.'

Beryl smiled, bit her lip, and gazed over the garden. As she gazed, she saw somebody, a man, leave the road, step along the paddock beside their palings as if he was coming straight towards her. Her heart beat. Who was it? Who could it be? It couldn't be a burglar, certainly not a burglar, for he was smoking and he strolled lightly. Beryl's heart leapt; it seemed to turn right over and then to stop. She recognised him.

'Good evening, Miss Beryl,' said the voice softly.

'Good evening.'

'Won't you come for a little walk?' it drawled.

Come for a walk – at that time of night! 'I couldn't. Everybody's in bed. Everybody's asleep.'

'Oh,' said the voice lightly, and a whiff of sweet smoke reached her. 'What does everybody matter? Do come! It's such a fine night. There's not a soul about.'

Beryl shook her head. But already something stirred in her, something reared its head.

The voice said, 'Frightened?' It mocked, 'Poor little girl!'

'Not in the least,' said she. As she spoke that weak thing within her seemed to uncoil, to grow suddenly tremendously strong; she longed to go!

And just as if this was quite understood by the other, the voice said, gently and softly, but finally, 'Come along!'

Beryl stepped over her low window, crossed the veranda, ran down the grass to the gate. He was there before her.

'That's right,' breathed the voice, and it teased, 'You're not frightened, are you? You're not frightened?'

She was; now she was here she was terrified and it seemed to her everything was different. The moonlight stared and glittered; the shadows were like bars of iron. Her hand was taken.

'Not in the least,' she said lightly. 'Why should I be?'

Her hand was pulled gently, tugged. She held back.

'No, I'm not coming any further,' said Beryl.

'Oh, rot!' Harry Kember didn't believe her. 'Come along! We'll just go as far as that fuchsia bush. Come along!'

The fuchsia bush was tall. It fell over the fence in a shower. There was a little pit of darkness beneath.

'No, really, I don't want to,' said Beryl.

For a moment Harry Kember didn't answer. Then he came close to her, turned to her, smiled and said quickly, 'Don't be silly! Don't be silly!'

His smile was something she'd never seen before. Was he drunk? That bright, blind, terrifying smile froze her with horror. What was she doing? How had she got here? The stern garden asked her as the gate pushed open, and quick as a cat Harry Kember came through and snatched her to him.

'Cold little devil! Cold little devil!' said the hateful voice.

But Beryl was strong. She slipped, ducked, wrenched free.

'You are vile, vile,' said she.

'Then why in God's name did you come?' stammered Harry Kember. Nobody answered him.

A cloud, small, serene, floated across the moon. In that moment of darkness the sea sounded deep, troubled. Then the cloud sailed away, and the sound of the sea was a vague murmur, as though it waked out of a dark dream. All was still.

(written 1921, first published in 1922, first book publication
The Garden Party and Other Stories, 1922)

The Voyage

The Picton boat was due to leave at half-past eleven. It was a beautiful night, mild, starry, only when they got out of the cab and started to walk down the Old Wharf that jutted out into the harbour, a faint wind blowing off the water ruffled under Fenella's hat, and she put up her hand to keep it on. It was dark on the Old Wharf, very dark; the wool sheds, the cattle trucks, the cranes standing up so high, the little squat railway engine, all seemed carved out of solid darkness. Here and there on a rounded wood-pile, that was like the stalk of a huge black mushroom, there hung a lantern, but it seemed afraid to unfurl its timid, quivering light in all that blackness; it burned softly, as if for itself.

Fenella's father pushed on with quick, nervous strides. Beside him her grandma bustled along in her crackling black ulster; they went so fast that she had now and again to give an undignified little skip to keep up with them. As well as her luggage strapped into a neat sausage, Fenella carried clasped to her her grandma's umbrella, and the handle, which was a swan's head, kept giving her shoulder a sharp little peck as if it too wanted her to hurry . . . Men, their caps pulled down, their collars turned up, swung by; a few women all muffled scurried along; and one tiny boy, only his little black arms and legs showing out of a white woolly shawl, was jerked along angrily between his father and mother; he looked like a baby fly that had fallen into the cream.

Then suddenly, so suddenly that Fenella and her grandma both leapt, there sounded from behind the largest wool shed, that had a trail of smoke hanging over it, *Mia-oo-oo-O-O!*

'First whistle,' said her father briefly, and at that moment they came in sight of the Picton boat. Lying beside the dark wharf, all strung, all beaded with round golden lights, the Picton boat looked as if she was more ready to sail among stars than out into the cold sea. People pressed along the gangway. First went her grandma, then her father, then Fenella. There was a high step down on to the deck, and an old sailor in a jersey standing by gave her his dry, hard hand. They were there; they stepped out of the way of the hurrying people, and standing under a little iron stairway that led to the upper deck they began to say goodbye.

'There, mother, there's your luggage!' said Fenella's father, giving grandma another strapped-up sausage.

'Thank you, Frank.'

'And you've got your cabin tickets safe?'

'Yes, dear.'

'And your other tickets?'

Grandma felt for them inside her glove and showed him the tips.

'That's right.'

He sounded stern, but Fenella, eagerly watching him, saw that he looked tired and sad. *Mia-oo-oo-O-O!* The second whistle blared just above their heads, and a voice like a cry shouted, 'Any more for the gangway?'

'You'll give my love to father,' Fenella saw her father's lips say. And her grandma, very agitated, answered, 'Of course I will, dear. Go now. You'll be left. Go now, Frank. Go now.'

'It's all right, mother. I've got another three minutes.' To her surprise Fenella saw her father take off his hat. He clasped grandma in his arms and pressed her to him. 'God bless you, mother!' she heard him say.

And grandma put her hand, with the black thread glove that was worn through on her ring finger, against his cheek, and she sobbed, 'God bless you, my own brave son!'

This was so awful that Fenella quickly turned her back on them, swallowed once, twice, and frowned terribly at a little green star on a mast head. But she had to turn round again; her father was going.

'Goodbye Fenella. Be a good girl.' His cold, wet moustache brushed her cheek. But Fenella caught hold of the lapels of his coat.

'How long am I going to stay?' she whispered anxiously. He wouldn't look at her. He shook her off gently, and gently said, 'We'll see about that. Here! Where's your hand?' He pressed something into her palm. 'Here's a shilling in case you should need it.'

A shilling! She must be going away for ever! 'Father!' cried Fenella. But he was gone. He was the last off the ship. The sailors put their shoulders to the gangway. A huge coil of dark rope went flying through the air and fell 'thump' on the wharf. A bell rang; a whistle shrilled. Silently the dark wharf began to slip, to slide, to edge away from them. Now there was a rush of water between. Fenella strained to see with all her might. 'Was that father turning round?' – or waving? – or standing alone? – or walking off by himself? The strip of water grew broader, darker. Now the Picton boat began to swing round steady, pointing out to sea. It was no good looking any longer. There was nothing to be seen but a few lights, the face of the town clock hanging in the air, and more lights, little patches of them, on the dark hills.

The freshening wind tugged at Fenella's skirts; she went back to her grandma. To her relief grandma seemed no longer sad. She had put the two sausages of luggage one on top of the other, and she was sitting on them, her hands folded, her head a little on one side. There was an intent, bright look on her face. Then Fenella saw that her lips were moving and guessed that she was praying. But the old woman gave her a bright nod as if to say the prayer was nearly over. She unclasped her hands, sighed, clasped them again, bent forward, and at last gave herself a soft shake.

'And now, child,' she said, fingering the bow of her bonnet-strings, 'I think we ought to see about our cabins. Keep close to me, and mind you don't slip.'

'Yes, grandma!'

'And be careful the umbrella isn't caught in the stair rail. I saw a beautiful umbrella broken in half like that on my way over.'

'Yes, grandma.'

Dark figures of men lounged against the rails. In the glow of their pipes a nose shone out, or the peak of a cap, or a pair of surprised-looking eyebrows. Fenella glanced up. High in the air a little figure, his hands thrust in his short jacket pockets, stood staring out to sea. The ship rocked ever so little and she thought the stars rocked too. And now a pale steward in a linen coat, holding a tray high in the palm of his hand, stepped out of a lighted doorway and skimmed past them. They went through that doorway. Carefully over the high brass-bound step on to the rubber mat and then down such a terribly steep flight of stairs that grandma had to put both feet on each step, and Fenella clutched the clammy brass rail and forgot all about the swan-necked umbrella.

At the bottom grandma stopped; Fenella was rather afraid she was going to pray again. But no, it was only to get out the cabin tickets. They were in the saloon. It was glaring bright and stifling; the air smelled of paint and burnt chop-bones and india-rubber. Fenella wished her grandma would go on, but the old woman was not to be hurried. An immense basket of ham sandwiches caught her eye. She went up to them and touched the top one delicately with her finger.

'How much are the sandwiches?' she asked.

'Tuppence!' bawled a rude steward, slamming down a knife and fork.

Grandma could hardly believe it.

'Twopence *each*?' she asked.

'That's right,' said the steward, and he winked at his companion.

Grandma made a small, astonished face. Then she whispered primly to Fenella, 'What wickedness!' And they sailed out at the further door and along a passage that had cabins on either side. Such a very nice stewardess came to meet them. She was dressed all in blue and her collar and cuffs were fastened with large brass buttons. She seemed to know grandma well.

'Well, Mrs Crane,' said she, unlocking their washstand. 'We've got you back again. It's not often you give yourself a cabin.'

'No,' said grandma. 'But this time my dear son's thoughtfulness –'

'I hope –' began the stewardess. Then she turned round and took a long, mournful look at grandma's blackness and at Fenella's black coat and skirt, black blouse, and hat with a crape rose.

Grandma nodded. 'It was God's will,' said she.

The stewardess shut her lips and, taking a deep breath, she seemed to expand.

'What I always say is,' she said, as though it was her own discovery, 'sooner or later each of us has to go, and that's a certingty.' She paused. 'Now, can I bring you anything, Mrs Crane? A cup of tea? I know it's no good offering you a little something to keep the cold out.'

Grandma shook her head. 'Nothing, thank you. We've got a few wine biscuits and Fenella has a very nice banana.'

'Then I'll give you a look later on,' said the stewardess; and she went out, shutting the door.

What a very small cabin it was! It was like being shut up in a box with grandma. The dark round eye above the washstand gleamed at them dully. Fenella felt shy. She stood against the door, still clasping her luggage and the umbrella. Were they going to get undressed in here? Already her grandma had taken off her bonnet, and, rolling up the strings, she fixed each with a pin to the lining before she hung the bonnet up. Her white hair shone like silk; the little bun at the back was covered with a black net. Fenella hardly ever saw her grandma with her head uncovered; she looked strange.

'I shall put on the woollen fascinator your dear mother crocheted for me,' said grandma, and, unstrapping the sausage, she took it out and wound it round her head; the fringe of grey bobbles danced at her eyebrows as she smiled tenderly and mournfully at Fenella. Then she undid her bodice, and something under that, and something else underneath that. Then there seemed a short, sharp tussle, and grandma flushed faintly. Snip! Snap! She had undone her stays. She breathed a sigh of relief and, sitting on the plush couch, she slowly and carefully pulled off her elastic-sided boots and stood them side by side.

By the time Fenella had taken off her coat and skirt and put on her flannel dressing-gown grandma was quite ready.

'Must I take off my boots, grandma? They're lace.'

Grandma gave them a moment's deep consideration. 'You'd feel a great deal more comfortable if you did, child,' said she. She kissed Fenella. 'Don't forget to say your prayers. Our dear Lord is with us when we are at sea even more than when we are on dry land. And because I am an experienced traveller,' said grandma briskly, 'I shall take the upper berth.'

'But, grandma, how ever will you get up there?'

Three little spider-like steps were all Fenella saw. The old woman gave a small silent laugh before she mounted them nimbly, and she peered over the high bunk at the astonished Fenella.

'You didn't think your grandma could do that, did you?' said she. And as she sank back Fenella heard her light laugh again.

The hard square of brown soap would not lather and the water in the bottle was like a kind of blue jelly. How hard it was, too, to turn down those stiff sheets; you simply had to tear your way in. If everything had been different, Fenella might have got the giggles ... At last she was inside, and while she lay there panting, there sounded from above a long, soft whispering, as though someone was gently, gently rustling among tissue paper to find something. It was grandma saying her prayers ...

A long time passed. Then the stewardess came in; she trod softly and leaned her hand on grandma's bunk.

'We're just entering the Straits,' she said.

'Oh!'

'It's a fine night, but we're rather empty. We may pitch a little.'

And indeed at that moment the Picton boat rose and rose and hung in the air just long enough to give a shiver before she swung down again, and there was the sound of heavy water slapping against her sides. Fenella remembered she had left that swan-necked umbrella standing up on the little couch. If it fell over, would it break? But grandma remembered too, at the same time.

'I wonder if you'd mind, stewardess, laying down my umbrella,' she whispered.

'Not at all, Mrs Crane.' And the stewardess, coming back to grandma, breathed, 'Your little granddaughter's in such a beautiful sleep.'

'God be praised for that!' said grandma.

'Poor little motherless mite!' said the stewardess. And grandma was still telling the stewardess all about what happened when Fenella fell asleep.

But she hadn't been asleep long enough to dream before she woke up again to see something waving in the air above her head. What was it? What could it be? It was a small grey foot. Now another joined it. They seemed to be feeling about for something; there came a sigh.

'I'm awake, grandma,' said Fenella.

'Oh, dear, am I near the ladder?' asked grandma. 'I thought it was this end.'

'No, grandma, it's the other. I'll put your foot on it. Are we there?' asked Fenella.

'In the harbour,' said grandma. 'We must get up, child. You'd better have a biscuit to steady yourself before you move.'

But Fenella had hopped out of her bunk. The lamp was still burning, but night was over, and it was cold. Peering through that round eye she could see far off some rocks. Now they were scattered over with foam; now a gull flipped by; and now there came a long piece of real land.

'It's land, grandma,' said Fenella, wonderingly, as though they had been at sea for weeks together. She hugged herself; she stood on one leg and rubbed it with the toes of the other foot; she was trembling. Oh, it had all been so sad lately. Was it going to change? But all her grandma said was, 'Make haste, child. I should leave your nice banana for the stewardess as you haven't eaten it.' And Fenella put on her black clothes again and a button sprang off one of her gloves and rolled to where she couldn't reach it. They went up on deck.

But if it had been cold in the cabin, on deck it was like ice. The sun was not up yet, but the stars were dim, and the cold pale sky was the same colour as the cold pale sea. On the land a white mist rose and fell. Now they could see quite plainly dark bush. Even the shapes of the umbrella ferns showed, and those strange silvery withered trees that are like skeletons . . . Now they could see the landing-stage and some little houses, pale too, clustered together, like shells on the lid of a box. The other passengers tramped up and down, but more slowly than they had the night before, and they looked gloomy.

And now the landing-stage came out to meet them. Slowly it swam towards the Picton boat and a man holding a coil of rope, and a cart with a small drooping horse and another man sitting on the step, came too.

'It's Mr Penreddy, Fenella, come for us,' said grandma. She sounded pleased. Her white waxen cheeks were blue with cold, her chin trembled, and she had to keep wiping her eyes and her little pink nose.

'You've got my –'

'Yes, grandma.' Fenella showed it to her.

The rope came flying through the air and 'smack' it fell on to the deck. The gangway was lowered. Again Fenella followed her grandma on to the wharf over to the little cart, and a moment later they were bowling away. The hooves of the little horse drummed over the wooden piles, then sank softly into the sandy road. Not a soul was to be seen; there was not even a feather of smoke. The mist rose and fell and the sea still sounded asleep as slowly it turned on the beach.

'I seen Mr Crane yestiddy,' said Mr Penreddy. 'He looked himself then. Missus knocked him up a batch of scones last week.'

And now the little horse pulled up before one of the shell-like houses. They got down. Fenella put her hand on the gate, and the big, trembling dew-drops soaked through her glove-tips. Up a little path of round white pebbles they went, with drenched sleeping flowers on either side. Grandma's delicate white picotees were so heavy with dew that they were fallen, but their sweet smell was part of the cold morning. The blinds were down in the little house; they mounted the steps on to the veranda. A pair of old bluchers was on one side of the door and a large red watering-can on the other.

'Tut! tut! Your grandpa,' said grandma. She turned the handle. Not a sound. She called, 'Walter!' And immediately a deep voice that sounded half stifled called back, 'Is that you, Mary?'

'Wait, dear,' said grandma. 'Go in there.' She pushed Fenella gently into a small dusky sitting-room.

On the table a white cat, that had been folded up like a camel, rose, stretched itself, yawned, and then sprang on to the tips of its toes. Fenella buried one cold little hand in the white, warm fur, and smiled timidly while she stroked and listened to grandma's gentle voice and the rolling tones of grandpa.

A door creaked. 'Come in, dear.' The old woman beckoned, Fenella followed. There, lying to one side of an immense bed, lay grandpa. Just his head with a white tuft and his rosy face and long silver beard showed over the quilt. He was like a very old, wide-awake bird.

'Well, my girl!' said grandpa. 'Give us a kiss!' Fenella kissed him. 'Ugh!' said grandpa. 'Her little nose is as cold as a button. What's that she's holding? Her grandma's umbrella?'

Fenella smiled again and crooked the swan neck over the bed-rail. Above the bed there was a big text in a deep black frame:

> Lost! One Golden Hour
> Set with Sixty Diamond Minutes.
> *No* Reward Is Offered
> For It Is *GONE FOR EVER!*

'Yer grandma painted that,' said grandpa. And he ruffled his white tuft and looked at Fenella so merrily she almost thought he winked at her.

(written 1921, first published in 1921, first book publication
The Garden Party and Other Stories, 1922)

A Married Man's Story

I

It is evening. Supper is over. We have left the small, cold dining-room, we have come back to the sitting-room where there is a fire. All is as usual. I am sitting at my writing-table which is placed across a corner so that I am behind it, as it were, and facing the room. The lamp with the green shade is alight; I have before me two large books of reference, both open, a pile of papers . . . All the paraphernalia, in fact, of an extremely occupied man. My wife, with her little boy on her lap, is in a low chair before the fire. She is about to put him to bed before she clears away the dishes and piles them up in the kitchen for the servant girl tomorrow morning. But the warmth, the quiet, and the sleepy baby, have made her dreamy. One of his red woollen boots is off, one is on. She sits, bent forward, clasping the little bare foot, staring into the glow, and as the fire quickens, falls, flares again, her shadow – an immense *Mother and Child* – is here and gone again upon the wall . . .

Outside it is raining. I like to think of that cold drenched window behind the blind, and beyond, the dark bushes in the garden, their broad leaves bright with rain, and beyond the fence, the gleaming road with the two hoarse little gutters singing against each other, and the wavering reflections of the lamps, like fishes' tails. While I am here, I am there, lifting my face to the dim sky, and it seems to me it must be raining all over the world – that the whole earth is drenched, is sounding with a soft, quick patter or hard, steady drumming, or gurgling and something that is like sobbing and laughing mingled together, and that light, playful splashing that is of water falling into still lakes and flowing rivers. And all at one and the same moment I am arriving in a strange city, slipping under the hood of the cab while the driver whips the cover off the breathing horse, running from shelter to shelter, dodging someone, swerving by someone else. I am conscious of tall houses, their doors and shutters sealed against the night, of dripping balconies and sodden flower-pots. I am brushing through deserted gardens and falling into moist smelling summer-houses (you know how soft and almost crumbling the wood of a summer-house is in the rain); I am standing on the dark quayside giving my ticket into the wet, red hand of the old sailor in an oilskin. How strong the sea smells! How loudly the tied-up boats knock against one another! I am crossing the wet stackyard, hooded in an old sack, carrying a lantern, while the house-dog, like a soaking doormat, springs, shakes himself over me. And now I am walking along a deserted road – it is impossible to miss the puddles, and the trees are stirring – stirring.

But one could go on with such a catalogue for ever – on and on – until one lifted the single arum lily leaf and discovered the tiny snails clinging, until one counted . . . and what then? Aren't those just the signs, the traces of my feeling? The bright green streaks made by someone who walks over the dewy grass? Not the feeling itself. And as I think that a mournful, glorious voice begins to sing in my bosom. Yes, perhaps that is nearer what I mean. What a voice! What power! What velvety softness! Marvellous!

Suddenly my wife turns round quickly. She knows – how long has she known? – that I am not 'working'. It is strange that with her full, open gaze she should smile so timidly – and that she should say in such a hesitating voice, 'What are you thinking?'

I smile and draw two fingers across my forehead in the way I have. 'Nothing,' I answer softly.

At that she stirs and, still trying not to make it sound important, she says, 'Oh, but you must have been thinking of something!'

Then I really meet her gaze, meet it fully, and I fancy her face quivers. Will she never grow accustomed to these simple – one might say – everyday little lies? Will she never learn not to expose herself – or to build up defences?

'Truly, I was thinking of nothing.'

There! I seem to see it dart at her. She turns away, pulls the other red sock off the baby, sits him up, and begins to unbutton him behind. I wonder if that little soft rolling bundle sees anything, feels anything? Now she turns him over on her knee, and in this light, his soft arms and legs waving, he is extraordinarily like a young crab. A queer thing is I can't connect him with my wife and myself – I've never accepted him as ours. Each time when I come into the hall and see the perambulator I catch myself thinking: 'H'm, someone has brought a baby!'

Or, when his crying wakes me at night, I feel inclined to blame my wife for having brought the baby in from outside. The truth is, that though one might suspect her of strong maternal feelings, my wife doesn't seem to me the type of woman who bears children in her own body. There's an immense difference! Where is that . . . animal ease and playfulness, that quick kissing and cuddling one has been taught to expect of young mothers? She hasn't a sign of it. I believe that when she ties its bonnet she feels like an aunt and not a mother. But of course I may be wrong; she may be passionately devoted . . . I don't think so. At any rate, isn't it a trifle indecent to feel like this about one's own wife? Indecent or not, one has these feelings. And one other thing. How can I reasonably expect my wife, *a broken-hearted woman,* to spend her time tossing the baby? But that is beside the mark. She never even began to toss when her heart was whole.

And now she has carried the baby to bed. I hear her soft, deliberate steps moving between the dining-room and the kitchen, there and back again, to the tune of the clattering dishes. And now all is quiet. What is happening now? Oh, I know just as surely as if I'd gone to see – she is standing in the middle of the kitchen facing the rainy window. Her head is bent, with one finger she is tracing something – nothing – on the table. It is cold in the kitchen; the gas jumps; the tap drips; it's a forlorn picture. And nobody is going to come behind her, to take her in his arms, to kiss her soft hair, to lead her to the fire and to rub her hands warm again. Nobody is going to call her or to wonder what she is doing out there. And she knows it. And yet, being a woman, deep down, deep down, she really does expect the miracle to happen; she really could embrace that dark, dark deceit, rather than live – like this.

II

To live like this . . . I write those words very carefully, very beautifully. For some reason I feel inclined to sign them, or to write underneath – Trying a New Pen. But, seriously, isn't it staggering to think what may be contained in one innocent-looking little phrase? It tempts me – it tempts me terribly. Scene: The supper-table. My wife has just handed me my tea. I stir it, lift the spoon, idly chase and then carefully capture a speck of tea-leaf, and having brought it ashore, I murmur, quite gently, 'How long shall we continue to live – like – this?' And immediately there is that famous 'blinding flash and deafening roar. Huge pieces of débris (I must say I like débris) are flung into the air . . . and when the dark clouds of smoke have drifted away . . .' But this will never happen; I shall never know it. It will be found upon me 'intact', as they say. 'Open my heart and you will see . . .'

Why? Ah, there you have me! There is the most difficult question of all to answer. Why do people stay together? Putting aside 'for the sake of the children', and 'the habit of years' and 'economic reasons' as lawyers' nonsense – it's not much more – if one really does try to find out why it is that people don't leave each other, one discovers a mystery. It is because they can't; they are bound. And nobody on earth knows what are the bonds that bind them except those two. Am I being obscure? Well, the thing itself isn't so frightfully crystal clear, is it? Let me put it like this. Supposing you are taken, absolutely, first into his confidence and then into hers. Supposing you know all there is to know about the situation. And having given it not only your deepest sympathy but your most honest impartial criticism, you declare, very calmly (but not without the slightest suggestion of relish – for there is – I swear there is – in the very best of us – something that leaps up and cries 'A-ahh!' for joy at the thought of destroying), 'Well, my opinion is that you two people ought to part. You'll do no earthly good together. Indeed, it seems to me, it's the duty of either to set the other free.' What happens then? He – and she – agree. It is their conviction too. You are only saying what they have been thinking all last night. And away they go to act on your advice, immediately . . . And the next time you hear of them they are still together. You see – you've reckoned without the unknown quantity – which is their secret relation to each other – and that they can't disclose even if they want to. Thus far you may tell and no further. Oh, don't misunderstand me! It need not necessarily have anything to do with their sleeping together . . . But this brings me to a thought I've often half entertained. Which is that human beings, as we know them, don't choose each other at all. It is the owner, the second self inhabiting them, who makes the choice for his own particular purposes, and – this may sound absurdly far-fetched – it's the second self in the other which responds.

Dimly – dimly – or so it has seemed to me – we realise this, at any rate to the extent that we realise the hopelessness of trying to escape. So that, what it all amounts to is – if the impermanent selves of my wife and me are happy – *tant mieux pour nous* – if miserable – *tant pis* . . . But I don't know, I don't know. And it may be that it's something entirely individual in me – this sensation (yes, it is even a sensation) of how extraordinarily *shell-like* we are as we are – little creatures, peering out of the sentry-box at the gate, ogling through our glass case at the entry, wan little servants, who never can say for certain, even, if the master is out or in . . .

The door opens . . . My wife. She says, 'I am going to bed.'

And I look up vaguely, and vaguely say, 'You are going to bed.'

'Yes.' A tiny pause. 'Don't forget – will you? – to turn out the gas in the hall.'

And again I repeat, 'The gas in the hall.'

There was a time – the time before – when this habit of mine – it really has become a habit now – it wasn't one then – was one of our sweetest jokes together. It began, of course, when on several occasions I really was deeply engaged and I didn't hear. I emerged only to see her shaking her head and laughing at me, 'You haven't heard a word!'

'No. What did you say?'

Why should she think that so funny and charming? She did – it delighted her. 'Oh, my darling, it's so like you! It's so – so –' And I knew she loved me for it. I knew she positively looked forward to coming in and disturbing me, and so – as one does – I played up. I was guaranteed to be wrapped away every evening at 10.30 p.m. But now? For some reason I feel it would be crude to stop my performance. It's simplest to play on. But what is she waiting for tonight? Why doesn't she go? Why prolong this? She is going. No, her hand on the door-knob, she turns round again, and she says in the most curious, small, breathless voice, 'You're not cold?'

Oh, it's not fair to be as pathetic as that! That was simply damnable. I shuddered all over before I managed to bring out a slow 'No-o!' while my left hand ruffles the reference pages.

She is gone; she will not come back again tonight. It is not only I who recognise that – the room changes too. It relaxes, like an old actor. Slowly the mask is rubbed off; the look of strained attention changes to an air of heavy, sullen brooding. Every line, every fold breathes fatigue. The mirror is quenched; the ash whitens; only my sly lamp burns on . . . But what a cynical indifference to me it all shows! Or should I perhaps be flattered? No, we understand each other. You know those stories of little children who are suckled by wolves and accepted by the tribe, and how for ever after they move freely among their fleet, grey brothers? Something like that has happened to me. But wait! That about the wolves won't do. Curious! Before I wrote it down, while it was still in my head, I was delighted with it. It seemed to express, and more, to suggest, just what I wanted to say. But written, I can smell the falseness immediately and the . . . source of the smell is in that word fleet. Don't you agree? Fleet, grey brothers! 'Fleet.' A word I never use. When I wrote 'wolves' it skimmed across my mind like a shadow and I couldn't resist it. Tell me! Tell me! Why is it so difficult to write simply – and not simply only but *sotto voce,* if you know what I mean? That is how I long to write. No fine effects – no bravura. But just the plain truth, as only a liar can tell it.

III

I light a cigarette, lean back, inhale deeply – and find myself wondering if my wife is asleep. Or is she lying in her cold bed, staring into the dark, with those trustful, bewildered eyes? Her eyes are like the eyes of a cow that is being driven along a road. 'Why am I being driven – what harm have I done?' But I really am not responsible for that look; it's her natural expression. One day, when she was turning out a cupboard, she found a little old photograph of herself, taken when she was a girl at school. In her confirmation dress, she explained. And there were the eyes, even then. I remember saying to her, 'Did you always look so sad?' Leaning over my shoulder, she laughed lightly, 'Do I look sad? I think it's just . . . me.' And she waited for me to say something about it. But I was marvelling at her courage at having shown it to me at all. It was a hideous photograph! And I wondered again if she realised how plain she was, and comforted herself with the idea that people who loved each other didn't criticise but accepted everything, or if she really rather liked her appearance and expected me to say something complimentary.

Oh, that was base of me! How could I have forgotten all the numberless times when I have known her turn away to avoid the light, press her face into my shoulders. And, above all, how could I have forgotten the afternoon of our wedding-day when we sat on the green bench in the Botanical Gardens and listened to the band; how, in an interval between two pieces, she suddenly turned to me and said in the voice in which one says, 'Do you think the grass is damp?' or 'Do you think it's time for tea?' . . . 'Tell me, do you think physical beauty is so very important?' I don't like to think how often she had rehearsed that question. And do you know what I answered? At that moment, as if at my command, there came a great gush of hard, bright sound from the band, and I managed to shout above it cheerfully, 'I didn't hear what you said.' Devilish! Wasn't it? Perhaps not wholly. She looked like the poor patient who hears the surgeon say, 'It will certainly be necessary to perform the operation – but not now!'

IV

But all this conveys the impression that my wife and I were never really happy together. Not true! Not true! We were marvellously, radiantly happy. We were a model couple. If you had seen us together, any time, any place, if you had followed us, tracked us down, spied, taken us off our guard, you still would have been forced to confess, 'I have never seen a more ideally suited pair.' Until last autumn.

But really to explain what happened then I should have to go back and back – I should have to dwindle until my two hands clutched the banisters, the stair-rail was higher than my head, and I peered through to watch my father padding softly up and down. There were coloured windows on the landings. As he came up, first his bald head was scarlet, then it was yellow. How frightened I was! And when they put me to bed, it was to dream that we were living inside one of my father's big coloured bottles. For he was a chemist. I was born nine years after my parents were married. I was an only child, and the effect to produce even me – small, withered bud I must have been – sapped all my mother's strength. She never left her room again. Bed, sofa, window, she moved between the three. Well I can see her, on the window days, sitting, her cheek in her hand, staring out. Her room looked over the street. Opposite there was a wall plastered with advertisements for travelling shows and circuses and so on. I stand beside her, and we gaze at the slim lady in a red dress hitting a dark gentleman over the head with her parasol, or at the tiger peering through the jungle while the clown, close by, balances a bottle on his nose, or at a little golden-haired girl sitting on the knee of an old black man in a broad cotton hat . . . She says nothing. On sofa days there is a flannel dressing-gown that I loathe and a cushion that keeps on slipping off the hard sofa. I pick it up. It has flowers and writing sewn on. I ask what the writing says, and she whispers, 'Sweet Repose!' In bed her fingers plait, in tight little plaits, the fringe of the quilt and her lips are thin. And that is all there is of my mother, except the last queer 'episode' that comes later.

My father . . . Curled up in the corner on the lid of a round box that held sponges, I stared at my father so long, it's as though his image, cut off at the waist by the counter, has remained solid in my memory. Perfectly bald, polished head, shaped like a thin egg, creased, creamy cheeks, little bags under the eyes, large pale ears like handles. His man-ner was discreet, sly, faintly amused and tinged with impudence. Long before I could appreciate it I knew the mixture . . . I even used to copy him in my corner, bending forward, with a small reproduction of his faint sneer. In the evening his customers were, chiefly, young women; some of them came in every day for his famous fivepenny pick-me-up. Their gaudy looks, their voices, their free ways fascinated me. I longed to be my father, handing them across the counter the little glass of blu-ish stuff they tossed off so greedily. God knows what it was made of. Years after I drank some, just to see what it tasted like, and I felt as though someone had given me a terrific blow on the head; I felt stunned.

One of those evenings I remember vividly. It was cold; it must have been autumn, for the flaring gas was lighted after my tea. I sat in my corner and my father was mixing something; the shop was empty. Suddenly the bell jangled and a young woman rushed in, crying so loud, sobbing so hard, that it didn't sound real. She wore a green cape trimmed with fur and a hat with cherries dangling. My father came from behind the screen. But she couldn't stop herself at first. She stood in the middle of the shop and wrung her hands and moaned; I've never heard such crying since. Presently she managed to gasp out, 'Give me

a pick-me-up!' Then she drew a long breath, trembled away from him
and quavered, 'I've had *bad news!*' And in the flaring gaslight I saw the
whole side of her face was puffed up and purple; her lip was cut and
her eyelid looked as though it was gummed fast over the wet eye. My
father pushed the glass across the counter, and she took the purse out
of her stocking and paid him. But she couldn't drink; clutching the
glass, she stared in front of her as if she could not believe what she saw.
Each time she put her head back the tears spurted out again. Finally
she put the glass down. It was no use. Holding the cape with one hand,
she ran in the same way out of the shop again. My father gave no sign.
But long after she had gone I crouched in my corner, and when I think
back it's as though I felt my whole body vibrating – 'So that's what it
is outside,' I thought. 'That's what it's like out there.'

V

Do you remember your childhood? I am always coming across these
marvellous accounts by writers who declare that they remember
'everything'. I certainly don't. The dark stretches, the blanks, are
much bigger than the bright glimpses. I seem to have spent most of my
time like a plant in a cupboard. Now and again, when the sun shone, a
careless hand thrust me out on to the window-sill, and a careless hand
whipped me in again – and that was all. But what happened in the
darkness – I wonder? Did one grow? Pale stem . . . timid leaves . . .
white reluctant bud. No wonder I was hated at school. Even the masters shrank from me. I somehow knew that my soft, hesitating voice
disgusted them. I knew, too, how they turned away from my shocked,
staring eyes. I was small and thin and I smelled of the shop; my nick-
name was Gregory Powder. School was a tin building, stuck on the
raw hillside. There were dark red streaks like blood in the oozing clay
banks of the playground. I hide in the dark passage, where the coats
hang, and am discovered there by one of the masters. 'What are you
doing there in the dark?' His terrible voice kills me; I die before his
eyes. I am standing in a ring of thrust-out heads; some are grinning,
some look greedy, some are spitting. And it is always cold. Big
crushed-up clouds press across the sky; the rusty water in the school

tank is frozen; the bell sounds numb. One day they put a dead bird in my overcoat pocket. I found it just when I reached home. Oh, what a strange flutter there was at my heart when I drew out that terribly soft, cold little body, with the legs thin as pins and the claws wrung. I sat on the back door step in the yard and put the bird in my cap. The feathers round the neck looked wet and there was a tiny tuft just above the closed eyes that stood up too. How tightly the beak was shut! I could not see the mark where it was divided. I stretched out one wing and touched the soft, secret down underneath; I tried to make the claws curl round my little finger. But I didn't feel sorry for it – no! I wondered. The smoke from our kitchen chimney poured downwards, and flakes of soot floated – soft, light in the air. Through a big crack in the cement yard a poor-looking plant with dull, reddish flowers had pushed its way. I looked at the dead bird again . . . And that is the first time that I remember singing – rather . . . listening to a silent voice inside a little cage that was me.

VI

But what has all this to do with my married happiness? How can all this affect my wife and me? Why – to tell what happened last autumn – do I run all this way back into the Past? The Past – what is the Past? I might say the star-shaped flake of soot on a leaf of the poor-looking plant, and the bird lying on the quilted lining of my cap, and my father's pestle and my mother's cushion belong to it. But that is not to say they are any less mine than they were when I looked upon them with my very eyes and touched them with these fingers. No, they are more – they are a living part of me. Who am I, in fact, as I sit here at this table, but my own past? If I deny that, I am nothing. And if I were to try to divide my life into childhood, youth, early manhood and so on, it would be a kind of affectation; I should know I was doing it just because of the pleasantly important sensation it gives one to rule lines and to use green ink for childhood, red for the next stage, and purple for the period of adolescence. For, one thing I have learnt, one thing I do believe is, Nothing Happens Suddenly. Yes, that is my religion, I suppose.

My mother's death, for instance. Is it more distant from me today than it was then? It is just as close, as strange, as puzzling, and, in spite of all the countless times I have recalled the circumstances, I know no more now than I did then, whether I dreamed them, or whether they really occurred. It happened when I was thirteen and I slept in a little strip of a room on what was called the half-landing. One night I woke up with a start to see my mother, in her nightgown, without even the hated flannel dressing-gown, sitting on my bed. But the strange thing which frightened me was, she wasn't looking at me. Her head was bent; the short, thin trail of hair lay between her shoulders; her hands were pressed between her knees and my bed shook; she was shivering. It was the first time I had ever seen her out of her own room. I said, or I think I said, 'Is that you, Mother?' And as she turned round, I saw in the moonlight how queer she looked. Her face looked small – quite different. She looked like one of the boys at the school baths, who sits on a step, shivering just like that, and wants to go in and yet is frightened.

'Are you awake?' she said. Her eyes opened; I think she smiled. She leaned towards me. 'I've been poisoned,' she whispered. 'Your father's poisoned me.' And she nodded. Then, before I could say a word, she was gone; I thought I heard the door shut. I sat quite still, I couldn't move, I think I expected something else to happen. For a long time I listened for something; there wasn't a sound. The candle was by my bed, but I was too frightened to stretch out my hand for the matches. But even while I wondered what I ought to do, even while my heart thumped – everything became confused. I lay down and pulled the blankets round me. I fell asleep, and the next morning my mother was found dead of failure of the heart.

Did that visit happen? Was it a dream? Why did she come to tell me? Or why, if she came, did she go away so quickly? And her expression – so joyous under the frightened look – was that real? I believed it fully the afternoon of the funeral, when I saw my father dressed up for his part, hat and all. That tall hat so gleaming black and round was like a cork covered with black sealing-wax, and the rest of my father was awfully like a bottle, with his face for the label – *Deadly Poison*. It flashed into my mind as I stood opposite him in the hall. And Deadly Poison, or old D. P., was my private name for him from that day.

VII

Late, it grows late. I love the night. I love to feel the tide of darkness rising slowly and slowly washing, turning over and over, lifting, floating, all that lies strewn upon the dark beach, all that lies hid in rocky hollows. I love, I love this strange feeling of drifting – whither? After my mother's death I hated to go to bed. I used to sit on the window-sill, folded up, and watch the sky. It seemed to me the moon moved much faster than the sun. And one big, bright green star I chose for my own. My star! But I never thought of it beckoning to me or twinkling merrily for my sake. Cruel, indifferent, splendid – it burned in the airy night. No matter – it was mine! But, growing close up against the window, there was a creeper with small, bunched-up pink and purple flowers. These did know me. These, when I touched them at night, welcomed my fingers; the little tendrils, so weak, so delicate, knew I would not hurt them. When the wind moved the leaves I felt I understood their shaking. When I came to the window, it seemed to me the flowers said among themselves, 'The boy is here.'

As the months passed there was often a light in my father's room below. And I heard voices and laughter. 'He's got some woman with him,' I thought. But it meant nothing to me. Then the gay voice, the sound of the laughter, gave me the idea it was one of the girls who used to come to the shop in the evenings – and gradually I began to imagine which girl it was. It was the dark one in the red coat and skirt who once had given me a penny. A merry face stooped over me – warm breath tickled my neck – there were little beads of black on her long lashes, and when she opened her arms to kiss me there came a marvellous wave of scent! Yes, that was the one.

Time passed, and I forgot the moon and my green star and my shy creeper – I came to the window to wait for the light in my father's window, to listen for the laughing voice, until one night I dozed and I dreamed she came again – again she drew me to her, something soft, scented, warm and merry hung over me like a cloud. But when I tried to see, her eyes only mocked me, her red lips opened and she hissed, 'Little sneak! Little sneak!' But not as if she were angry, – as if she understood, and her smile somehow was like a rat – hateful!

The night after, I lighted the candle and sat down at the table instead. By and by, as the flame steadied, there was a small lake of liquid wax, surrounded by a white, smooth wall. I took a pin and made little holes in this wall and then sealed them up faster than the wax could escape. After a time I fancied the candle flame joined in the game; it leapt up, quivered, wagged; it even seemed to laugh. But while I played with the candle and smiled and broke off the tiny white peaks of wax that rose above the wall and floated them on my lake, a feeling of awful dreariness fastened on me – yes, that's the word. It crept up from my knees to my thighs, into my arms; I ached all over with misery. And I felt so strangely that I couldn't move. Something bound me there by the table – I couldn't even let the pin drop that I held between my finger and thumb. For a moment I came to a stop, as it were.

Then the shrivelled case of the bud split and fell, the plant in the cupboard came into flower. 'Who am I?' I thought. 'What is all this?' And I looked at my room, at the broken bust of the man called Hahnemann on top of the cupboard, at my little bed with the pillow like an envelope. I saw it all, but not as I had seen before . . . Everything lived, everything. But that was not all. I was equally alive and – it's the only way I can express it – the barriers were down between us – I had come into my own world!

VIII

The barriers were down. I had been all my life a little outcast; but until that moment no one had 'accepted' me; I had lain in the cupboard – or the cave forlorn. But now I was taken, I was accepted, claimed. I did not consciously turn away from the world of human beings; I had never known it; but I from that night did beyond words consciously turn towards my silent brothers . . .

(written 1921, first published in *The Doves' Nest and Other Stories*, 1923)

The Garden Party

And after all the weather was ideal. They could not have had a more perfect day for a garden-party if they had ordered it. Windless, warm, the sky without a cloud. Only the blue was veiled with a haze of light gold, as it is sometimes in early summer. The gardener had been up since dawn, mowing the lawns and sweeping them, until the grass and the dark flat rosettes where the daisy plants had been seemed to shine. As for the roses, you could not help feeling they understood that roses are the only flowers that impress people at garden-parties; the only flowers that everybody is certain of knowing. Hundreds, yes, literally hundreds, had come out in a single night; the green bushes bowed down as though they had been visited by archangels.

Breakfast was not yet over before the men came to put up the marquee.

'Where do you want the marquee put, mother?'

'My dear child, it's no use asking me. I'm determined to leave everything to you children this year. Forget I am your mother. Treat me as an honoured guest.'

But Meg could not possibly go and supervise the men. She had washed her hair before breakfast, and she sat drinking her coffee in a green turban, with a dark wet curl stamped on each cheek. Jose, the butterfly, always came down in a silk petticoat and a kimono jacket.

'You'll have to go, Laura; you're the artistic one.'

Away Laura flew, still holding her piece of bread-and-butter. It's so delicious to have an excuse for eating out of doors and, besides, she loved having to arrange things; she always felt she could do it so much better than anybody else.

Four men in their shirt-sleeves stood grouped together on the garden path. They carried staves covered with rolls of canvas and they had big tool-bags slung on their backs. They looked impressive. Laura wished now that she was not holding that piece of bread-and-butter, but there was nowhere to put it and she couldn't possibly throw it away. She blushed and tried to look severe and even a little bit short-sighted as she came up to them.

'Good morning,' she said, copying her mother's voice. But that sounded so fearfully affected that she was ashamed, and stammered like a little girl, 'Oh – er – have you come – is it about the marquee?'

'That's right, miss,' said the tallest of the men, a lanky, freckled fellow, and he shifted his tool-bag, knocked back his straw hat and smiled down at her. 'That's about it.'

His smile was so easy, so friendly, that Laura recovered. What nice eyes he had, small, but such a dark blue! And now she looked at the others, they were smiling too. 'Cheer up, we won't bite,' their smile seemed to say. How very nice workmen were! And what a beautiful morning! She mustn't mention the morning; she must be business-like. The marquee.

'Well, what about the lily-lawn? Would that do?'

And she pointed to the lily-lawn with the hand that didn't hold the bread-and-butter. They turned, they stared in the direction. A little fat chap thrust out his underlip and the tall fellow frowned.

'I don't fancy it,' said he. 'Not conspicuous enough. You see, with a thing like a marquee' – and he turned to Laura in his easy way – 'you want to put it somewhere where it'll give you a bang slap in the eye, if you follow me.'

Laura's upbringing made her wonder for a moment whether it was quite respectful of a workman to talk to her of bangs slap in the eye. But she did quite follow him.

'A corner of the tennis-court,' she suggested. 'But the band's going to be in one corner.'

'H'm, going to have a band, are you?' said another of the workmen. He was pale. He had a haggard look as his dark eyes scanned the tennis-court. What was he thinking?

'Only a very small band,' said Laura gently. Perhaps he wouldn't mind so much if the band was quite small. But the tall fellow interrupted.

'Look here, miss, that's the place. Against those trees. Over there. That'll do fine.'

Against the karakas. Then the karaka trees would be hidden. And they were so lovely, with their broad, gleaming leaves, and their clusters of yellow fruit. They were like trees you imagined growing on a desert island, proud, solitary, lifting their leaves and fruits to the sun in a kind of silent splendour. Must they be hidden by a marquee?

They must. Already the men had shouldered their staves and were making for the place. Only the tall fellow was left. He bent down, pinched a sprig of lavender, put his thumb and forefinger to his nose and snuffed up the smell. When Laura saw that gesture she forgot all about the karakas in her wonder at him caring for things like that – caring for the smell of lavender. How many men that she knew would have done such a thing. Oh, how extraordinarily nice workmen were, she thought. Why couldn't she have workmen for friends rather than the silly boys she danced with and who came to Sunday night supper? She would get on much better with men like these.

It's all the fault, she decided, as the tall fellow drew something on the back of an envelope, something that was to be looped up or left to hang, of these absurd class distinctions. Well, for her part, she didn't feel them. Not a bit, not an atom . . . And now there came the chock-chock of wooden hammers. Someone whistled, someone sang out, 'Are you right there, matey?' 'Matey!' The friendliness of it, the – the – Just to prove how happy she was, just to show the tall fellow how at home she felt, and how she despised stupid conventions, Laura took a big bite of her bread-and-butter as she stared at the little drawing. She felt just like a work-girl.

'Laura, Laura, where are you? Telephone, Laura!' a voice cried from the house.

'Coming!' Away she skimmed, over the lawn, up the path, up the steps, across the veranda and into the porch. In the hall her father and Laurie were brushing their hats ready to go to the office.

'I say, Laura,' said Laurie very fast, 'you might just give a squiz at my coat before this afternoon. See if it wants pressing.'

'I will,' said she. Suddenly she couldn't stop herself. She ran at Laurie and gave him a small, quick squeeze. 'Oh, I do love parties, don't you?' gasped Laura.

'Ra-ther,' said Laurie's warm, boyish voice, and he squeezed his sister too and gave her a gentle push. 'Dash off to the telephone, old girl.'

The telephone. 'Yes, yes; oh yes. Kitty? Good morning, dear. Come to lunch? Do, dear. Delighted, of course. It will only be a very scratch meal – just the sandwich crusts and broken meringue-shells and what's left over. Yes, isn't it a perfect morning? Your white? Oh, I certainly should. One moment – hold the line. Mother's calling.' And Laura sat back. 'What, mother? Can't hear.'

Mrs Sheridan's voice floated down the stairs. 'Tell her to wear that sweet hat she had on last Sunday.'

'Mother says you're to wear that *sweet* hat you had on last Sunday. Good. One o'clock. Bye-bye.'

Laura put back the receiver, flung her arms over her head, took a deep breath, stretched and let them fall. 'Huh,' she sighed, and the moment after the sigh she sat up quickly. She was still, listening. All the doors in the house seemed to be open. The house was alive with soft, quick steps and running voices. The green baize door that led to the kitchen regions swung open and shut with a muffled thud. And now there came a long, chuckling absurd sound. It was the heavy piano being moved on its stiff castors. But the air! If you stopped to notice, was the air always like this? Little faint winds were playing chase in at the tops of the windows, out at the doors. And there were two tiny spots of sun, one on the inkpot, one on a silver photograph frame, playing too. Darling little spots. Especially the one on the ink-pot lid. It was quite warm. A warm little silver star. She could have kissed it.

The front door bell pealed and there sounded the rustle of Sadie's print skirt on the stairs. A man's voice murmured; Sadie answered, careless, 'I'm sure I don't know. Wait. I'll ask Mrs Sheridan.'

'What is it, Sadie?' Laura came into the hall.

'It's the florist, Miss Laura.'

It was, indeed. There, just inside the door, stood a wide, shallow tray full of pots of pink lilies. No other kind. Nothing but lilies – canna lilies, big pink flowers, wide open, radiant, almost frighteningly alive on bright crimson stems.

'O-oh, Sadie!' said Laura, and the sound was like a little moan. She crouched down as if to warm herself at that blaze of lilies; she felt they were in her fingers, on her lips, growing in her breast.

'It's some mistake,' she said faintly. 'Nobody ever ordered so many. Sadie, go and find mother.'

But at that moment Mrs Sheridan joined them.

'It's quite right,' she said calmly. 'Yes, I ordered them. Aren't they lovely?' She pressed Laura's arm. 'I was passing the shop yesterday, and

I saw them in the window. And I suddenly thought for once in my life I shall have enough canna lilies. The garden party will be a good excuse.'

'But I thought you said you didn't mean to interfere,' said Laura. Sadie had gone. The florist's man was still outside at his van. She put her arm round her mother's neck and gently, very gently, she bit her mother's ear.

'My darling child, you wouldn't like a logical mother, would you? Don't do that. Here's the man.'

He carried more lilies still, another whole tray.

'Bank them up, just inside the door, on both sides of the porch, please,' said Mrs Sheridan. 'Don't you agree, Laura?'

'Oh, I *do*, mother.'

In the drawing-room Meg, Jose and good little Hans had at last succeeded in moving the piano.

'Now, if we put this chesterfield against the wall and move everything out of the room except the chairs, don't you think?'

'Quite.'

'Hans, move these tables into the smoking-room, and bring a sweeper to take these marks off the carpet and – one moment, Hans –' Jose loved giving orders to the servants and they loved obeying her. She always made them feel they were taking part in some drama. 'Tell mother and Miss Laura to come here at once.'

'Very good, Miss Jose.'

She turned to Meg. 'I want to hear what the piano sounds like, just in case I'm asked to sing this afternoon. Let's try over "This Life is Weary." '

Pom! Ta-ta-ta *Tee*-ta! The piano burst out so passionately that Jose's face changed. She clasped her hands. She looked mournfully and enigmatically at her mother and Laura as they came in.

> This Life is *Wee*-ary,
> A Tear – a Sigh.
> A Love that *Chan*-ges,
>   This Life is *Wee*-ary,
> A Tear – a Sigh.
> A Love that *Chan*-ges,
> And then . . . Goodbye!

But at the word 'Goodbye,' and although the piano sounded more desperate than ever, her face broke into a brilliant, dreadfully unsympathetic smile.

'Aren't I in good voice, mummy?' she beamed.

> This Life is *Wee*-ary,
> Hope comes to Die.
> A Dream — a *Wa*-kening.

But now Sadie interrupted them. 'What is it, Sadie?'

'If you please, m'm, cook says have you got the flags for the sandwiches?'

'The flags for the sandwiches, Sadie?' echoed Mrs Sheridan dreamily. And the children knew by her face that she hadn't got them. 'Let me see.' And she said to Sadie firmly, 'Tell cook I'll let her have them in ten minutes.'

Sadie went.

'Now, Laura,' said her mother quickly, 'come with me into the smoking-room. I've got the names somewhere on the back of an envelope. You'll have to write them out for me. Meg, go upstairs this minute and take that wet thing off your head. Jose, run and finish dressing this instant. Do you hear me, children, or shall I have to tell your father when he comes home tonight? And — and, Jose, pacify cook if you do go into the kitchen, will you? I'm terrified of her this morning.'

The envelope was found at last behind the dining-room clock, though how it had got there Mrs Sheridan could not imagine.

'One of you children must have stolen it out of my bag, because I remember vividly — cream-cheese and lemon-curd. Have you done that?'

'Yes.'

'Egg and —' Mrs Sheridan held the envelope away from her. 'It looks like mice. It can't be mice, can it?'

'Olive, pet,' said Laura, looking over her shoulder.

'Yes, of course, olive. What a horrible combination it sounds. Egg and olive.'

They were finished at last, and Laura took them off to the kitchen. She found Jose there pacifying the cook, who did not look at all terrifying.

'I have never seen such exquisite sandwiches,' said Jose's rapturous voice. 'How many kinds did you say there were, cook? Fifteen?'

'Fifteen, Miss Jose.'

'Well, cook, I congratulate you.'

Cook swept up crusts with the long sandwich knife, and smiled broadly.

'Godber's has come,' announced Sadie, issuing out of the pantry. She had seen the man pass the window.

That meant the cream puffs had come. Godber's were famous for their cream puffs. Nobody ever thought of making them at home.

'Bring them in and put them on the table, my girl,' ordered cook.

Sadie brought them in and went back to the door. Of course Laura and Jose were far too grown-up to really care about such things. All the same, they couldn't help agreeing that the puffs looked very attractive. Very. Cook began arranging them, shaking off the extra icing sugar.

'Don't they carry one back to all one's parties?' said Laura.

'I suppose they do,' said practical Jose, who never liked to be carried back. 'They look beautifully light and feathery, I must say.'

'Have one each, my dears,' said cook in her comfortable voice. 'Yer ma won't know.'

Oh, impossible. Fancy cream puffs so soon after breakfast. The very idea made one shudder. All the same, two minutes later Jose and Laura were licking their fingers with that absorbed inward look that only comes from whipped cream.

'Let's go into the garden, out by the back way,' suggested Laura. 'I want to see how the men are getting on with the marquee. They're such awfully nice men.'

But the back door was blocked by cook, Sadie, Godber's man and Hans.

Something had happened.

'Tuk-tuk-tuk,' clucked cook like an agitated hen. Sadie had her hand clapped to her cheek as though she had toothache. Hans's face was screwed up in the effort to understand. Only Godber's man seemed to be enjoying himself; it was his story.

'What's the matter? What's happened?'

'There's been a horrible accident,' said cook. 'A man killed.'

'A man killed! Where? How? When?'

But Godber's man wasn't going to have his story snatched from under his very nose.

'Know those little cottages just below here, miss?' Know them? Of course she knew them. 'Well, there's a young chap living there, name of Scott, a carter. His horse shied at a traction-engine, corner of Hawke Street this morning, and he was thrown out on the back of his head. Killed.'

'Dead!' Laura stared at Godber's man.

'Dead when they picked him up,' said Godber's man with relish. 'They were taking the body home as I come up here.' And he said to the cook, 'He's left a wife and five little ones.'

'Jose, come here.' Laura caught hold of her sister's sleeve and dragged her through the kitchen to the other side of the green baize door. There she paused and leaned against it. 'Jose!' she said, horrified, 'however are we going to stop everything?'

'Stop everything, Laura!' cried Jose in astonishment. 'What do you mean?'

'Stop the garden-party, of course.' Why did Jose pretend?

But Jose was still more amazed. 'Stop the garden-party? My dear Laura, don't be so absurd. Of course we can't do anything of the kind. Nobody expects us to. Don't be so extravagant.'

'But we can't possibly have a garden-party with a man dead just outside the front gate.'

That really was extravagant, for the little cottages were in a lane to themselves at the very bottom of a steep rise that led up to the house. A broad road ran between. True, they were far too near. They were the greatest possible eyesore and they had no right to be in that neighbourhood at all. They were little mean dwellings painted a chocolate brown. In the garden patches there was nothing but cabbage stalks, sick hens and tomato cans. The very smoke coming out of their chimneys was poverty-stricken. Little rags and shreds of smoke, so unlike the great silvery plumes that uncurled from the Sheridans' chimneys. Washerwomen lived in the lane and sweeps and a cobbler and a man whose house-front was studded all over with minute bird-cages. Children swarmed. When the Sheridans were little they were forbidden to set foot there because of the revolting language and of what they might catch. But since they were grown-up Laura and Laurie on their prowls sometimes walked through. It was disgusting and sordid. They came out with a shudder. But still one must go everywhere; one must see everything. So through they went.

'And just think of what the band would sound like to that poor woman,' said Laura.

'Oh, Laura!' Jose began to be seriously annoyed. 'If you're going to stop a band playing every time someone has an accident, you'll lead a very strenuous life. I'm every bit as sorry about it as you. I feel just as sympathetic.' Her eyes hardened. She looked at her sister just as she used to when they were little and fighting together. 'You won't bring a drunken workman back to life by being sentimental,' she said softly.

'Drunk! Who said he was drunk?' Laura turned furiously on Jose. She said just as they had used to say on those occasions, 'I'm going straight up to tell mother.'

'Do, dear,' cooed Jose.

'Mother, can I come into your room?' Laura turned the big glass door-knob.

'Of course, child. Why, what's the matter? What's given you such a colour?' And Mrs Sheridan turned round from her dressing-table. She was trying on a new hat.

'Mother, a man's been killed,' began Laura.

'*Not* in the garden?' interrupted her mother.

'No, no!'

'Oh, what a fright you gave me!' Mrs Sheridan sighed with relief and took off the big hat and held it on her knees.

'But listen, mother,' said Laura. Breathless, half choking, she told the dreadful story. 'Of course, we can't have our party, can we?' she pleaded. 'The band and everybody arriving. They'd hear us, mother; they're nearly neighbours!'

To Laura's astonishment her mother behaved just like Jose; it was harder to bear because she seemed amused. She refused to take Laura seriously.

'But, my dear child, use your common sense. It's only by accident we've heard of it. If someone had died there normally — and I can't understand how they keep alive in those poky little holes — we should still be having our party, shouldn't we?'

Laura had to say 'yes' to that, but she felt it was all wrong. She sat down on her mother's sofa and pinched the cushion frill.

'Mother, isn't it really terribly heartless of us?' she asked.

'Darling!' Mrs Sheridan got up and came over to her, carrying the hat. Before Laura could stop her she had popped it on. 'My child!' said her mother, 'the hat is yours. It's made for you. It's much too young for me. I have never seen you look such a picture. Look at yourself!' And she held up her hand-mirror.

'But, mother,' Laura began again. She couldn't look at herself; she turned aside.

This time Mrs Sheridan lost patience just as Jose had done.

'You are being very absurd, Laura,' she said coldly. 'People like that don't expect sacrifices from us. And it's not very sympathetic to spoil everybody's enjoyment as you're doing now.'

'I don't understand,' said Laura, and she walked quickly out of the room into her own bedroom. There, quite by chance, the first thing she saw was this charming girl in the mirror, in her black hat trimmed with gold daisies and a long black velvet ribbon. Never had she imagined she could look like that. Is mother right? she thought. And now she hoped her mother was right. Am I being extravagant? Perhaps it was extravagant. Just for a moment she had another glimpse of that poor woman and those little children and the body being carried into the house. But it all seemed blurred, unreal, like a picture in the newspaper. I'll remember it again after the party's over, she decided. And somehow that seemed quite the best plan . . .

Lunch was over by half-past one. By half-past two they were all ready for the fray. The green-coated band had arrived and was established in a corner of the tennis-court.

'My dear!' trilled Kitty Maitland, 'aren't they too like frogs for words? You ought to have arranged them round the pond with the conductor in the middle on a leaf.'

Laurie arrived and hailed them on his way to dress. At the sight of him Laura remembered the accident again. She wanted to tell him. If Laurie agreed with the others, then it was bound to be all right. And she followed him into the hall.

'Laurie!'

'Hallo!' He was half-way upstairs, but when he turned round and saw Laura he suddenly puffed out his cheeks and goggled his eyes at her. 'My word, Laura! You do look stunning,' said Laurie. 'What an absolutely topping hat!'

Laura said faintly 'Is it?' and smiled up at Laurie and didn't tell him after all.

Soon after that people began coming in streams. The band struck up; the hired waiters ran from the house to the marquee. Wherever you looked there were couples strolling, bending to the flowers, greeting, moving on over the lawn. They were like bright birds that had alighted in the Sheridans' garden for this one afternoon, on their way to – where? Ah, what happiness it is to be with people who all are happy, to press hands, press cheeks, smile into eyes.

'Darling Laura, how well you look!'

'What a becoming hat, child!'

'Laura, you look quite Spanish. I've never seen you look so striking.'

And Laura, glowing, answered softly, 'Have you had tea? Won't you have an ice? The passion-fruit ices really are rather special.' She ran to her father and begged him: 'Daddy darling, can't the band have something to drink?'

And the perfect afternoon slowly ripened, slowly faded, slowly its petals closed.

'Never a more delightful garden-party . . .' 'The greatest success . . .' 'Quite the most . . .'

Laura helped her mother with the goodbyes. They stood side by side in the porch till it was all over.

'All over, all over, thank heaven,' said Mrs Sheridan. 'Round up the others, Laura. Let's go and have some fresh coffee. I'm exhausted. Yes, it's been very successful. But oh, these parties, these parties! Why will you children insist on giving parties!' And they all of them sat down in the deserted marquee.

'Have a sandwich, daddy dear. I wrote the flag.'

'Thanks.' Mr Sheridan took a bite and the sandwich was gone. He took another. 'I suppose you didn't hear of a beastly accident that happened today?' he said.

'My dear,' said Mrs Sheridan, holding up her hand, 'we did. It nearly ruined the party. Laura insisted we should put it off.'

'Oh, mother!' Laura didn't want to be teased about it.

'It was a horrible affair all the same,' said Mr Sheridan. 'The chap was married too. Lived just below in the lane, and leaves a wife and half a dozen kiddies, so they say.'

An awkward little silence fell. Mrs Sheridan fidgeted with her cup. Really, it was very tactless of father . . .

Suddenly she looked up. There on the table were all those sandwiches, cakes, puffs, all uneaten, all going to be wasted. She had one of her brilliant ideas.

'I know,' she said. 'Let's make up a basket. Let's send that poor creature some of this perfectly good food. At any rate, it will be the greatest treat for the children. Don't you agree? And she's sure to have neighbours calling in and so on. What a point to have it all ready prepared. Laura!' She jumped up. 'Get me the big basket out of the stairs cupboard.'

'But, mother, do you really think it's a good idea?' said Laura.

Again, how curious, she seemed to be different from them all. To take scraps from their party. Would the poor woman really like that?

'Of course! What's the matter with you today? An hour or two ago you were insisting on us being sympathetic.'

Oh well! Laura ran for the basket. It was filled, it was now heaped by her mother.

'Take it yourself, darling,' said she. 'Run down just as you are. No, wait, take the arum lilies too. People of that class are so impressed by arum lilies.'

'The stems will ruin her lace frock,' said practical Jose.

So they would. Just in time. 'Only the basket, then. And, Laura!' – her mother followed her out of the marquee – 'don't on any account –'

'What, mother?'

No, better not put such ideas into the child's head! 'Nothing! Run along.'

It was just growing dusky as Laura shut their garden gates. A big dog ran by like a shadow. The road gleamed white, and down below in the hollow the little cottages were in deep shade. How quiet it seemed after the afternoon. Here she was going down the hill to somewhere where a man lay dead, and she couldn't realise it. Why couldn't she? She stopped a minute. And it seemed to her that kisses, voices, tinkling spoons, laughter, the smell of crushed grass were somehow inside her. She had no room for anything else. How strange! She looked up at the pale sky, and all she thought was, 'Yes, it was the most successful party.'

Now the broad road was crossed. The lane began, smoky and dark.

Women in shawls and men's tweed caps hurried by. Men hung over the palings; the children played in the doorways. A low hum came from the mean little cottages. In some of them there was a flicker of light, and a shadow, crab-like, moved across the window. Laura bent her head and hurried on. She wished now she had put on a coat. How her frock shone! And the big hat with the velvet streamer – if only it was another hat! Were the people looking at her? They must be. It was a mistake to have come; she knew all along it was a mistake. Should she go back even now?

No, too late. This was the house. It must be. A dark knot of people stood outside. Beside the gate an old, old woman with a crutch sat in a chair, watching. She had her feet on a newspaper. The voices stopped as Laura drew near. The group parted. It was as though she was expected, as though they had known she was coming here.

Laura was terribly nervous. Tossing the velvet ribbon over her shoulder, she said to a woman standing by, 'Is this Mrs Scott's house?' and the woman, smiling queerly, said, 'It is, my lass.'

Oh, to be away from this! She actually said, 'Help me, God,' as she walked up the tiny path and knocked. To be away from those staring eyes, or to be covered up in anything, one of those women's shawls even. I'll just leave the basket and go, she decided. I shan't even wait for it to be emptied.

Then the door opened. A little woman in black showed in the gloom.

Laura said, 'Are you Mrs Scott?' But to her horror the woman answered, 'Walk in, please, miss,' and she was shut in the passage.

'No,' said Laura, 'I don't want to come in. I only want to leave this basket. Mother sent –'

The little woman in the gloomy passage seemed not to have heard her. 'Step this way, please, miss,' she said in an oily voice, and Laura followed her.

She found herself in a wretched little low kitchen, lighted by a smoky lamp. There was a woman sitting before the fire.

'Em,' said the little creature who had let her in. 'Em! It's a young lady.' She turned to Laura. She said meaningly, 'I'm 'er sister, miss. You'll excuse 'er, won't you?'

'Oh, but of course!' said Laura. 'Please, please don't disturb her. I – I only want to leave –'

But at that moment the woman at the fire turned round. Her face, puffed up, red, with swollen eyes and swollen lips, looked terrible. She seemed as though she couldn't understand why Laura was there. What did it mean? Why was this stranger standing in the kitchen with a basket? What was it all about? And the poor face puckered up again.

'All right, my dear,' said the other. 'I'll thenk the young lady.'

And again she began, 'You'll excuse her, miss, I'm sure,' and her face, swollen too, tried an oily smile.

Laura only wanted to get out, to get away. She was back in the passage. The door opened. She walked straight through into the bedroom, where the dead man was lying.

'You'd like a look at 'im, wouldn't you?' said Em's sister, and she brushed past Laura over to the bed. 'Don't be afraid, my lass' – and now her voice sounded fond and sly, and fondly she drew down the sheet – ''e looks a picture. There's nothing to show. Come along, my dear.'

Laura came.

There lay a young man, fast asleep – sleeping so soundly, so deeply, that he was far, far away from them both. Oh, so remote, so peaceful. He was dreaming. Never wake him up again. His head was sunk in the pillow, his eyes were closed; they were blind under the closed eyelids. He was given up to his dream. What did garden-parties and baskets and lace frocks matter to him? He was far from all those things. He was wonderful, beautiful. While they were laughing and while the band was playing, this marvel had come to the lane. Happy . . . happy . . . All is well, said that sleeping face. This is just as it should be. I am content.

But all the same you had to cry, and she couldn't go out of the room without saying something to him. Laura gave a loud childish sob.

'Forgive my hat,' she said.

And this time she didn't wait for Em's sister. She found her way out of the door, down the path past all those dark people. At the corner of the lane she met Laurie.

He stepped out of the shadow. 'Is that you, Laura?'

'Yes.'

'Mother was getting anxious. Was it all right?'

'Yes, quite. Oh, Laurie!' She took his arm, she pressed up against him.

'I say, you're not crying, are you?' asked her brother.

Laura shook her head. She was.

Laurie put his arm round her shoulder. 'Don't cry,' he said in his warm, loving voice. 'Was it awful?'

'No,' sobbed Laura. 'It was simply marvellous. But, Laurie –' She stopped, she looked at her brother. 'Isn't life,' she stammered, 'isn't life –' But what life was she couldn't explain. No matter. He quite understood.

'*Isn't* it, darling?' said Laurie.

(written 1921, first published in 1922, first book publication
The Garden Party and Other Stories, 1922)

The Doll's House

When dear old Mrs Hay went back to town after staying with the Burnells she sent the children a doll's house. It was so big that the carter and Pat carried it into the courtyard, and there it stayed, propped up on two wooden boxes beside the feed-room door. No harm could come to it; it was summer. And perhaps the smell of paint would have gone off by the time it had to be taken in. For, really, the smell of paint coming from that doll's house ('Sweet of old Mrs Hay, of course; most sweet and generous!') – but the smell of paint was quite enough to make anyone seriously ill, in Aunt Beryl's opinion. Even before the sacking was taken off. And when it was . . .

There stood the doll's house, a dark, oily, spinach green, picked out with bright yellow. Its two solid little chimneys, glued on to the roof, were painted red and white, and the door, gleaming with yellow varnish, was like a little slab of toffee. Four windows, real windows, were divided into panes by a broad streak of green. There was actually a tiny porch, too, painted yellow, with big lumps of congealed paint hanging along the edge.

But perfect, perfect little house! Who could possibly mind the smell. It was part of the joy, part of the newness.

'Open it quickly, someone!'

The hook at the side was stuck fast. Pat prised it open with his pen-knife, and the whole house front swung back, and – there you were, gazing at one and the same moment into the drawing-room and dining-room, the kitchen and two bedrooms. That is the way for a house to open! Why don't all houses open like that? How much more exciting than peering through the slit of a door into a mean little hall with a hat-stand and two umbrellas! That is – isn't it? – what you long to know about a house when you put your hand on the knocker. Perhaps it is the way God opens houses at the dead of night when He is taking a quiet turn with an angel . . .

'Oh-oh!' The Burnell children sounded as though they were in despair. It was too marvellous; it was too much for them. They had never seen anything like it in their lives. All the rooms were papered. There were pictures on the walls, painted on the paper, with gold frames complete. Red carpet covered all the floors except the kitchen; red plush chairs in the drawing-room, green in the dining-room; tables, beds with real bedclothes, a cradle, a stove, a dresser with tiny plates and one big jug. But what Kezia liked more than anything, what she liked frightfully, was the lamp. It stood in the middle of the dining-room table, an exquisite little amber lamp with a white globe. It was even filled all ready for lighting, though, of course, you couldn't light it. But there was something inside that looked like oil and moved when you shook it.

The father and mother dolls, who sprawled very stiff as though they had fainted in the drawing-room, and their two little children asleep upstairs, were really too big for the doll's house. They didn't look as though they belonged. But the lamp was perfect. It seemed to smile at Kezia, to say, 'I live here.' The lamp was real.

The Burnell children could hardly walk to school fast enough the next morning. They burned to tell everybody, to describe, to – well – to boast about their doll's house before the school-bell rang.

'I'm to tell,' said Isabel, 'because I'm the eldest. And you two can join in after. But I'm to tell first.'

There was nothing to answer. Isabel was bossy, but she was always right, and Lottie and Kezia knew too well the powers that went with being eldest. They brushed through the thick buttercups at the road edge and said nothing.

'And I'm to choose who's to come and see it first. Mother said I might.'

For it had been arranged that while the doll's house stood in the courtyard they might ask the girls at school, two at a time, to come and look. Not to stay to tea, of course, or to come traipsing through the house. But just to stand quietly in the courtyard while Isabel pointed out the beauties, and Lottie and Kezia looked pleased . . .

But hurry as they might, by the time they had reached the tarred palings of the boys' playground the bell had begun to jangle. They only just had time to whip off their hats and fall into line before the roll was called. Never mind. Isabel tried to make up for it by looking very important and mysterious and by whispering behind her hand to the girls near her, 'Got something to tell you at playtime.'

Playtime came and Isabel was surrounded. The girls of her class nearly fought to put their arms round her, to walk away with her, to beam flatteringly, to be her special friend. She held quite a court under the huge pine trees at the side of the playground. Nudging, giggling together, the little girls pressed up close. And the only two who stayed outside the ring were the two who were always outside, the little Kelveys. They knew better than to come anywhere near the Burnells.

For the fact was, the school the Burnell children went to was not at all the kind of place their parents would have chosen if there had been any choice. But there was none. It was the only school for miles. And the consequence was all the children of the neighbourhood, the Judge's little girls, the doctor's daughters, the store-keeper's children, the milkman's, were forced to mix together. Not to speak of there being an equal number of rude, rough little boys as well. But the line had to be drawn somewhere. It was drawn at the Kelveys. Many of the children, including the Burnells, were not allowed even to speak to them. They walked past the Kelveys with their heads in the air, and as they set the fashion in all matters of behaviour, the Kelveys were shunned by everybody. Even the teacher had a special voice for them, and a special smile for the other children when Lil Kelvey came up to her desk with a bunch of dreadfully common-looking flowers.

They were the daughters of a spry, hard-working little washer-woman, who went about from house to house by the day. This was awful enough. But where was Mr Kelvey? Nobody knew for certain. But everybody said he was in prison. So they were the daughters of a washerwoman and a gaolbird. Very nice company for other people's children! And they looked it. Why Mrs Kelvey made them so conspicuous was hard to understand. The truth was they were dressed in 'bits' given to her by the people for whom she worked. Lil, for instance, who was a stout, plain child, with big freckles, came to school in a dress made from a green art-serge tablecloth of the Burnells', with red plush sleeves from the Logans' curtains. Her hat, perched on top of her high forehead, was a grown-up woman's hat, once the property of Miss Lecky, the postmistress. It was turned up at the back and trimmed with a large scarlet quill. What a little guy she looked! It was impossible not to laugh. And her little sister, our Else, wore a long white dress, rather like a nightgown, and a pair of little boy's boots. But whatever our Else wore she would have looked strange. She was a tiny wishbone of a child, with cropped hair and enormous solemn eyes — a little white owl. Nobody had ever seen her smile; she scarcely ever spoke. She went through life holding on to Lil, with a piece of Lil's skirt screwed up in her hand. Where Lil went, our Else followed. In the playground, on the road going to and from school, there was Lil marching in front and our Else holding on behind. Only when she wanted anything, or when she was out of breath, our Else gave Lil a tug, a twitch, and Lil stopped and turned round. The Kelveys never failed to understand each other.

Now they hovered at the edge; you couldn't stop them listening. When the little girls turned round and sneered, Lil, as usual, gave her silly, shamefaced smile, but our Else only looked.

And Isabel's voice, so very proud, went on telling. The carpet made a great sensation, but so did the beds with real bedclothes, and the stove with an oven door.

When she finished Kezia broke in. 'You've forgotten the lamp, Isabel.'

'Oh yes,' said Isabel, 'and there's a teeny little lamp, all made of yellow glass, with a white globe that stands on the dining-room table. You couldn't tell it from a real one.'

'The lamp's best of all,' cried Kezia. She thought Isabel wasn't making half enough of the little lamp. But nobody paid any attention. Isabel was choosing the two who were to come back with them that afternoon and see it. She chose Emmie Cole and Lena Logan. But when the others knew they were all to have a chance, they couldn't be nice enough to Isabel. One by one they put their arms round Isabel's waist and walked her off. They had something to whisper to her, a secret. 'Isabel's *my* friend.'

Only the little Kelveys moved away forgotten; there was nothing more for them to hear.

Days passed, and as more children saw the doll's house, the fame of it spread. It became the one subject, the rage. The one question was, 'Have you seen Burnells' doll's house? Oh, ain't it lovely!' 'Haven't you seen it? Oh, I say!'

Even the dinner hour was given up to talking about it. The little girls sat under the pines eating their thick mutton sandwiches and big slabs of johnny cake spread with butter. While always, as near as they could get, sat the Kelveys, our Else holding on to Lil, listening too, while they chewed their jam sandwiches out of a newspaper soaked with large red blobs.

'Mother,' said Kezia, 'can't I ask the Kelveys just once?'

'Certainly not, Kezia.'

'But why not?'

'Run away, Kezia; you know quite well why not.'

At last everybody had seen it except them. On that day the subject rather flagged. It was the dinner hour. The children stood together under the pine trees, and suddenly, as they looked at the Kelveys eating out of their paper, always by themselves, always listening, they wanted to be horrid to them. Emmie Cole started the whisper.

'Lil Kelvey's going to be a servant when she grows up.'

'O-oh, how awful!' said Isabel Burnell, and she made eyes at Emmie.

Emmie swallowed in a very meaning way and nodded to Isabel as she'd seen her mother do on those occasions.

'It's true – it's true – it's true,' she said.

Then Lena Logan's little eyes snapped. 'Shall I ask her?' she whispered.

'Bet you don't,' said Jessie May.

'Pooh, I'm not frightened,' said Lena. Suddenly she gave a little squeal and danced in front of the other girls. 'Watch! Watch me! Watch me now!' said Lena. And sliding, gliding, dragging one foot, giggling behind her hand, Lena went over to the Kelveys.

Lil looked up from her dinner. She wrapped the rest quickly away. Our Else stopped chewing. What was coming now?

'Is it true you're going to be a servant when you grow up, Lil Kelvey?' shrilled Lena.

Dead silence. But instead of answering, Lil only gave her silly, shamefaced smile. She didn't seem to mind the question at all. What a sell for Lena! The girls began to titter.

Lena couldn't stand that. She put her hands on her hips; she shot forward. 'Yah, yer father's in prison!' she hissed spitefully.

This was such a marvellous thing to have said that the little girls rushed away in a body, deeply, deeply excited, wild with joy. Someone found a long rope, and they began skipping. And never did they skip so high, run in and out so fast, or do such daring things as on that morning.

In the afternoon Pat called for the Burnell children with the buggy and they drove home. There were visitors. Isabel and Lottie, who liked visitors, went upstairs to change their pinafores. But Kezia thieved out at the back. Nobody was about; she began to swing on the big white gates of the courtyard. Presently, looking along the road, she saw two little dots. They grew bigger, they were coming towards her. Now she could see that one was in front and one close behind. Now she could see that they were the Kelveys. Kezia stopped swinging. She slipped off the gate as if she was going to run away. Then she hesitated. The Kelveys came nearer, and beside them walked their shadows, very long, stretching right across the road with their heads in the buttercups. Kezia clambered back on the gate; she had made up her mind; she swung out.

'Hullo,' she said to the passing Kelveys.

They were so astounded that they stopped. Lil gave her silly smile. Our Else stared.

'You can come and see our doll's house if you want to,' said Kezia, and she dragged one toe on the ground. But at that Lil turned red and shook her head quickly.

'Why not?' asked Kezia.

Lil gasped, then she said, 'Your ma told our ma you wasn't to speak to us.'

'Oh, well,' said Kezia. She didn't know what to reply. 'It doesn't matter. You can come and see our doll's house all the same. Come on. Nobody's looking.'

But Lil shook her head still harder.

'Don't you want to?' asked Kezia.

Suddenly there was a twitch, a tug at Lil's skirt. She turned round. Our Else was looking at her with big, imploring eyes; she was frowning; she wanted to go. For a moment Lil looked at our Else very doubtfully. But then our Else twitched her skirt again. She started forward. Kezia led the way. Like two little stray cats they followed across the courtyard to where the doll's house stood.

'There it is,' said Kezia.

There was a pause. Lil breathed loudly, almost snorted; our Else was still as stone.

'I'll open it for you,' said Kezia kindly. She undid the hook and they looked inside.

'There's the drawing-room and the dining-room, and that's the –'

'Kezia!'

Oh, what a start they gave!

'Kezia!'

It was Aunt Beryl's voice. They turned round. At the back door stood Aunt Beryl, staring as if she couldn't believe what she saw.

'How dare you ask the little Kelveys into the courtyard!' said her cold, furious voice. 'You know as well as I do, you're not allowed to talk to them. Run away, children, run away at once. And don't come back again,' said Aunt Beryl. And she stepped into the yard and shooed them out as if they were chickens.

'Off you go immediately!' she called, cold and proud.

They did not need telling twice. Burning with shame, shrinking together, Lil huddling along like her mother, our Else dazed, somehow they crossed the big courtyard and squeezed through the white gate.

'Wicked, disobedient little girl!' said Aunt Beryl bitterly to Kezia, and she slammed the doll's house to.

The afternoon had been awful. A letter had come from Willie Brent, a terrifying, threatening letter, saying if she did not meet him that evening in Pulman's Bush, he'd come to the front door and ask the reason why! But now that she had frightened those little rats of Kelveys and given Kezia a good scolding, her heart felt lighter. That ghastly pressure was gone. She went back to the house humming.

When the Kelveys were well out of sight of the Burnells', they sat down to rest on a big red drainpipe by the side of the road. Lil's cheeks were still burning; she took off the hat with the quill and held it on her knee. Dreamily they looked over the hay paddocks, past the creek, to the group of wattles where Logan's cows stood waiting to be milked. What were their thoughts?

Presently our Else nudged up close to her sister. But now she had forgotten the cross lady. She put out a finger and stroked her sister's quill; she smiled her rare smile.

'I seen the little lamp,' she said softly.

Then both were silent once more.

(written 1921, first published in 1922, first book publication
The Doves' Nest and Other Stories, 1923)

A Cup of Tea

Rosemary Fell was not exactly beautiful. No, you couldn't have called her beautiful. Pretty? Well, if you took her to pieces . . . But why be so cruel as to take anyone to pieces? She was young, brilliant, extremely modern, exquisitely well dressed, amazingly well read in the newest of the new books, and her parties were the most delicious mixture of the really important people and . . . artists – quaint creatures, discoveries of hers, some of them too terrifying for words, but others quite presentable and amusing.

Rosemary had been married two years. She had a duck of a boy. No, not Peter – Michael. And her husband absolutely adored her. They were rich, really rich, not just comfortably well off, which is odious and stuffy and sounds like one's grandparents. But if Rosemary wanted to shop she would go to Paris as you and I would go to Bond Street. If she wanted to buy flowers, the car pulled up at that perfect shop in Regent Street, and Rosemary inside the shop just gazed in her dazzled, rather exotic way, and said: 'I want those and those and those. Give me four bunches of those. And that jar of roses. Yes, I'll have all the roses in the jar. No, no lilac. I hate lilac. It's got no shape.' The attendant bowed and put the lilac out of sight, as though this was only too true; lilac was dreadfully shapeless. 'Give me those stumpy little tulips. Those red and white ones.' And she was followed to the car by a thin shop-girl staggering under an immense white paper armful that looked like a baby in long clothes . . .

One winter afternoon she had been buying something in a little antique shop in Curzon Street. It was a shop she liked. For one thing, one usually had it to oneself. And then the man who kept it was ridiculously fond of serving her. He beamed whenever she came in. He clasped his hands; he was so gratified he could scarcely speak. Flattery, of course. All the same, there was something . . .

'You see, madam,' he would explain in his low respectful tones, 'I love my things. I would rather not part with them than sell them to someone who does not appreciate them, who has not that fine feeling

which is so rare . . .' And, breathing deeply, he unrolled a tiny square
of blue velvet and pressed it on the glass counter with his pale
finger-tips.

Today it was a little box. He had been keeping it for her. He had
shown it to nobody as yet. An exquisite little enamel box with a glaze
so fine it looked as though it had been baked in cream. On the lid a
minute creature stood under a flowery tree, and a more minute creature still had her arms round his neck. Her hat, really no bigger than a
geranium petal, hung from a branch; it had green ribbons. And there
was a pink cloud like a watchful cherub floating above their heads.
Rosemary took her hands out of her long gloves. She always took off
her gloves to examine such things. Yes, she liked it very much. She
loved it; it was a great duck. She must have it. And, turning the creamy
box, opening and shutting it, she couldn't help noticing how charming her hands were against the blue velvet. The shopman, in some dim
cavern of his mind, may have dared to think so too. For he took a
pencil, leaned over the counter, and his pale bloodless fingers crept
timidly towards those rosy, flashing ones, as he murmured gently: 'If
I may venture to point out to madam, the flowers on the little lady's
bodice.'

'Charming!' Rosemary admired the flowers. But what was the
price? For a moment the shopman did not seem to hear. Then a murmur reached her. 'Twenty-eight guineas, madam.'

'Twenty-eight guineas.' Rosemary gave no sign. She laid the little
box down; she buttoned her gloves again. Twenty-eight guineas. Even
if one is rich . . . She looked vague. She stared at a plump tea-kettle
like a plump hen above the shopman's head, and her voice was dreamy
as she answered: 'Well, keep it for me – will you? I'll . . .'

But the shopman had already bowed as though keeping it for her
was all any human being could ask. He would be willing, of course, to
keep it for her for ever.

The discreet door shut with a click. She was outside on the step,
gazing at the winter afternoon. Rain was falling, and with the rain it
seemed the dark came too, spinning down like ashes. There was a cold
bitter taste in the air, and the new-lighted lamps looked sad. Sad were
the lights in the houses opposite. Dimly they burned as if regretting
something. And people hurried by, hidden under their hateful umbrellas. Rosemary felt a strange pang. She pressed her muff against her

breast; she wished she had the little box, too, to cling to. Of course, the car was there. She'd only to cross the pavement. But still she waited. There are moments, horrible moments in life, when one emerges from shelter and looks out, and it's awful. One oughtn't to give way to them. One ought to go home and have an extra-special tea. But at the very instant of thinking that, a young girl, thin, dark, shadowy – where had she come from? – was standing at Rosemary's elbow and a voice like a sigh, almost like a sob, breathed: 'Madam, may I speak to you a moment?'

'Speak to me?' Rosemary turned. She saw a little battered creature with enormous eyes, someone quite young, no older than herself, who clutched at her coat-collar with reddened hands, and shivered as though she had just come out of the water.

'M-madam,' stammered the voice. 'Would you let me have the price of a cup of tea?'

'A cup of tea?' There was something simple, sincere in that voice; it wasn't in the least the voice of a beggar. 'Then have you no money at all?' asked Rosemary.

'None, madam,' came the answer.

'How extraordinary!' Rosemary peered through the dusk, and the girl gazed back at her. How more than extraordinary! And suddenly it seemed to Rosemary such an adventure. It was like something out of a novel by Dostoevsky, this meeting in the dusk. Supposing she took the girl home? Supposing she did do one of those things she was always reading about or seeing on the stage, what would happen? It would be thrilling. And she heard herself saying afterwards to the amazement of her friends: 'I simply took her home with me,' as she stepped forward and said to that dim person beside her: 'Come home to tea with me.'

The girl drew back startled. She even stopped shivering for a moment. Rosemary put out a hand and touched her arm. 'I mean it,' she said, smiling. And she felt how simple and kind her smile was. 'Why won't you? Do. Come home with me now in my car and have tea.'

'You – you don't mean it, madam,' said the girl, and there was pain in her voice.

'But I do,' cried Rosemary. 'I want you to. To please me. Come along.'

The girl put her fingers to her lips and her eyes devoured Rosemary. 'You're – you're not taking me to the police station?' she stammered.

'The police station!' Rosemary laughed out. 'Why should I be so cruel? No, I only want to make you warm and to hear – anything you care to tell me.'

Hungry people are easily led. The footman held the door of the car open, and a moment later they were skimming through the dusk.

'There!' said Rosemary. She had a feeling of triumph as she slipped her hand through the velvet strap. She could have said, 'Now I've got you,' as she gazed at the little captive she had netted. But of course she meant it kindly. Oh, more than kindly. She was going to prove to this girl that – wonderful things did happen in life, that – fairy godmothers were real, that – rich people had hearts, and that women *were* sisters. She turned impulsively, saying: 'Don't be frightened. After all, why shouldn't you come back with me? We're both women. If I'm the more fortunate, you ought to expect . . .'

But happily at that moment, for she didn't know how the sentence was going to end, the car stopped. The bell was rung, the door opened, and with a charming, protecting, almost embracing movement, Rosemary drew the other into the hall. Warmth, softness, light, a sweet scent, all those things so familiar to her she never even thought about them, she watched that other receive. It was fascinating. She was like the rich little girl in her nursery with all the cupboards to open, all the boxes to unpack.

'Come, come upstairs,' said Rosemary, longing to begin to be generous. 'Come up to my room.' And, besides, she wanted to spare this poor little thing from being stared at by the servants; she decided as they mounted the stairs she would not even ring for Jeanne, but take off her things by herself. The great thing was to be natural!

And 'There!' cried Rosemary again, as they reached her beautiful big bedroom with the curtains drawn, the fire leaping on her wonderful lacquer furniture, her gold cushions and the primrose and blue rugs.

The girl stood just inside the door; she seemed dazed. But Rosemary didn't mind that.

'Come and sit down,' she cried, dragging her big chair up to the fire, 'in this comfy chair. Come and get warm. You look so dreadfully cold.'

'I daren't, madam,' said the girl, and she edged backwards.

'Oh, please,' – Rosemary ran forward – 'you mustn't be frightened, you mustn't, really. Sit down, and when I've taken off my things we shall go into the next room and have tea and be cosy. Why are you afraid?' And gently she half pushed the thin figure into its deep cradle.

But there was no answer. The girl stayed just as she had been put, with her hands by her sides and her mouth slightly open. To be quite sincere, she looked rather stupid. But Rosemary wouldn't acknowledge it. She leaned over her, saying: 'Won't you take off your hat? Your pretty hair is all wet. And one is so much more comfortable without a hat, isn't one?'

There was a whisper that sounded like 'Very good, madam,' and the crushed hat was taken off.

'And let me help you off with your coat, too,' said Rosemary.

The girl stood up. But she held on to the chair with one hand and let Rosemary pull. It was quite an effort. The other scarcely helped her at all. She seemed to stagger like a child, and the thought came and went through Rosemary's mind, that if people wanted helping they must respond a little, just a little, otherwise it became very difficult indeed. And what was she to do with the coat now? She left it on the floor, and the hat too. She was just going to take a cigarette off the mantelpiece when the girl said quickly, but so lightly and strangely: 'I'm very sorry, madam, but I'm going to faint. I shall go off, madam, if I don't have something.'

'Good heavens, how thoughtless I am!' Rosemary rushed to the bell.

'Tea! Tea at once! And some brandy immediately!'

The maid was gone again, but the girl almost cried out: 'No, I don't want no brandy. I never drink brandy. It's a cup of tea I want, madam.' And she burst into tears.

It was a terrible and fascinating moment. Rosemary knelt beside her chair.

'Don't cry, poor little thing,' she said. 'Don't cry.' And she gave the other her lace handkerchief. She really was touched beyond words. She put her arm round those thin, bird-like shoulders.

Now at last the other forgot to be shy, forgot everything except that they were both women, and gasped out: 'I can't go on no longer like this. I can't bear it. I can't bear it. I shall do away with myself. I can't bear no more.'

'You shan't have to. I'll look after you. Don't cry any more. Don't you see what a good thing it was that you met me? We'll have tea and you'll tell me everything. And I shall arrange something. I promise. *Do* stop crying. It's so exhausting. Please!'

The other did stop just in time for Rosemary to get up before the tea came. She had the table placed between them. She plied the poor little creature with everything, all the sandwiches, all the bread and butter, and every time her cup was empty she filled it with tea, cream and sugar. People always said sugar was so nourishing. As for herself she didn't eat; she smoked and looked away tactfully so that the other should not be shy.

And really the effect of that slight meal was marvellous. When the tea-table was carried away a new being, a light, frail creature with tangled hair, dark lips, deep, lighted eyes, lay back in the big chair in a kind of sweet languor, looking at the blaze. Rosemary lit a fresh cigarette; it was time to begin.

'And when did you have your last meal?' she asked softly.

But at that moment the door-handle turned.

'Rosemary, may I come in?' It was Philip.

'Of course.'

He came in. 'Oh, I'm so sorry,' he said, and stopped and stared.

'It's quite all right,' said Rosemary, smiling. 'This is my friend, Miss –'

'Smith, madam,' said the languid figure, who was strangely still and unafraid.

'Smith,' said Rosemary. 'We are going to have a little talk.'

'Oh yes,' said Philip. 'Quite,' and his eye caught sight of the coat and hat on the floor. He came over to the fire and turned his back to it. 'It's a beastly afternoon,' he said curiously, still looking at that listless figure, looking at its hands and boots, and then at Rosemary again.

'Yes, isn't it?' said Rosemary enthusiastically. 'Vile.'

Philip smiled his charming smile. 'As a matter of fact,' said he, 'I wanted you to come into the library for a moment. Would you? Will Miss Smith excuse us?'

The big eyes were raised to him, but Rosemary answered for her: 'Of course she will.' And they went out of the room together.

'I say,' said Philip, when they were alone. 'Explain. Who is she? What does it all mean?'

Rosemary, laughing, leaned against the door and said: 'I picked her up in Curzon Street. Really. She's a real pickup. She asked me for the price of a cup of tea, and I brought her home with me.'

'But what on earth are you going to do with her?' cried Philip.

'Be nice to her,' said Rosemary quickly. 'Be frightfully nice to her. Look after her. I don't know how. We haven't talked yet. But show her – treat her – make her feel –'

'My darling girl,' said Philip, 'you're quite mad, you know. It simply can't be done.'

'I knew you'd say that,' retorted Rosemary. 'Why not? I want to. Isn't that a reason? And besides, one's always reading about these things. I decided –'

'But,' said Philip slowly, and he cut the end of a cigar, 'she's so astonishingly pretty.'

'Pretty?' Rosemary was so surprised that she blushed. 'Do you think so? I – I hadn't thought about it.'

'Good Lord!' Philip struck a match. 'She's absolutely lovely. Look again, my child. I was bowled over when I came into your room just now. However . . . I think you're making a ghastly mistake. Sorry, darling, if I'm crude and all that. But let me know if Miss Smith is going to dine with us in time for me to look up *The Milliner's Gazette*.'

'You absurd creature!' said Rosemary, and she went out of the library, but not back to her bedroom. She went to her writing-room and sat down at her desk. Pretty! Absolutely lovely! Bowled over! Her heart beat like a heavy bell. Pretty! Lovely! She drew her cheque-book towards her. But no, cheques would be no use, of course. She opened a drawer and took out five pound notes, looked at them, put two back, and holding the three squeezed in her hand, she went back to her bedroom.

Half an hour later Philip was still in the library, when Rosemary came in.

'I only wanted to tell you,' said she, and she leaned against the door again and looked at him with her dazzled exotic gaze, 'Miss Smith won't dine with us tonight.'

Philip put down the paper. 'Oh, what's happened? Previous engagement?'

Rosemary came over and sat down on his knee. 'She insisted on going,' said she, 'so I gave the poor little thing a present of money. I couldn't keep her against her will, could I?' she added softly.

Rosemary had just done her hair, darkened her eyes a little, and put on her pearls. She put up her hands and touched Philip's cheeks.

'Do you like me?' said she, and her tone, sweet, husky, troubled him.

'I like you awfully,' he said, and he held her tighter. 'Kiss me.'

There was a pause.

Then Rosemary said dreamily: 'I saw a fascinating little box today. It cost twenty-eight guineas. May I have it?'

Philip jumped her on his knee. 'You may, little wasteful one,' said he.

But that was not really what Rosemary wanted to say.

'Philip,' she whispered, and she pressed his head against her bosom, 'am I *pretty*?'

(written 1922, first published in 1922, first book publication
The Doves' Nest and Other Stories, 1923)

The Fly

'Y'are very snug in here,' piped old Mr Woodifield, and he peered out of the great, green-leather armchair by his friend the boss's desk as a baby peers out of its pram. His talk was over; it was time for him to be off. But he did not want to go. Since he had retired, since his . . . stroke, the wife and the girls kept him boxed up in the house every day of the week except Tuesday. On Tuesday he was dressed and brushed and allowed to cut back to the City for the day. Though what he did there the wife and girls couldn't imagine. Made a nuisance of himself to his friends, they supposed . . . Well, perhaps so. All the same, we cling to our last pleasures as the tree clings to its last leaves. So there sat old Woodifield, smoking a cigar and staring almost greedily at the boss, who rolled in his office chair, stout, rosy, five years older than he, and still going strong, still at the helm. It did one good to see him.

Wistfully, admiringly, the old voice added, 'It's snug in here, upon my word!'

'Yes, it's comfortable enough,' agreed the boss, and he flipped the *Financial Times* with a paper-knife. As a matter of fact he was proud of his room; he liked to have it admired, especially by old Woodifield. It gave him a feeling of deep, solid satisfaction to be planted there in the midst of it in full view of that frail old figure in the muffler.

'I've had it done up lately,' he explained, as he had explained for the past – how many? – weeks. 'New carpet,' and he pointed to the bright red carpet with a pattern of large white rings. 'New furniture,' and he nodded towards the massive bookcase and the table with legs like twisted treacle. 'Electric heating!' He waved almost exultantly towards the five transparent, pearly sausages glowing so softly in the tilted copper pan.

But he did not draw old Woodifield's attention to the photograph over the table of a grave-looking boy in uniform standing in one of those spectral photographers' parks with photographers' storm-clouds behind him. It was not new. It had been there for over six years.

'There was something I wanted to tell you,' said old Woodifield, and his eyes grew dim remembering. 'Now what was it? I had it in my mind when I started out this morning.' His hands began to tremble, and patches of red showed above his beard.

Poor old chap, he's on his last pins, thought the boss. And, feeling kindly, he winked at the old man, and said jokingly, 'I tell you what. I've got a little drop of something here that'll do you good before you go out into the cold again. It's beautiful stuff. It wouldn't hurt a child.' He took a key off his watch-chain, unlocked a cupboard below his desk, and drew forth a dark, squat bottle. 'That's the medicine,' said he. 'And the man from whom I got it told me on the strict Q.T. it came from the cellars at Windsor Castle.'

Old Woodifield's mouth fell open at the sight. He couldn't have looked more surprised if the boss had produced a rabbit.

'It's whisky, ain't it?' he piped feebly.

The boss turned the bottle and lovingly showed him the label. Whisky it was.

'D'you know,' said he, peering up at the boss wonderingly, 'they won't let me touch it at home.' And he looked as though he was going to cry.

'Ah, that's where we know a bit more than the ladies,' cried the boss, swooping across for two tumblers that stood on the table with the water-bottle, and pouring a generous finger into each. 'Drink it down. It'll do you good. And don't put any water with it. It's sacrilege to tamper with stuff like this. Ah!' He tossed off his, pulled out his handkerchief, hastily wiped his moustaches, and cocked an eye at old Woodifield, who was rolling his in his chaps.

The old man swallowed, was silent a moment, and then said faintly, 'It's nutty!'

But it warmed him; it crept into his chill old brain – he remembered.

'That was it,' he said, heaving himself out of his chair. 'I thought you'd like to know. The girls were in Belgium last week having a look at poor Reggie's grave, and they happened to come across your boy's. They're quite near each other, it seems.'

Old Woodifield paused, but the boss made no reply. Only a quiver in his eyelids showed that he heard.

'The girls were delighted with the way the place is kept,' piped the old voice. 'Beautifully looked after. Couldn't be better if they were at home. You've not been across, have yer?'

'No, no!' For various reasons the boss had not been across.

'There's miles of it,' quavered old Woodifield, 'and it's all as neat as a garden. Flowers growing on all the graves. Nice broad paths.' It was plain from his voice how much he liked a nice broad path.

The pause came again. Then the old man brightened wonderfully.

'D'you know what the hotel made the girls pay for a pot of jam?' he piped. 'Ten francs! Robbery, I call it. It was a little pot, so Gertrude says, no bigger than a half-crown. And she hadn't taken more than a spoonful when they charged her ten francs. Gertrude brought the pot away with her to teach 'em a lesson. Quite right, too; it's trading on our feelings. They think because we're over there having a look round we're ready to pay anything. That's what it is.' And he turned towards the door.

'Quite right, quite right!' cried the boss, though what was quite right he hadn't the least idea. He came round by his desk, followed the shuffling footsteps to the door, and saw the old fellow out. Woodifield was gone.

For a long moment the boss stayed, staring at nothing, while the grey-haired office messenger, watching him, dodged in and out of his cubby-hole like a dog that expects to be taken for a run. Then: 'I'll see nobody for half an hour, Macey,' said the boss. 'Understand? Nobody at all.'

'Very good, sir.'

The door shut, the firm heavy steps recrossed the bright carpet, the fat body plumped down in the spring chair, and leaning forward, the boss covered his face with his hands. He wanted, he intended, he had arranged to weep . . .

It had been a terrible shock to him when old Woodifield sprang that remark upon him about the boy's grave. It was exactly as though the earth had opened and he had seen the boy lying there with Woodifield's girls staring down at him. For it was strange. Although over six years had passed away, the boss never thought of the boy except as lying unchanged, unblemished in his uniform, asleep for ever. 'My son!' groaned the boss. But no tears came yet. In the past, in the first months and even years after the boy's death, he had only to say those words to be overcome by such grief that nothing short of a violent fit of weeping could relieve him. Time, he had declared then, he had told everybody, could make no difference. Other men perhaps might recover, might live their loss down, but not he. How was it possible?

His boy was an only son. Ever since his birth the boss had worked at building up this business for him; it had no other meaning if it was not for the boy. Life itself had come to have no other meaning. How on earth could he have slaved, denied himself, kept going all those years without the promise for ever before him of the boy's stepping into his shoes and carrying on where he left off?

And that promise had been so near being fulfilled. The boy had been in the office learning the ropes for a year before the war. Every morning they had started off together; they had come back by the same train. And what congratulations he had received as the boy's father! No wonder; he had taken to it marvellously. As to his popularity with the staff, every man jack of them down to old Macey couldn't make enough of the boy. And he wasn't in the least spoilt. No, he was just his bright natural self, with the right word for everybody, with that boyish look and his habit of saying, 'Simply splendid!'

But all that was over and done with as though it never had been. The day had come when Macey had handed him the telegram that brought the whole place crashing about his head. 'Deeply regret to inform you . . .' And he had left the office a broken man, with his life in ruins.

Six years ago, six years . . . How quickly time passed! It might have happened yesterday. The boss took his hands from his face; he was puzzled. Something seemed to be wrong with him. He wasn't feeling as he wanted to feel. He decided to get up and have a look at the boy's photograph. But it wasn't a favourite photograph of his; the expression was unnatural. It was cold, even stern-looking. The boy had never looked like that.

At that moment the boss noticed that a fly had fallen into his broad inkpot, and was trying feebly but desperately to clamber out again. Help! help! said those struggling legs. But the sides of the inkpot were wet and slippery; it fell back again and began to swim. The boss took up a pen, picked the fly out of the ink, and shook it on to a piece of blotting-paper. For a fraction of a second it lay still on the dark patch that oozed round it. Then the front legs waved, took hold, and, pulling its small, sodden body up, it began the immense task of cleaning the ink from its wings. Over and under, over and under, went a leg along a wing as the stone goes over and under the scythe. Then there was a pause, while the fly, seeming to stand on the tips of its toes, tried to expand first one wing and then the other. It succeeded at last, and, sitting down, it began, like a minute cat, to clean its face. Now one could imagine that the little front legs rubbed against each other lightly, joyfully. The horrible danger was over; it had escaped; it was ready for life again.

But just then the boss had an idea. He plunged his pen back into the ink, leaned his thick wrist on the blotting-paper, and as the fly tried its wings down came a great heavy blot. What would it make of that? What indeed! The little beggar seemed absolutely cowed, stunned, and afraid to move because of what would happen next. But then, as if painfully, it dragged itself forward. The front legs waved, caught hold, and, more slowly this time, the task began from the beginning.

He's a plucky little devil, thought the boss, and he felt a real admiration for the fly's courage. That was the way to tackle things; that was the right spirit. Never say die; it was only a question of . . . But the fly had again finished its laborious task, and the boss had just time to refill his pen, to shake fair and square on the new-cleaned body yet another dark drop. What about it this time? A painful moment of suspense followed. But behold, the front legs were again waving; the boss felt a rush of relief. He leaned over the fly and said to it tenderly, 'You artful little b . . .' And he actually had the brilliant notion of breathing on it to help the drying process. All the same, there was something timid and weak about its efforts now, and the boss decided that this time should be the last, as he dipped the pen deep into the inkpot.

It was. The last blot fell on the soaked blotting-paper, and the draggled fly lay in it and did not stir. The back legs were stuck to the body; the front legs were not to be seen.

'Come on,' said the boss. 'Look sharp!' And he stirred it with his pen – in vain. Nothing happened or was likely to happen. The fly was dead.

The boss lifted the corpse on the end of the paper-knife and flung it into the waste-paper basket. But such a grinding feeling of wretchedness seized him that he felt positively frightened. He started forward and pressed the bell for Macey.

'Bring me some fresh blotting-paper,' he said sternly, 'and look sharp about it.' And while the old dog padded away he fell to wondering what it was he had been thinking about before. What was it? It was . . . He took out his handkerchief and passed it inside his collar. For the life of him he could not remember.

(written 1922, first published in 1922, first book publication
The Doves' Nest and Other Stories, 1923)

VINTAGE CLASSICS

Vintage launched in the United Kingdom in 1990, and was originally the paperback home for the Random House Group's literary authors. Now, Vintage is comprised of some of London's oldest and most prestigious literary houses, including Chatto & Windus (1855), Hogarth (1917), Jonathan Cape (1921) and Secker & Warburg (1935), alongside the newer or relaunched hardback and paperback imprints: The Bodley Head, Harvill Secker, Yellow Jersey, Square Peg, Vintage Paperbacks and Vintage Classics.

From Angela Carter, Graham Greene and Aldous Huxley to Toni Morrison, Haruki Murakami and Virginia Woolf, Vintage Classics is renowned for publishing some of the greatest writers and thinkers from around the world and across the ages – all complemented by our beautiful, stylish approach to design. Vintage Classics' authors have won many of the world's most revered literary prizes, including the Nobel, the Man Booker, the Prix Goncourt and the Pulitzer, and through their writing they continue to capture imaginations, inspire new perspectives and incite curiosity.

In 2007 Vintage Classics introduced its distinctive red spine design, and in 2012 Vintage Children's Classics was launched to include the much-loved authors of our childhood. Random House joined forces with the Penguin Group in 2013 to become Penguin Random House, making it the largest trade publisher in the United Kingdom.

@vintagebooks

penguin.co.uk/vintage-classics